Prais

Sha

"Mr. Rushdie's style [is] a source of delight, a bright stream of words . . . a voice at once whimsical, sly and exclamatory, full of apostrophes and asides, flexible enough to incorporate the up-to-date slang and obscenities of the warring men and the peculiar speech rhythms . . . of the Pakistani ladies in a state of excitement."
—*The New York Times Book Review*

"The extravagantly tragicomic nightmare evoked by *Shame* . . . does for Pakistan what Mr. Rushdie's equally remarkable . . . *Midnight's Children* did for India. The narrative voice of *Shame* creates its own irresistible logic. In a postscript to his story, the author acknowledges having quoted Milan Kundera, Franz Kafka, Nikolai Erdmann and Georg Büchner. Here and there in the text, one can't help thinking of Gabriel García Márquez. These are extraordinary writers with whom to be associated, but it's company that Salman Rushdie deserves."
—*The New York Times*

"Revelation and obscurity, affairs of honor, blushings of all parts, the recession of erotic life, the open violence of public life, create the extraordinary Rushdie mood." —*The Guardian* (London)

"*Shame* should consolidate [Rushdie's] position as one of the finest young writers around. This novel of crossed family destinies in contemporary Pakistan teems with interesting characters, dramatic events, and marvelous verbal inventions. Like its predecessor, it recreates an exotic but thoroughly believable world that is a delight to experience. . . . A wonderful book." —*Quill & Quire*

By Salman Rushdie

FICTION

Grimus
Midnight's Children
The Satanic Verses
Shame
Haroun and the Sea of Stories
East, West
The Moor's Last Sigh
The Ground Beneath Her Feet
Fury
Shalimar the Clown
The Enchantress of Florence
Luka and the Lake of Fire

NONFICTION

Joseph Anton
The Jaguar Smile
Imaginary Homelands
The Wizard of Oz
Step Across This Line

SCREENPLAY

Midnight's Children

ANTHOLOGY

Mirrorwork (co-editor)

SHAME

SALMAN RUSHDIE

SHAME

A NOVEL

Random House Trade Paperbacks
New York

2008 Random House Trade Paperback Edition

Published in the United States by Random House Trade Paperbacks, an imprint of The Random House Publishing Group, a division of Random House, Inc., New York.

RANDOM HOUSE TRADE PAPERBACKS and colophon are trademarks of Random House, Inc.

Originally published in hardcover in the United States by Alfred A. Knopf, a division of Random House, Inc., and in the United Kingdom by Jonathan Cape Ltd. in 1983.

LIBRARY OF CONGRESS CATALOGING-IN-PUBLICATION DATA

Rushdie, Salman.
Shame: a novel / Salman Rushdie.
p. cm.
ISBN 978-0-8129-7670-0
I. Title
PR6068.U757S5
823'.914—dc21   97-5633

Printed in the United States of America

www.atrandom.com

6 8 9 7

For Sameen

CONTENTS

I

ESCAPES FROM THE
MOTHER COUNTRY

1

❦

THE DUMB-WAITER

In the remote border town of Q., which when seen from the air resembles nothing so much as an ill-proportioned dumb-bell, there once lived three lovely, and loving, sisters. Their names . . . but their real names were never used, like the best household china, which was locked away after the night of their joint tragedy in a cupboard whose location was eventually forgotten, so that the great thousand-piece service from the Gardner potteries in Tsarist Russia became a family myth in whose factuality they almost ceased to believe . . . the three sisters, I should state without further delay, bore the family name of Shakil, and were universally known (in descending order of age) as Chhunni, Munnee and Bunny.

And one day their father died.

Old Mr Shakil, at the time of his death a widower for eighteen years, had developed the habit of referring to the town in which he lived as 'a hell hole'. During his last delirium he embarked on a ceaseless and largely incomprehensible monologue amidst whose turbid peregrinations the household servants could make out long passages of obscenity, oaths and curses of a ferocity that made the air boil violently around his bed. In this peroration the embittered

3

old recluse rehearsed his lifelong hatred for his home town, now calling down demons to destroy the clutter of low, dun-coloured, 'higgling and piggling' edifices around the bazaar, now annihilating with his death-encrusted words the cool whitewashed smugness of the Cantonment district. These were the two orbs of the town's dumb-bell shape: old town and Cantt, the former inhabited by the indigenous, colonized population and the latter by the alien colonizers, the Angrez, or British, sahibs. Old Shakil loathed both worlds and had for many years remained immured in his high, fortress-like, gigantic residence which faced inwards to a well-like and lightless compound yard. The house was positioned beside an open maidan, and it was equidistant from the bazaar and the Cantt. Through one of the building's few outward-facing windows Mr Shakil on his death-bed was able to stare out at the dome of a large Palladian hotel, which rose out of the intolerable Cantonment streets like a mirage, and inside which were to be found golden cuspidors and tame spider-monkeys in brass-buttoned uniforms and bellhop hats and a full-sized orchestra playing every evening in a stuccoed ballroom amidst an energetic riot of fantastic plants, yellow roses and white magnolias and roof-high emerald-green palms – the Hotel Flashman, in short, whose great golden dome was cracked even then but shone nevertheless with the tedious pride of its brief doomed glory; that dome under which the suited-and-booted Angrez officers and white-tied civilians and ringleted ladies with hungry eyes would congregate nightly, assembling here from their bungalows to dance and to share the illusion of being colourful – whereas in fact they were merely white, or actually grey, owing to the deleterious effect of that stony heat upon their frail cloud-nurtured skins, and also to their habit of drinking dark Burgundies in the noonday insanity of the sun, with a fine disregard for their livers. The old man heard the music of the imperialists issuing from the golden hotel, heavy with the gaiety of despair, and he cursed the hotel of dreams in a loud, clear voice.

'Shut that window,' he shouted, 'so that I don't have to die listening to that racket,' and when the old womanservant Hashmat

Bibi had fastened the shutters he relaxed slightly and, summoning up the last reserves of his energy, altered the course of his fatal, delirious flow.

'Come quickly,' Hashmat Bibi ran from the room yelling for the old man's daughters, 'your fatherji is sending himself to the devil.' Mr Shakil, having dismissed the outside world, had turned the rage of his dying monologue against himself, calling eternal damnation down upon his soul. 'God knows what got his goat,' Hashmat despaired, 'but he is going in an incorrect way.'

The widower had raised his children with the help of Parsee wet-nurses, Christian ayahs and an iron morality that was mostly Muslim, although Chhunni used to say that he had been made harder by the sun. The three girls had been kept inside that labyrinthine mansion until his dying day; virtually uneducated, they were imprisoned in the zenana wing where they amused each other by inventing private languages and fantasizing about what a man might look like when undressed, imagining, during their pre-pubertal years, bizarre genitalia such as holes in the chest into which their own nipples might snugly fit, 'because for all we knew in those days,' they would remind each other amazedly in later life, 'fertilization might have been supposed to happen through the breast.' This interminable captivity forged between the three sisters a bond of intimacy that would never completely be broken. They spent their evenings seated at a window behind a lattice-work screen, looking towards the golden dome of the great hotel and swaying to the strains of the enigmatic dance music . . . and there are rumours that they would indolently explore each other's bodies during the languorous drowsiness of the afternoons, and, at night, would weave occult spells to hasten the moment of their father's demise. But evil tongues will say anything, especially about beautiful women who live far away from the denuding eyes of men. What is almost certainly true is that it was during these years, long before the baby scandal, that the three of them, all of whom longed for children with the abstract passion of their virginity, made their secret compact to remain triune, forever bound by the intimacies of their youth, even after the children came: that is to say, they resolved to share the babies. I cannot prove or disprove the foul story that this treaty was written down and signed in the commingled menstrual blood of the isolated trinity, and then burned to ashes, being preserved only in the cloisters of their memories.

But for twenty years, they would have only one child. His name would be Omar Khayyam.

All this happened in the fourteenth century. I'm using the Hegiran calendar, naturally: don't imagine that stories of this type always take place longlong ago. Time cannot be homogenized as easily as milk, and in those parts, until quite recently, the thirteen-hundreds were still in full swing.

When Hashmat Bibi told them that their father had arrived at his final moments, the sisters went to visit him, dressed in their brightest clothes. They found him in the grip of an asphyxiating fist of shame, demanding of God, in gasps of imperious gloominess, that he be consigned for all eternity to some desert outpost of Jahannum, some borderland of hell. Then he fell silent, and Chhunni, the eldest daughter, quickly asked him the only question of any interest to the three young women: 'Father, we are going to be very rich now, is that not so?'

'Whores,' the dying man cursed them, 'don't count on it.'

The bottomless sea of wealth on which everyone had supposed the Shakil family fortunes to be sailing proved, on the morning after his foulmouthed death, to be an arid crater. The fierce sun of his financial incompetence (which he had successfully concealed for decades behind his imposing patriarchal façade, his filthy temper and the overweening hauteur which was his most poisonous legacy to his daughters) had dried out all the oceans of cash, so that Chhunni, Munnee and Bunny spent the entire period of mourning settling the debts for which his creditors had never dared to press the old man while he lived, but for payment of which (plus compound interest) they now absolutely refused to wait one moment longer. The girls emerged from their lifelong sequestration wearing expressions of well-bred disgust for these vultures swooping down to feast upon the carcass of their parent's great improvidence; and because they had been raised to think of money as one of the two subjects that it is forbidden to discuss with strangers, they signed away their fortune without even troubling to read the documents which the money-lenders presented. At the end of it all the vast estates around Q., which comprised approximately eighty-five per cent of the only good orchards and rich agricultural lands in that largely infertile region, had been lost in their entirety; the three sisters were left with nothing but the unmanageably infinite mansion stuffed from floor to ceiling with possessions and haunted by the few servants who refused to leave, less out of loyalty than from that terror of the life-prisoner for the outside world. And – as is perhaps the universal custom of aristocratically bred persons – they reacted to the news of their ruin by resolving to throw a party.

In later years, they told each other the story of that notorious gala night with a simple glee that restored to them the illusion of being young. 'I had invitations printed in the Cantt,' Chhunni Shakil would begin, seated beside her sisters on an old wooden swing-seat. Giggling happily about the old adventure, she continued, 'And what invitations! Embossed, with gold lettering, on cards stiff as wood. They were like spits in the eye of fate.'

'Also in the closed eyes of our dead father,' Munnee added. 'To him it would have seemed like a completely shameless going-on, an abhorrence, the proof of his failure to impose his will on us.'

'Just as,' Bunny continued, 'our ruin proved his failure in another sphere.'

At first it seemed to them that the dying shame of their father had been born of his knowledge of the coming bankruptcy. Later, however, they began to consider less prosaic possibilities. 'Maybe,' Chhunni hypothesized, 'he saw on his death-bed a vision of the future.'

'Good,' her sisters said, 'then he will have died as miserably as he made us live.'

The news of the emergence into society of the Shakil sisters spread rapidly through the town. And on the much-anticipated evening, the old house was invaded by an army of musical geniuses, whose three-stringed dumbirs, seven-stringed sarandas, reed flutes and drums filled that puritanical mansion with celebratory music for the first time in two decades; regiments of bakers and confectioners and snack-wallahs marched in with arsenals of eats, denuding the shop-counters of the town and filling up the interior of the huge multicoloured shamiana tent that had been erected in the central compound, its mirrorworked fabric reflecting the glory of the arrangements. It became clear, however, that the snobbishness which their father had bred into the sisters' bone-marrow had fatally infected the guest list. Most of the burghers of Q. had already been mortally insulted to find themselves deemed unworthy of the company of the three lustrous ladies, whose gilt-edged invitations were the talk of the town. Now the crimes of omission were compounded by those of commission, because it was seen that the sisters had committed the ultimate solecism: invitations, scorning the doormats of the indigenous worthies, had found their way into the Angrez Cantonment, and into the ballroom of the dancing sahibs. The long-forbidden household remained barred to all but a few locals; but after the cocktail hour at Flashman's, the sisters were visited by a uniformed and ball-gowned crowd of foreigners. The imperialists! – the grey-skinned sahibs and their gloved begums! – raucous-voiced and glittering with condescension, they entered the mirrorworked marquee.

'Alcohol was served.' Old mother Chhunni, reminiscing, clapped her hands delightedly at the horror of the memory. But that was the point at which the reminiscing always ceased, and all three ladies became curiously vague; so that I am unable to clear away the improbabilities which have mushroomed around that party during the dark passage of the years.

Can it really have been the case that the few non-white guests – local zamindars and their wives, whose wealth had once been trifling in comparison with the Shakil crores – stood together in a tight clump of rage, gazing balefully at the cavorting sahibs?

That all these persons left simultaneously after a very few moments, without having broken bread or eaten salt, abandoning the sisters to the colonial authorities? How likely is it that the three sisters, their eyes shining with antimony and arousal, moved in grave silence from officer to officer, as though they were sizing them up, as if mustachioes were being checked for glossiness and jaws evaluated by the angles of their jutting? – And then (the legend goes) that they, the Shakil girls, clapped their hands in unison and ordered the musicians to start playing Western-style dance music, minuets, waltzes, fox-trots, polkas, gavottes, music that acquired a fatally demonic quality when forced out of the virtuosi's outraged instruments?

All night, they say, the dancing continued. The scandal of such an event would have placed the newly orphaned girls beyond the pale in any case, but there was worse to come. Shortly after the party ended, after the infuriated geniuses has departed and the mountains of uneaten food had been thrown to the pie-dogs – for the sisters in their grandeur would not permit food intended for their peers to be distributed among the poor – it began to be bruited about the bazaars of Q. that one of the three nose-in-air girls had been put, on that wild night, into the family way.

O shame, shame, poppy-shame!

But if the sisters Shakil were overwhelmed by any feelings of dishonour, they gave no sign of it. Instead, they dispatched Hashmat Bibi, one of the servants who had refused to leave, into Q., where she commissioned the services of the town's finest handyman, a certain Mistri Yakoob Balloch, and also purchased the largest imported padlock to be found in the God-Willing Ironmongery Store. This padlock was so large and heavy that Hashmat Bibi was obliged to have it carried home on the back of a rented mule, whose owner inquired of the servant woman: 'For what your begums want this lock-shock now? Invasion has already occurred.' Hashmat replied, crossing her eyes for emphasis: 'May your grandsons urinate upon your pauper's grave.'

The hired handyman, Mistri Yakoob, was so impressed by the ferocious calm of the antediluvian crone that he worked willingly under her supervision without daring to pass a comment. She had him construct a strange external elevator, or dumb-waiter, large enough to hold three grown adults, by means of which items could be winched by a system of motorized pulleys from the street into the upper storeys of the house, or vice versa. Hashmat Bibi stressed the importance of constructing the whole contraption in such a way that it could be operated without requiring the mansion's inhabitants to show themselves an any window – not so much as a little finger must be capable of being glimpsed. Then she listed the unusual security features which she wished him to install in the bizarre mechanism. 'Put here,' she ordered him, 'a spring release which can be worked from inside the house. When triggered, it should make the whole bottom of the lift fall off just-likethat. Put there, and there, and there, some secret panels which can shoot out eighteen-inch stiletto blades, sharp sharp. My ladies must be defended against intruders.'

The dumb-waiter contained, then, many terrible secrets. The Mistri completed his work without once laying eyes on any of the three sisters Shakil, but when he died a few weeks later, clutching his stomach and rolling about in a gully, spitting blood on to the dirt, it got about that those shameless women had had him poisoned to ensure his silence on the subject of his last and most mysterious commission. It is only fair to state, however, that the medical evidence in the case runs strongly against this version of events. Yakoob Balloch, who had been suffering for some time from sporadic pains in the region of the appendix, almost certainly died of natural causes, his death-throes caused not by the spectral poisons of the putatively murderous sisters, but by the genuinely fatal banality of peritonitis. Or some such thing.

The day came when the three remaining male employees of the Shakil sisters were seen pushing shut the enormous front doors of solid teak and brass. Just before those gates of solitude closed upon the sisters, to remain unopened for more than half a century, the little crowd of curious townsfolk outside caught sight of a wheelbarrow on which there gleamed, dully, the outsize lock of their withdrawal. And when the doors were shut, the sounds of the great lock being hauled into place, and of the key being turned, heralded the beginning of the strange confinement of the scandalous ladies and their servants too.

It turned out that on her last trip into town Hashmat Bibi had left a number of sealed envelopes containing detailed instructions at the establishments of the community's leading suppliers of goods and services; so that afterwards, on the appointed days and at the hours specified, the chosen washerwoman, the tailor, the cobbler, as well as the selected vendors of meats, fruits, haberdashery, flowers, stationery, vegetables, pulses, books, flat drinks, fizzy drinks, foreign magazines, newspapers, unguents, perfumes, antimony, strips of eucalyptus bark for tooth-cleaning, spices, starch, soaps, kitchen utensils, picture frames, playing cards and strings for musical instruments, would present themselves at the foot of Mistri Yakoob's last construction. They would emit coded whistles, and the dumb-waiter would descend, humming, to street level bearing written instructions. In this way the Shakil ladies managed to recede entirely and for all time from the world, returning of their own volition into that anchoritic existence whose end they had been so briefly able to celebrate after their father's death; and such was the hauteur of their arrangements that their withdrawal seemed like an act not of contrition but of pride.

There arises a delicate question: how did they pay for it all?

With some embarrassment on their behalf, and purely to show that the present author, who has already been obliged to leave many questions in a state of unanswered ambiguity, is capable of giving clear replies when absolutely necessary, I reveal that Hashmat Bibi had delivered a last sealed envelope to the door of the town's least savoury establishment, wherein the Quranic strictures against usury counted for nothing, whose shelves and storage chests groaned under the weight of the accumulated debris of innumerable decayed histories . . . damn and blast it. To be frank – she went to the pawnshop. And he, the pawnbroker, the ageless, pencil-thin, innocently wide-eyed Chalaak Sahib, would also present himself thereafter at the dumb-waiter (under cover of night, as instructed), to assess the worth of the items he found therein, and to send up into the heart of the silent house cash monies on the nail to a total of eighteen point five per cent approx. of the market value of the irredeemably pawned treasures. The three mothers of the imminent Omar Khayyam Shakil were using the past, their only remaining capital, as a means of purchasing the future.

But who was pregnant?

Chhunni, the eldest, or Munnee-in-the-middle, or 'little' Bunny, the baby of the three? – Nobody ever discovered, not even the child that was born. Their closing of ranks was absolute, and effected with the most meticulous attention to detail. Just imagine: they made the servants swear loyalty oaths on the Book. The servants joined them in their self-imposed captivity, and only left the house feet first, wrapped in white sheets, and via, of course, the route constructed by Yakoob Balloch. During the entire term of that pregnancy, no doctor was summoned to the house. And as it proceeded, the sisters, understanding that unkept secrets always manage to escape, under a door, through a keyhole or an open window, until everyone knows everything and nobody knows how ... the sisters, I repeat, displayed the uniquely passionate solidarity that was their most remarkable characteristic by feigning – in the case of two of them – the entire range of symptoms that the third was obliged to display.

Although some five years separated Chhunni from Bunny, it was at this time that the sisters, by virtue of dressing identically and through the incomprehensible effects of their unusual, chosen life, began to resemble each other so closely that even the servants made mistakes. I have described them as beauties; but they were not the moon-faced almond-eyed types so beloved of poets in that neck of the woods, but rather strong-chinned, powerfully built, purposefully striding women of an almost oppressively charismatic force. Now the three of them began, simultaneously, to thicken at the waist and in the breast; when one was sick in the morning, the other two began to puke in such perfectly synchronized sympathy that it was impossible to tell which stomach had heaved first. Identically, their wombs ballooned towards the pregnancy's full term. It is naturally possible that all this was achieved with the help of physical contrivances, cushions and padding and even faint-inducing vapours; but it is my unshakeable opinion that such an analysis grossly demeans the love that existed between the sisters. In spite of biological improbability, I am prepared to swear that so wholeheartedly did they wish to share the motherhood of their sibling – to transform the public shame of unwedlocked concep-tion into the private triumph of the longed-for group baby – that, in short, twin phantom pregnancies accompanied the real one; while the simultaneity of their behavior suggests the operation of some form of communal mind.

They slept in the same room. They endured the same crav-ings – marzipan, jasmine-petals, pine-kernels, mud – at the same times; their metabolic rates altered in parallel. They began to weigh the same, to feel exhausted at the same moment, and to awake together, each morning, as if somebody had rung a bell. They felt identical pains; in three wombs, a single baby and its two ghostly mirror-images kicked and turned with the precision of a well-drilled dance troupe . . . suffering identically, the three of them – I will go so far as to say – fully earned the right to be con-sidered joint mothers of the forthcoming child. And when one – I will not even guess at the name – came to her time, nobody else saw whose waters broke; nor whose hand locked a bedroom door from the inside. No outside eyes witnessed the passage of the three labours, two phantom one genuine; or the moment when empty balloons subsided, while between a third pair of thighs, as if in an alleyway, there appeared the illegitimate child; or when hands lifted Omar Khayyam Shakil by the ankles, held him upside-down, and thumped him on the back.

Our hero, Omar Khayyam, first drew breath in that improbable mansion which was too large for its rooms to be counted; opened his eyes; and saw, upside-down through an open window, the macabre peaks of the Impossible Mountains on the horizon. One – but which? – of his three mothers had picked him up by the ankles, had pummelled the first breath into his lungs . . . until, still staring at the inverted summits, the baby began to scream.

When Hashmat Bibi heard a key turning in the door and came timidly into the room with food and drink and fresh sheets and sponges and soap and towels, she found the three sisters sitting up together in the capacious bed, the same bed in which their father had died, a huge mahogany four-poster around whose columns carved serpents coiled upwards to the brocade Eden of the canopy. They were all wearing the flushed expression of dilated joy that is the mother's true prerogative; and the baby was passed from breast to breast, and none of the six was dry.

Young Omar Khayyam was gradually made aware that certain irregularities had both preceded and succeeded his birth. We have dealt with the pre-; and as for the suc-:

'I refused completely,' his eldest mother Chhunni told him on his seventh birthday, 'to whisper the name of God into your ear.'

On his eighth birthday, middle-Munnee confided: 'There was no question of shaving your head. Such beautiful black-black hair you came with, nobody was cutting it off under my nose, no sir!'

Exactly one year later, his youngest mother adopted a stern expression. 'Under no circs,' Bunny announced, 'would I have permitted the foreskin to be removed. What is this idea? It is not like banana peel.'

Omar Khayyam Shakil entered life without benefit of mutilation, barbery or divine approval. There are many who would consider this a handicap.

Born in a death-bed, about which there hung (as well as curtains and mosquito-netting) the ghost-image of a grandfather who, dying, had consigned himself to the peripheries of hell; his first sight the spectacle of a range of topsy-turvy mountains . . . Omar Khayyam Shakil was afflicted, from his earliest days, by a sense of inversion, of a world turned upside-down. And by something worse: the fear that he was living at the edge of the world, so close that he might fall off at any moment. Through an old telescope, from the upper-storey windows of the house, the child Omar Khayyam surveyed the emptiness of the landscape around Q., which convinced him that he must be near the very Rim of Things, and that beyond the Impossible Mountains on the horizon must lie the great nothing into which, in his nightmares, he had begun to tumble with monotonous regularity. The most alarming aspect of these dreams was the sleep-sense that his plunges into the void were somehow appropriate, that he deserved no better . . . he awoke amidst mosquito-netting, sweating freely and even shrieking at the realization that his dreams were informing him of his worthlessness. He did not relish the news.

So it was in those half-formed years that Omar Khayyam took the never-to-be-reversed decision to cut down on his sleeping time, a lifelong endeavor which had brought him, by the end, by the time his wife went up in smoke – but no, ends must not be permitted to precede beginnings and middles, even if recent scientific experiments have shown us that within certain types of closed systems, under intense pressure, time can be persuaded to run backwards, so that effects precede their causes. This is precisely the sort of unhelpful advance of which storytellers must take no notice whatsoever; that way madness lies! – to the point at which a mere forty minutes a night, the famous forty winks, sufficed to refresh him. How young he was when he made the surprisingly adult resolution to escape from the unpalatable reality of dreams into the slightly more acceptable illusions of his everyday, waking life! 'Little bat,' his three mothers called him tolerantly when they learned of his nocturnal flittings through the inexhaustible chambers of their home, a dark-grey chadar flapping around his shoulders, providing protection against the cold of the winter nights; but as to whether he grew up into caped crusader or cloaked bloodsucker, into Batman or Dracula, I leave it to the reader to decide.

(His wife, the elder daughter of General Raza Hyder, was an insomniac too; but Omar Khayyam's sleeplessness is not to be compared with hers, for while his was willed, she, foolish Sufiya Zinobia, would lie in bed squeezing her eyelids shut between her thumbs and forefingers, as if she could extrude consciousness through her eyelashes, like motes of dust, or tears. And she burned, she fried, in that very room of her husband's birth and his grandfather's death, beside that bed of snakes and Paradise ... a plague on this disobedient Time! I command this death scene back into the wings at once: shazam!)

By the age of ten young Omar had already begun to feel grateful for the enclosing, protective presence of the mountains on the western and southern skyline. The Impossible Mountains: you will not find that name in your atlases, no matter how large-scale. Geographers have their limitations, however; the young Omar Khayyam, who fell in love with a miraculously shiny brass telescope which he unearthed from the wild abundance of things that clogged his home, was always aware that any silicon creatures or gas monsters inhabiting the stars of the Milky Way which flowed overhead each night would never have recognized their homes by the names in his much-thumbed star charts. 'We had our reasons,' he said throughout his life, 'for the name we gave to our personal mountain range.'

The thin-eyed, rock-hard tribals who dwelt in those mountains and who were occasionally to be seen in the streets of Q. (whose softer inhabitants crossed streets to avoid the tribals' mountainous stench and barging, unceremonious shoulders) also called the range 'the roof of Paradise'. The mountains, in fact the whole region, even Q. itself, suffered from periodic earthquakes; it was a zone of instability, and the tribals believed that the tremors were caused by the emergence of angels through fissures in the rocks. Long before his own brother saw a winged and golden-glowing man watching him from a rooftop, Omar Khayyam Shakil had become aware of the plausible theory that Paradise was located not in the sky but beneath his very feet, so that the earth movements were proof of the angels' interest in scrutinizing world affairs. The shape of the mountain range altered constantly under this angelic pressure. From its crumpled ochre slopes rose an infinite number of stratified pillar-like formations whose geological strata were so sharply defined that the titanic columns seemed to have been erected by colossi skilled in stonemasonry . . . these divine dream-temples, too, rose and fell as the angels came and went.

Hell above, Paradise below; I have lingered on this account of Omar Khayyam's original, unstable wilderness to underline the propositions that he grew up between twin eternities, whose conventional order was, in his experience, precisely inverted; that such headstandings have effects harder to measure than earthquakes, for what inventor has patented a seismograph of the soul?; and that, for Omar Khayyam, uncircumcised, unwhispered-to, unshaven, their presence heightened his feeling of being a person apart.

But I have been out of doors for quite long enough now, and must get my narrative out of the sun before it is afflicted by mirages or heat-stroke. – Afterwards, at the other end of his life (it seems that the future cannot be restrained, and insists on seeping back into the past), when he got his name into all the papers over the scandal of the headless murders, the customs official's daughter Farah Rodrigues unlocked her lips and released from her custody the story of the day on which the adolescent Omar Khayyam, even then a fat fellow with a missing shirt-button at navel height, had accompanied her to her father's post at the land border forty miles to the west of Q. She sat in an illicit brandy den and spoke to the room in general, in the cackle of splintered glass to which time and the wilderness air had reduced her formerly crystal laugh: 'Incredible, I swear,' she reminisced, 'we just reached there in the jeep and at once a cloud came down and sat on the ground, right along the frontier, like it couldn't get across without a visa, and that Shakil was so scared he passed out, he got vertigo and fainted, even though both his feet had been on solid ground.'

Even in the days of his greatest distinction, even when he married Hyder's daughter, even after Raza Hyder became President, Omar Khayyam Shakil was sometimes plagued by that improbable vertigo, by the sense of being a creature of the edge: a peripheral man. Once, during the time of his drinking and carousing friendship with Iskander Harappa, millionaire playboy, radical thinker, Prime Minister and finally miracle-working corpse, Omar Khayyam in his cups described himself to Isky. 'You see before you,' he confided, 'a fellow who is not even the hero of his own life; a man born and raised in the condition of being out of things. Heredity counts, dontyouthinkso?'

'That is an oppressive notion,' Iskander Harappa replied.

Omar Khayyam Shakil was raised by no fewer than three mothers, with not a solitary father in sight, a mystery which was later deepened by the birth, when Omar was already twenty years old, of a younger brother who was likewise claimed by all three female parents and whose conception seemed to have been no less immaculate. Equally disturbing, for the growing youth, was his first experience of falling in love, of pursuing with waddling and heated resolution the voluptuously unattainable figure of a certain Farah the Parsee (née Zoroaster), an occupation known to all the local lads, with the solitary exception of his congenitally isolated self, as: 'courting Disaster'.

Dizzy, peripheral, inverted, infatuated, insomniac, stargazing, fat: what manner of hero is this?

2

A NECKLACE OF SHOES

A few weeks after Russian troops entered Afghanistan, I returned home, to visit my parents and sisters and to show off my firstborn son. My family lives in 'Defence', the Pakistan Defence Services Officers' Co-Operative Housing Society, although it is not a military family. 'Defence' is a fashionable part of Karachi; few of the soldiers who were permitted to buy land there at rock-bottom prices could afford to build on it.

But they weren't allowed to sell the empty plots, either. To buy an officer's piece of 'Defence', you had to draw up a complex contract. Under the terms of this contract the land remained the property of the vendor, even though you had paid him the full market price and were now spending a small fortune building your own house on it to your own specifications. In theory you were just being a nice guy, a benefactor who had chosen to give the poor officer a home out of your boundless charity. But the contract also obliged the vendor to name a third party who would have plenipotentiary authority over the property once the house was finished. This third party was your nominee, and when the construction workers went home he simply handed the property over to you. Thus two separate acts of goodwill were necessary to the process. 'Defence' was almost entirely developed on this nice-guy basis. This spirit of comradeship, of working selflessly together towards a common goal, is worthy of remark.

It was an elegant procedure. The vendor got rich, the interme-diary got his fee, you got your house, and nobody broke any laws. So naturally nobody ever questioned how it came about that the city's most highly desirable development zone had been allotted to the defence services in this way. This attitude, too, remains a part of the foundations of 'Defence': the air there is full of unasked questions. But their smell is faint, and the flowers in the many maturing gardens, the trees lining the avenues, the perfumes worn by the beautiful soignée ladies of the neighbourhood quite over-power this other, too-abstract odour. Diplomats, international businessmen, the sons of former dictators, singing stars, textile moguls, Test cricketers come and go. There are many new Datsun and Toyota motor cars. And the name 'Defence Society', which might sound to some ears like a symbol (representing the mutually advantageous relationship between the country's establishment and its armed forces), holds no such resonance in the city. It is only a name.

One evening, soon after my arrival, I visited an old friend, a poet. I had been looking forward to one of our long conversa-tions, to hearing his views about recent events in Pakistan, and about Afghanistan, of course. His house was full of visitors as usual; nobody seemed interested in talking about anything except the cricket series between Pakistan and India. I sat down at a table with my friend and began an idle game of chess. But I really wanted to get the low-down on things, and at length I brought up the stuff that was on my mind, beginning with a question about the execution of Zulfikar Ali Bhutto. But only half the question got past my lips; the other half joined the ranks of the area's many unasked queries, because I felt an extremely painful kick land on my shins and, without crying out, switched in mid-sentence back to sporting topics. We also discussed the incipient video boom.

People entered, excited, circled, laughed. After about forty minutes my friend said, 'It's O.K. now.' I asked, 'Who was it?' He

gave me the name of the informer who had infiltrated this par-
ticular group. They treated him civilly, without hinting that they
knew why he was there, because otherwise he would vanish,
and the next time they might not know who the informer was.
Later, I met the spy. He was a nice guy, pleasantly spoken, honest-
faced, and no doubt happy that he was hearing nothing worth
reporting. A kind of equilibrium had been achieved. Once again, I
was struck by how many nice guys there were in Pakistan, by the
civility growing in those gardens, perfuming the air.

Since my last visit to Karachi, my friend the poet had spent
many months in jail, for social reasons. That is to say, he knew
somebody who knew somebody who was the wife of the second
cousin by marriage of the step-uncle of somebody who might or
might not have shared a flat with someone who was running guns
to the guerrillas in Baluchistan. You can get anywhere in Pakistan
if you know people, even into jail. My friend still refuses to talk
about what happened to him during those months; but other
people told me that he was in bad shape for a long time after he
got out. They said he had been hung upside-down by the ankles
and beaten, as if he were a new-born baby whose lungs had to be
coerced into action so that he could squeal. I never asked him if
he screamed, or if there were upside-down mountain peaks visible
through a window.

Wherever I turn, there is something of which to be ashamed.
But shame is like everything else; live with it for long enough and
it becomes part of the furniture. In 'Defence', you can find shame
in every house, burning in an ashtray, hanging framed upon a
wall, covering a bed. But nobody notices it any more. And
everyone is civilized.

Maybe my friend should be telling this story, or another one,
his own; but he doesn't write poetry any more. So here I am
instead, inventing what never happened to me, and you will note
that my hero has already been ankle-hung, and that his name is
the name of a famous poet; but no quatrains ever issued or will
issue from his pen.

Outsider! Trespasser! You have no right to this subject! . . . I know:

nobody ever arrested me. Nor are they ever likely to. *Poacher! Pirate! We reject your authority. We know you, with your foreign language wrapped around you like a flag: speaking about us in your forked tongue, what can you tell but lies?* I reply with more questions: is history to be considered the property of the participants solely? In what courts are such claims staked, what boundary commissions map out the territories?

Can only the dead speak?

I tell myself this will be a novel of leavetaking, my last words on the East from which, many years ago, I began to come loose. I do not always believe myself when I say this. It is a part of the world to which, whether I like it or not, I am still joined, if only by elastic bands.

As to Afghanistan: after returning to London, I met a senior British diplomat at a dinner, a career specialist in 'my' part of the world. He said it was quite proper, 'post-Afghanistan', for the West to support the dictatorship of President Zia ul-Haq. I should not have lost my temper, but I did. It wasn't any use. Then, as we left the table, his wife, a quiet civil lady who had been making pacifying noises, said to me, 'Tell me, why don't people in Pakistan get rid of Zia in, you know, the usual way?'

Shame, dear reader, is not the exclusive property of the East.

The country in this story is not Pakistan, or not quite. There are two countries, real and fictional, occupying the same space, or almost the same space. My story, my fictional country exist, like myself, at a slight angle to reality. I have found this off-centring to be necessary; but its value is, of course, open to debate. My view is that I am not writing only about Pakistan.

I have not given the country a name. And Q. is not really Quetta at all. But I don't want to be precious about this: when I arrive at the big city, I shall call it Karachi. And it will contain a 'Defence'.

Omar Khayyam's position as a poet is curious. He was never very popular in his native Persia; and he exists in the West in a translation that is really a complete reworking of his verses, in many cases very different from the spirit (to say nothing of the content) of the original. I, too, am a translated man. I have been *borne across*. It is generally believed that something is always lost in translation; I cling to the notion – and use, in evidence, the success of Fitzgerald-Khayyam – that something can also be gained.

'The sight of you through my beloved telescope,' Omar Khayyam Shakil told Farah Zoroaster the day he declared his love, 'gave me the strength to break my mothers' power.'

'Voyeur,' she replied, 'I shit on your words. Your balls dropped too soon and you got the hots, no more to it than that. Don't load your family problems on to me.' She was two years his senior, but Omar Khayyam was nevertheless forced to concede that his darling had a dirty mouth . . .

. . . As well as the name of a great poet, the child had been given his mothers' family name. And as if to underline what they meant by calling him after the immortal Khayyam the three sisters gave a name, too, to that underlit corridory edifice that was now all the country they possessed: the house was named 'Nishapur'. Thus a second Omar grew up in a second place of that name, and every so often, as he grew, would catch a strange look in his three mothers' six eyes, a look that seemed to say Hurry up, we are waiting for your poems. But (I repeat) no rubaiyat ever issued from his pen.

His childhood had been exceptional by any standards, because what applied to mothers and servants wentwithoutsaying for our peripheral hero as well. Omar Khayyam passed twelve long years, the most crucial years of his development, trapped inside that reclusive mansion, that third world that was neither material nor spiritual, but a sort of concentrated decrepitude made up of the decomposing remnants of those two more familiar types of cosmos, a world in which he would constantly run into – as well as the mothballed, spider-webbed, dust-shrouded profusion of crumbling objects – the lingering, fading miasmas of discarded ideas and forgotten dreams. The finely-calculated gesture with which his three mothers had sealed themselves off from the world had created a sweltering, entropical zone in which, despite all the rotting-down of the past, nothing new seemed capable of growth, and from which it became Omar Khayyam's most cherished youthful ambition quickly to escape. Unaware, in that hideously indeterminate frontier universe, of the curvature of space and time, thanks to which he who runs longest and hardest inevitably ends up, gaspingpanting, with wrenched and screaming tendons, at the starting line, he dreamed of exits, feeling that in the claustrophobis of 'Nishapur' his very life was at stake. He was, after all, something new in that infertile and time-eroded labyrinth.

Have you heard of those wolf-children, suckled – we must suppose – on the feral multiple breasts of a hairy moon-howling dam? Rescued from the Pack, they bit their saviours vilely in the arm; netted and caged, they are brought stinking of raw meat and faecal matter into the emancipated light of the world, their brains too imperfectly formed to be capable of acquiring more than the most fundamental rudiments of civilization . . . Omar Khayyam, too, fed at too-many mammary glands; and he wandered for some four thousand days in the thing-infested jungle that was 'Nishapur', his walled-in wild place, his mother-country; until he succeeded in getting the frontiers opened by making a birthday wish that could not be satisfied by anything lifted up in the machine of Mistri Balloch.

'Drop this jungle-boy business,' Farah sneered when Omar tried it on her, 'you're no fucking ape-man, sonny jim.' And, educationally speaking, she was right; but she had also denied the wildness, the evil within him; and he proved upon her own body that she was wrong.

First things first: for twelve years, he had the run of the house. Little (except freedom) was denied him. A spoiled and vulpine brat; when he howled, his mothers caressed him . . . and after the nightmares began and he started giving up sleep, he plunged deeper and deeper into the seemingly bottomless depths of that decaying realm. Believe me when I tell you that he stumbled down corridors so long untrodden that his sandalled feet sank into the dust right up to his ankles; that he discovered ruined staircases made impassable by longago earthquakes which had caused them to heave up into tooth-sharp mountains and also to fall away to reveal dark abysses of fear . . . in the silence of the night and the first sounds of dawn he explored beyond history into what seemed the positively archaeological antiquity of 'Nishapur', discovering in almirahs the wood of whose doors disintegrated beneath his tentative fingers the impossible forms of painted neolithic pottery in the Kotdiji style; or in kitchen quarters whose existence was no longer even suspected he would gaze ignorantly upon bronze implements of utterly fabulous age; or in regions of that colossal palace which had been abandoned long ago because of the collapse of their plumbing he would delve into the quake-exposed intricacies of brick drainage systems that had been out of date for centuries.

On one occasion he lost his way completely and ran wildly about like a time-traveller who has lost his magic capsule and fears he will never emerge from the disintegrating history of his race – and came to a dead stop, staring in horror at a room whose outer wall had been partly demolished by great, thick, water-seeking tree-roots. He was perhaps ten years old when he had this first glimpse of the unfettered outside world. He had only to walk through the shattered wall – but the gift had been sprung upon him without sufficient warning, and, taken unawares by the shocking promise of the dawn light streaming through the hole, he turned tail and fled, his terror leading him blindly back to his own comforting, comfortable room. Afterwards, when he had had time to consider things, he tried to retrace his steps, armed with a purloined ball of string; but try as he might, he never again found his way to that place in the maze of his childhood where the minotaur of forbidden sunlight lived.

'Sometimes I found skeletons,' he swore to disbelieving Farah, 'human as well as animal.' And even where bones were absent, the house's long-dead occupants dogged his steps. Not in the way you think! – No howls, no clanking chains! – But disembodied feelings, the choking fumes of ancient hopes, fears, loves; and finally, made wild by the ancestor-heavy, phantom oppressions of these far recesses of the run-down building, Omar Khayyam took his revenge (not long after the episode of the broken wall) on his unnatural surroundings. I wince as I record his vandalism: armed with broomstick and misappropriated hatchet, he rampaged through dusty passages and maggoty bedrooms, smashing glass cabinets, felling oblivion-sprinkled divans, pulverizing wormy libraries; crystal, paintings, rusty helmets, the paper-thin remnants of priceless silken carpets were destroyed beyond all possibility of repair. 'Take that,' he screeched amidst the corpses of his useless, massacred history, 'take that, old stuff!' – and then burst (dropping guilty hatchet and clean-sweeping broom) into illogical tears.

It must be stated that even in those days nobody believed the boy's stories about the far-flung infinities of the house. 'Only child,' Hashmat Bibi creaked, 'always always they live in their poor head.' And the three male servants laughed too: 'Listening to you, baba, we are thinking this house has grown so huge huge, there mustn't be room for anywhere else in the world!' And three mothers, sitting tolerantly in their favourite swingseat, stretched out patting hands and sealed the matter: 'At least he has a vivid imagination,' said Munnee-in-the-middle, and Mother Bunny concurred: 'Comes from his poetic name.' Worried that he might be sleep-walking, Chhunni-ma detailed a servant to place his sleeping-mat outside Omar Khayyam's room; but by then he had placed the more fantasticated zones of 'Nishapur' off-limits for ever. After he descended upon the cohorts of history like a wolf (or wolf-child) on the fold, Omar Khayyam Shakil confined himself to the well-trodden, swept and dusted, used regions of the house.

Something – conceivably remorse – led him to his grandfather's dark-panelled study, a book-lined room which the three sisters had never entered since the old man's death. Here he discovered that Mr Shakil's air of great learning had been a sham, just like his supposed business acumen; because the books all bore the *ex libris* plates of a certain Colonel Arthur Greenfield, and many of their pages were uncut. It was a gentleman's library, bought *in toto* from the unknown Colonel, and it had remained unused throughout its residence in the Shakil household. Now Omar Khayyam fell upon it with a will.

Here I must praise his autodidactic gifts. For by the time he left 'Nishapur' he had learned classical Arabic and Persian; also Latin, French and German; all with the aid of leather-bound dictionaries and the unused texts of his grandfather's deceptive vanity. In what books the young fellow immersed himself! Illuminated manuscripts of the poetry of Ghalib; volumes of letters written by Mughal emperors to their sons; the Burton translation of the *Alf laylah wa laylah*, and the *Travels* of Ibn Battuta, and the Qissa or tales of the legendary adventurer Hatim Tai . . . yes, yes, I see that I must withdraw (as Farah instructed Omar to withdraw) the misleading image of the mowgli, the junglee boy.

The continual passage of items from living quarters via dumbwaiter to pawnshop brought concealed matter to light at regular intervals. Those outsize chambers stuffed brim-full with the material legacy of generations of rapaciously acquisitive forebears were being slowly emptied, so that by the time Omar Khayyam was ten and a half there was enough space to move around without bumping into the furniture at every step. And one day the three mothers sent a servant into the study to remove from their lives an exquisitely carved walnut screen on which was portrayed the mythical circular mountain of Qaf, complete with the thirty birds playing God thereupon. The flight of the bird-parliament revealed to Omar Khayyam a little bookcase stuffed with volumes on the theory and practice of hypnosis: Sanskrit mantras, compendiums of the lore of the Persian Magi, a leathern copy of the *Kalevala* of the Finns, an account of the hypno-exorcisms of Father Gassner of Klosters and a study of the 'animal magnetism' theory of Franz Mesmer himself; also (and most usefully) a number of cheaply printed do-it-yourself manuals. Greedily, Omar Khayyam began to devour these books, which alone in the library did not bear the name of the literary Colonel; they were his grandfather's true legacy, and they led him into his lifelong involvement with that arcane science which has so awesome a power for good or ill.

The household servants were as under-occupied as he; his mothers had gradually become very lax about such matters as cleanliness and cuisine. The trio of menservants became, therefore, Omar Khayyam's first, willing subjects. Practising with the aid of a shiny four-anna coin he put them under, discovering with some pride his talent for the art: effortlessly keeping his voice on a flat, monotonous plane, he lulled them into trances, learning, among other things, that the sexual drives which his mothers appeared to have lost completely since his birth had not been similarly stilled in these men. Entranced, they happily confessed the secrets of their mutual caresses, and blessed the maternal trinity for having so altered the circumstances of their lives that their true desires could be revealed to them. The contented three-way love of the male servants provided a curious balance for the equal, but wholly platonic, love of the three sisters for one another. (But Omar Khayyam continued to grow bitter, despite being surrounded by so many intimacies and affections.)

Hashmat Bibi also agreed to 'go under'. Omar made her imagine she was floating on a soft pink cloud. 'You are sinking deeper,' he intoned as she lay upon her mat, 'and deeper into the cloud. It is good to be in the cloud; you want to sink lower and lower.' These experiments had a tragic side-effect. Soon after his twelfth birthday, his mothers were informed by the three loving menservants, who stared accusingly at the young master as they spoke, that Hashmat had apparently willed herself into death; at the very end she had been heard muttering, '. . . deeper and deeper into the heart of the rosy cloud.' The old lady, having been given glimpses of non-being through the mediating powers of the young hypnotist's voice, had finally relaxed the iron will with which she had clung to life for what she had claimed was more than one hundred and twenty years. The three mothers stopped swinging in their seat and ordered Omar Khayyam to abandon mesmerism. But by then the world had changed. I must go back a little way to describe the alteration.

What was also found in the slowly emptying rooms: a previously mentioned telescope. With which Omar Khayyam spied out of upper-storey windows (those on the ground floor being permanently shuttered and barred): the world seen as a bright disc, a moon for his delight. He watched kite-fights between colourful, tailed *patangs* whose strings were black and dipped in glass to make them razor sharp; he heard the victors' cries – 'Boi-oi-oi! Boi-oi!' – come towards him on the gritty breeze; once a green and white kite, its string severed, dropped in through his open window. And when, shortly before his twelfth birthday, there strolled on to this ocular moon the incomprehensibly appealing figure of Farah Zoroaster, at that time no more than fourteen but already possessed of a body that moved with the physical wisdom of a woman, then, in that exact moment, he felt his voice break in his throat, while below his belt other things slid downwards too, to take their appointed places, somewhat ahead of schedule, in hitherto-empty sacs. His longing for the outside was immediately transformed into a dull ache in the groin, a tearing in his loins; what followed was perhaps inevitable.

He was not free. His roving freedom-of-the-house was only the pseudo-liberty of a zoo animal; and his mothers were his loving, caring keepers. His three mothers: who else implanted in his heart the conviction of being a sidelined personality, a watcher from the wings of his own life? He watched them for a dozen years, and, yes, it must be said, he hated them for their closeness, for the way they sat with arms entwined on their swinging, creaking seat, for their tendency to lapse giggling into the private languages of their girlhood, for their way of hugging each other, of putting their three heads together and whispering about whoknowswhat, of finishing one another's sentences. Omar Khayyam, walled up in 'Nishapur' had been excluded from human society by his mothers' strange resolve; and this, his mothers' three-in-oneness, redoubled that sense of exclusion, of being, in the midst of objects, out of things.

Twelve years take their toll. At first the high pride which had driven Chhunni, Munnee and Bunny to reject God, their father's memory and their place in society had enabled them to maintain the standards of behaviour which were just about their father's only legacy to them. They would rise, each morning, within seconds of one another, brush their teeth up, down and sideways fifty times each with eucalyptus sticks, and then, identically attired, would oil and comb each other's hair and twine white flowers into the coiled black buns they made of their locks. They addressed the servants, and also each other, by the polite form of the second-person pronoun. The rigidity of their bearing and the precision of their household instructions gave a legitimizing sheen to all their actions, including (which was no doubt the point) the production of an illegitimate child. But slowly, slowly, they slipped.

On the day of Omar Khayyam's departure for the big city, his eldest mother told him a secret that put a date to the beginning of their decline. 'We never wanted to stop breast-feeding you,' she confessed. 'By now you know that it is not usual for a six-year-old boy to be still on the nipple; but you drank from half a dozen, one for each year. On your sixth birthday we renounced this greatest of pleasures, and after that nothing was the same, we began to forget the point of things.'

During the next six years, as breasts dried and shrank, the three sisters lost that firmness and erectness of body which had accounted for a good deal of their beauty. They became soft, there were knots in their hair, they lost interest in the kitchen, the servants got away with murder. But still they declined at the same rate and in identical fashion; the bonds of their identity remained unbroken.

Remember this: the Shakil sisters had never received a proper education, except in manners; while their son, by the time his voice broke, was already something of a self-taught prodigy. He attempted to interest his mothers in his learning; but when he set out the most elegant proofs of Euclidian theorems or expatiated eloquently on the Platonic image of the Cave, they rejected the unfamiliar notions out of hand. 'Angrez double-dutch,' said Chhunni-ma, and the three mothers shrugged as one. 'Who is to understand the brains of those crazy types?' asked Munnee-in-the-middle, in tones of final dismissal. 'They read books from left to right.'

The philistinism of his mothers accentuated Omar Khayyam's feelings, inchoate and half-articulated, of being extraneous, both because he was a gifted child whose gifts were being returned-to-sender by his parents, and because, for all his learning, he guessed that his mothers' point of view was holding him back. He suffered the sensation of being lost inside a cloud, whose curtains parted occasionally to offer tantalizing glimpses of the sky . . . in spite of what he murmured to Hashmat Bibi, cloudiness was not attractive to the boy.

Now then. Omar Khayyam Shakil is almost twelve. He is over-weight, and his generative organ, newly potent, also possesses a fold of skin that should have been removed. His mothers are growing vague about the reasons for their life; while he, in con-trast, has overnight become capable of levels of aggression previ-ously foreign to his complaisant fat-boy nature. I offer (have already hinted at) three causes: one, his sighting of fourteen-year-old Farah on the moon of his telescopic lens; two, his awkward-ness about his altered speech, which swings out of control between croaks and squeaks while an ugly lump bobs in his throat like a cork; and one must not forget three, namely the time-honoured (or dishonoured) mutations wrought by pubertal bio-chemistry upon the adolescent male personality . . . ignorant of this conjunction of diabolic forces within their son, the three mothers make the mistake of asking Omar Khayyam what he wants for his birthday.

He surprises them by being sullen: 'You'll never give it, what's the point?' Horrified maternal gasps. Six hands fly to three heads and take up hear-no-see-no-speak-no-evil positions. Mother Chhunni (hands over ears): 'How can he say this? The boy, what's he talking?' And middling-Munnee, peeping tragically through her fingers: 'Somebody has upset our angel, plain to see.' And Baby Bunny removes hands from lips to speaknoevil: 'Ask! Ask only! What can we refuse? What's so big that we won't do?'

It bursts out of him then: howling, 'To let me out of this horrible house,' and then, much more quietly, into the aching silence that his words have brought into being, 'and to tell my father's name.'

'Cheek! Cheek of the chappie!' – this from Munnee his middle mother; then her sisters draw her into an inward-facing huddle, arms round waists in that pose of obscene unity which the watching boy finds so hard to stomach.

'Didn't I tell?' – in grunts and falsettos of anguish – 'Then why get it out of me in the first place?'

But now it is possible to observe a change. Quarrelsome syllables fly out of the maternal huddle, because the boy's requests have divided the sisters for the first time in more than a decade. They are arguing, and the argument is a rusty, difficult business, a dispute between women who are trying to remember the people they once were.

When they emerge from the rubble of their exploded identity they make heroic attempts to pretend to Omar, and to themselves, that nothing serious has happened; but although all three of them stick by the collective decision that has been made, the boy can see that this unanimity is a mask which is being held in place with considerable difficulty.

'These are reasonable requests,' Baby Bunny speaks first, 'and one, at least, should be granted.'

His triumph terrifies him; the cork in his throat jumps, almost as far as his tongue. 'Whichwhichwhich?' Fearfully, he asks.

Munnee takes over. 'A new satchel will be ordered and will come in the Mistri's machine,' she states gravely, 'and you will go to school. You need not be too happy,' she adds, 'because when you leave this house you will be wounded by many sharp names, which people will throw at you, like knives, in the street.' Munnee, the fiercest opponent of his freedom, has had her own tongue sharpened on the steel of her defeat.

Finally, his eldest mother says her piece. 'Come home without hitting anyone,' she instructs, 'or we will know that they have lowered your pride and made you feel the forbidden emotion of shame.'

'That would be a completely debased effect,' middle-Munnee says.

This word: shame. No, I must write it in its original form, not in this peculiar language tainted by wrong concepts and the accumulated detritus of its owners' unrepented past, this Angrezi in which I am forced to write, and so for ever alter what is written . . .

Sharam, that's the word. For which this paltry 'shame' is a wholly inadequate translation. Three letters, *shìn rè mìm* (written, naturally, from right to left); plus *zabar* accents indicating the short vowel sounds. A short word, but one containing encyclopaedias of nuance. It was not only shame that his mothers forbade Omar Khayyam to feel, but also embarrassment, discomfiture, decency, modesty, shyness, the sense of having an ordained place in the world, and other dialects of emotion for which English has no counterparts. No matter how determinedly one flees a country, one is obliged to take along some hand-luggage; and can it be doubted that Omar Khayyam (to concentrate on him), having been barred from feeling shame (vb. int.: *sharmàna*) at an early age, continued to be affected by that remarkable ban throughout his later years, yes, long after his escape from his mothers' zone of influence?

Reader: it cannot.

What's the opposite of shame? What's left when *sharam* is subtracted? That's obvious: shamelessness.

Owing to the pride of his parents and the singular circumstances of his life, Omar Khayyam Shakil, at the age of twelve, was wholly unfamiliar with the emotion in which he was now being forbidden to indulge.

'What does it feel like?' he asked – and his mothers, seeing his bewilderment, essayed explanations. 'Your face gets hot,' said Bunny-the-youngest, 'but your heart starts shivering.'

'It makes women feel like to cry and die,' said Chhunni-ma, 'but men, it makes them go wild.'

'Except sometimes,' his middle mother muttered with prophetic spite, 'it happens the other way around.'

The division of the three mothers into separate beings became, in the following years, more and more plaintosee. They squabbled over the most alarming trifles, such as who should write the notes that were placed in the dumb-waiter, or whether to take their mid-morning mint tea and biskuts in the drawing room or on the landing. It was as if by sending their son out into the sunlit arenas of the town they had exposed themselves to the very thing they denied him the freedom to experience; as if on the day when the world laid eyes for the first time on their Omar Khayyam the three sisters were finally pierced by the forbidden arrows of *sharam*. Their quarrels died down when he made his second escape; but they were never properly reunited until they decided to repeat the act of motherhood . . .

And there is an even stranger matter to report. It is this: when they were divided by Omar Khayyam's birthday wishes, they had been indistinguishable too long to retain any exact sense of their former selves – and, well, to come right out with it, the result was that they divided up in the wrong way, they got all mixed up, so that Bunny, the youngest, sprouted the premature grey hairs and took on the queenly airs that ought to have been the prerogative of the senior sibling; while big Chhunni seemed to become a torn, uncertain soul, a sister of middles and vacillations; and Munnee developed the histrionic gadfly petulance that is the traditional characteristic of the baby in any generation, and which never ceases to be that baby's right, no matter how old she gets. In the chaos of their regeneration the wrong heads ended up on the wrong bodies; they became psychological centaurs, fish-women, hybrids; and of course this confused separation of personalities carried with it the implication that they were still not genuinely discrete, because they could only be comprehended if you took them as a whole.

Who would not have wanted to escape from such mothers? –

In later years, Omar Khayyam would remember his childhood as a lover, abandoned, remembers his beloved: changeless, incapable of ageing, a memory kept prisoner in a circle of heart's fire. Only he remembered with hatred instead of love; not with flames, but icily, icily. The other Omar wrote great things out of love; our hero's story is poorer, no doubt because it was marinated in bile.

– And it would be easy to argue that he developed pronounced misogynist tendencies at an early age. – That all his subsequent dealings with women were acts of revenge against the memory of his mothers. – But I say in Omar Khayyam's defence: all his life, whatever he did, whoever he became, he did his filial duty and paid their bills. The pawnbroker Chalaak Sahib ceased to pay visits to the dumb-waiter; which indicates the existence of love, love of some sort . . . but he is not grown-up yet. Just now the satchel has arrived via the Mistri's machine; now it hangs over the shoulder of the twelve-year-old escapologist; now he enters the dumb-waiter and the satchel begins its descent back to earth. Omar Khayyam's twelfth birthday brought him freedom instead of cake; also, inside the satchel, blue-lined copybooks, a slate, a washable wooden board and some quill pens with which to practise the sinuous script of his mother tongue, chalks, pencils, a wooden ruler and a box of geometry instruments, protractor, dividers, compass. Plus a small aluminum etherizing box in which to murder frogs. With the weapons of learning hanging over his shoulder, Omar Khayyam left his mothers, who wordlessly (and still in unison) waved goodbye.

Omar Khayyam Shakil never forgot the moment of his emergence from the dumb-waiter into the dust of the no-man's-land around the high mansion of his childhood which stood like a pariah between the Cantonment and the town; or the first sight of the reception committee, one of whose members was carrying a most unexpected sort of garland.

When the wife of Q.'s finest leather-goods merchant received the sisters' order for a school satchel from the peon whom she dispatched to the dumb-waiter once a fortnight in accordance with the Shakils' standing orders, she, Zeenat Kabuli, at once ran round to the house of her best friend, the widow Farida Balloch, who lived with her brother Bilal. The three of them, who had never ceased to believe that Yakoob Balloch's street-death was the direct result of his getting mixed up with the anchoritic sisters, agreed that the flesh-and-blood product of the longago scandal must be about to emerge into plain daylight. They stationed themselves outside the Shakil household to await this event, but not before Zeenat Kabuli had pulled out from the back of her shop a gunny sack filled with old rotting shoes and sandals and slippers of no conceivable value to anyone, annihilated footwear that had been awaiting just such an occasion, and which was now strung together to form the worst of all insults, that is, a necklace of shoes. 'The shoe garland,' the widow Balloch swore to Zeenat Kabuli, 'just see if I don't hang it on that child's neck, personal.'

The week-long vigil of Farida, Zeenat and Bilal inevitably attracted attention, so that by the time Omar Khayyam jumped out of the dumb-waiter they had been joined by divers other gawpers and taunters, raggedy urchins and unemployed clerks and washerwomen on their way to the ghats. Also present was the town postman, Muhammad Ibadalla, who bore upon his forehead the *gatta* or permanent bruise which revealed him to be a religious fanatic who pressed brow to prayer-mat on at least five occasions per diem, and probably at the sixth, optional time as well. This Ibadalla had found his job through the malign influence of the beardy serpent who stood beside him in the heat, the local divine, the notorious Maulana Dawood who rode around town on a motor-scooter donated by the Angrez shabis, threatening the citizens with damnation. It turned out that this Ibadalla had been incensed by the Shakil ladies' decision not to send their letter to the headmaster of the Cantt school via the postal services. It had been included, instead, in the envelope they had sent down in the dumb-waiter to the flower-girl Azra, along with a small extra fee. Ibadalla had been wooing this Azra for some time, but she laughed at him, 'I don't care for a type who spends so much time with his backside higher than his head.' So the sisters' decision to place their letter in her care struck the postman as a personal insult, a way of undermining his status, and also as further proof of their Godlessness, for had they not allied themselves by this infamous act of correspondence with a slut who cracked jokes about prayer? 'Behold,' Ibadalla yelled energetically as Omar Khayyam touched the ground, 'there stands the Devil's seed.'

There now occurred an unfortunate incident. Ibadalla, incensed by the Azra business, had spoken up first, thus incurring the displeasure of his patron Maulana Dawood, a loss of divine support which ruined the postman's chance of future promotion and intensified his hatred of all Shakils; because of course the Maulana thought it his right to begin the assault on the poor, fat, prematurely-pubescent symbol of incarnate sin. In an attempt to regain the initiative Dawood flung himself to his knees in the dust at Omar's feet; he ground his forehead ecstatically into the dirt by Omar's toes, and called out: 'O God! O scourging Lord! Bring down upon this human abomination Thy sizzling fountain of fire!' Etcetera. This grotesque display greatly irritated the three who had kept the original vigil. 'Whose husband died for a dumb-waiter?' Farida Balloch hissed to her friend. 'That shouting oldie's? Then who should be speaking now?' Her brother Bilal did not stop for speech; rope of shoes in hand, he strode forward, bellowing in that stentorian voice that was almost the equal of the fabled voice of his namesake, that first, black Bilal, the Prophet's muezzin: 'Boy! Flesh of infamy! Think yourself lucky I do no more than this! You think I couldn't squash you flat like one mosquito?' – And in the background, like raucous echoes, urchins washerwomen clerks were chanting: 'Devil's seed! – Fountain of fire! – Whose husband died? – Like one mosquito!' – They were all closing in, Ibadalla and Maulana and three vengeful vigilantes, while Omar stood like a cobra-hypnotized mongoose, but all around him things were unfreezing, the twelve-year-old, suspended prejudices of the town were springing back to life . . . and Bilal could wait no longer, he rushed up to the boy as Dawood prostrated himself for the seventeenth time; the garland of shoes was hurled in Omar's direction; and just then the Maulana straightened up to howl at God, interposing scrawny gizzard between insulting footwear and its target, and there, next thing anyone knew, was the fateful necklace, hanging around the divine's accidental neck.

Omar Khayyam began to giggle: such can be the effects of fear. And urchins giggled with him; even the widow Balloch had to fight back the laughter until it came out as water from her eyes. In those days, people were not so keen on the servants of God as we are told they have become at present . . . Maulana Dawood rose up with murder in his face. Being no fool, however, he quickly turned this face away from the giant Bilal and reached out his claws for Omar Khayyam – who was saved by the blessed figure, shouldering its way through the mob, of Mr Eduardo Rodrigues, schoolmaster, who had arrived as arranged to fetch the new pupil to class. And with Rodrigues was a vision of such joy that moon-struck Khayyam at once forgot the danger that had come so close. 'This is Farah,' Rodrigues told him, 'she is two standards senior to you.' The vision looked at Omar; then at the shoe-necked Maulana, who in his rage had neglected to remove the garland; then put back its head and roared.

'God, yaar,' she said to Omar, her first word a casual blasphemy, 'why you didn't sit on at home? This town was already full of fools.'

3

MELTING ICE

Cool, white as a refrigerator, it stood amidst offensively green lawns: the Cantonment School. In its gardens trees also flourished, because the Angrez sahibs had diverted large quantities of the region's sparse water supplies into the hoses with which the Cantt gardeners strolled around all day. It was clear that those curious grey beings from a wet northern world could not survive unless grass and bougainvillaea and tamarind and jackfruit thrived as well. As for the human saplings nurtured in the School: white (grey) as well as brown, they ranged from age-three to age-nineteen. But after the age of eight, the numbers of Angrez children fell away sharply, and the children in the upper standards were almost uniformly brown. What happened to the fair-skinned children after their eighth birthdays? Death, vanishment, a sudden surge of melanin production in their skins?—No, no. For the real answer it would be necessary to conduct extensive research into the old ledgers of steamship companies and the diaries of long-extinct ladies in what the Angrez colonialists always called the mother country, but what was in fact a land of maiden aunts and other, more distant female relatives, on whom children could be billeted to save them from the perils of an Oriental upbringing . . .

but such research is beyond the resources of the author, who must avert his eyes from such side-issues without further delay.

School is school; everyone knows what goes on there. Omar Khayyam was a fat boy, so he got what fat boys get, taunts, ink-pellets in the back of the neck, nicknames, a few beatings, nothing special. When his schoolfellows found that he had no intention of rising to any gibes about his unusual origins they simply left him alone, contenting themselves with the occasional schoolyard rhyme. This suited him excellently. Unashamed, accustomed to solitude, he began to enjoy his near-invisibility. From his position at the edge of the school's life, he took vicarious pleasure in the activities of those around him, silently celebrating the rise or fall of this or that playground emperor, or the examination failures of particularly unappetizing classfellows: the delights of the spectator.

Once, by chance, he stood in a shadowed corner of the tree-heavy grounds and observed two seniors canoodling energetically behind a flame-of-the-forest. Watching their fondlings, he felt a strangely warm satisfaction, and decided to look for other oppor-tunities of indulging in this new pastime. As he grew older, and was permitted to stay out later, he became skilled in his chosen pursuit; the town yielded up its secrets to his omnipresent eyes. Through inefficient chick-blinds he spied on the couplings of the postman Ibadalla with the widow Balloch, and also, in another place, with her best friend Zeenat Kabuli, so that the notorious occasion on which the postman, the leather-goods merchant and the loud-mouthed Bilal went at one another with knives in a gully and ended up stone dead, all three of them, was no mystery to him; but he was too young to understand why Zeenat and Farida, who should by rights have hated each other like poison once it all came out, shacked up together instead and lived, after that triple killing, in unbreakable friendship and celibacy for the rest of their days.

To be frank: what a telescope began at long distance, Omar Khayyam continued in close-up. Let us not be afraid to mention the word 'voyeur', remembering that it has already been men-tioned (in telescopic context) by Farah Zoroaster. But now that we have named him peeping-tom, we should also say that he was never caught, unlike that bold fellow in Agra who, they say, looked over a high wall to spy on the building of the Taj Mahal. He had his eyes put out, or so the story goes; whereas Omar Khayyam's peepers were opened wide by his voyeurism, which revealed to him both the infinitely rich and cryptic texture of human life and also the bitter-sweet delights of living through other human beings.

He had one total failure. Needless to say, what mothers had hidden from him for twelve years, schoolboys unveiled in twelve minutes: that is, the story of the legendary party at which musta-chioed officers had been eyed, sized up, and afterwards . . . Omar Khayyam Shakil, obeying maternal orders, engaged in no fisticuffs when taunted with this saga. He existed in a kind of Eden of the morals, and shrugged the insults off; but after that he began watching the Angrez gentlemen for signs, examining them for facial resemblances to himself, waiting to pounce on some casual or inadvertent expression or gesture that might reveal the identity of his unknown male progenitor. He had no success. Perhaps the father was long gone, and living, if still alive, in some seaside bun-galow lapped by tides of nostalgia for the horizons of his departed glory, fingering the few miserable artifacts – ivory hunting horns, kukri knives, a photograph of himself at a Maharaja's tiger hunt – which preserved, on the mantels of his declining years, the dying echoes of the past, like seashells that sing of distant seas . . . but these are fruitless speculations. Unable to locate a father, the boy selected one for himself out of available personnel, bestowing the accolade without any reservations upon Mr Eduardo Rodrigues the schoolmaster, who was himself a recent arrival in Q., having alighted jauntily from a bus one day some years previously, dressed in whites, with a white fedora on his head and an empty birdcage in his hand.

And one last word about Omar Khayyam's peepings: because of course his three mothers had begun to live vicariously too, they couldn't help themselves, in those days of their weakening resolve they quizzed him eagerly upon his return from Outside about ladies' fashions and all the minutiae of town life, and had he heard anything about *them*; from time to time they covered their faces with their shawls, so that it was evident that they could no longer seal themselves off from the emotion they had anathematized . . . spying on the world through the unreliable eyes of their son (and naturally he did not tell them everything), their own voyeurism-by-proxy had the effect that such things are classically supposed to have: that is, it weakened their moral fibre. Perhaps this is why they were able to contemplate a repetition of their crime.

Mr Eduardo Rodrigues was as slim and sharp as his enormous collection of pencils, and nobody knew his age. According to the angle at which the light caught his face he could take on the bright-eyed insolent appearance of a teenager or the doleful aspect of a man drowning in half-spent yesterdays. An unexplained southerner, he cut a mysterious figure in the town, having gone directly from the bus depot of his arrival to the Cantonment School, where he had succeeded in talking his way into a teaching post before night fell. 'It is necessary to be unusual,' was all the explanation he would give, 'if one wants to spread the Word.'

He lived in a puritanical room as the paying guest of one of the less fortunate Angrez sahibs. On his walls he hung a crucifix, and also glued up a number of cheap pictures, excised from calendars, of a balmy coastal land in which palm trees swayed against impossibly orange sunsets and a Baroque cathedral stood, partially overgrown by creepers, on an ocean inlet crowded with flame-sailed dhows. Omar Khayyam Shakil and Farah Zoroaster, the only students who ever entered this sanctum, saw no signs of anything more personal; it seemed as if Eduardo were hiding his past from the fierce rays of the desert sun, to prevent it from fading. Such was the blinding emptiness of the teacher's quarters that Omar Khayyam did not notice until his third visit the cheap birdcage sitting on top of the room's one cupboard, a cage from which the gold paint had long ago begun to peel, and which was just as empty as it had been on the day of his arrival at the bus depot, 'As if,' Farah whispered scornfully, 'he came up here to catch a bird, and couldn't, the stupid type.'

Eduardo and Omar, each in his separate way an outsider in Q., may have been drawn to each other by the half-conscious perception of their likeness; but there were also other forces at work. These forces may all be conveniently collected under a single heading, and this phrase, too, has been mentioned before: it is 'courting Disaster'.

It had not escaped the notice of the town gossips that Eduardo had arrived, birdcage in hand, fedora on head, a mere two months after the customs officer Zoroaster had been sent up to these parts, minus wife, plus eight-year-old daughter. So it wasn't long before mule-wallahs and ironmongers and scootered divines had worked out that this Zoroaster's previous posting had been in the same zone of creepery cathedrals and coconut beaches whose memory could be smelled on Rodrigues's white suit and in his Portuguese name. Tongues began to wag: 'So where is that customs-wallah's wife? Divorced, sent back to her mother, murdered in a rage of the passions? Look at that Farah, she doesn't look like her daddy, not one bit!' But these tongues were also obliged to admit that Farah Zoroaster did not look one bit like the teacher either, so that avenue was reluctantly closed off, especially when it became plain that Rodrigues and Zoroaster were on extremely cordial terms. 'So why does a customs officer get shunted out here to this end-of-the-earth job?' Farah had a simple answer. 'My stupid father is a type who goes on dreaming after he has woken up. He thinks one day we will return to where we have never been, that damn land of Ahuramazda, and this no-good Irani frontier is the closest we could get. Can you imagine?' she howled, 'He *volunteered*.'

Gossip is like water. It probes surfaces for their weak places, until it finds the breakthrough point; so it was only a matter of time before the good people of Q. hit upon the most shameful, scandalous explanation of all. 'O God, a grown man in love with a little child. Eduardo and Farah — what do you mean it can't happen, happens every day, only a few years back there was that other — yes, that must be it, these Christians are big perverts, God preserve us, he follows his little floozy up here to the backyard of the universe, and who knows what encouragement she gives, because a woman knows how to tell a man if he is wanted or not wanted, of course, even at eight years old, these things are in the blood.'

Neither Eduardo nor Farah gave, in their behaviour, the slightest indication that the rumours were rooted in fact. It is true that Eduardo did not marry during the years of Farah's growing towards womanhood; but it is also true that Farah, known as 'Disaster', was also called 'the ice block' on account of her sub-zero coldness towards her many admirers, a frigidity which extended also to her relations with Eduardo Rodrigues. 'But of course they put up a good front, what do you think?' — the gossips were able to point out, triumphantly, that they had been justified by events in the end.

Omar Khayyam Shakil, for all his love of watching-and-listening, pretended to turn a deaf ear to all these stories; such are the effects of love. But they got inside him anyway, they got under his skin and into his blood and worked their way, like little splinters, to his heart; until he, too, proved himself guilty of the alleged Christian perversions of the schoolteacher Rodrigues. Choose yourself a father and you also choose your inheritance. (But Sufiya Zinobia must wait for a few pages yet.)

I have idled away too many paragraphs in the company of gossips; let's get back on to solid ground: Eduardo Rodrigues, accompanied gossip-feedingly by Farah, collecting Omar Khayyam on his first schoolday, a fact which bore witness to the residual influence of the Shakil name in the town. In the following months, Eduardo discovered the boy's exceptional aptitude for learning, and wrote to his mothers offering his services as a private tutor who could help realize their child's potential. It is a matter of record that this mothers agreed to the schoolteacher's suggestion; also that Eduardo's only other private pupil was Farah Zoroaster, whose father was excused from paying any fee, because Eduardo was a genuinely dedicated teacher; and thirdly, that as the years passed the threesome of Omar, Eduardo and Farah became a common sight in the town.

It was Rodrigues, who had the ability of speaking in capital letters, who steered Omar towards a medical career. 'To Succeed in Life,' he told the boy amid beach-postcards and empty birdcage, 'one must be Of the Essence. Yes, make yourself Essential, that's the Ticket . . . and who is most Indispensable? Why, the fellow who does the Dispensing! I mean of Advice, Diagnosis, Restricted Drugs. Be a Doctor; it is what I have Seen in You.'

What Eduardo saw in Omar (in my opinion): the possibilities of his true, peripheral nature. What's a doctor, after all? – A legitimized voyeur, a stranger whom we permit to poke fingers and even hands into places where we would not permit most people to insert so much as a finger-tip, who gazes on what we take most trouble to hide; a sitter-at-bedsides, an outsider admitted to our most intimate moments (birthdeathetc.), anonymous, a minor character, yet also, paradoxically, central, especially at the crisis . . . yes, yes. Eduardo was a far-sighted teacher, and no mistake. And Omar Khayyam, who had picked Rodrigues for a father, never once considered going against his tutor's wishes. This is how lives are made.

But not only in this way; also by dog-eared books discovered accidentally at home, and by long-suppressed first loves . . . when Omar Khayyam Shakil was sixteen years old, he was flung into a great vortex of fearful joy, because Farah the Parsee, Disaster Zoroaster, invited him one day to come out and see her father's customs post.

'. . . and fainted, though both his feet had been on solid ground.' We have already been told something of what transpired at the frontier: how a cloud descended, and Omar Khayyam, mistaking it for his childhood nightmare of the void at the end of the earth, passed out. It is possible that this fainting fit gave him the idea for what he did later that day.

Details first: what was the tone of Farah's invitation? – Grace-less, curt, I–don't–care–if–you–don't. Its motivation, whence? – From Eduardo, who had urged her privately: 'That is one lonely boy, be nice. You bright ones should stick together.' (Omar Khayyam was the brighter of the pair; although two years still stood between them, he had caught up Farah in other ways, and was now in the self-same standard.) How rapidly did Omar Khayyam accept? – Ek dum. Fut-a-fut. At once, or even quicker.

On weekdays, during term, Farah lodged in Q. at the home of a Parsee mechanic and his wife, with whom her father had culti-vated a friendship for this very purpose. This mechanic, an unim-portant Jamshed who does not even merit a description, drove them out to the frontier on the selected holiday in a jeep he was repairing. And as they neared the border, Farah's spirits rose while Omar's fell . . .

. . . His fear of the Edge mounted, irrationally, as they drove, as he sat behind her in the roofless vehicle while her open, wind-whipped hair flickered in front of him like black fire. Whereas her mood was lightened by the drive, around a spur of the mountains, through a pass in which they were watched by the invisible eyes of suspicious tribals. The emptiness of the frontier pleased Farah, no matter how openly she sneered at her father for having taken this dead-end job. She even began to sing; revealing that she had a melodious voice.

At the frontier: clouds, fainting fit, water sprinkled on face, reawakening, whereamI. Omar Khayyam comes round to find that the cloud has lifted, so that it is possible to see that the frontier is an unimpressive place: no wall, no police, no barbed wire or floodlights, no red-and-white striped barriers, nothing but a row of concrete bollards at hundred-foot intervals, bollards driven into the hard and barren ground. There is a small customs house, and a railhead that has turned brown with rust; on the rails stands a single forgotten goods van, also browned by oblivion. 'The trains don't come any more,' Farah says, 'the international situation does not permit it.'

A customs officer depends, for a decent income, on traffic. Goods pass through, he not unreasonably impounds them, their owners see reason, an accommodation is reached, the customs man's family gets new clothes. Nobody minds this arrangement; everyone knows how little public officials are paid. Negotiations are honourably conducted on both sides.

But very little in the way of dutiable items passes through the small brick building that is Mr Zoroaster's power centre. Under cover of night, tribals stroll back and forth between the countries through bollards and rocks. Who knows what they carry forth and back? This is Zoroaster's tragedy; and, in spite of her scholarship, he has trouble financing his daughter's fine education. How he consoles himself: 'Soon, soon the railway line will open . . .' But the rust is accumulating on this belief as well; he gazes across bollards to the ancestral land of Zarathustra and tries to gain solace from its proximity, but there is, these days, a strain in his expression . . . Farah Zoroaster claps her hands and runs in and out between the interminable bollards. 'Fun, na?' she yells, 'Teep-taap!' Omar Khayyam, for the sake of maintaining her affable mood, agrees that the place is quite tip-top. Zoroaster shrugs without bitterness and retreats into his office with the jeep-driver, warning the young people not to stay out too long in the sun.

Perhaps they stayed out too long, and that was what gave Omar Khayyam the courage to declare his love: 'The sight of you through my telescope,' etc., but there is no need to repeat his speech, or Farah's coarse reply. Rejected, Omar Khayyam unleashes piteous questions: 'Why? Why not? Because I'm fat?' And Farah replies, 'Fat would be all right; but there is something ugly about you, you know that?' – 'Ugly?' – 'Don't ask me what, I dunno. Something. Must be in your personality or somewhere.'

Silence between them until late afternoon. Omar meandering in Farah's wake between bollards. He notices that broken pieces of mirrors have been tied to many of the posts with pieces of string; as Farah approaches each fragment she sees shards of herself reflected in the glass, and smiles her private smile. Omar Khayyam Shakil understands that his beloved is a being too self-contained to succumb to any conventional assault; she and her mirrors are twins and need no outsiders to make them feel complete . . . and then, in the late afternoon, inspired by too-much-sun or fainting fit, he has his idea. 'Have you ever,' he asks Farah Zoroaster, 'been hypnotized?' – And for the first time in history, she looks at him with interest.

Afterwards, when her womb began to swell; when an outraged headmaster called her into his office and expelled her for calling down shame upon the school; when she was thrown out by her father, who had suddenly found that his empty customs house was too full to accommodate a daughter whose belly revealed her adherence to other, unacceptable customs; when Eduardo Rodrigues had taken her, pulling and fighting against his inexorable, gripping hand, to the Cantt padre and married her by force; Eduardo, having thus declared himself the guilty party for all to see, was dismissed from his job for conduct unbecoming; when Farah and Eduardo had left for the railway station in a tonga notable for the almost total absence of luggage (although a birdcage, still empty, was present, and malicious tongues said that Eduardo Rodrigues had finally caught two birds instead of one); when they had gone and the town had settled back into ashen nothingness, after the brief blaze of the wicked drama that had been played out in its streets . . . then Omar Khayyam tried, futilely, to find consolation in the fact that, as every hypnotist knows, one of the first reassurances in the hypnotic process, a formula which is repeated many times, runs as follows:

'You will do anything that I ask you to do, but I will ask you to do nothing that you will be unwilling to do.'

'She was willing,' he told himself. 'Then where's the blame? She must have been willing, and everybody knows the risk.'

But in spite of nothing-that-you-will-be-unwilling-to-do; in spite, too, of the actions of Eduardo Rodrigues, which had been at once so resolute and so resigned that Omar Khayyam had almost been convinced that the teacher really was the father–why not, after all? A woman who is willing with one will be willing with two! – in spite of everything, I say, Omar Khayyam Shakil was possessed by a demon which made him shake in the middle of breakfast and go hot in the night and cold in the day and sometimes cry out for no reason in the street or while ascending in the dumb-waiter. Its fingers reached outwards from his stomach to clutch, without warning, various interior parts of himself, from adam's-apple to large (and also small) intestine, so that he suffered from moments of near-strangulation and spent long unproductive hours on the pot. It made his limbs mysteriously heavy in the mornings so that sometimes he was unable to get out of bed. It made his tongue dry and his knees knock. It led his teenage feet into cheap brandy shops. Tottering drunkenly home to the rage of his three mothers, he would be heard telling a swaying group of fellow-sufferers: 'The only thing about this business is that it has made me understand my mothers at last. This must be what they locked themselves up to avoid, and baba, who would not?' Vomiting out the thin yellow fluid of his shame while the dumb-waiter descended, he swore to his companions, who were falling asleep in the dirt: 'Me, too, man. I've got to escape this also.'

On the evening when Omar Khayyam, eighteen years old and already fatter than fifty melons, came home to inform Chhunni, Munnee and Bunny that he had won a scholarship at the best medical college in Karachi, the three sisters were only able to hide their grief at his imminent departure by erecting around it a great barrier of objects, the most valuable jewels and paintings in the house, which they scurried to collect from room to room until a pile of ancient beauty stood in front of their old, favourite swing-seat. 'Scholarship is all very well,' his youngest mother told him, 'but we also can give money to our boy when he goes into the world.' 'What do these doctors think?' Chhunni demanded in a king of fury. 'We are too poor to pay for your education? Let them take charity to the devil, your family has money in abundance.' 'Old money,' Munnee concurred. Unable to persuade them that the award was an honour he did not wish to refuse, Omar Khayyam was obliged to leave for the railway station with his pockets bulging with the pawnbroker's banknotes. Around his neck was a garland whose one-hundred and one fresh-cut flowers gave off an aroma which quite obliterated the memory-stink of the necklace of shoes which had once so narrowly missed his neck. The perfume of this garland was so intense that he forgot to tell his mothers a last bit of gossip, which was that Zoroaster the customs officer had fallen sick under the spell of the bribeless desert and had taken to standing stark naked on top of concrete bollards while mirror-fragments ripped his feet. Arms outstretched and daughterless, Zoroaster addressed the sun, begging it to come down to earth and engulf the planet in its brilliant cleansing fire. The tribals who bore this tale into the bazaar of Q. were of the opinion that the customs-wallah's fervour was so great that he would undoubtedly succeed, so that it was worth making preparations for the end of the word.

The last person to whom Omar Khayyam spoke before making his escape from the town of shame was a certain Chand Moham-mad who said afterwards, 'That fat guy didn't look so hot when I started talking to him and he looked twice as sick when I finished.' This Chand Mohammad was a vendor of ice. As Omar Khayyam, still unable to shake off the terribly debility which had gripped him ever since the incident at the frontier, hauled his obesity into a first-class carriage, Chand ran up and said, 'Hot day, sahib. Ice is needed.' At first, Shakil, out of breath and gloomy, told him, 'Be off and sell other fools your frozen water.' But Chand persisted: 'Sahib, in the afternoon the Loo wind will blow, and if you do not have my ice at your feet the heat will melt the marrow out of your bones.'

Persuaded by this convincing argument, Omar Khayyam pur-chased a long tin tub, four feet long, eighteen inches wide, one foot deep, in which there lay a solid slab of ice, sprinkled with sawdust and sand to prolong its life. Grunting as he heaved it into the carriage, the ice vendor made a joke. 'Such is life,' he said, 'one ice block returns to town and another sets off in the opposite direction.'

Omar Khayyam unbuckled his sandals and placed his bare feet on the ice, feeling the healing solace of its coldness. Peeling off too many rupees for Chand Mohammad as he cheered up, he asked idly, 'What rubbish are you talking? How can a block of ice return unmelted after the journey? The tin tub, empty, or full of melted water, you must be meaning that.'

'O, no, sahib, great lord,' the ice-vendor grinned as he pocketed the cash, 'this is one ice block that goes everywhere without melting at all.'

Colour drained from fat cheeks. Plump feet jumped off ice. Omar Khayyam, looking around fearfully as if he thought she might materialize at any moment, spoke in tones so altered by fury that the ice-vendor backed off, frightened. 'Her? When? You are trying to insult . . . ?' He caught the ice-man by his ragged shirt, and the poor wretch had no option but to tell it all, to reveal that on this very train, a few hours back, Mrs Farah Rodrigues (née Zoroaster) had returned shamelessly to the scene of her infamy and headed straight out to her father's frontier post, 'even though he threw her in the street like a bucket of dirty water, sahib, just think.'

When Farah came back, she brought neither husband nor child. Nobody ever found out what had become of Eduardo and the baby for which he had sacrificed everything, so of course the stories could circulate without fear of disproof: a miscarriage, an abortion in spite of Rodrigues's Catholic faith, the baby exposed on a rock after birth, the baby stifled in its crib, the baby given to the orphanage or left in the street, while Farah and Eduardo like wild lovers copulated on the postcard beaches or in the aisle of the vegetation-covered house of the Christian God, until they tired of each other, she gave him the boot, he (tired of her lascivious flirtings) gave her the boot, they gave each other simultaneous boots, who cares who it was, she is back so lock up your sons.

Farah Rodrigues in her pride spoke to no one in Q. except to order food and supplies in the shops; until, in her old age, she began to frequent the covert liquor joints, which was where she

would reminisce, years later, about Omar Khayyam, after his
name got into the papers. On her rare visits to the bazaar she made
her purchases without looking anyone in the eye, pausing only to
gaze at herself in every available mirror with a frank affection
which proved to the town that she regretted nothing. So even
when it got about that she had come back to look after her crazy
father and to run the customs post, to prevent his dismissal by his
Angrez bosses, even then the town's attitude did not soften; who
knows what they get up to out there, people said, naked father
and whore-child, best place for them is out there in the desert
where nobody has to look except God and the Devil, and they
know it all already.

And on his train, his feet once more resting on a block of
melting ice, Omar Khayyam Shakil was borne away into the
future, convinced that he had finally managed to escape, and the
cool pleasure of that notion and also of the ice brought a smile to
his lips, even while the hot wind blew.

Two years later, his mothers wrote to tell him that he had a
brother, whom they had named Babar after the first Emperor of
the Mughals who had marched over the Impossible Mountains
and conquered wherever he went. After that the three sisters, uni-
fied once again by motherhood, were happy and indistinguishable
for many years within the walls of 'Nishapur'.

When Omar Khayyam read the letter, his first reaction was to
whistle softly with something very like admiration.

'The old witches,' he said aloud, 'they managed to do it again.'

II

THE DUELLISTS

4

❖

BEHIND THE SCREEN

This is a novel about Sufiya Zinobia, elder daughter of General Raza Hyder and his wife Bilquìs, about what happened between her father and Chairman Iskander Harappa, formerly Prime Minister, now defunct, and about her surprising marriage to a certain Omar Khayyam Shakil, physician, fat man, and for a time the intimate crony of that same Isky Harappa, whose neck had the miraculous power of remaining unbruised, even by a hangman's rope. Or perhaps it would be more accurate, if also more opaque, to say that Sufiya Zinobia is about this novel.

At any rate, it is not possible even to begin to know a person without first gaining some knowledge of her family background; so I must proceed in this way, by explaining how it was that Bilquìs grew frightened of the hot afternoon wind called the Loo:

On the last morning of his life, her father Mahmoud Kemal, known as Mahmoud the Woman, dressed as usual in a shiny blue two-piece suit shot with brilliant streaks of red, looked approvingly at himself in the ornate mirror which he had removed from the foyer of his theatre on account of its irresistible frame of naked cherubs shooting arrows and blowing golden horns, hugged his eighteen-year-old daughter, and announced: 'So you see, girl, your father dresses finely, as befits the chief administrative officer of a glorious Empire.' And at breakfast, when she began dutifully to spoon khichri on to his plate, he roared in good-natured fury, 'Why do you lift your hand, daughter? A princess does not serve.' Bilquìs bowed her head and stared out of the bottom left-hand corner of her eyes, whereupon her father applauded loudly. 'O, too good, Billoo! What elite acting, I swear!'

It's a fact, strange-but-true, that the city of idolaters in which this scene took place – call it Indraprastha, Puranaqila, even Delhi – had often been ruled by men who believed (like Mahmoud) in Al-Lah, The God. Their artifacts litter the city to this day, ancient observatories and victory towers and of course that great red fortress, Al-Hambra, the red one, which will play an important part in our story. And, what is more, many of these godly rulers had come up from the humblest of origins; every schoolchild knows about the Slave Kings . . . but anyway, the point is that this whole business of ruling-an-Empire was just a family joke, because of course Mahmoud's domain was only the Empire Talkies, a fleapit of a picture theatre in the old quarter of the town.

'The greatness of a picture house,' Mahmoud liked to say, 'can be deduced from the noisiness of its customers. Go to those deelux palaces in the new city, see their velvet thrones of seats and the mirror tiling all over the vestibules, feel the air-conditioning and you'll understand why the audiences sit as quiet as hell. They are tamed by the splendour of the surroundings, also by the price of the seats. But in the Empire of Mahmoud the paying customers make the very devil of a din, except during the hit song numbers. We are not absolute monarchs, child, don't forget it; especially in these days when the police are turning against us and refuse to come and eject even the biggest badmashes, who make whistlings that split your ears. Never mind. It is a question of freedom of individuals, after all.'

Yes: it was a fifth-rate Empire. But to Mahmoud it was quite something, a Slave King's estate, for had he not begun his career out on the suppurating streets as one of those no-account types who push the movie adverts around town on wheelbarrows, shouting, 'It is now-showing!' and also 'Plans filling up fast!' – and did he not now sit in a manager's office, complete with cashbox and keys? You see: even family jokes run the risk of being taken seriously, and there lurked in the natures of both father and daughter a literalism, a humourlessness owing to which Bilquìs grew up with an unspoken fantasy of queenhood simmering in the corners of her downcast eyes. 'I tell you,' she would apostrophize the angelic mirror after her father had left for work, 'with me it would be absolute control or zero! These badmashes would not get away with their whistling shistling if it was my affair!' Thus Bilquìs invented a secret self far more imperious than her father the emperor. And in the darkness of his Empire, night after night, she studied the giant, shimmering illusions of princesses who danced before the rackety audience beneath the gold-painted equestrian figure of an armoured medieval knight who bore a pennant on which was inscribed the meaningless word *Excelsior*. Illusions fed illusions, and Bilquìs began to carry herself with the grandeur befitting a dream-empress, taking as compliments the taunts of the street-urchins in the gullies around her home: 'Tantara!' they greeted her as she sailed by, 'Have mercy, O gracious lady, O Rani of Khansi!' *Khansi-ki-Rani*, they named her: queen of coughs, that is to say of expelled air, of sickness and hot wind.

'Be careful,' her father warned her, 'things are changing in this city; even the most affectionate nicknames are acquiring new and so-dark meanings.'

This was the time immediately before the famous moth-eaten partition that chopped up the old country and handed Al-Lah a few insect-nibbled slices of it, some dusty western acres and jungly eastern swamps that the ungodly were happy to do without. (Al-Lah's new country: two chunks of land a thousand miles apart. A country so improbable that it could almost exist.) But let's be unemotional and state merely that feelings were running so high that even going to the pictures had become a political act. The one-godly went to these cinemas and the washers of stone gods to those; movie-fans had been partitioned already, in advance of the tired old land. The stone-godly ran the movie business, that goes without saying, and being vegetarians they made a very famous film: *Gai-Wallah*. Perhaps you've heard of it? An unusual fantasy about a lone, masked hero who roamed the Indo-Gangetic plain liberating herds of beef-cattle from their keepers, saving the sacred, horned, uddered beasts from the slaughterhouse. The stone-gang packed out the cinemas where this movie was shown; the one-godly riposted by rushing to see imported, non-vegetarian Westerns in which cows got massacred and the good guys feasted on steaks. And mobs of irate film buffs attacked the cinemas of their enemies . . . well, it was a time for all types of craziness, that's all.

Mahmoud the Woman lost his Empire because of a single error, which arose out of his fatal personality flaw, namely tolerance. 'Time to rise above all this partition foolishness,' he informed his mirror one morning, and that same day he booked a double bill into his Talkies: Randolph Scott and Gai-Wallah would succeed one another on his screen.

On the opening day of the double bill of his destruction the meaning of his nickname changed for ever. He had been named The Woman by the street urchins because, being a widower, he had been obliged to act as a mother to Bilquìs ever since his wife died when the girl was barely two. But now this affectionate title came to mean something more dangerous, and when children spoke of Mahmoud the Woman they meant Mahmoud the Weakling, the Shameful, the Fool. 'Woman,' he sighed resignedly to his daughter, 'what a term! Is there no end to the burdens this word is capable of bearing? Was there ever such a broad-backed and also such a dirty word?'

How the double bill was settled: both sides, veg and non-veg, boycotted the Empire. For five, six, seven days films played to an empty house in which peeling plaster and slowly rotating ceiling fans and the intermission gram-vendors gazed down upon rows of undoubtedly rickety and equally certainly unoccupied seats; three-thirty, six-thirty and nine-thirty shows were all the same, not even the special Sunday-morning show could tempt anyone through the swing doors. 'Give it up,' Bilquìs urged her father. 'What do you want? You miss your wheelbarrow or what?'

But now an unfamiliar stubbornness entered Mahmoud the Woman, and he announced that the double bill would be held over for a Second Sensational Week. His own barrow-boys deserted him; nobody was willing to cry these ambiguous wares through the electric gullies; no voice dared announce, 'Plans now open!' or, 'Don't wait or it's too late!'

Mahmoud and Bilquìs lived in a high thin house behind the Empire, 'straight through the screen,' as he said; and on that afternoon when the world ended and began again the emperor's daughter, who was alone with the servant at home, was suddenly choked by the certainty that her father had chosen, with the mad logic of his romanticism, to persist with his crazy scheme until it killed him. Terrified by a sound like the beating wings of an angel, a sound for which she could afterwards find no good explanation but which pounded in her ears until her head ached, she ran out of her house, pausing only to wrap around her shoulders the green dupatta of modesty; which was how she came to be standing, catching her breath, in front of the heavy doors of the cinema behind which her father sat grimly amidst vacant seats watching the show, when the hot firewind of apocalypse began to blow.

The walls of her father's Empire puffed outwards like a hot puri while that wind like the cough of a sick giant burned away her eyebrows (which never grew again), and tore the clothes off her body until she stood infant-naked in the street; but she failed to notice her nudity because the universe was ending, and in the echoing alienness of the deadly wind her burning eyes saw everything come flying out, seats, ticket books, fans, and then pieces of her father's shattered corpse and the charred shards of the future. 'Suicide!' she cursed Mahmoud the Woman at the top of a voice made shrieky by the bomb. 'You chose this!' – and turning and running homewards she saw that the back wall of the cinema had been blown away, and embedded in the topmost storey of her high thin house was the figure of a golden knight on whose pennant she did not need to read the comically unknown word *Excelsior*.

Don't ask who planted the bomb; in those days there were many such planters, many gardeners of violence. Perhaps it was even a one-godly bomb, seeded in the Empire by one of Mahmoud's more fanatical co-religionists, because it seems that the timer reached zero during a particularly suggestive love scene, and we know what the godly think of love, or the illusion of it, especially when admission money must be paid to see it . . . they are Against. They cut it out. Love corrupts.

O Bilquìs. Naked and eyebrowless beneath the golden knight, wrapped in the delirium of the firewind, she saw her youth flying past her, borne away on the wings of the explosion which were still beating in her ears. All migrants leave their pasts behind, although some try to pack it into bundles and boxes – but on the journey something seeps out of the treasured mementoes and old photographs, until even their owners fail to recognize them, because it is the fate of migrants to be stripped of history, to stand naked amidst the scorn of strangers upon whom they see the rich clothing, the brocades of continuity and the eyebrows of belonging – at any rate, my point is that Bilquìs's past left her even before she left that city; she stood in a gully, denuded by the suicide of her father, and watched it go. In later years it would visit her sometimes, the way a forgotten relative comes to call, but for a long time she was suspicious of history, she was the wife of a hero with a great future, so naturally she pushed the past away, as one rebuffs those poor cousins when they come to borrow money.

She must have walked, or run, unless a miracle occurred and she was lifted by some divine power out of that wind of her desolation. Returning to her senses, she felt the pressure of red stone against her skin; it was night, and the stone was cool upon her back in the dark dry heat. People were surging past her in great herds, a crowd so large and urgent that her first thought was that it was being propelled by some unimaginable explosion: 'Another bomb, my God, all these persons blown away by its power!' But it was not a bomb. She understood that she was leaning against the endless wall of the red fortress that dominated the old city, while soldiers shepherded the crowd through its yawning gates; her feet began to move, faster than her brain, and led her into the throng. An instant later she was crushed by the reborn awareness of her nudity, and began to cry out: 'Give me a cloth!', until she saw that nobody was listening, nobody even glanced at the body of the singed, but still beautiful, naked girl. Yet she clutched at herself for shame, holding on to herself in that rushing sea as if she were a straw; and felt around her neck the remnants of a length of muslin. The dupatta of modesty had stuck to her body, fixed there by the congealed blood of the many cuts and scratches of whose very existence she had been unaware. Holding the blackened remnants of the garment of womanly honour over her secret places, she entered the dull redness of the fort, and heard the boom of its closing doors.

In Delhi, in the days before partition, the authorities rounded up any Muslims, for their own safety, it was said, and locked them up in the red fortress, away from the wrath of the stonewashers. Whole families were sealed up there, grandmothers, young children, wicked uncles . . . including members of my own family. It's easy to imagine that as my relatives moved through the Red Fort in the parallel universe of history, they might have felt some hint of the fictional presence of Bilquìs Kemal, rushing cut and naked past them like a ghost . . . or vice versa. Yes. Or vice versa.

The tide of human beings carried Bilquìs along as far as the large, low, ornately rectangular pavilion that had once been an emperor's hall of public audience; and in that echoing *diwan*, overwhelmed by the humiliation of her undress, she passed out. In that generation many women, ordinary decent respectable ladies of the type to whom nothing ever happens, to whom nothing is supposed to happen except marriage children death, had this sort of strange story to tell. It was a rich time for stories, if you lived to tell your tale.

Shortly before the scandalous marriage of her younger daughter, Good News Hyder, Bilquìs told the girl the story of her meeting with her husband. 'When I woke up,' she said, 'it was daytime and I was wrapped in an officer's coat. But whose do you think, goof, of course his, your own father Raza's; what to tell you, he saw me lying there, with all my goods on display in the window, you know, and I suppose the bold fellow just liked what there was to see.' Good News went *haa!* and *tch tch!*, feigning shock at her mother's sauciness, and Bilquìs said shyly: 'Such encounters were not uncommon then.' Good News dutifully replied, 'Well, Amma, as for his being impressed, I'm not one bit surprised.'

Raza arriving in the hall of public audience came to attention before Bilquìs, who was decently coated; he clicked his heels, saluted, grinned. 'It is normal during a courtship,' he told his future wife, 'for clothes to be worn. It is the privilege of a husband eventually to remove . . . but in our case, the reverse procedure will be true. I must dress you, top to toe, as befits a blushing bride.' (Good News, full of marriage juices, sighed when she heard this. 'His first words! My God, too romantic!')

How he seemed to military-coated Bilquìs: 'So tall! So fair-skinned! So proud, like a king!' No photographs were taken of their meeting, but allowances must be made for her state of mind. Raza Hyder was five foot eight: no giant, you'll agree. And as for his skin – it was certainly darker than Bilquìs's adoring eyes were willing to concede. But proud, like a king? That is likely. He was only a Captain then; but it is, nevertheless, a plausible description.

What may also be said fairly of Raza Hyder: that he possessed enough energy to light up a street; that his manners were always impeccable – even when he became President, he met people with such an air of humility (which is not irreconcilable with pride) that very few were willing to speak ill of him afterwards, and those that did so would feel, as they spoke, as if they were betraying a friend; and that he bore, upon his forehead, the light but permanent bruise which we have previously noted on the devout forehead of Ibadalla, the postman of Q.: the *gatta* marked Raza for a religious man.

One last detail. It was said of Captain Hyder that he did not sleep for four hundred and twenty hours after the Muslims were gathered in the red fortress, which would explain the black pouches under his eyes. These pouches would grow blacker and baggier as his power increased, until he no longer needed to wear sunglasses the way the other top brass did, because he looked like he had a pair on anyway, all the time, even in bed. The future General Hyder: Razzoo, Raz-Matazz, Old Razor Guts himself! How could Bilquìs have resisted such a one? She was conquered in double-quick time.

During their days in the fort, the pouch-eyed Captain visited Bilquìs regularly, always bringing with him some item of clothing or beautification: blouses, saris, sandals, eyebrow pencils with which to replace the lost hairs, brassières, lipsticks were showered on her. Saturation bombing techniques are designed to force an early surrender . . . when her wardrobe had grown large enough to permit the removal of the military overcoat, she paraded for him in the hall. 'Come to think of it,' Bilquìs told Good News, 'maybe that was when he made that dressing-up remark.' Because she remembered how she had replied: lowering her eyes in the elite actressy manner which her father had once praised, she said sadly, 'But what husband could I, without hope of dowry, ever find? Certainly not such a generous Captain who outfits strange ladies like queens.'

Raza and Bilquìs were betrothed beneath the bitter eyes of the dispossessed multitudes; and afterwards the gifts continued, sweet-meats as well as bangles, soft drinks and square meals as well as henna and rings. Raza established his fiancée behind a screen of stone lattice-work, and set a young foot-soldier on guard to defend her territory. Isolated behind this screen from the dull, debilitated anger of the mob, Bilquìs dreamed of her wedding day, defended against guilt by that old dream of queenliness which she had invented long ago. 'Tch tch,' she reproached the glowering refugees, 'but this envy is a too terrible thing.'

Barbs were flung through the stone lattice: 'Ohé, madam! Where do you think he gets your grand-grand clothes? From handicraft emporia? Watch the mud-flats of the river beneath the fortress walls, count the looted naked bodies flung there every night!' Dangerous words, penetrating lattice-work: scavenger, harlot, whore. But Bilquìs set her jaw against such coarseness and told herself: 'How bad-mannered it would be to ask a man from where he brought his gifts! Such cheapness, I will never do it, no.' This sentiment, her reply to the gibes of her fellow refugees, never actually passed her lips, but it filled up her mouth, making it puff up into a pout.

I do not judge her. In those days, people survived any way they could.

The Army was partitioned like everything else, and Captain Hyder went west to the new, moth-nibbled land of God. There was a marriage ceremony, and then Bilquìs Hyder sat beside her new husband in a troop transport, a new woman, newly-wed, flying to a bright new world.

'What things won't you do there, Raz!' she cried. 'What greatness, no? What fame!' Raza's ears went red under the eyes (hot with amusement) of his companions in that bumping, rackety Dakota; but he looked pleased all the same. And Bilquìs's prophecy came true, after all. She, whose life had blown up, emptying her of history and leaving in its place only that dark dream of majesty, that illusion so powerful that it demanded to enter the sphere of what-was-real – she, rootless Bilquìs, who now longed for stability, for no-more-explosions, had discerned in Raza a boulder-like quality on which she would build her life. He was a man rooted solidly in an indeflectible sense of himself, and that made him seem invincible, 'A giant absolutely,' she flattered him, whispering in his ear so as not to set off the giggles of the other officers in the cabin, 'shining, like the actors on the screen.'

I am wondering how best to describe Bilquìs. As a woman who was unclothed by change, but who wrapped herself in certainties; or as a girl who became a queen, but lost the ability possessed by every beggar-woman, that is, the power of bearing sons; or as that lady whose father was a Woman and whose son turned out to be girl as well; and whose man of men, her Razzoo or Raz-Matazz, was himself obliged, in the end, to put on the humiliating black shroud of womanhood; or perhaps as a being in the secret grip of fate—for did not the umbilical noose that stifled her son find its echo, or twin, in another and more terrible rope? . . . But I find that I must, after all, return to my starting point, because to me she is, and will always be, the Bilquìs who was afraid of the wind.

I'll be fair: nobody likes the Loo, that hot afternoon breath-that-chokes. We pull down our shutters, hang damp cloths over the windows, try to sleep. But as she grew older the wind awak-ened strange terrors in Bilquìs. Her husband and children noticed how nervous and snappish she became in the afternoons; how she took to pacing about, slamming and locking doors, until Raza Hyder protested against living in a house where you had to ask your wife for a key before you could go to the pot. From her slender wrist there hung, jingling, the ten-ton key-ring of her neurosis. She developed a horror of movement, and placed an embargo on the relocation of even the most trivial of household items. Chairs, ashtrays, flowerpots took root, rendered immobile by the force of her fearful will. 'My Hyder likes everything in its place,' she would say, but the disease of fixity was hers. And there were days when she had to be kept indoors as a virtual prisoner, because it would have been a shame and a scandal if any outsider had seen her in that state; when the Loo blew she would screech like a hoosh or an afrit or some such demon, she would shout for the household servants to come and hold down the furniture in case the wind blew it away like the contents of a long-lost Empire, and scream at her daughters (when they were present) to cling tight to something heavy, something fixed, lest the firewind bear them off into the sky.

The Loo is an evil wind.

If this were a realistic novel about Pakistan, I would not be writing about Bilquìs and the wind; I would be talking about my youngest sister. Who is twenty-two, and studying engineering in Karachi; who can't sit on her hair any more, and who (unlike me) is a Pakistani citizen. On my good days, I think of her as Pakistan, and then I feel very fond of the place, and find it easy to forgive its (her) love of Coca-Cola and imported motor cars.

Although I have known Pakistan for a long time, I have never lived there for longer than six months at a stretch. Once I went for just two weeks. Between these sixmonthses and fortnights there have been gaps of varying duration. I have learned Pakistan in slices, the same way as I have learned my growing sister. I first saw her at the age of zero (I, at fourteen, bent over her crib as she screamed into my face); then at three, four, six, seven, ten, fourteen, eighteen and twenty-one. So there have been nine youngest-sisters for me to get to know. I have felt closer to each successive incarnation than to the one before. (This goes for the country, too.)

I think what I'm confessing is that, however I choose to write about over-there, I am forced to reflect that world in fragments of broken mirrors, the way Farah Zoroaster saw her face at the bollarded frontier. I must reconcile myself to the inevitability of the missing bits.

But suppose this were a realistic novel! Just think what else I might have to put in. The business, for instance, of the illegal installation, by the richest inhabitants of 'Defence', of covert, subterranean water pumps that steal water from their neighbours' mains – so that you can always tell the people with the most pull by the greenness of their lawns (such clues are not confined to the Cantonment of Q.). – And would I also have to describe the Sind Club in Karachi, where there is still a sign reading 'Woman and Dogs Not Allowed Beyond This Point'? Or to analyse the subtle logic of an industrial programme that builds nuclear reactors but cannot develop a refrigerator? O dear – and the school text-books which say, 'England is not an agricultural country', and the teacher who once docked two marks from my youngest sister's geography essay because it differed at two points from the exact wording of this same text-book . . . how awkward, dear reader, all this could turn out to be.

How much real-life material might become compulsory! – About, for example, the longago Deputy Speaker who was killed in the National Assembly when the furniture was flung at him by elected representatives; or about the film censor who took his red pencil to each frame of the scene in the film *Night of the Generals* in which General Peter O'Toole visits an art gallery, and scratched out all the paintings of naked ladies hanging on the walls, so that audiences were dazzled by the surreal spectacle of General Peter strolling through a gallery of dancing red blobs; or about the TV chief who once told me solemnly that pork was a four-letter word; or about the issue of *Time* magazine (or was it *Newsweek?*) which never got into the country because it carried an article about President Ayub Khan's alleged Swiss bank account; or about the bandits on the trunk roads who are condemned for doing, as private enterprise, what the government does as public policy; or about genocide in Baluchistan; or about the recent preferential awards of State scholarships, to pay for postgraduate studies abroad, to members of the fanatical Jamaat party; or about the attempt to declare the sari an obscene garment; or about the extra hangings – the first for twenty years – that were ordered purely to legitimize the execution of Mr Zulfikar Ali Bhutto; or about why Bhutto's hangman has vanished into thin air, just like the many street-urchins who are being stolen every day in broad daylight; or about anti-Semitism, an interesting phenomenon, under whose influence people who have never met a Jew vilify all Jews for the sake of maintaining solidarity with the Arab states which offer Pakistan workers, these days, employment and much-needed foreign exchange; or about smuggling, the boom in heroin exports, military dictators, venal civilians, corrupt civil servants, bought judges, newspapers of whose stories the only thing that can confidently be said is that they are lies; or about the apportioning of the national budget, with special reference to the percentages set aside for defence (huge) and for education (not huge). Imagine my difficulties!

By now, if I had been writing a book of this nature, it would have done me no good to protest that I was writing universally, not only about Pakistan. The book would have been banned, dumped in the rubbish bin, burned. All that effort for nothing! Realism can break a writer's heart.

Fortunately, however, I am only telling a sort of modern fairy-tale, so that's all right; nobody need get upset, or take anything I say too seriously. No drastic action need be taken, either.

What a relief!

And now I must stop saying what I am not writing about, because there's nothing so special about that; every story one chooses to tell is a kind of censorship, it prevents the telling of other tales . . . I must get back to my fairy-story, because things have been happening while I've been talking too much.

On my way back to the story, I pass Omar Khayyam Shakil, my sidelined hero, who is waiting patiently for me to get to the point at which his future bride, poor Sufiya Zinobia, can enter the narrative, head first down the birth canal. He won't have to wait long; she's almost on her way.

I shall pause only to note (because it is not inappropriate to mention this here) that during his married life Omar Khayyam was forced to accept without argument Sufiya Zinobia's childlike fondness for moving the furniture around. Intensely aroused by these forbidden deeds, she rearranged tables, chairs, lamps, when-ever nobody was watching, like a favourite secret game, which she played with a frightening stubborn gravity. Omar Khayyam found protests rising to his lips, but he bit them back, knowing that to say anything would be useless: 'Honestly, wife,' he wanted to exclaim, 'God knows what you'll change with all this shifting shifting.'

5

❧

THE WRONG MIRACLE

Bilquìs is lying wide awake in the dark of a cavernous bedroom, her hands crossed upon her breasts. When she sleeps alone her hands habitually find their way into this position, even though her in-laws disapprove. She can't help it, this hugging of herself to herself, as though she were afraid of losing something.

All around her in the darkness are the dim outlines of other beds, old charpoys with thin mattresses, on which other women lie under single white sheets; a grand total of forty females clustered around the majestically tiny form of the matriarch Bariamma, who snores lustily. Bilquìs already knows enough about this chamber to be sure that most of the shapes tossing vaguely in the dark are no more asleep than she. Even Bariamma's snores might be a deception. The women are waiting for the men to come.

The turning door-knob rattles like a drum. At once there is a change in the quality of the night. A delicious wickedness is in the air. A cool breeze stirs, as if the entry of the first man has suc-ceeded in dispelling some of the intense treacly heat of the hot season, enabling the ceiling fans to move a little more efficiently through the soupy atmosphere. Forty women, one of them

Bilquìs, stir damply under their sheets . . . more men enter. They are tiptoeing along the midnight avenues of the dormitory and the women have become very still, except for Bariamma. The matriarch is snoring more energetically then ever. Her snores are sirens, sounding the all-clear and giving necessary courage to the men.

The girl in the bed next to Bilquìs, Rani Humayun, who is unmarried and therefore expects no visit tonight, whispers across the blackness: 'Here come the forty thieves.'

And now there are tiny noises in the dark: charpoy ropes yielding fractionally beneath the extra weight of a second body, the rustle of clothing, the heavier exhalations of the invading husbands. Gradually the darkness acquires a kind of rhythm, which accelerates, peaks, subsides. Then there is a multiple padding towards the door, several times the drum-roll of the turning doorknob, and at last silence, because Bariamma, now that it is polite to do so, has quite ceased to snore.

Rani Humayun, who has landed one of the prize catches of the marriage season and will shortly leave this dormitory to wed the fair-skinned, foreign-educated, sensually full-lipped young millionaire Iskander Harappa, and who is, like Bilquìs, eighteen years old, has befriended her cousin Raza's new bride. Bilquìs enjoys (while pretending to be scandalized) Rani's malicious ruminations on the subject of the household sleeping arrangements. 'Imagine, in that darkness,' Rani giggles while the two of them grind the daily spices, 'who would know if her real husband had come to her? And who could complain? I tell you, Billoo, these married men and ladies are having a pretty good time in this joint family set-up. I swear, maybe uncles with nieces, brothers with their brothers' wives, we'll never know who the children's daddies really are!' Bilquìs blushes gracefully and covers Rani's mouth with a coriander-scented hand. 'Stop, darling, what a dirtyfilthy mind!'

But Rani is inexorable. 'No, Bilquìs, I tell you, you are new here but I have grown up in this place, and by the hairs of our Bariamma's head I vow that this arrangement which is supposed to be made for decency etcetera is just the excuse for the biggest orgy on earth.'

Bilquìs does not point out (how rude it would be to do so) that the minuscule, almost dwarfish Bariamma is not only toothless and blind but no longer has a single hair on her ancient head, either. The matriarch wears a wig.

Where are we, and when? – In a large family house in the old quarter of the coastal city which, having no option, I must call Karachi. Raza Hyder, an orphan like his wife, has brought her (immediately after descending from the Dakota of their flight into the west) into the bosom of his maternal relations; Bariamma is his grandmother on his late mother's side. 'You must stay here,' he told Bilquìs, 'until things settle down and we can see what is what and what is not.' So these days Hyder is in temporary quarters at the Army base while his bride lies amid sleep-feigning in-laws, knowing that no man will visit her in the night. – And yes, I see that I have brought my tale into a second infinite mansion, which the reader will perhaps already be comparing to a faraway house in the border town of Q.; but what a complete contrast it affords! For this is no sealed-off redoubt; it bursts, positively bursts with family members and related personnel.

'They still live in the old village way,' Raza warned Bilquìs before depositing her in that house in which it was believed that the mere fact of being married did not absolve a woman of the shame and dishonour that results from the knowledge that she sleeps regularly with a man; which was why Bariamma had devised, without once discussing it, the idea of the forty thieves. And of course all the women denied that anything of 'that nature' ever took place, so that when pregnancies occurred they did so as if by magic, as if all conceptions were immaculate and all births virgin. The idea of parthenogenesis had been accepted in this house in order to keep out certain other, unpleasantly physical notions.

Bilquìs, the girl with the dream of queenhood, thought but did not say; 'O God. Ignoramuses from somewhere. Backward types, village idiots, unsophisticated completely, and I am stuck with them.' Aloud, she told Raza meekly: 'Much to be said for the old traditions.' Raza nodded seriously in simple agreement; her heart sank further after that.

In the empire of Bariamma, Bilquìs, the newest arrival, the junior member, was of course not treated like a queen.

'See if we don't have sons,' Raza told Bilquìs, 'In my mother's family boys grow on trees.'

Lost in the forest of new relatives, wandering in the blood-jungle of the matriarchal home, Bilquìs consulted the family Quran in search of these family trees, and found them there, in their traditional place, monkey-puzzle groves of genealogy inscribed in the back of the holy book. She discovered that since the generation of Bariamma, who had two sisters, Raza's maternal great-aunts, both widowed, as well as three brothers – a landlord, a wastrel and a mental-case fool – since that sexually-balanced generation, only two girls had been born in the entire family. One of these was Raza's deceased mother; the other, Rani Humayun, who could not wait to escape from that house which was never left by its sons, who imported their wives to live and breed in battery conditions, like shaver chickens. On his mother's side, Raza had a total of eleven legitimate uncles and, it was believed, at least nine illegitimate ones, the brood of the wastrel, philandering great-uncle. Besides Rani, he could point to a grand total of thirty-two male cousins born in wedlock. (The putative offspring of the bastard uncles did not rate a mention in the Quran.) Of this enormous stock of relatives, a sizeable percentage was in residence under Bariamma's short but omnipotent shadow; wastrel and fool were unmarried, but when the landlord came to stay his wife occupied one of the beds in Bariamma's zenana wing. At the time of which I am speaking, landlord and wife were present; also eight of the eleven legitimate uncles, plus wives; and (Bilquìs had difficulty with her counting) around twenty-nine male cousins, and Rani Humayun. Twenty-six cousinly wives stuffed the wicked bedchamber, and Bilquìs herself made forty, once the three sisters of the oldest generation were included.

Bilquìs Hyder's head whirled. Trapped in a language which contained a quite specific name for each conceivable relative, so that the bewildered newcomer was unable to hide behind such generic appellations as 'uncle', 'cousin', 'aunt', but was continually caught out in all her insulting ignorance, Bilquìs's tongue was silenced by the in-law mob. She virtually never spoke except when alone with Rani or Raza; and thus acquired the triple reputation of sweet-innocent-child, doormat and fool. Because Raza was often away for days at a time, depriving her of the protection and flattery the other women got from their husbands on a daily basis, she also attained the status of poor-thing, which her lack of eyebrows (that no amount of pencilled artistry could disguise) did nothing to diminish. Thanks to this she was given slightly more than her fair share of household duties and also slightly more than her fair share of the rough edge of Bariamma's tongue. But she was also admired, grudgingly, because the family had a high opinion of Raza, the women admitted that he was a good man who did not beat his wife. This definition of goodness alarmed Bilquìs, to whom it had never occurred that she might be beaten, and she raised the subject with Rani. 'Oh yes,' her cousin-in-law replied, 'how they all hit! Tharaap! Tharaap! Sometimes it does your heart good to watch. But one must also watch out. A good man can go bad, like meat, if you do not keep him cool.'

As the officially designated poor-thing, Bilquìs was also obliged to sit each evening at Bariamma's feet while the blind old lady recounted the family tales. These were lurid affairs, featuring divorces, bankruptcies, droughts, cheating friends, child mortality, diseases of the breast, men cut down in their prime, failed hopes, lost beauty, women who grew obscenely fat, smuggling deals, opium-taking poets, pining virgins, curses, typhoid, bandits, homosexuality, sterility, frigidity, rape, the high price of food, gamblers, drunks, murders, suicides and God. Bariamma's mildly droning recital of the catalogue of family horrors had the effect of somehow defusing them, making them safe, embalming them in the mummifying fluid of her own incontrovertible respectability. The telling of the tales proved the family's ability to survive them, to retain, in spite of everything, its grip on its honour and its unswerving moral code. 'To be of the family,' Bariamma told Bilquìs, 'you must know our things, and tell us yours.' So Bilquis was forced, one evening (Raza was present but made no attempt to protect her), to recount the end of Mahmoud the Woman and her nudity in the Delhi streets. 'Never mind,' Bariamma pronounced approvingly, when Bilquìs was shaking with the shame of her revelations, 'at least you managed to keep your dupatta on.'

After that Bilquìs often heard her story being retold, wherever one or two of the family were gathered, in the hot lizardy corners of the courtyard or on the starlit roofs of the summer nights, in the nurseries to frighten the children and even in the boudoir of jewel-heavy, hennaed Rani on the morning of her wedding; because stories, such stories, were the glue that held the clan together, binding the generations in webs of whispered secrets. Her story altered, at first, in the retellings, but finally it settled down, and after that nobody, neither teller nor listener, would tolerate any deviation from the hallowed, sacred text. This was when Bilquìs knew that she had become a member of the family; in the sanctification of her tale lay initiation, kinship, blood. 'The recounting of histories,' Raza told his wife, 'is for us a rite of blood.'

But neither Raza nor Bilquìs could have known that their story had scarcely begun, that it would be the juiciest and goriest of all the juicygory sagas, and that, in time to come, it would always begin with the following sentence (which, in the family's opinion, contained all the right resonances for the opening of such a narrative):

'It was the day on which the only son of the future President Raza Hyder was going to be reincarnated.'

'Yes, yes,' the audience would cheer, 'tell us that one, that's the best.'

⚜

In that hot season, the two newly-partitioned nations announced the commencement of hostilities on the Kashmiri frontier. You can't beat a northern war in the hot season; officers, foot-soldiers, cooks all rejoiced as they headed for the coolness of the hills. 'Yara, this is luck, na?' 'Shit, sisterfucker, at least this year I won't die in that damn heat.' O backslapping camaraderie of the meteorologically fortunate! Jawans went to war with the devil-may-care abandon of holidaymakers. There were, inevitably, deaths; but the organizers of the war had catered for these as well. Those who fell in battle were flown directly, first-class, to the perfumed gardens of Paradise, to be waited on for all eternity by four gorgeous Houris, untouched by man or djinn. 'Which of your Lord's blessings,' the Quran inquires, 'would you deny?'

Army morale was high; but Rani Humayun was most put out, because it would have been unpatriotic to hold a wedding reception in wartime. The function had been postponed, and she stamped her feet. Raza Hyder, however, stepped contentedly into the camouflaged jeep of his flight from the boiling insanity of the summer city, and just then his wife whispered into his ear that she was expecting another sort of happy event. (Taking a leaf out of Bariamma's book, I have turned a blind eye and snored loudly while Raza Hyder visited the dormitory of the forty women and made this miracle possible.)

Raza let fly a yell so swollen by triumph that Bariamma, seated indoors on her takht, became convinced in the confusion of her sweating blindness that her grandson had already received news of some famous victory, so that when such news did in fact come through, weeks later, she replied simply: 'Did you just find that out? I knew it one month back.' (This was in the days before the people learned that their side almost always lost, so that the national leaders, rising brilliantly to the challenge, perfected no fewer than one thousand and one ways of salvaging honour from defeat.)

'He's coming!' Raza deafened his wife, causing earthen pitchers to topple from the heads of womenservants and frightening the geese. 'What did I tell you, Mrs?' He set his cap more jauntily on his head, slapped his wife too firmly on the stomach, joined the palms of his hands together and made diving gestures. 'Whoosh!' he shouted. 'Voom, wife! Here he comes!' And he roared off into the north, promising to win a great victory in honour of his forthcoming son, and leaving behind him a Bilquìs who, being washed for the first time by the solipsistic fluids of motherhood, had neglected to notice the tears in her husband's eyes, the tears turning his black eye-pouches into velvet bags, the tears which were among the earliest pointers that the future strong-man of the nation was of the type that cried too easily . . . in private with the frustrated Rani Humayun, Bilquìs crowed proudly: 'Never mind this war foolishness; the important news is that I am making a boy to marry your unborn daughter.'

An extract from the family's saga of Raza and Bilquìs, given in the formulaic words which it would be a gross sacrilege to alter:
  'When we heard that our Razzoo had pulled off an attacking coup so daring that there was no option but to call it a triumph, we started off by refusing to believe our ears, – for already in those days even the sharpest ears had developed the fault of becoming wholly unreliable when they were attuned to the radio news bulletins; – on such occasions everybody heard things that could not possibly have been the case. – But then we nodded our heads, understanding that a man whose wife is about to bear him a son is capable of anything. Yes, it was the unborn boy who was responsible for this, the only victory in the history of our armed forces, – which formed the basis of Raza's reputation for invincibility, a reputation which quickly became invincible itself, – so that not even the long humiliating years of his decline proved capable of destroying it. – He returned a hero, having seized for our holy new land a mountain valley so high and inaccessible that even goats had difficulty in breathing up there; so intrepid he was, so tremendous, that all true patriots had to gasp – and you must not believe that propaganda which says that the enemy did not bother

to defend the place; – the fighting was fierce as ice – and with twenty men only he took the valley! That little band of giants, that daredevil crew, and Old Razor Guts at their head – who could have denied them? Who could have stood in their path?

'For all peoples, there are places that mean too much. "Aansu!" we wept with pride; with true patriotism we sobbed, "Only imagine – he has taken the Aansu-ki-Wadi!" It's true: the capture of that fabled "valley of tears" made us all weep as uncontrollably as, in later years, its conqueror became famous for doing. – But after a while it was clear that nobody knew what to do with that place where your spit froze before it hit the ground; except Iskander Harappa, of course; – who, dry-eyed as ever, went off to the Tribal Agencies Department and purchased more or less the whole caboodle, dirt-cheap, snow-cheap, for cash money on the nail, – and a few years later there were ski-lodges up there, and scheduled air flights, and European goings-on at night that made the local tribals faint for shame. – But did Raz, our great hero, see anything of that foreign exchange?' (Here the teller invariably smites her forehead with the palm of her hand.) 'No, how would he, that great Army dumbo? Isky always got there first. But' (and now the narrator adopts the most cryptic, menacing tone of which she is capable), 'it is being there last that counts.'

At this point I must interrupt the legend. The duel between Raza Hyder (promoted to Major for his Aansu exploit) and Iskander Harappa, which began, but certainly did not end, in Aansu, will have to wait yet awhile; because now that Old Razor Guts is back in town, and it is peacetime again, the wedding is about to be celebrated which will make the mortal adversaries into cousins-in-laws: into *family*.

Rani Humayun, eyes downcast, watches in a mirror-ring her bridegroom approaching her; borne shoulder-high by a turbaned retinue of friends, he sits on a golden plate. Later, after she had fainted under the weight of her jewellery; been revived by the pregnant Bilquìs who then passed out herself; had money thrown in her lap by every member of her family in turn; watched through her veil as her ancient lecherous great-uncle pinched the bottoms of her new husband's female relations, knowing that his grey hairs would prevent them from complaining; and finally lifted the veil beside her while a hand raised her own, and looked long and hard into the face of Iskander Harappa, whose over-powering sexual appeal owed much to the unlined softness of his twenty-five-year-old cheeks – around which curled long hair that was already, and freakishly, the colour of pure silver, and thinning on top to reveal the golden dome of his skull – and between which, also curled, she discovered lips whose patrician cruelty was alleviated by their sensual thickness, the lips, she thought, of a black *hubshee*, and idea which gave her a peculiarly sinful frisson of delight . . . later, after she had ridden with him to a bedchamber opulent with ancient swords and imported French tapestries and Russian novels, after she had descended full of terror from a white stallion whose sex was quite patently standing to attention, after she had heard the doors of her marriage closing behind her in this other home whose grandeur made Bariamma's place look like a village hovel – then, oiled and naked on a bed before which the man who had just turned her into a grown woman stood staring indolently down upon her beauty, she, Rani Harappa, made her first genuinely wifely remark.

'Who was that fellow,' she asked, 'the fat one, whose horse sat down under him when your procession arrived? I think it must be that bad chap, that doctor or something, that everybody in town is calling such a bad influence on you.'

Iskander Harappa turned his back on her and lit a cigar. 'Get one thing clear,' she heard him say, 'you don't pick and choose my friends.'

But Rani, seized by helpless laughter under the influence of the remembered image of the proud horse that gave up and subsided, legs splayed to the four points of the compass, under the colossal weight of Omar Khayyam Shakil – and also basking in the soft heat of their recent lovemaking – made mollifying sounds: 'I only meant, Isky, what a shameless type he must be, to carry all that tummy about and all.'

Omar Khayyam at thirty: five years the senior of Iskander Harappa and more than a decade older than Isky's bride, re-enters our little tale as a character with a high reputation as a doctor and a low reputation as a human being, a degenerate of whom it is often said that he appears to be entirely without shame, 'fellow doesn't know the meaning of the word,' as if some essential part of his education has been overlooked; or perhaps he has deliberately chosen to expunge the word from his vocabulary, lest its explosive presence there amid the memories of his past and present actions shatter him like an old pot. Rani Harappa has correctly identified her enemy, and now remembers, shuddering, and for the hundred and first time since it happened, the moment during her wedding celebrations when a bearer brought Iskander Harappa a telephone message informing him that the Prime Minister had been assassinated. When Iskander Harappa stood, called for silence and relayed the message to the appalled guests, an awkward hush persisted for fully thirty seconds, and then the voice of Omar Khayyam Shakil, on which everyone could hear the splashing of alcohol, cried out, 'That bastard! If he's dead he's dead. Why does he want to come here and spoil the party?'

Back then everything was smaller than it is today; even Raza Hyder was only a Major. But he was like the city itself, going places, growing fast, but in a stupid way, so that the bigger they both got, the uglier they became. I must tell you what things were like in those early days after the partition: the city's old inhabitants, who had become accustomed to living in a land older than time, and were therefore being slowly eroded by the implacably revenant tides of the past, had been given a bad shock by independence, by being told to think of themselves, as well as the country itself, as new.

Well, their imaginations simply weren't up to the job, you can

understand that; so it was the ones who really were new, the distant cousins and half-acquaintances and total strangers who poured
in from the east to settle in the Land of God, who took over and
got things going. The newness of those days felt pretty unstable; it
was a dislocated, rootless sort of thing. All over the city (which
was, of course, the capital then) builders were cheating on the
cement in the foundations of new houses, people – and not only
Prime Ministers – got shot from time to time, throats got themselves slit in gullies, bandits became billionaires, but all this was
expected. History was old and rusted, it was a machine nobody
had plugged in for thousands of years, and here all of a sudden it
was being asked for maximum output. Nobody was surprised that
there were accidents . . . well, there were a few voices saying, if
this is the country we dedicated to our God, what kind of God is
it that permits – but these voices were silenced before they had
finished their questions, kicked on the shins under tables, for their
own sakes, because there are things that cannot be said. No, it's
more than that: there are things that cannot be permitted to
be true.

At any rate: Raza Hyder has already shown, in the taking of
Aansu, the advantages of the energy-giving influx of immigrants,
of novel beings; but energy or no energy, he was unable to prevent his first-born son from being strangled to death in the womb.

Once again (in the opinion of his maternal grandmother) he cried
too easily. Just when he should have been demonstrating the stiff-
ness of his upper lip be began to bawl his eyes out, even in public.
Tears were seen sliding off the wax on his bulbous moustache, and
his black eye-pouches glistened once more like little pools of oil.
His wife, Bilquìs, however, did not let fall a single tear.

'Hey, Raz,' she consoled her husband in words iced with the
brittle certainty of her desperation, 'Razzoo, chin up. We'll get
him back the next time.'

'Old Razor Guts, my toe,' Bariamma scoffed to all and
sundry. 'You know he invented that name for himself and forced

his troops to call him so, by order? Old Leaky Water Reservoir, more like.'

An umbilical cord wound itself around a baby's neck and was transformed into a hangman's noose (in which other nooses are prefigured), into the breath-stopping silken rumal of a Thug; and an infant came into the world handicapped by the irreversible misfortune of being dead before he was born. 'Who knows why God will do such things?' Bariamma, mercilessly, told her grandson. 'But we submit, we must submit. And not take out baby-tears before women.'

However: being stone dead was a handicap which the boy managed, with commendable gallantry, to surmount. Within a matter of months, or was it only weeks, the tragically cadaverous infant had 'topped' in school and at college, had fought bravely in war, had married the wealthiest beauty in town and risen to a high position in the government. He was dashing, popular, handsome, and the fact of his being a corpse now seemed of no more consequence than would a slight limp or a minor speech impediment.

Of course I know perfectly well that the boy had in reality perished before he even had time to be given a name. His subsequent feats were performed entirely within the distracted imaginations of Raza and Bilquìs, where they acquired an air of such solid actuality that they began to insist on being provided with a living human being who would carry them out and make them real. Possessed by the fictive triumphs of their stillborn son, Raza and Bilquìs went at one another with a will, heaving silently in the blind-eyed dormitory of the family wives, having convinced themselves that a second pregnancy would be an act of replacement, that God (for Raza was, as we know, devout) had consented to send them a free substitute for the damaged goods they had received in the first delivery, as though He were the manager of a reputable mail-order firm. Bariamma, who found out everything, clicked her tongue noisily over this reincarnation nonsense, aware that is was something they had imported, like a germ, from that land of idolaters they had left; but curiously she was never harsh with them, understanding that the mind will find strange means of coping with grief. So she must bear her share of responsibility for what followed, she should not have neglected her duty just because it was painful, she should have dished that rebirth notion while she could, but it took root so fast, and then it was too late, not a matter for discussion any more.

Many years later, when Iskander Harappa stood in the dock of the courtroom in which he was on trial for his life, his face as grey as the imported suit he wore, which had been tailored for him when he weighed twice as much, he taunted Raza with the memory of this reincarnation obsession. 'This leader who prays six times a day, and on national television too!' Isky said in a voice whose siren melodies had been untuned by jail. 'I recall when I had to remind him that the idea of avatars was a heresy. Of course he never listened, but then Raza Hyder has made a custom of not listening to friendly advice.' And outside the courtroom, the bolder members of Harappa's disintegrating entourage were heard to mutter that General Hyder had been raised in the enemy state across the border, after all, and there was evidence of a Hindu great-grandmother on his father's side, so those ungodly philosophies had long ago infected his blood.

And it is true that Iskander and Rani both tried to argue with the Hyders, but Bilquìs's lips just got stretched tight as a drum by her obstinacy. At that time Rani Harappa was expecting, she had managed it like a shot, and Bilquìs was already making it a matter of principle not to do what her old dormitory buddy advised, one reason for which may have been that she, Bilquìs, in spite of all the nocturnal goings-on, was finding it very difficult to conceive.

When Rani gave birth to a daughter, her failure to produce a male child offered Bilquìs a little consolation, but not much, because another dream had bitten the dust, the fantasy of a marriage between their firstborn children. Now, of course, the newborn Miss Arjumand Harappa was older than any future male Hyder could ever be, so the match was out of the question. Rani had, in fact, delivered her side of the deal; her efficiency deepened Bilquìs's well-like gloom.

And under Bariamma's roof little sneers and comments began to be aimed at this unnatural female who could produce nothing but dead babies; the family was proud of its fecundity. One night, after Bilquìs had retired to bed, having washed the eyebrows off her face and regained her appearance of a startled rabbit, she was staring jealously at the empty bed which had once been occupied by Rani Harappa when, from her other flank, a particularly vicious cousin named Duniyazad Begum hissed night-dark insults: 'The disgrace of your barrenness, Madam, is not yours alone. Don't you know that shame is collective? The shame of any one of us sits on us all and bends our backs. See what you're doing to your husband's people, how you repay the ones who took you in when you came penniless and a fugitive from that godless country over there.'

Bariamma had switched the lights out – the master-switch hung on a cord above her bed – and her snoring dominated the blackness of the zenana chamber. But Bilquìs did not lie still in her bed; she arose and fell upon Duniyazad Begum, who had been awaiting her eagerly, and the two of them, hands entangled in hair, knees driving into yielding fleshy zones, tumbled softly to the floor. The fight was conducted soundlessly, such was the power of the matriarch over the night; but the news spread through the room on ripples of darkness and the women sat up in their beds and watched. When the men came they, too, became mute spectators of this mortal combat, during which Duniyazad lost several handfuls of hair from her luxuriant armpits and Bilquìs broke a tooth on her adversary's clawing fingers; until Raza Hyder entered the dormitory and pulled them apart. It was at this point that Bariamma ceased to snore and switched on the light, releasing into the illuminated air all the noise, all the cheers and screams, that had been held back by the darkness. As women rushed to prop up the bald, blind matriarch with gaotakia bolsters, Bilquìs, trembling in her husband's arms, refused to go on living under that roof of her calumniation. 'Husband, you know it,' she pulled about herself the tattered shreds of her queenly childhood, 'I was raised in a higher fashion than this; and if my children do not come it is because I cannot make them here, in this zoo, like they all do, like animals or what.'

'Yes, yes, we know how you think yourself toogood for us,' Bariamma, subsiding into gaotakias with a hissing noise, as of a deflating balloon, had the last word. 'Then you take her away, Raza, boy,' she said in her hornet's whine of a voice. 'You, Billoo Begum, begone. When you leave this house your shame leaves with you, and our dear Duniya, whom you attacked for speaking the truth, will sleep more easily. Come on, *mohajir*! Immigrant! Pack up double-quick and be off to what gutter you choose.'

I, too, know something of this immigrant business. I am an emigrant from one country (India) and a newcomer in two (England, where I live, and Pakistan, to which my family moved against my will). And I have a theory that the resentments we *mohajirs* engender have something to do with our conquest of the force of gravity. We have performed the act of which all men anciently dream, the thing for which they envy the birds; that is to say, we have flown.

I am comparing gravity with belonging. Both phenomena observably exist: my feet stay on the ground, and I have never been angrier than I was on the day my father told me he had sold my childhood home in Bombay. But neither is understood. We know the force of gravity, but not its origins; and to explain why we become attached to our birthplaces we pretend that we are trees and speak of roots. Look under your feet. You will not find gnarled growths sprouting through the soles. Roots, I sometimes think, are a conservative myth, designed to keep us in our places.

The anti-myths of gravity and of belonging bear the same name: flight. *Migration, n., moving, for instance in flight, from one place to another.* To fly and to flee: both are ways of seeking freedom . . . an odd thing about gravity, incidentally, is that while it remains uncomprehended everybody seems to find it easy to comprehend the notion of its theoretical counter-force: anti-gravity. But anti-belonging is not accepted by modern science . . . suppose ICI or

Ciba-Geigy or Pfizer or Roche or even, I guess, NASA came up with an anti-gravity pill. The world's airlines would go broke overnight, of course. Pill-poppers would come unstuck from the ground and float upwards until they sank into the clouds. It would be necessary to devise special waterproof flying garments. And when the effects of the pill wore off one would simply sink gently down to earth again, but in a different place, because of prevailing windspeeds and planetary rotation. Personalized international travel could be made possible by manufacturing pills of different strengths for different lengths of journey. Some kind of directional booster-engine would have to be constructed, perhaps in back-pack form. Mass production could bring this within the reach of every household. You see the connection between gravity and 'roots': the pill would make migrants of us all. We would float upwards, use our boosters to get ourselves to the right latitude, and let the rotating planet do the rest.

When individuals come unstuck from their native land, they are called migrants. When nations do the same thing (Bangladesh), the act is called secession. What is the best thing about migrant peoples and seceded nations? I think it is their hopefulness. Look into the eyes of such folk in old photographs. Hope blazes undimmed through the fading sepia tints. And what's the worst thing? It is the emptiness of one's luggage. I'm speaking of invisible suitcases, not the physical, perhaps cardboard, variety containing a few meaning-drained mementoes: we have come unstuck from more than land. We have floated upwards from history, from memory, from Time.

I may be such a person. Pakistan may be such a country.

It is well known that the term 'Pakistan', an acronym, was originally thought up in England by a group of Muslim intellectuals. P for the Punjabis, A for the Afghans, K for the Kashmiris, S for Sind and the 'tan', they say, for Baluchistan. (No mention of the East Wing, you notice; Bangladesh never got its name in the title, and so, eventually, it took the hint and seceded from the secessionists. Imagine what such a double secession does to people!) – So it was a word born in exile which then went East, was borne-across or trans-lated, and imposed itself on history; a returning migrant, settling down on partitioned land, forming a palimpsest on the past. A palimpsest obscures what lies beneath. To build Pakistan it was necessary to cover up Indian history, to deny that Indian centuries lay just beneath the surface of Pakistani Standard Time. The past was rewritten; there was nothing else to be done.

Who commandeered the job of rewriting history? – The immigrants, the *mohajirs*. In what languages? – Urdu and English, both imported tongues, although one travelled less distance than the other. It is possible to see the subsequent history of Pakistan as a duel between two layers of time, the obscured world forcing its way back through what-had-been-imposed. It is the true desire of every artist to impose his or her vision on the world; and Pakistan, the peeling, fragmenting palimpsest, increasingly at war with itself, may be described as a failure of the dreaming mind. Perhaps the pigments used were the wrong ones, impermanent, like Leonardo's; or perhaps the place was just *insufficiently imagined*, a picture full of irreconcilable elements, midriffbaring immigrant saris versus demure, indigenous Sindhi shalwar-kurtas, Urdu versus Punjabi, now versus then: a miracle that went wrong.

As for me: I, too, like all migrants, am a fantasist. I build imaginary countries and try to impose them on the ones that exist. I, too, face the problem of history: what to retain, what to dump, how to hold on to what memory insists on relinquishing, how to deal with change. And to come back to the 'roots' idea, I should say that I haven't managed to shake myself free of it completely. Sometimes I do see myself as a tree, even, rather grandly, as the ash Yggdrasil, the mythical world-tree of Norse legend. The ash Yggdrasil has three roots. One falls into the pool of knowledge by Valhalla, where Odin comes to drink. A second is being slowly consumed in the undying fire of Muspellheim, realm of the flame-god Surtur. The third is gradually being gnawed through by a fearsome beast called the Nidhögg. And when fire and monster have destroyed two of the three, the ash will fall, and darkness will descend. The twilight of the gods: a tree's dream of death.

My story's palimpsest-country has, I repeat, no name of its own. The exiled Czech writer Kundera once wrote: 'A name means continuity with the past and people without a past are people without a name.' But I am dealing with a past that refuses to be suppressed, that is daily doing battle with the present; so it is perhaps unduly harsh of me to deny my fairyland a title.

There's an apocryphal story that Napier, after a successful campaign in what is now the south of Pakistan, sent back to England the guilty, one-word message, 'Peccavi'. *I have Sind.* I'm tempted to name my looking-glass Pakistan in honour of this bilingual (and fictional, because never really uttered) pun. Let it be *Peccavistan.*

It was the day on which the only son of the future General Raza Hyder was going to be reincarnated.

Bilquìs had moved out of Bariamma's contraceptive presence into a simple residence for married officers and wives in the compound of the Army base; and not long after her escape she had conceived, just as prophesied. 'What did I say?' she triumphed, 'Raz, he's coming back, the little angel, just you wait and see.' Bilquìs put her new-found fertility down to the fact that she was finally able to make a noise during their lovemaking, 'so that the little angel, waiting to be born, can hear what's going on and respond accordingly,' she told her husband fondly, and the happiness of the remark prevented him from replying that it was not only angels who were within earshot of her passionate love-moans and ululations, but also every other married officer on the base, including his immediate superior and also some junior chaps, so that he had been obliged to put up with a fair amount of raillery in the mess.

Bilquìs entered labour – the rebirth was imminent – Raza Hyder awaited it, stiffly seated in an anteroom of the military hospital's maternity ward. And after eight hours of howling and heaving and bursting blood-vessels in her cheeks and using the filthy language that is permitted to ladies only during parturition, at last, pop! she managed it, the miracle of life. Raza Hyder's daughter was born at two-fifteen in the afternoon, and born, what's more, as vivaciously alive and kicking as her big brother had been dead.

When the swaddled child was handed to Bilquìs, that lady could not forbear to cry, faintly, 'Is that all, my God? So much huffery and puffery to push out only this mouse?'

The heroine of our story, the wrong miracle, Sufiya Zinobia, was as small a baby as anyone had ever seen. (She remained small when she grew up, taking after her near-midget paternal great-grandmother, whose name, Bariamma, Big Mother, had always been a sort of family joke.)

A surprisingly small bundle was returned by Bilquìs to the mid-wife, who bore it out to the anxious father. 'A daughter, Major Sahib, and so beautiful, like the day, dontyouthinkso?' In the delivery room, silence flooded from the pores of the exhausted mother; in the anteroom, Raza was quiet, too. Silence: the ancient language of defeat.

Defeat? But this was Old Razor Guts himself, conqueror of glaciers, vanquisher of frosty meadows and ice-fleeced mountain sheep! Was the future strong-man of the nation so easily crushed? Not a bit of it. Did the midwife's bombshell lead to unconditional surrender? Certainly not. Raza began to argue; and the words came in rushes, inexorable as tanks. The walls of the hospital shook and retreated; horses shied, unseating riders, on the nearby polo fields.

'Mistakes are often made!' Raza shouted. 'Terrible blunders are not unknown! Why, my own fifth cousin by marriage when he was born. . . ! But me no buts, woman, I demand to see the hospital supervisor!'

And even louder: 'Babies do not come clean into this world!'

And blasted from his lips like cannonballs: 'Genitalia! Can! Be! Obscured!'

Raza Hyder raging roaring. The midwife stiffened, saluted; this was a military hospital, don't forget, and Raza outranked her, so she admitted yes, what the Major Sahib was saying was possible certainly. And fled. Hope rose in the moist eyes of the father, also in the dilated pupils of Bilquìs, who had heard the noise, of course. And now it was the baby, its very essence in doubt, who fell silent and began to muse.

The supervisor (a Brigadier) entered the quaking room in which the future President was trying to affect biology by a super-human act of will. His words, weighty, final, outranking Raza's murdered hope. The stillborn son died again, even his ghost snuffed out by the medico's fatal speech: 'No possibility of error. Please to note that the child has been washed. Prior to swaddling procedure. Matter of sex is beyond dispute. Permit me to tender my congratulations.' But what father would allow his son, twice-conceived, to be executed thus, without a fight? Raza tore away swaddling cloth; having penetrated to the baby within, he jabbed at its nether zones: 'There! I ask you, sir, what is that?' – 'We see here the expected configuration, also the not uncommon post-natal swelling, of the female . . .' – 'A bump!' Raza shrieked hope-lessly. 'Is it not, doctor, an absolute and unquestionable *bump*?'

But the Brigadier had left the room.

'And at this point' – I am quoting from the family legend again – 'when her parents had to admit the immutability of her gender, to submit, as faith demands, to God; at this very instant the extremely new and soporific being in Raza's arms began – it's true! – to blush.'

O rubescent Sufiya Zinobia!

It is possible that the above incident has been a little embell-ished during its many tellings and retellings; but I shall not be the one to question the veracity of oral tradition. They say the baby blushed at birth.

Then, even then, she was too easily shamed.

6

AFFAIRS OF HONOUR

There is a saying that the frog who croaks in the shaft of a well will be frightened by the booming voice of the giant frog who answers him.

When the great gas fields were discovered in Needle Valley in the district of Q., the unpatriotic behaviour of the intemperate local tribals became a matter for national concern. After the team of drilling engineers, surveyors and gas scientists which was sent to Needle to plan the construction of the butane mines had been attacked by the tribals, who raped each member of the team eighteen point six times on average (of which thirteen point nine seven assaults were from the rear and only four point six nine in the mouth) before slitting one hundred per cent of the expert gullets, the State Chief Minister Aladdin Gichki requested military assistance. The commander of the forces appointed for the protection of the invaluable gas resources was none other than Raza Hyder, hero of the Aansu-ki-Wadi expedition, and already a full Colonel. It was a popular appointment. 'Who better to defend one precious mountain valley,' the nation's premier daily paper *War* rhetorically inquired, 'than the conqueror of another such jewel?' Old Razor Guts himself made the following statement, to a reporter from the same journal, on the steps of the newly air-conditioned mail train to the west: 'These brigands are the frogs in the well, good sir, and, God willing, I intend to be the giant who scares off their pants.'

At that time his daughter Sufiya Zinobia was fifteen months old. She, and his wife Bilquìs, accompanied Colonel Hyder on his journey towards the Impossible Mountains. And no sooner had their train pulled out of the station than sounds of 'Godless carousing' (Raza's phrase) began to filter into their compartment. Raza asked the guard for the identities of his neighbours. 'Very big persons, sir,' was the reply, 'certain executives and also lady stars of a famous bioscope company.' Raza Hyder shrugged. 'Then we must put up with the racket, because I will not lower myself by disputing with filmi types.' When she heard this Bilquìs set her lips in a tight and bloodless smile, and her eyes stared ferociously through the mirror on the wall which divided her from the empires of her past.

The carriage was a new model with a corridor running past the compartment doors, and a few hours later Bilquìs was returning from the Ladies when a youth with lips as fat as Iskander Harappa's leaned out of the depraved compartment of the cinema people and made kissing noises at her, whispering whiskied endearments: 'I swear, yaar, you can keep your goods from foreign, the home produce is the best, no question.' Bilquìs could feel his eyes squeezing her breasts, but for some unaccountable reason she did not mention this insult to her honour when she returned to her husband's side.

Raza Hyder's honour also received an insulting blow on that trip, or, to be precise, at its conclusion, because when they arrived at the Cantt station in Q. they found a crowd of locust proportions awaiting them on the platform, singing hit songs and throwing flowers and waving banners and flags of welcome, and although Bilquìs could see Raza twirling his moustache her smiling lips never moved to warn him of the obvious truth, which was that the welcome was not for the Colonel but for the cheap riff-raff next door. Hyder descended from the train with arms spread wide and a speech guaranteeing the safety of the crucial gas seams dripping from his lips, and was almost knocked over by the rush of autograph hunters and hem-kissers towards the demure lady actresses. (Off balance, he failed to notice a fat-lipped youth wiggling his fingers in farewell in the direction of Bilquìs.) The injury sustained here by his pride explained much of what followed; in the illogical manner of the humiliated, he began taking it out on his wife, who shared a bioscopic background with his adversaries – whereupon his rage at the botched reincarnation of his only son awoke again, and crossed over the newly-established bridge between his wife and the cinema fans, until Raza began, unconsciously, to hold his progenitorial difficulties against the shallow moviegoers of Q.

Trouble in a marriage is like monsoon water accumulating on a flat roof. You don't realize it's up there, but it gets heavier and heavier, until one day, with a great crash, the whole roof falls in on your head . . . leaving Sindbad Mengal, the kiss-lipped boy who was the youngest son of the president of the bioscope corporation, and who had arrived to take charge of cinematic activity in that region, making promises of weekly programme changes, new picture palaces, and regular personal appearances by top stars and playback singers, the Hyders packed away their own assurances of triumph and pushed their way out of the station through the rejoicing crowd.

At Flashman's Hotel, they were shown into a honeymoon suite which smelled oppressively of naphthalene balls by an enfeebled bearer who was accompanied by the last of the trained monkeys in bellhop uniform, and who could not, in the depths of his despair, resist touching Raza Hyder on the arm and inquiring, 'Please, great sir, do you know, when are the Angrez sahibs coming back?'

And Rani Harappa?

Wherever she looks are peering faces; wherever she listens, voices, using a vocabulary of such multicoloured obscenity that it dyes her listening ears in rainbow colours. She wakes up one morning soon after her arrival at her new home to find peasant girls rummaging through her clothes drawers, taking out and holding up lacy imported lingerie, examining ruby lipsticks. 'What do you think you're doing?' – The two girls, unashamed, turn to stare, still holding garments, cosmetics, combs. 'O, Isky's wife, nothing to worry, Isky's ayah said to look.' 'We polished floors and so she gave permission.' 'Ohé, Isky's wife, look out on those floors we polished! Slipperier than a monkey's bottom, I swear.' – Rani rises to her elbows in bed; her voice fights off sleep. 'Get out! Don't you blush to be here? Go on, flee before I.' The girls fan themselves as if a fire were blazing in the room. 'O, God, too hot!' 'Hey, Isky's wife, dip your tongue in water!' She shouts, 'Don't be insol . . .', but they interrupt. 'Never mind all that, lady, in this house it's still what Isky's ayah says.' The girls move, wiggling cheeky hips, towards the door. And pause in the doorway for a parting shot: 'Shit, but Isky gives his wife good clothes, the best of everything, no mistake.' 'That is true. But if a peacock dances in the jungle, there is nobody to see its tail.'

'And tell Isky's – tell the ayah I want to see my daughter,' she cries, but the girls have closed the door, and one of them shouts through it, 'Why be so high and mighty? The child will come when she's ready.'

Rani Harappa no longer weeps, no longer tells her mirror *This can't be happening* or sighs with inaccurate nostalgia for the dormitory of the forty thieves. Plus daughter, minus husband, she is stranded in this backyard of the universe: Mohenjo, the Harappa country estate in Sind, stretching from horizon to horizon, afflicted by a chronic water shortage, populated by laughing scornful monsters, 'Frankensteins, absolutely.' She no longer imagines that Iskander does not know how she is treated here. 'He knows,' she says to her mirror. Her beloved husband, her groom on the golden plate. 'A woman becomes looser after having a child,' she confides to the glass, 'and my Isky, he likes things tight.' Then her hand covers her lips and she runs to door and windows to make sure nobody has heard.

Later, she sits in shalwar and kurta of Italian crêpe-de-chine on the coolest porch, embroidering a shawl, watching a little dust cloud on the horizon. No, how can it be Isky, he is in town with his bosom pal Shakil; I knew trouble, knew it the moment I saw him, the fat pigmeat tub. Probably just one of those little whirlwinds that skip across the scrub.

Mohenjo earth is obstinate. It bakes its people hard as rocks in the heat. The horses in the stables are made of iron, the cattle have diamond bones. The birds here beak up clods of earth, spit, build nests out of mud; there are few trees, except in the little haunted wood, where even the iron horses bolt . . . an owl, while Rani embroiders, lies sleeping in a burrow in the ground. Only a wingtip can be seen.

'If I was murdered here, the news would never leave the estate.' Rani is uncertain whether or not she has spoken aloud. Her thoughts, loosened by solitude, often burst these days through her unconscious lips; and often contradict one another, because the very next notion to form in her mind as she sits on the heavy-eaved verandah is this: 'I love the house.'

Verandahs run along all four walls; a long covered mosquito-netted walkway joins the house to the kitchen bungalow. It is one of the miracles of the place that chapatis do not cool down on their journey along this wood-floored avenue to the dining hall; nor do soufflés ever fall. And oil paintings and chandeliers and high ceilings and a flat tar-macadamed roof upon which, once, before he abandoned her there, she knelt giggling through a morning skylight at her husband still in bed. Iskander Harappa's family home. 'At least I have this piece of him, this soil, his first place. Bilquìs, what a shameless person I must be, to settle for such a small part of my man.' And Bilquìs, on the telephone from Q.: 'Maybe it's O.K. for you, darling, but I could never put up with it, no sir, anyway my Raza is away at the gas, but spare me your sympathy, dear, when he comes home he may be tired as hell but never so tired, you understand what I mean.'

The dust cloud has reached Mir Village now, so it is a visitor and not a whirlwind. She tries to suppress her excitement. The village bears the name of Iskander's father, Sir Mir Harappa, now deceased, once proudly knighted by the Angrez authorities for services rendered. The birdshit is cleaned off his equestrian statue every day. Sir Mir in stone gazes with equal hauteur upon village hospital and brothel, the epitome of an enlightened zamindar . . . 'A visitor.' She claps her hands, rings a bell. Nothing. Until at length Isky's ayah, a heavy-boned woman with soft uncallused hands, brings out a jug of pomegranate water. 'No need to make such noise, Isky's wife, your husband's household knows how to entertain.' Behind the ayah is old Gulbaba, deaf, half-blind, and behind him a trail of spilled pistachio nuts leading to the half-empty dish in his hands. 'O God your servants darling,' Bilquìs has offered long-distance views, 'all those fogey types left over from five hundred years ago. I swear you should take them to the doctor and give the painless injections. What you put up with! Queen by name, you must make yourself queen by fame.'

She rocks in her verandah chair, the needle moving unhurriedly, and feels the youth and gaiety being crushed out of her, drop by drop, by the pressure of the passing moments, and then the horsemen ride into the courtyard and she recognizes Iskander's cousin, Little Mir Harappa from the Daro estate that begins just over the northern horizon. In these parts horizons serve as boundary fences.

'Rani Begum,' Little Mir shouts from horseback, 'no point you blaming me for this. Blame your husband, you should keep him on a tighter rein. Excuse me, but the fellow's a real motherfucker, he's got me all worked up.'

A dozen armed horsemen dismount and begin to loot the house, while Mir wheels and rears his mount and hurls justifications at his cousin's wife, in the throes of a giddy, neighing frenzy that sets his tongue free of all constraints. 'What do you know about that bullock's arsehole, madam? Fuck me in the mouth, but I know. That pizzle of a homosexual pig. Ask the villagers how his great father locked up his wife and spent every night in the brothel, how a whore disappeared when her fat stomach couldn't be explained by what she ate, and then the next thing Lady

Harappa was holding the baby even though everyone knew she hadn't been screwed in a decade. Like father, like son, my honest opinion, sorry if you don't like it. Sisterfucking bastard spawn of corpse-eating vultures. Does he think he can insult me in public and get away with it? Who is the elder, me or that sucker of shit from the rectums of diseased donkeys? Who is the bigger landowner, me or him with his six inches of land on which even the lice cannot grow fat? You tell him who is king in these parts. Tell him who can do what he likes round here, and that he should come crawling to kiss my feet like a murdering rapist of his own grandmother and beg for pardon. That nibbler of a crow's left nipple. This day shows him who's the boss.'

Looters cut from gilded frames paintings of the school of Rubens; Sheraton chairs have their legs amputated. Antique silver is placed in worn old saddle-bags. Cut-glass decanters splinter on thousand-knot carpets. She, Rani, goes on with her embroidery in the midst of the punitive riot. The old servants, the ayah, Gul-baba, the polishing girls, syces, villagers from Mir Village stand and watch, squat and listen. Little Mir, a proud equestrian figure, the tall hawkish avatar of the statue in the village, does not fall silent until his men are back upon their horses. 'A man's honour is in his women,' he shouts. 'So when he took that whore from me he took my honour, tell him that, the little jumped-up piss drinker. Tell him about the frog in the well, and how the giant frog replied. Tell him to be afraid and to think himself lucky I am a mild-mannered man. I could have regained my honour by depriving him of his. Lady, I could do to you anything, anything, and who would dare say no? Here it is my law, Mir's law, that runs. Salaam aleikum.' The dust of the departing horsemen settles on the surface of the untouched pomegranate water, then sinks to form a thick sediment at the bottom of the jug. 'I just can't tell him yet,' Rani tells Bilquìs on the telephone. 'It makes me feel too ashamed.'

'O, Rani, you got your problems, darling,' Bilquìs sympathizes down the Army telephone line. 'What do you mean you don't know? Here I am, stuck away just like you, and even in this zero-town I know what the whole of Karachi is saying. Darling, who hasn't seen how your Isky and that fat doctor run around, belly-dancer shows, international hotel swimming-pools where the naked white women go, why do you think he puts you where you are? Alcohol, gambling, opium, who knows that. Those women in their waterproof fig leaves. Excuse me darling but somebody has to tell you. Cock-fights, bear-fights, snake-and-mongoose fights, that Shakil fixes everything like a pimp or what. And how many women? O baba. Under banquet tables he grabs their thighs. They say the two of them go to the red-light district with movie cameras. Of course it's clear what that Shakil is up to, that nobody from nowhere is getting the high life on a plate, maybe some of those women are willing to be passed on, crumbs from the rich man's table, you understand my meaning. Anyway the point is darling your Isky pinched his cousin's juiciest little French tart from right under his nose, at some big cultural event, I'm sorry to say it but it was all over town, so funny to see Mir standing there while Isky walked off with the floozy, O God I don't know why you don't just cry and cry. Now what's to get worked up about, honestly you should know who is your friend and who is poisoning your name behind your back. You should hear me on the phone, darling, how I defend you, like a tiger, you've got no idea, sweetie, sitting up there and lording it over your antique Gulbabas and all.'

She encounters the ayah clucking ruefully in the wreckage of the dining hall. 'Went too far,' the ayah says. 'My Isky, such a naughty boy. Always always he got his cousin's goat. Went too far. The little hooligan.'

Wherever she looks are peering faces; wherever she listens, voices. She is watched as, blushing with the humiliation of it, she calls Iskander to give him the news. (It has taken her five days to build up her courage.) Iskander Harappa says just three words.

'Life is long.'

Raza Hyder led his gas soldiers out to Needle Valley after a week in which their activities had so alarmed the town that State Chief

Minister Gichki had ordered Raza to get moving double-quick before the stock of virgins available to the bachelors of Q. dwindled to a point at which the moral stability of the region would be jeopardized. Accompanying the soldiers were numerous architects, engineers and construction workers, all of whom were in a condition of moist-trousered panic, because for security reasons none of them had been informed of the fate of the advance party until they arrived in Q., where they were immediately given magnificently elaborated versions of the tale by every street-corner paan-wallah. The construction personnel sobbed inside locked vans; soldiers, on guard, jeered: 'Cowards! Babies! Women!' Raza in his flagbearing jeep heard none of this. He was unable to turn his thoughts away from the events of the preceding day, when he had visited at the hotel by an obsequious gnome whose loose garments smelled powerfully of motor-scooter exhaust fumes: Maulana Dawood, the ancient divine, around whose chicken-thin neck had once hung a necklace of shoes.

'Sir, great sir, I look upon your hero's brow and am inspired.' The *gatta*, the bruise of devotion on Raza's forehead, did not go unremarked.

'No, O most wise, it is I who am at once humbled and exalted by your visit.' Raza Hyder would have been prepared to continue in this vein for at least eleven minutes, and felt a little disappointed when the holy man nodded and said briskly, 'So then, to business. You know about this Gichki of course. Not to be trusted.'

'Not?'

'Completely not. Most corrupt individual. But your files will show this.'

'Allow me to benefit from the knowledge of the man on the spot . . .'

'Like all our politicos these days. No fear of God and big smuggling rackets. This is boring for you; the Army is well up in such matters.'

'Please proceed.'

'Foreign devilments, sir. Nothing less. Devil things from abroad.'

What Gichki was accused of bringing illicitly into God's pure land: iceboxes, foot-operated sewing machines, American popular music recorded at 78 revolutions per minute, love-story picture books that inflamed the passions of the local virgins, domestic air-conditioning units, coffee percolators, bone china, skirts, German sunglasses, cola concentrates, plastic toys, French cigarettes, contraceptive devices, untaxed motor vehicles, big ends, Axminster carpets, repeating rifles, sinful fragrances, brassières, rayon pants, farm machinery, books, eraser-tipped pencils and tubeless bicycle tyres. The customs officer at the border post was mad and his shameless daughter was willing to turn a blind eye in return for regular gratuities. As a result all these items from hell could arrive in broad daylight, on the public highway, and find their way into the gypsy markets, even in the capital itself. 'Army,' Dawood said in a voice that had dropped to a whisper, 'must not stop at stamping out tribal wild men. In God's name, sir.'

'Sir, put your point.'

'Sir, it is this. Prayer is the sword of the faith. By the same token, is not the faithful sword, wielded for God, a form of holy prayer?'

Colonel Hyder's eyes became opaque. He turned away to look out of the window towards an enormous silent house. From an upper window of the house a young boy was training field-glasses on the hotel. Raza turned back towards the Maulana. 'Gichki, you say.'

'Here it is Gichki. But everywhere things are the same. Ministers!'

'Yes,' Hyder said absently, 'they are ministers, that's true.'

'Then I have said my piece and take my leave, abasing myself before you for the privilege of this encounter. God is great.'

'Be in the hands of God.'

Raza headed for the threatened gas fields with the above conversation in his mind's ear; and in his mind's eye the picture of a small boy with binoculars, alone at an upstairs window. A boy who was someone's son: a drop appeared on Old Razor Guts's cheek and was blown off by the wind.

❧

'Gone for three months minimum,' Bilquìs sighed into her telephone. 'What to do? I am young, I can't sit all day like a water-buffalo in mud. Thank God I can go to the movies.' Every night, leaving her child in the care of a locally hired ayah, Bilquìs sat in the brand-new cinema called Mengal Mahal. But Q. was a small town; eyes saw things, even in the dark . . . but I shall return to this theme at a later point, because I can no longer avoid the story of my poor heroine:

Two months after Raza Hyder departed into the wilderness to do battle with the gas-field dacoits, his only child Sufiya Zinobia contracted a case of brain fever that turned her into an idiot. Bilquìs, rending hair and sari with equal passion, was heard to utter a mysterious sentence: 'It is a judgment,' she cried beside her daughter's bed. Despairing of military and civilian doctors she turned to a local Hakim who prepared an expensive liquid distilled from cactus roots, ivory dust and parrot feathers, which saved the girl's life but which (as the medicine man had warned) had the effect of slowing her down for the rest of her years, because the unfortunate side-effect of a potion so filled with elements of longevity was to retard the progress of time inside the body of anyone to whom it was given. By the day of Raza's return on furlough Sufiya Zinobia had shaken off the fever, but Bilquìs was convinced she could already discern in her not-yet-two-year-old-child the effects of that inner deceleration which could never be reversed. 'And if there is this effect,' she feared, 'who knows what else? Who can say?'

In the clutches of a guilt so extreme that even the affliction of her only child seemed insufficient to explain it, a guilt in which, were I possessed of a scandalously wagging tongue, I would say that something Mengalian, something to do with visits to the cinema and fat-mouthed youths, was also present, Bilquìs Hyder spent the night before Raza's return pacing sleeplessly around the honeymoon suite of Flashman's Hotel, and it should perhaps be noted that one of her hands, acting, apparently, of its own volition, continually caressed the region around her navel. At four a.m. she obtained a long-distance line to Rani Harappa in Mohenjo and made the following injudicious remarks:

'Rani, a judgment, what else? He wanted a hero of a son; I gave him an idiot female instead. That's the truth, excuse me, I can't help it. Rani, a simpleton, a goof! Nothing upstairs. Straw instead of cabbage between the ears. Empty in the breadbin. To be done? But darling, there is nothing. That birdbrain, that mouse! I must accept it: she is my shame.'

When Raza Hyder returned to Q. the boy was standing at the window of the great solitary house once again. One of the local guides, in answer to the Colonel's inquiry, told Raza that the house was owned by three crazy sinful witches who never came outside but who managed to produce children nevertheless. The boy at the window was their second son: witch-fashion, they claimed to share their offspring. 'But the story is, sir, that in that house is more wealth than in the treasury of Alexander the Great.' Hyder replied with what sounded like contempt: 'So. But if a pea-cock dances in the jungle, who will see its tail?' Still, his eyes never left the boy at the window until the jeep arrived at the hotel, where he found his wife awaiting him with her hair loose and her face washed clean of eyebrows, so that she was the very incarnation of tragedy, and he heard what she had been too ashamed to send word of. The illness of his daughter and the vision of the fieldglass-eyed young boy combined in Hyder's spirits with the bitterness of his ninety days in the desert and sent him storming out of the honeymoon suite bursting with a rage so terrible that for the sake of his personal safety it was necessary to find a release for it as soon as possible. He ordered a staff car to drive him to the residence of Chief Minister Gichki in the Cantonment, and, without waiting on ceremony, he informed the Minister that although construction work at Needle was well advanced the threat from the tribals could never be eliminated unless he, Hyder, were empowered to take draconian punitive measures. 'With God's help we are defending the site, but now we must stop this pussyfooting. Sir, you must place the law in my hands. Carte blanche. At certain moments civil law must bend before military necessity. Violence is the language of these savages; but the law obliges us to speak in the discredited womanly tongue of minimum-force. No good, sir. I cannot guarantee results.' And when Gichki responded that on no account were the laws of the State to be flouted by the armed forces – 'We'll have no barbarisms in those hills, sir! No tortures, no stringings-up by toes, not while I am Chief Minister here!' – then Raza, in discourteously loud tones that escaped through the doors and windows of Gichki's office and terrified the peons outside because they had issued from the lips of one so habitually polite, gave the Chief Minister a warning. 'Army is watching these days, Gichki Sahib. All over the country the eyes of honest soldiers see what they see, and we are not pleased, no sir. The people stir, sir. And if they look away from politicians, where will they turn for purity?'

Raza Hyder in his wrath left Gichki – small, bullet-cropped hair, flat Chinese face – formulating his never-to-be-delivered reply; and found Maulana Dawood awaiting him by the staff car. Soldier and divine rode on the back seat, their words shielded from the driver by a sheet of glass. But it seems probable that behind this screen a name passed from divine tongue into martial ear: a name, carrying with it intimations of scandal. Did Maulana Dawood tell Hyder about the meetings of Bilquìs and her Sindbad? I say only that it seems probable. Innocent until proven guilty is an excellent rule.

That night the cinema executive Sindbad Mengal left his office at Mengal Mahal by the back door as usual, emerging into a dark gully behind the cinema screen. He was whistling a sad tune, the melody of a man who cannot meet his beloved even though the moon is full. In spite of the loneliness of the tune he had dressed up to the nines, as was his custom: his bright European garb, bush-shirt and duck pants, was radiant in the gully, and the melancholy moonlight bounced off the oil in his hair. It is likely that he never even noticed that the shadows in the gully had begun to close in on him; the knife, which the moon would have illuminated, was clearly kept sheathed until the last instant. We know this because Sindbad Mengal did not stop whistling until the knife entered his guts, whereupon someone else began to whistle the same tune, just in case anybody was passing by and got curious. A hand covered Sindbad's mouth as the knife went to work. In the next few days Mengal's absence from his office inevitably attracted attention, but it was not until several moviegoers had complained about the deterioration in the cinema's stereophonic sound quality that an engineer inspected the loudspeakers behind the screen and discovered segments of Sindbad Mengal's white shirt and duck pants concealed within them, as well as black Oxford shoes. The knife-sliced garments still contained the appropriate pieces of the cinema manager's body. The genitals had been severed and inserted into the rectum. The head was never found, nor was the murderer brought to justice.

Life is not always long.

That night Raza made love to Bilquìs with a coarseness which she was willing to put down to his months in the wilderness. The name of Mengal was never mentioned between them, not even when the town was buzzing with the murder story, and soon afterwards Raza returned to Needle Valley. Bilquìs stopped going to the cinema, and although in this period she retained her queenly composure it seemed as though she were standing on a crumbling outcrop over an abyss, because she became prone to dizzy spells. Once, when she picked up her damaged daughter to play the traditional game of water-carrier, slinging Sufiya Zinobia on her back and pretending she was a water-skin, she collapsed to the floor beneath the delighted child before she had finished pouring her out. Soon afterwards she called Rani Harappa to announce that she was pregnant. While she was imparting this information, the lid of her left eye began, inexplicably, to nictate.

An itchy palm means money in the offing. Shoes crossed on the floor mean a journey; shoes turned upside-down warn of tragedy. Scissors cutting empty air mean a quarrel in the family. And a winking left eye means there will be bad news soon.

'On my next leave,' Raza wrote to Bilquìs, 'I shall be going to Karachi. There are family duties, and also Marshal Aurangzeb is giving a reception. One does not refuse one's Commander-in-Chief's invitation. If your condition, however, you will do better to rest. It would be thoughtless of me to ask you to accompany me on this non-compulsory and arduous trip.'

Politeness can be a trap, and Bilquìs was caught in the web of her husband's courtesy. 'As you wish,' she wrote back, and what made her write this was not entirely guilt, but also something untranslatable, a law which obliged her to pretend that Raza's words meant no more than they said. This law is called *takallouf.* To unlock a society, look at its untranslatable words. *Takallouf* is a member of that opaque, world-wide sect of concepts which refuse to travel across linguistic frontiers: it refers to a form of tongue-typing formality, a social restraint so extreme as to make it impossible for the victim to express what he or she really means, a species of compulsory irony which insists, for the sake of good form, on being taken literally. When *takallouf* gets between a husband and a wife, look out.

Raza travelled alone to the capital . . . and now that an untranslatable word has brought Hyder and Harappa, unencumbered by spouses, very near to meeting once again, it is time to take stock of the situation, because our two duellists will shortly find themselves doing battle. Even now, the cause of their first altercation is allowing a servant girl to oil and braid her hair. She, Atiyah Aurangzeb, known to her intimates as "Pinkie', is contemplating, coolly, the soirée which she has decided to arrange in the name of her almost senile husband, the crumbling Marshal Aurangzeb, Joint Chief of Staff. Pinkie Aurangzeb is in her middle thirties, several years older than Raza and Iskander, but this does not diminish her allure; mature women have charms of their own, as is well known. Trapped in a marriage with a dotard, Pinkie finds her pleasures wherever she can.

Meanwhile, two wives are abandoned in their separate exiles, each with a daughter who should have been a son (more needs to be said about young Arjumand Harappa, more will certainly be written about poor, idiot Sufiya Zinobia). Two different approaches to the matter of revenge have been outlined. And while Iskander Harappa consorts with a fat pigment tub named Omar Khayyam Shakil for purposes of debauchery etc., Raza Hyder would seem to have fallen under the influence of a grey eminence, who whispers austere secrets in the backs of Army limousines. Cinemas, sons of witches, bruises on foreheads, frogs, peacocks have all worked to create an atmosphere in which the stink of honour is all-pervasive.

Yes, it is high time the combatants took the field.

The fact is that Raza Hyder was smitten right between the eyes by Pinkie Aurangzeb. He desired her so badly that it made the bruise on his forehead ache, but he lost her to Iskander Harappa, right there at the Marshall's reception, while the old soldier slept in an armchair, relegated to a corner of the glittering throng, but even in that condition of somnolent cuckolded dotage never spilling a drop from the brimming tumbler of whisky-soda he clutched in his sleeping hand.

On that fateful occasion began a duel which was to continue at least until both protagonists were dead, if not longer. Its initial prize was the body of the Marshall's wife, but after that it moved on to higher things. First things first, however: and Pinkie's body, excitingly on display, in a green sari worn dangerously low upon the hips in the fashion of the women of the East Wing; with silver-and-diamond earrings in the form of crescent-and-star hanging brightly from pierced lobes; and bearing upon irresistibly vulnerable shoulders a light shawl whose miraculous work could only have been the product of the fabled embroiderers of Aansu, because amidst its miniscule arabesques a thousand and one stories had been portrayed in threads of gold, so vividly that it seemed the tiny horsemen were actually galloping along her collarbone, while minute birds appeared to be flying, actually flying, down the graceful meridian of her spine . . . this body is worth lingering over.

And lingering over it, when Raza had managed to fight his way through the whirlpools and eddies of young bucks and jealous women surrounding Pinkie Aurangzeb, was the half-drunk Iskander Harappa, city playboy number one, at whom the vision of loveliness was smiling with a warmth that froze the thick perspiration of his arousal on to Raza's waxed moustache, while that notorious degenerate with his filthy tongue that put even his cousin Mir to shame told the goddess dirty jokes.

Raza Hyder stiff, at embarrassed attention, the garment of his lust rendered rigid by the starch of *takallouf* . . . but Isky hiccuped, 'Look who's here! Our goddamn hero, the tilyar!' Pinkie tittered as Iskander adopted a professional stance, adjusting invisible pincenez: 'The tilyar, madam, as you are possibly aware, is a skinny little migrating bird good for nothing but shooting out of the sky.' Ripples of laughter spread outwards through the eddying bucks. Pinkie, annihilating Raza with a look, murmured, 'Pleased to meet,' and Raza found himself replying with a ruinously awkward and bombastic formality, 'My honour, lady, and may I say that in my opinion and with the grace of God the new blood is going to be the making of our great new nation,' but Pinkie Aurangzeb was pretending to stifle a laugh. 'Fuck me in the mouth, tilyar,' Iskander Harappa shouted gaily, 'this is a party, yaar, no motherfucking speeches, for God's sake.' The rage buried beneath Hyder's good manners was bubbling higher, but it was impotent against this sophistication that permitted obscenity and blasphemy and could murder a man's desire and his pride with clever laughter. 'Cousin,' he attempted catastrophically, 'I am just a simple soldier,' but now his hostess stopped pretending not to laugh at him, drew the shawl tighter around her shoulders, put a hand on Iskander Harappa's arm and said, 'Take me into the garden, Isky. The air-conditioning is too cold in here, and outside it's nice and warm.'

'Then into the warm, pronto!' Harappa cried gallantly, pressing his glass into Raza's hand for safe-keeping. 'For you, Pinkie, I would enter the furnaces of hell, if you desire protection when you get there. My teetotal relative Raza is no less brave,' he added over his departing shoulder, 'only he goes to hell not for ladies, but for gas.'

Watching from the sidelines as Iskander Harappa bore his prize away into the close, musky twilight of the garden was the flabby Himalayan figure of our peripheral hero, the doctor, Omar Khayyam Shakil.

Do not form too low an opinion of Atiyah Aurangzeb. She remained faithful to Iskander Harappa even after he turned serious and dispensed with her services, and retired without a word of complaint into the stoic tragedy of her private life, until the day of his death, when after setting fire to an old embroidered shawl she hacked out her own heart with a nine-inch kitchen knife. And Isky, too, was faithful to her in his fashion. From the time that she became his mistress he stopped sleeping with his wife Rani altogether, thus ensuring that she would have no more children, and that he would be the last of his line, an idea which, he told Omar Khayyam Shakil, was not without a certain appeal.

(Here I should explain the matter of daughters-who-should-have-been-sons. Sufiya Zinobia was the 'wrong miracle' because her father had wanted a boy; but this was not Arjumand Harappa's problem. Arjumand, the famous 'virgin Ironpants', regretted her female sex for wholly non-parental reasons. 'This woman's body,' she told her father on the day she became a grown woman, 'it brings a person nothing but babies, pinches and shame.')

Iskander reappeared from the garden as Raza was preparing to leave, and attempted to make peace. With a formality the equal of Raza's own, he said: 'Dear fellow, before you go back to Needle you must come up to Mohenjo; Rani would be so happy. Poor girl, I wish she enjoyed this city life . . . and I insist that you call your Billoo there also. Let the ladies have a good chat while we shoot tilyars all day long. What do you say?'

And takallouf obliged Raza Hyder to answer: 'Thank you, yes.'

The day before they passed the sentence of death Iskander Harappa would be permitted to telephone his daughter for one minute exactly. The last words he ever addressed to her in private were acrid with the hopeless nostalgia of those shrunken times:

'Arjumand, my love, I should have gone out to fight this buffalo-fucker Hyder when he staked himself to the ground. I left that business unfinished; it was my biggest mistake.'

Even in his playboy period Iskander occasionally felt bad about his sequestered wife. At such moments he rounded up a few cronies, bundled them into station-wagons and led a convoy of urban gaiety up to his country estate. Pinkie Aurangzeb was conspicuous by her absence; and Rani was queen for a day.

When Raza Hyder accepted Isky's invitation to Mohenjo, the two of them drove up together, followed by five other vehicles containing an ample supply of whisky, film starlets, sons of textile magnates, European diplomats, soda siphons and wives. Bilquìs, Sufiya Zinobia and the ayah were met at the private railway station Sir Mir Harappa had constructed on the main line from the capital to Q. And, for one day, nothing bad happened at all.

After the death of Isky Harappa, Rani and Arjumand Harappa were kept locked up in Mohenjo for several years, and to fill the silences the mother told the daughter about the business of the shawl. 'I had begun to embroider it before I heard that I was sharing my husband with Little Mir's woman, but it turned out to be a premonition of another woman entirely.' By that time Arjumand Harappa had already reached the stage of refusing to hear anything bad about her father. She snapped back: 'Allah, mother, all you can do is bitch about the Chairman. If he did not love you, you must have done something to deserve it.' Rani Harappa shrugged. 'Chairman Iskander Harappa, your father, whom I always loved,' she replied, 'was world champion of shamelessness; he was international rogue and bastard number one. You see, daughter, I remember those days, I remember Raza Hyder when he was not a devil with horns and a tail, and also Isky, before he became a saint.'

The bad thing that happened at Mohenjo when the Hyders were there was started by a fat man who had had too much to drink. It happened on the second evening of that visit, on the very verandah on which Rani Harappa had gone on with her embroi-

dery while Little Mir's men looted her home – an incursion
whose effects could still be seen, in the empty picture-frames with
fragments of canvas adhering to the corners, in the sofas whose
stuffing stuck out through the ripped leather, in the odd assort-
ment of cutlery at the dining table and the obscene slogans in the
hall, which could still be made out beneath the coats of white-
wash. The partial wreckage of the Mohenjo house gave the guests
the feeling of holding a celebration in the midst of a disaster, and
made them expect more trouble, so that the bright laughter of the
film starlet Zehra acquired an edge of hysteria and the men all
drank too fast. And all the time Rani Harappa sat in her rocking-
chair and worked on her shawl, leaving the organization of
Mohenjo to the ayah who was fawning over Iskander as if he were
three years old, or a deity, or both. And finally the trouble did
come, and because it was the fate of Omar Khayyam Shakil to
affect, from his position on the periphery, the great events whose
central figures were other people but which collectively made up
his own life, it was he who said with a tongue made too loose by
the neurotic drinking of the evening that Mrs Bilquìs Hyder was a
lucky woman, Iskander had done her a favour by pinching Pinkie
Aurangzeb from under Raza's nose. 'If Isky hadn't been there
maybe our hero's Begum would have to console herself with children, because there would be no man to fill her bed.' Shakil had
spoken too loud, to gain the attention of the starlet Zehra, who
was more interested in the over-bright looks she was getting from
a certain Akbar Junejo, a well-known gambler and film producer;
when Zehra moved away without bothering to make any excuses,
Shakil was faced with the spectacle of a wide-eyed Bilquìs, who
had just emerged on to the verandah after seeing her daughter
into bed, and on whom the pregnancy was showing much too
early . . . so who knows if that was the reason for Bilquìs's stand, if
she was just trying to transfer her own guilt on to the shoulders of
a husband whose probity was now also the subject of gossip? –
Anyway, what happened was this: after it became clear to
the guests that Omar Khayyam's words had been heard and
understood by the woman who stood blazing on the evening

verandah, a silence fell, and a stillness which reduced the party to a tableau of fear, and into that stillness Bilquìs Hyder shrieked her husband's name.

It must not be forgotten that she was a woman to whom the dupatta of womanly honour had clung even when the rest of her clothing had been torn off her body; not a woman to turn a deaf ear to public slanders. Raza Hyder and Iskander Harappa stared wordlessly at each other while Bilquìs pointed a long-nailed index finger at the heart of Omar Khayyam Shakil.

'You hear that man, husband? Hear what shame he is making for me.'

O, the hush, the muteness, like a cloud that obscured the horizon! Even the owls forbore to screech.

Raza Hyder came to attention, because once the afrit of honour has been summoned from its sleep, it will not depart until satisfied. 'Iskander,' Raza said, 'I will not fight inside your house.' Then he did a strange and a wild thing. He marched off the verandah, entered the stables, returned with a wooden stake, a mallet and a length of good stout rope. The stake was driven into the rock-hard earth; and then Colonel Hyder, future President, tethered himself to it by the ankle and hurled the mallet away.

'Here I stand,' he shouted, 'let the one who slanders my honour come out and find me.' And there, all night long, he remained; because Omar Khayyam Shakil rushed indoors, to faint of alcohol and fright.

Hyder like a bull paced in circles, the rope a radius stretching taut from ankle to stake. The night thickened; the guests, embarrassed, drifted away to bed. But Isky Harappa stayed on the verandah, knowing that although the folly had been the fat man's, the true quarrel stood between the Colonel and himself. The starlet Zehra, on her way to a bed which it would be unforgivably loose-tongued of me to suggest was already occupied – so I shall say nothing at all on the subject – offered her host a warning. 'Don't go getting any stupid ideas, Isky darling, you hear? Don't you dare go out there. He's a soldier, look at him, like a tank, he'll

kill you for sure. Just let him cool off, O.K.?' But Rani Harappa
gave her husband no advice. ('You see, Arjumand,' she told her
daughter, years later, 'I recall your daddy when he was too
mousey to take his medicine like a man.')

How it ended: badly, as it had to. Just before dawn. You can
understand: Raza had been awake all night, stamping in the circle
of his pride, his eyes red with rage and fatigue. Red eyes don't see
clearly – and the light was poor – and who sees servants coming,
anyway? – what I'm trying to say is that old Gulbaba woke early
and walked across the yard with a brass lotah jug, on his way to
ablute before saying his prayers; and, seeing Colonel Hyder tied to
a stake, crept up behind him to ask, sir, what are you doing, will it
not be better if you come . . . ? Old servants take liberties. It is the
privilege of their years. But Raza, sleep-deafened, heard only
steps, a voice; felt a tap on his shoulder; swung round; and with
one terrible blow, felled Gulbaba like a twig. The violence loosened something inside the old man; let us call it life, because
within a month old Gul was dead, with a confused expression on
his face, like a man who knows he has mislaid an important possession and can't remember what it is.

In the aftermath of that murderous punch Bilquìs relented,
emerging from the shadow of the house to persuade Raza to
unhitch himself from his post. 'The poor girl, Raza, don't make
her see this thing.' And when Raza came back to the verandah,
Iskander Harappa, himself unslept and unshaven, offered his arms
in embrace, and Raza, with considerable grace, hugged Isky,
shoulder against shoulder, allowing their necks to meet, as the
saying goes.

When Rani Harappa emerged from her boudoir the next day
to say goodbye to her husband, Iskander went pale at the sight of
the shawl she had wrapped around her shoulders, a completed
shawl as delicately worked as anything made by the craftswomen
of Aansu, a masterpiece amidst whose minuscule arabesques a
thousand and one stories had been portrayed, so artfully that it
seemed as though horsemen were galloping along her collarbone,

while tiny birds flew along the soft meridian of her spine. 'Good-bye, Iskander,' she told him, 'and do not forget that the love of some women is not blind.'

Well, well, friendship is a bad word for the thing between Raza and Iskander, but for a long time after the incident of the stake it was the word they both used. Sometimes the good words can't be found.

She has always wanted to be a queen, but now that Raza Hyder is at last a sort of prince the ambition has gone sour on her lips. A second baby has been born, six weeks early, but Raza has uttered no word of suspicion. Another daughter, but he hasn't complained about that either, saying only that it is quite proper that the first should be a boy and the second a girl, so one must not blame the new arrival for her elder sister's mistake. The girl has been named Naveed, that is Good News, and she is a model baby. But the mother has been damaged by this birth. Something has been torn inside, and the medical opinion is that she must have no more children. Raza Hyder will never have a son. He has spoken, just once, of the boy with field-glasses at the window of the witches' house, but this subject, too, has been closed. He is withdrawing from her down the corridors of his mind, closing the doors behind him. Sindbad Mengal, Mohenjo, love: all these doors are closed. She sleeps alone, so that her old fears have her at their mercy, and it is in these days that she begins to be afraid of the hot afternoon wind that flows so fiercely out of her past.

Martial law has been declared. Raza has arrested Chief Minister Gichki and been appointed administrator of the region. He has moved into the Ministerial residence with his wife and children, abandoning to its memories that cracking hotel in which the last trained monkey has taken to wandering listlessly amidst the dying palms of the dining hall while ageing musicians scratch at their rotting fiddles for an audience of empty tables. She does not see much of Raza these days. He has work to do. The gas pipeline is progressing well, and now that Gichki is out of the way a programme of making examples of arrested tribals has been inaugurated. She fears that the bodies of hanged men will turn the citizens of Q. against her husband, but she does not say this to him. He is taking a firm line, and Maulana Dawood gives him all the advice he needs.

The last time I visited Pakistan, I was told this joke. God came down to Pakistan to see how things were going. He asked General Ayub Khan why the place was in such a mess. Ayub replied: 'It's these no-good corrupt civilians, sir. Just get rid of them and leave the rest to me.' So God eliminated the politicos. After a while, He returned; things were even worse than before. This time He asked Yahya Khan for an explanation. Yahya blamed Ayub, his sons and their hangers-on for the troubles. 'Do the needful,' Yahya begged, 'and I'll clean the place up good and proper.' So God's thunderbolts wiped out Ayub. On His third visit, He found a catastrophe, so He agreed with Zulfikar Ali Bhutto that democracy must return. He turned Yahya into a cockroach and swept him under a carpet; but, a few years later, he noticed the situation was still pretty awful. He went to General Zia and offered him supreme power: on one condition. 'Anything, God,' the General replied, 'You name it.' So God said, 'Answer me one question and I'll flatten Bhutto for you like a chapati.' Zia said: 'Fire away.' So God whispered in his ear: 'Look, I do all these things for this country, but what I don't understand is: why don't people seem to love me any more?'

It seems clear that the President of Pakistan managed to give God a satisfactory answer. I wonder what it was.

III

SHAME, GOOD NEWS
AND THE VIRGIN

7

BLUSHING

Not so long ago, in the East End of London, a Pakistani father murdered his only child, a daughter, because by making love to a white boy she had brought such dishonour upon her family that only her blood could wash away the stain. The tragedy was intensified by the father's enormous and obvious love for his butchered child, and by the beleaguered reluctance of his friends and relatives (all 'Asians', to use the confusing term of these trying days) to condemn his actions. Sorrowing, they told radio microphones and television cameras that they understood the man's point of view, and went on supporting him even when it turned out that the girl had never actually 'gone all the way' with her boyfriend. The story appalled me when I heard it, appalled me in a fairly obvious way. I had recently become a father myself and was therefore newly capable of estimating how colossal a force would be required to make a man turn a knife-blade against his own flesh and blood. But even more appalling was my realization that, like the interviewed friends etc., I, too, found myself understanding the killer. The news did not seem alien to me. We who have grown up on a diet of honour and shame can still grasp what must seem unthinkable to peoples living in the aftermath of the death of God and of tragedy: that men will sacrifice their dearest love on the implacable altars of their pride. (And not only men. I have since heard of a case in which a woman committed the identical crime for identical reasons.) Between shame and shamelessness lies the axis upon which we turn; meteorological conditions at both these poles are of the most extreme, ferocious type. Shamelessness, shame: the roots of violence.

My Sufiya Zinobia grew out of the corpse of that murdered girl, although she will not (have no fear) be slaughtered by Raza Hyder. Wanting to write about shame, I was at first haunted by the imagined spectre of that dead body, its throat slit like a halal chicken, lying in a London night across a zebra crossing, slumped across black and white, black and white, while above her a Belisha beacon blinked, orange, not-orange, orange. I thought of the crime as having been committed right there, publicly, ritually, while at the windows eyes. And no mouth opened in protest. And when the police knocked on doors, what hope of assistance had they? Inscrutability of the 'Asian' face under the eyes of the foe. It seems even the insomniacs at their windows closed their eyelids and saw nothing. And the father left with blood-cleansed name and grief.

I even went so far as to give the dead girl a name: Anahita Muhammad, known as Anna. In my imagination she spoke with an East London accent but wore jeans, blue brown pink, out of some atavistic reluctance to show her legs. She would certainly have understood the language her parents spoke at home, but would obstinately have refused to utter a word of it herself. Anna Muhammad: lively, no doubt attractive, a little too dangerously so at sixteen. Mecca meant ballrooms to her, rotating silver balls, strobe lighting, youth. She danced behind my eyes, her nature changing each time I glimpsed her: now innocent, now whore, then a third and a fourth thing. But finally she eluded me, she became a ghost, and I realized that to write about her, about shame, I would have to go back East, to let the idea breathe its favourite air. Anna, deported, repatriated to a country she had never seen, caught brain-fever and turned into a sort of idiot.

Why did I do that to her? – Or maybe the fever was a lie, a figment of Bilquìs Hyder's imagination, intended to cover up the damage done by repeated blows to the head: hate can turn a miracle-gone-wrong into a basket case. And that hakimi potion sounds pretty unconvincing. How hard to pin down the truth, especially when one is obliged to see the world in slices; snapshots conceal as much as they make plain.

All stories are haunted by the ghosts of the stories they might have been. Anna Muhammad haunts this book; I'll never write about her now. And other phantoms are here as well, earlier and now ectoplasmic images connecting shame and violence. These ghosts, like Anna, inhabit a country that is entirely unghostly: no spectral 'Peccavistan', but Proper London. I'll mention two: a girl set upon in a late-night underground train by a group of teenage boys is the first. The girl 'Asian' again, the boys predictably white. Afterwards, remembering her beating, she feels not angry but ashamed. She does not want to talk about what happened, she makes no official complaint, she hopes the story won't get out: it is a typical reaction, and the girl is not one girl but many. Looking at smoking cities on my television screen, I see groups of young people running through the streets, the shame burning on their brows and setting fire to shops, police shields, cars. They remind me of my anonymous girl. Humiliate people for long enough and a wildness bursts out of them. Afterwards, surveying the wreckage of their rage, they look bewildered, uncomprehending, young. Did we do such things? Us? But we're just ordinary kids, nice people, we didn't know we could . . . then, slowly, pride dawns on them, pride in their power, in having learned to hit back. And I imagine what would have happened if such a fury could have been released in that girl on her underground train – how she would have thrashed the white kids within an inch of their lives, breaking arms legs noses balls, without knowing whence the violence came, without seeing how she, so slight a figure, could command such awesome strength. And they, what would they have done? How to tell the police they were beaten up by a mere girl, just one weak female against the lot of them? How to look their comrades in the face? I feel gleeful about this notion: it's a seductive, silky thing, this violence, yes it is.

I never gave this second girl a name. But she, too, is inside my Sufiya Zinobia now, and you'll recognize her when she pops out.

The last ghost inside my heroine is male, a boy from a news clipping. You may have read about him, or at least his prototype: he was found blazing in a parking lot, his skin on fire. He burned to death, and the experts who examined his body and the scene of the incident were forced to accept what seemed impossible: namely that the boy had simply ignited of his own accord, without dousing himself in petrol or applying any external flame. We are energy; we are fire; we are light. Finding the key, stepping through into that truth, a boy began to burn.

Enough. Ten years have slipped by in my story while I've been seeing ghosts. — But one last word on the subject: the first time I sat down to think about Anahita Muhammad, I recalled the last sentence of *The Trial* by Franz Kafka, the sentence in which Joseph K. is stabbed to death. My Anna, like Kafka's Joseph, died under a knife. Not so Sufiya Zinobia Hyder; but that sentence, the ghost of an epigraph, hangs over her story still:

' "*Like a dog!*" *he said: it was as if he meant the shame of it to outlive him.*'

By the year of the Hyders' return from Q. the capital had grown, Karachi had become fat, so that people who had been there from the beginning could no longer recognize the slender girlish town of their youth in this obese harridan of a metropolis. The great fleshy folds of its endless expansion had swallowed up the primeval salt marshes, and all along the sandspit there erupted, like boils, the gaudily painted beach houses of the rich. The streets were full of the darkened faces of young men who had been drawn to the painted lady by her overblown charms, only to find that her price was too high for them to pay; something puritan and violent sat on their foreheads and it was frightening to walk amongst their disillusions in the heat. The night held smugglers who rode in scooter-rickshaws to the coast; and the Army, of course, was in power.

Raza Hyder got off the railway train from the west wreathed in rumours. This was the period shortly after the disappearance of the former Chief Minister Aladdin Gichki, who had finally been released from captivity for lack of hard evidence against him; he lived quietly with his wife and dog for several weeks until the day he went out to walk the Alsatian and never returned, even though his last words to Begum Gichki had been, 'Tell the cook to make a dozen extra meatballs for dinner, I'm starving to death today.' Meatballs, one to twelve, steamed expectantly in a dish, but something must have spoiled Gichki's appetite, because he never ate them. Possibly he was unable to resist the pangs of hunger and ate the Alsatian instead, because they never found the dog either, not so much as a hair of its tail. The Gichki mystery kept cropping up in conversations, and Hyder's name often got into these chats, perhaps because the mutual hatred between Gichki and the divine Maulana Dawood was well known, and Dawood's intimacy with Hyder was no secret either. Strange stories filtered back to Karachi from Q. and hung in the air-conditioned urban air.

The official version of Hyder's period of power in the west was that it had been an unmitigated success, and his career was continuing along its upward path. Dacoity had been eliminated, the mosques were full, the organs of state had been purged of Gichkism, of the corruption disease, and separatism was a dead duck. Old Razor Guts was now a Brigadier . . . but, as Iskander Harappa was fond of telling Omar Khayyam Shakil when the pair of them were in their cups, 'Fuck me in the mouth, yaar, everybody knows those tribals are running wild out there because Hyder kept hanging innocent people by the balls.' There were also whispers about marital troubles in the Hyder household. Even Rani Harappa in exile heard the rumours of dissension, of the idiot child whose mother called her 'Shame' and treated her like mud, of the internal injury which made sons impossible and which was leading Bilquìs down dark corridors towards a crack-up; but she, Rani, did not know how to talk to Bilquìs about these things, and the telephone receiver remained untouched on its hook.

Some things did not get talked about. Nobody mentioned a fat-mouthed boy called Sindbad Mengal, or speculated on the parentage of the younger Hyder girl ... Brigadier Raza Hyder was driven directly from the station to the inner sanctum of the President, Field-Marshal Mohammad A., where according to some reports he was hugged affectionately and had his cheeks pulled in friendship, while others hinted that the blast of angry air issuing from the keyholes of that room was so intensely hot that Raza Hyder, standing to attention before his outraged President, must have been badly singed. What is certain is that he emerged from the Presidential presence as the national minister of education, information and tourism, while someone else climbed aboard a westbound train to assume the governorship of Q. And Raza Hyder's eyebrows remained intact.

Also intact: the alliance between Raza and Maulana Dawood, who had accompanied the Hyders to Karachi and who, once he was installed in the official residence of the new minister, at once distinguished himself by launching a vociferous public campaign against the consumption of prawns and blue-bellied crabs, which, being scavengers, were as unclean as any pig, and which, although understandably unavailable in far-off Q., were both plentiful and popular in the capital by the sea. The Maulana was deeply affronted to find these armoured monsters of the deep freely available in the fishmarkets, and succeeded in enlisting the support of urban divines who did not know how to object. The city's fishermen found that the sales of shellfish began to drop alarmingly, and were therefore obliged to rely more than ever on the income they gained from the smuggling of contraband goods. Illicit booze and cigarettes replaced blue crabs in the holds of many dhows. No booze or cigarettes found their way into the Hyder residence, however. Dawood made unheralded raids on the servants' quarters to check that God was in charge. 'Even a city of scuttling monstrosities,' he assured Raza Hyder, 'can be purified with the help of the Almighty.'

Three years after Raza Hyder's return to Q., it became clear that his star had secretly been in decline, because the rumours from Q. (Mengal, Gichki, ball-hung tribals) never died down entirely; so that when the capital was shifted away from Karachi and taken up north into the clean mountain air and placed in hideous new buildings specially constructed for the purpose, Raza Hyder stayed put on the coast. The ministry of education, information and tourism went north along with the rest of the administration; but Raza Hyder (to be blunt) was sacked. He was returned to military duty, and given the futureless job of commanding the Military Training Academy. They permitted him to keep his house, but Maulana Dawood told him: 'So what if you still have the marble walls? They have made you a crab in this marble shell. *Na-pak*: unclean.'

We have leapt too far ahead: it is time to conclude our remarks about rumours and shellfish. Sufiya Zinobia, the idiot, is blushing.

I did it to her, I think, to make her pure. Couldn't think of another way of creating purity in what is supposed to be the Land of the Pure ... and idiots are, by definition, innocent. Too romantic a use to make of mental disability? Perhaps; but it's too late for such doubts. Sufiya Zinobia has grown, her mind more slowly than her body, and owing to this slowness she remains, for me, somehow clean *(pak)* in the midst of a dirty world. See how, growing, she caresses a pebble in her hand, unable to say why goodness seems to lie within this smooth flat stone; how she glows with pleasure when she hears loving words, even though they are almost always meant for someone else ... Bilquìs poured all her affection over her younger daughter, Naveed. 'Good News' – the nickname had stuck, like a pulled face in the wind – was soaked in it, a monsoon of love, while Sufiya Zinobia, her parents' burden, her mother's shame, remained as dry as the desert. Groans, insults, even the wild blows of exasperation rained on her instead; but such rain yields no moisture. Her spirit parched for lack of affection, she nevertheless managed, when love was in her vicinity, to glow happily just to be near the precious thing.

She also blushed. You recall she blushed at birth. Ten years later, her parents were still perplexed by these reddenings, these blushes like petrol fires. The fearful incandescence of Sufiya Zinobia had been, it seemed, intensified by the desert years in Q. When the Hyders paid the obligatory courtesy call on Bariamma and her tribe, the ancient lady bent to kiss the girls and was alarmed to find that her lips had been mildly burned by a sudden rush of heat to Sufiya Zinobia's cheek; the burn was bad enough to necessitate twice-daily applications of lip salve for a week. This misbehaviour of the child's thermostatic mechanisms roused in her mother what looked like a practised wrath: 'That moron,' Bliquìs shouted beneath the amused gaze of Duniyad Begum and the rest, 'just don't even look at her now! What is this? Anyone puts eyes on her or tells her two words and she goes red, red like a chilli! I swear. What normal child goes so beetroot hot that her clothes can smell of burning? But what to do, she went wrong and that's that, we must just grin and bear.' The disappointment of the Hyders in their elder daughter had also been hardened in the noonday rays of the wilderness into a thing as pitiless as that shadow-frying sun.

The affliction was real enough. Miss Shahbanou, the Parsee ayah whom Bliquìs had employed on her return to Karachi, complained on her first day that when she gave Sufiya Zinobia a bath the water had scalded her hands, having been brought close to boiling point by a red flame of embarrassment that spread from the roots of the damaged girl's hair to the tips of her curling toes.

To speak plainly: Sufiya Zinobia Hyder blushed uncontrollably whenever her presence in the world was noticed by others. But she also, I believe, blushed for the world.

Let me voice my suspicion: the brain-fever that made Sufiya Zinobia preternaturally receptive to all sorts of things that float around in the ether enabled her to absorb, like a sponge, a host of unfelt feelings.

Where do you imagine they go? – I mean emotions that should

have been felt, but were not – such as regret for a harsh word, guilt for a crime, embarrassment, propriety, shame? – Imagine shame as a liquid, let's say a sweet fizzy tooth-rotting drink, stored in a vending machine. Push the right button and a cup plops down under a pissing stream of the fluid. How to push the button? Nothing to it. Tell a lie, sleep with a white boy, get born the wrong sex. Out flows the bubbling emotion and you drink your fill ... but how many human beings refuse to follow these simple instructions! Shameful things are done: lies, loose living, disrespect for one's elders, failure to love one's national flag, incorrect voting at elections, over-eating, extramarital sex, autobiographical novels, cheating at cards, maltreatment of womenfolk, examination failures, smuggling, throwing one's wicket away at the crucial point of a Test Match: and they are done *shamelessly*. Then what happens to all that unfelt shame? What of the unquaffed cups of pop? Think again of the vending machine. The button is pushed; but then in comes the shameless hand and jerks away the cup! The button-pusher does not drink what was ordered; and the fluid of shame spills, spreading in a frothy lake across the floor.

But we are discussing an abstract, an entirely ethereal vending machine; so into the ether goes the unfelt shame of the world. Whence, I submit, it is siphoned off by the misfortunate few, janitors of the unseen, their souls the buckets into which squeegees drip what-was-spilled. We keep such buckets in special cupboards. Nor do we think much of them, although they clean up our dirty waters.

Well then: Sufiya the moron blushed. Her mother said to the assembled relatives, 'She does it to get attention. O, you don't know what it's like, the mess, the anguish, and for what? For no reward. For air. Thank God for my Good News.' But goof or no goof, Sufiya Zinobia – by blushing furiously each time her mother looked sidelong at her father – revealed to watching family eyes that something was piling up between those two. Yes. Idiots can feel such things, that's all.

❧

Blushing is slow burning. But it is also another thing: it is a *psychosomatic event*. I quote: 'A sudden shut-down of the arterio-venous anastomoses of the face floods the capillaries with the blood that produces the characteristically heightened colour. People who do not believe in psychosomatic events and do not believe that the mind can influence the body by direct nervous pathways should reflect upon blushing, which in people of heightened sensibility can be brought on even by the recollection of an embarrassment of which they have been the subject – as clear an example of mind over matter as one could wish for.'

Like the authors of the above words, our hero, Omar Khayyam Shakil, is a practitioner of medicine. He is, furthermore, interested in the action of mind over matter: in behaviour under hypnosis, for example; in the entranced self-mutilations of those fanatical Shias whom Iskander Harappa disparagingly calls 'bedbugs'; in blushing. So it will not be long before Sufiya Zinobia and Omar Khayyam, patient and doctor, future wife and husband, come together. As they must; because what I have to tell is – cannot be described as anything but – a love story.

An account of what happened that year, the fortieth year in the life of Isky Harappa as well as Raza Hyder, probably ought to begin with the moment when Iskander heard that his cousin Little Mir had ingratiated himself with President A., and was about to be elevated to high office. He jumped clean out of bed when he heard the news, but Pinkie Aurangzeb, the owner of the bed and the source of the information, did not budge, even though she knew that a crisis had burst upon her, and that her forty-three-year-old body which Iskander had unveiled by jumping out of bed without letting go of the sheet no longer radiated the kind of light that could get men's minds off whatever was bugging them. 'Shit on my mother's grave,' Iskander Harappa yelled, 'first Hyder becomes a minister and now him. Life gets serious when a man is pushing forty.'

'Things are starting to fade,' Pinkie Aurangzeb thought as she lay smoking eleven consecutive cigarettes while Iskander stalked the room wrapped in the bedsheet. She lit her twelfth cigarette as Isky absently let the sheet fall. Then she watched him in the nudity of his prime as he silently broke his ties with his present, and turned towards the future. Pinkie was a widow; old Marshal Aurangzeb had kicked the bucket at last, and nowadays her soirées were not quite such essential affairs, and the city gossip had begun to reach her late. 'The ancient Greeks,' Iskander said out of the blue, making Pinkie spill the ash off her cigarette-tip, 'kept, in the Olympic games, no records of runners-up.' Then he dressed quickly, but with the meticulous dandyism that she had always loved, and left her for good; that sentence was the only explanation she ever got. But in the years of her isolation she worked it out, she knew that History had been waiting for Iskander Harappa to notice Her, and a man who catches History's eye is thereafter bound to a mistress from whom he will never escape. History is natural selection. Mutant versions of the past struggle for dominance; new species of fact arise, and old, saurian truths go to the wall, blindfolded and smoking last cigarettes. Only the mutations of the strong survive. The weak, the anonymous, the defeated leave few marks: field-patterns, axe-heads, folk-tales, broken pitchers, burial mounds, the fading memory of their youthful beauty. History loves only those who dominate her: it is a relationship of mutual enslavement. No room in it for Pinkies; or, in Isky's view, for the likes of Omar Khayyam Shakil.

Reborn Alexanders, would-be Olympic champions must conform to the most stringent of training routines. So after he left Pinkie Aurangzeb, Isky Harappa also vowed to eschew everything else that could erode his spirit. His daughter Arjumand would always remember that that was when he gave up stud poker, chemin de fer, private roulette evenings, horse-race fixing, French food, opium and sleeping pills; when he broke his habit of seeking out beneath silver-heavy banqueting tables the excited ankles and compliant knees of society beauties, and when he stopped visiting the whores whom he had been fond of photographing with an eight millimetre Paillard Bolex movie camera while they performed, singly or in threes, upon his own person or that of Omar Khayyam, their musky languid rites. It was the beginning of that legendary political career which would culminate in his victory over death itself. These first triumphs, being merely victories over himself, were necessarily smaller. He expunged from his public, urban vocabulary his encyclopaedic repertoire of foul green village oaths, imprecations which could detach brim-full cut-glass tumblers from men's hands and shatter them before they reached the floor. (But when campaigning in the villages he allowed the air to turn green with obscenity once again, understanding the vote-getting powers of the filth.) He stifled for ever the high-pitched giggle of his unreliable playboy self and substituted a rich, full-throated, statesmanlike guffaw. He gave up fooling around with the women servants in his city home.

Did any man ever sacrifice more for his people? He gave up cock-fights, bear-fights, snake-and-mongoose duels; plus disco dancing, and his monthly evenings at the home of the chief film censor, where he had watched special compilations of the juiciest bits excised from incoming foreign films.

He also decided to give up Omar Khayyam Shakil. 'When that degenerate comes to call,' Iskander instructed the gatekeeper, 'just throw the badmash out on his fat bottom and watch him bounce.' Then he retired into the white-and-gilt rococo bedroom at the cool heart of his mansion in 'Defence', an edifice of reinforced cement concrete and stone cladding that resembled a split-level Telefunken radiogram, and sank into meditation.

But, for a long time, surprisingly, Omar Khayyam neither visited nor telephoned his old friend. Forty days passed before the doctor was made aware of the change in his carefree, shame-free world . . .

Who sits at her father's feet while, elsewhere, Pinkie Aurangzeb grows old in an empty house? Arjumand Harappa: thirteen years old and wearing an expression of huge satisfaction, she sits cross-legged on the marble-chip floor of a rococo bedroom, watching

Isky complete the process of remaking himself; Arjumand, who has not yet acquired the notorious nickname (the 'virgin Ironpants') that will stick to her for most of her life. She has always known in the precocity of her years that there is a second man inside her father, growing, waiting, and now at last bursting out, while the old Iskander slips rustling and discarded to the floor, a shrivelled snakeskin in a hard diamond of sunlight. So what pleasure she takes in his transformation, in finally acquiring the father she deserves! 'I did this,' she tells Iskander, 'my wanting it so badly finally made you see.' Harappa smiles at his daughter, pats her hair. 'That happens sometimes.' 'And no more Omar-uncle,' Arjumand adds. 'Good riddance to bad rubbish.'

Arjumand Harappa, the virgin Ironpants, will always be ruled by extremes. Already, at thirteen, she has a gift for loathing; also for adulation. Whom she loathes: Shakil, the fat monkey who has been sitting on her father's shoulders, holding him down in the slime; and also her own mother, Rani in her Mohenjo of burrowing owls, the epitome of defeat. Arjumand has persuaded her father to let her live and go to school in the city; and for this father she bears a reverence bordering on idolatry. Now that her worship is at last acquiring an object worthy of itself, Arjumand cannot restrain her joy. 'What things won't you do!' she cries. 'Just wait and see!' Omar Khayyam's absent bulk carries with it the shadows of the past.

Iskander, supine in white-and-gold bed and sunk in frenzied reverie, states with sudden clarity: 'It's a man's world, Arjumand. Rise above your gender as you grow. This is no place to be a woman in.' The rueful nostalgia of these sentences marks the last death-throes of Iskander's love for Pinkie Aurangzeb, but his daughter takes him at his word, and when her breasts begin to swell she will bind them tightly in linen bandages, so fiercely that she blushes with pain. She will come to enjoy the war against her body, the slow provisional victory over the soft, despised flesh . . . but let us leave them there, father and daughter, she already building in her heart that Alexandrine god-myth of Harappa to which she will only be able to give free rein after his death, he devising in the councils of his new cleanness the strategies of his future triumph, of his wooing of the age.

Where is Omar Khayyam Shakil? What has become of our peripheral hero? He has aged, too; like Pinkie, he's in his middle forties now. Age has treated him well, silvering his hair and goatee beard. Let us remind ourselves that he was a brilliant student in his day, and that scholarly brightness remains undimmed; lecher and rakehell he may be, but he is also the top man at the city's leading hospital, and an immunologist of no small international renown. In the time since we last knew him well he has travelled to American seminars, published papers on the possibility of psycho-somatic events occurring within the body's immune system, becoming an important chap. He is still fat and ugly, but he dresses now with some distinction; some of Isky's snappy sarto-rial ways have rubbed off on him. Omar Khayyam wears greys: grey suits, hats, ties, grey suede shoes, grey silk underpants, as if he hopes that the muteness of the colour will tone down the garish effect of his physiognomy. He carries a present from his friend Iskander: a silver-headed swordstick from the Aansu valley, twelve inches of polished steel concealed in intricately-carved walnut.

By this time he is sleeping for barely two and a half hours a night, but the dream of falling off the world's end still troubles him from time to time. Sometimes it comes to him when he is awake, because people who sleep too little can find the boundaries between the waking and sleeping worlds get difficult to police. Things skip between the unguarded bollards, avoiding the cus-toms post . . . at such times he is assailed by a terrible vertigo, as if he were on top of a crumbling mountain, and then he leans heavily on his sword-concealing cane to prevent himself from falling. It should be said that his professional success, and his friendship with Iskander Harappa, have had the effect of reducing the frequency of these giddy spells, of keeping our hero's feet a little more firmly on the ground. But still the dizziness comes, now and then, to remind him how close he is, will always be, to the edge.

But where has he got to? Why does he not telephone, visit, get bounced out on his behind? – I discover him in Q., in the fortress home of his three mothers, and at once I know that a disaster has taken place, because nothing else could have lured Omar Khayyam into the mother country once again. He has not visited 'Nishapur' since the day he left with his feet on a cooling ice-block; bankers' drafts have been sent in his stead. His money has paid for his absence . . . but there are other prices, too. And no escape is final. His willed severance from his past mingles with the chosen insomnia of his nights: their joint effect is to glaze his moral sense, to transform him into a kind of ethical zombie, so that his very act of distancing helps him to obey his mothers' ancient injunction: the fellow feels no shame.

He retains his mesmeric eyes, his level hypnotist's voice. For many years now Iskander Harappa has accompanied those eyes, that voice to the Intercontinental Hotel and allowed them to go to work on his behalf. Omar Khayyam's outsize ugliness, com-bined with eyes-and-voice, makes him attractive to white women of a certain type. They succumb to his flirtatious offers of hyp-nosis, his unspoken promises of the mysteries of the East; he takes them to a rented hotel suite and puts them under. Released from admittedly scanty inhibitions they provide Isky and Omar with some highly charged sex. Shakil defends his behaviour: 'Impos-sible to persuade a subject to do anything she is unwilling to do.' Iskander Harappa, however, has never bothered with excuses . . . this, too, is a part of what Isky – as yet unbeknownst to Omar Khayyam – has forsaken. For History's sake.

Omar Khayyam is in 'Nishapur' because his brother, Babar, is dead. The brother whom he has never seen, dead before his twenty-third birthday, and all that is left of him is a bundle of dirty notebooks, which Omar Khayyam will bring with him when he returns to Karachi after the forty days of mourning. A brother reduced to tattered, scribbled words. Babar has been shot, and the order to fire was given by . . . but no, the notebooks first:

When they brought his body down from the Impossible Mountains, smelling of corruption and goats, the notebooks they discovered in his pockets were returned to his family with many of their pages missing. Among the tattered remnants of these brutalized volumes it was possible to decipher a series of love-poems addressed to a famous playback singer whom he, Babar Shakil, could not possibly have met. And interspersed with the unevenly metrical expressions of this abstract love, in which hymns to the spirituality of her voice mingled uneasily with free verse of a distinctly pornographic sensuality, was to be found an account of his sojourn in an earlier hell, a record of the torment of having been the kid brother of Omar Khayyam.

The shade of his elder sibling had haunted every corner of 'Nishapur'. Their three mothers, who now subsisted on the doctor's remittances and had no more dealings with the pawn-broker, had conspired in their gratitude to make Babar's childhood a motionless journey through an unchanging shrine whose walls were impregnated by applause for the glorious, departed elder son. And because Omar Khayyam was so much his senior and had long since fled that provincial dustiness in whose streets, nowadays, drunken gas-field workers brawled desultorily with off-duty miners of coal, bauxite, onyx, copper and chrome, and over whose rooftops the cracked dome of Flashman's Hotel presided with ever-increasing mournfulness, the younger child, Babar, had the feeling of having been at once oppressed and abandoned by a second father; and in that household of women atrophied by yesterdays he celebrated his twentieth birthday by carrying examination certificates and gold medals and newspaper cuttings and old schoolbooks and files of letters and cricket bats and, in short, all the souvenirs of his illustrious sibling into the shadowed lightlessness of the central compound, and setting fire to the whole lot before his three mothers could stop him. Turning his back on the inglorious spectacle of old crones scrabbling amongst hot ashes for the charred corners of snapshots and for medallions which the fire had transmuted from gold into lead, Babar made his way via the dumb-waiter into the streets of Q., his anniversary thoughts slow with uncertainties about the future. He was wandering aimlessly, brooding upon the narrowness of his possibilities, when the earthquake began.

At first he mistook it for a shudder within his own body, but a blow to his cheek, inflicted by a tiny splinter of plunging sharpness, cleared the mists of self-absorption from the would-be poet's eyes. 'It's raining glass,' he thought in surprise, blinking rapidly at the lanes of the thieves' bazaar into which his feet had led him without knowing it, lanes of little shanty-stalls among which his supposed inner shudder was making a fine mess: melons burst at his feet, pointy slippers fell from trembling shelves, gemstones and brocades and earthenware and combs tumbled pell-mell into the glass-dusted alleys. He stood stupidly in that vitreous downpour of broken windows, unable to shake off the feeling of having imposed his private turmoils on the world around him, resisting the insane compulsion to seize hold of someone, anyone, in the milling, panicky crowd of pickpockets, salesmen and shoppers, to apologize for the trouble he had caused.

'That earthquake,' Babar Shakil wrote in his notebook, 'shook something loose inside me. A minor tremor, but maybe it also shook something into place.'

When the world was still again he made for a cheap brandy den, picking his way through fragments of glass and past the equally piercing howls of the proprietor; and as he entered (the notebooks stated) he caught sight through the corner of his left eye of a winged and golden-glowing man looking down on him from a rooftop; but when he twisted his head upwards the angel was no longer to be seen. Later, when he was in the mountains with the separatist tribal guerrillas, he was told the story of the angels and the earthquakes and the subterranean Paradise; their belief that the golden angels were on their side gave the guerrillas an unshakeable certainty of the justice of their cause, and made it easy for them to die for it. 'Separatism,' Babar wrote, 'is the belief that you are good enough to escape from the clutches of hell.'

Babar Shakil spent his birthday getting drunk in that den of broken bottles, picking out, more than once, long splinters of glass from his mouth, so that by the evening's end his chin was streaked with blood; but the splashing liquor disinfected the cuts and minimized the risk of tetanus. In the brandy shop: tribals, a wall-eyed whore, travelling jokers with drums and horns. The jokes grew louder as the night wore on, and the mixture of humour and booze was a cocktail that gave Babar a hangover of such colossal proportions that he never recovered from it.

What jokes! Hee-hee-what-you-talking-man-someone-will-hear ribaldry: – Listen, yaar, you know when children get circumcised the circumciser speaks holy words? – Yah, man, I know. – Then what did he say when he did the cut on Old Razor Guts? – I don't know, what what? – Just one word only, yaar, one word and he got thrown out of the house! – God, must have been a bad word, man, come on, tell. – This was it, sir: 'Oops.'

Babar Shakil in a dangerous veil of brandy. Comedy enters his bloodstream, effects a permanent mutation. – Hey mister, you know what they say about us tribals, too little patriotism and too much sex-drive, well, it's all true, want to know why? – Yes. – So take patriotism. Number one, government takes our rice for Army troops, we should be proud, na, but we just complain there is none for us. Number two, government mines our minerals and economy gets a boost, but we just beef that nobody here sees the cash. Number three, gas from Needle now provides sixty per cent of national requirement, but still we are not happy, moaning all the time how the gas is not domestically available in these parts. Now how could people be less patriotic, you must agree. But fortunately our government loves us still, so much that it has made our sex-drive the top national priority. – How's that? – But it is obvious to see: this government is happy to go on screwing us from now till doomsday.

– O, too good, yaar, too good.

The next day Babar left home before dawn to join the guerrillas and his family never saw him alive again. From the bottomless chests of 'Nishapur' he took an old rifle and its accompanying cartridge boxes, a few books and one of Omar Khayyam's academic medallions, which had been transmuted into base metal by a fire; no doubt to remind himself of the causes of his own act of separatism, of the origins of a hatred which had been powerful enough to cause an earthquake. In his hideout in the Impossible Mountains Babar grew a beard, studied the complex structure of the hill clans, wrote poetry, rested between raids on military outposts and railway lines and water reservoirs, and eventually, thanks to the exigencies of that dislocated existence, was able to discuss in his notebooks the relative merits of copulation with sheep and with goats. There were guerrillas who preferred the passivity of sheep; for others the goats' greater friskiness was impossible to resist. Many of Babar's companions went so far as to fall in love with four-legged mistresses, and although they were all wanted men they would risk their lives in the bazaars of Q. in order to purchase gifts for their loved ones: combs for fleeces were acquired, also ribbons and bells for darling nannies who never deigned to express their gratitude. Babar's spirit (if not his body) rose above such things; he poured his reservoir of unspent passion over the mental image of a popular singer of whose features he remained ignorant to his dying day, because he had only heard her sing on a crackling transistor radio.

The guerrillas gave Babar a nickname of which he was inordinately proud: they called him 'the emperor', in memory of that other Babar whose throne was usurped, who took to the hills with a ragged army and who at last founded that renowned dynasty of monarchs whose family name is still used as an honorific title bestowed on film tycoons. Babar, the Mogul of the Impossible Mountains ... two days before the departure of Raza Hyder from Q., a sortie led for the last time by the great commander himself was responsible for firing the bullet which knocked Babar down.

But it didn't matter, because he had spent too long with the angels; up in the shifting, treacherous mountains he had watched them, golden-breasted and with gilded wings. Archangels flapped over his head as he sat doing sentry duty on a fierce outcrop of rock. Yes, perhaps Jibreel himself had hovered benignly over him like a golden helicopter while he violated a sheep. And shortly before his death the guerrillas noticed that their bearded comrade's skin had begun to give off a yellow light; the little buds of new wings were visible on his shoulders. It was a transformation familiar to the denizens of the Impossible Mountains. 'You won't be here much longer,' they told Babar with traces of envy in their voices, 'Emperor, you're off; no more woolly fucks for you.' The angeling of Babar must have been just about complete by the time of his death, when his guerrilla unit attacked a seemingly broken-down goods train and so fell into Raza Hyder's trap, because although eighteen bullets pierced his body, which made an easy target because it glowed yellow through his clothing in the night, it was easy for him to skip out of his skin and soar lucent and winged into the eternity of the mountains, where a great cloud of seraphs rose up as the world shook and roared, and where to the music of heavenly reed-flutes and celestial seven-stringed sarandas and three-stringed dumbirs he was received into the elysian bosom of the earth. His body, when they brought it down, was said to be as insubstantial and feathery as an abandoned snakeskin, such as cobras and playboys leave behind them when they change; and he was gone, gone for good, the fool.

Of course his death was not described in any notebook; it was enacted within the grieving imaginations of his three mothers, because, as they told Omar while recounting the tale of their son's transformation into an angel, 'We have the right to present him with a good death, a death with which the living can live.' Under the impact of the tragedy, Chhunni, Munnee and Bunny began to crumble inside, becoming mere façades, beings as insubstantial as the sloughed-off corpse of their son. (But they pulled themselves together at the end.)

The body was returned to them some weeks after eighteen bullets had entered it. They also received a letter on official notepaper. 'Only the memory of the former prestige of your family name protects you from the consequences of your son's great infamy. It is our opinion that the families of these gangsters have much to answer for.' The letter had been signed, before his departure, by the former governor, Raza Hyder himself; who must therefore have known that he had engineered the death of the boy whom he had seen, years previously, watching him through field-glasses from the upper windows of the sealed mansion between the Cantt and the bazaar.

Out of pity for Omar Khayyam Shakil – to spare, let us say, his blushes – I shall not describe the scene at the gate of the Harappa town house that took place when the doctor finally turned up in a taxi-cab holding his brother's notebooks in his hand. He has been bounced in enough dirt for the moment; suffice to say that under the cold weight of Iskander's rejection, Omar Khayyam suffered an attack of vertigo so severe that he was sick in the back of the taxi. (Over that, too, I draw a fastidious veil.) Once again others had acted and by so doing had shaped the story of his life: Babar's flight, Hyder's bullets, the exaltation of Mir Harappa and the resulting alteration in Iskander added up, as far as our hero was concerned, to a kick in his personal teeth. Later, in his own home (we have not yet visited the Shakil residence: an unglamorous apartment in one of the city's older housing zones, four rooms notable for the complete absence of all but the most essential items of furniture, as though Shakil in his adulthood were rebelling against the fantasticated clutter of his mothers' home, and choosing, instead, the bare-walled asceticism of his selected father, the vanished, birdcaged schoolteacher Eduardo Rodrigues. A father is both a warning and a lure), which he had been obliged by the outraged taxi-driver to reach stinking and on foot, he retired to bed, heat-drained, his head still spinning; he placed a bundle of tattered notebooks on his bedside table and said as he drifted into sleep: 'Babar, life is long.'

The next day he returned to work; and the day after that he began to fall in love.

Once upon a time there was a plot of land. It was attractively situated in the heart of the First Phase of the Defense Services Officers' Co-operative Housing Society; to its right stood the official residence of the national minister for education, information and tourism, an imposing building whose walls were clad in green onyx marble streaked with red, and to its left was the home of the widow of the late Joint Chief of Staff, Marshal Aurangzeb. Despite location and neighbours, however, the plot of land remained empty; no foundations had been dug there, no shuttering raised to build walls of reinforced cement concrete. The plot of land lay, tragically for its owner, in a small hollow; so that when the two days of pouring rain which the city enjoyed each year arrived, the waters flooded into the empty plot and formed a muddy lake. This unusual phenomenon of a lake which came into being for two days a year and which was then boiled away by the sun, leaving behind a thin mulch of water-transported garbage and faeces, was enough to discourage all potential builders, even though the plot was, as stated above, congenially sited: the Aga Khan owned the lodge at the top of the nearby hill, and the eldest son of the President, Field-Marshal Mohammad A., also lived nearby. It was on this hapless patch of earth that Pinkie Aurangzeb decided to raise turkeys.

Deserted by living lover as well as dead husband, the Marshal's widow elected to turn her hand to business. Much taken by the success of the new shaver-chicken scheme which the national airline had recently begun to operate from batteries on the periphery of the airport, Pinkie decided to go for bigger birds. The officers of the housing society were incapable of resisting Mrs Aurangzeb's allure (it might have been fading, but it was still too much for clerks), and turned blind eyes to the clouds of gobbling fowls which she released into the vacant, walled-in property. The arrival of the turkeys was treated by Mrs Bilquìs Hyder as a personal insult. A highly-strung lady, of whom it was said that troubles in her marriage were placing her brain under increasing stress, she took to leaning out of windows and abusing the noisy birds. 'Shoo! Shut up, crazy fellows! Turkeys making God knows what-all racket right next to a minister's house! See if I don't slit your throats!'

When Bilquìs appealed to her husband to do something about the eternally gobbling birds who were destroying what remained of her peace of mind, Raza Hyder replied calmly, 'She is the widow of our great Marshal, wife. Allowances must be made.' The minister for education, information and tourism was tired at the end of a hard day's work in which he had approved measures which would legalize the piracy by the government of Western scientific text-books, personally supervised the smashing of one of the small portable presses on which anti-state propaganda was illicitly printed and which had been discovered in the basement of an England-returned arts graduate who had been corrupted by foreign ideas, and discussed with the city's leading art dealers the growing problem of pilferage of antiquities from the country's archaeological sites – discussed the issue, one should add, with such sensitivity that the dealers had been moved to present him, in recognition of his attitude, with a small stone head from Taxila, dating from the time of Alexander the Great's expedition into the north. In short, Raza Hyder was in no mood for turkeys.

Bilquìs had not forgotten what a fat man had hinted about her husband and Mrs Aurangzeb on the verandah of Mohenjo years ago; she remembered the time when her husband had been willing to stake himself to the ground on her behalf; and she was also, in her thirty-second year, becoming increasingly shrill. That was the year in which the Loo blew more fiercely than ever before, and cases of fever and madness increased by four hundred and twenty per cent . . . Bilquìs placed her hands upon her hips and yelled at Raza in the presence of both her daughters: 'O, a fine day for me! Now you humiliate me with birds.' Her elder daughter, the mental case, began to blush, because it was evident that the gobbling turkeys did indeed represent one more victory for Pinkie Aurangzeb over other men's wives, the last such victory, of which the victor was wholly unaware.

And once upon a time there was a retarded daughter, who for twelve years had been given to understand that she embodied her mother's shame. Yes, now I must come to you, Sufiya Zinobia, in your outsize cot with the rubber sheeting, in that ministerial residence of marble walls, in an upstairs bedroom through whose windows turkeys gobbled at you, while at a dressing table of onyx marble your sister screamed at the ayah to pull her hair.

Sufiya Zinobia at the age of twelve had formed the unattractive habit of tearing her hair. When her dark-brown locks were being washed by Shahbanou the Parsee ayah, she would continually kick and scream; the ayah was always forced to give up before the last of the soap had been rinsed out. The constant presence of sandalwood-scented detergent gave Sufiya Zinobia an appalling case of split ends, and she would sit in the enormous cot which her parents had constructed for her (and which they had brought all the way from Q., complete with expanses of rubber undersheets and large-size babies' comforters) and tear each damaged hair in two, all the way down to the root. This she did seriously, systematically, as if inflicting ritual injury upon herself like one of Iskander Harappa's bedbugs, the Shia dervishes in the processions of 10 Muharram. Her eyes, while she worked, acquired a dull glint, a gleam of distant ice or fire from far below their habitually opaque surface; and the torn cloud of hairs stood out around her face and formed in the sunlight a kind of halo of destruction.

It was the day after the turkey outburst of Bilquìs Hyder. Sufiya Zinobia tore her hair in her cot; but Good News, plain-faced as a chapati, was determined to prove that her great thick mane had grown long enough to sit upon. Straining her head backwards she shouted at pale Shahbanou: 'Pull down! Hard as you can! What're you waiting for, stupid? *Yank!*' – and the ayah, hollow-eyed, frail, tried to tuck hair-tips under Good News's bony rump. Tears of pain stood in the girl's determined eyes: 'A woman's beauty,' Good News gasped, 'grows down from the top of her head. It is well known that men go crazy for shiny hair that you can put under your bums.' Shahbanou in flat tones stated: 'No good, bibi, won't go.' Good News pummelling the ayah turned on her sister in her wrath: 'You. Thing. Look at you. Who would marry you with that hair, even if you had a brain? Turnip. Beetroot. Angrez radish. See how you make trouble for me with your tearing. Elder sister should marry first but who will come for her, ayah? I swear, my tragedy, what do you know. Come on now, pull again, this time don't pretend it won't reach – no, never mind that fool now, leave her with her stinky blushes and her wetting. She doesn't understand, what could she understand, zero.' And Shahbanou, shrugging, impervious to Naveed Hyder's blows: 'You shouldn't talk so bad to your sister, bibi, one day your tongue will go black and fall off.'

Two sisters in a room while outside the hot wind begins to blow. Shutters are put up against the wildness of the blast, and over the garden wall turkeys panic in the feverish clutches of the gale. As the Loo increases in fury, the house subsides into sleep. Shahbanou on a mat on the floor beside Sufiya Zinobia's cot; Good News, exhausted by hair-pullery, sprawls on her ten-year-old's bed.

Two sisters asleep: in repose, the younger girl's face revealed its plainness, stripped of its waking determination to be attractive; while the simpleton lost, in sleep, the bland vacuity of her expression, and the severe classicism of her features would have pleased any watching eye. What contrasts in these girls! Sufiya Zinobia, embarrassingly small (no, we shall avoid, at all costs, comparing her to an Oriental miniature), and Good News rangy, elongated. Sufiya and Naveed, shame and good news: the one slow and silent, the other quick with her noise. Good News would stare brazenly at her elders; Sufiya averted her eyes. But Naveed Hyder was her mother's little angel, she got away with everything. 'Imagine,' Omar Khayyam would think in later years, 'if that marriage scandal had happened to Sufiya Zinobia! They'd have cut her skin off and sent it to the dhobi.'

Listen: you could have taken the whole quantity of sisterly love inside Good News Hyder, sealed it in an envelope and posted it anywhere in the world for one rupee airmail, that's how much it weighed . . . where was I? Oh, yes, the hot wind blew, its howl a maw of sound that swallowed all other noise, that dry gale bearing disease and madness upon its sand-sharp wings, the worst Loo in living memory, releasing demons into the world, forcing its way through shutters to plague Bilquìs with the insupportable phantoms of her past, so that although she buried her head under a pillow she still saw before her eyes a golden equestrian figure carrying a pennant on which there flamed the terrifyingly cryptic word *Excelsior*. Not even the gobbling of the turkeys could be heard above the gale, as the world took shelter; then the searing fingers of the wind penetrated a bedroom in which two sisters slept, and one of them began to stir.

It's easy to blame trouble on a wind. Maybe that pestilential blast did have something to do with it – maybe, when it touched Sufiya Zinobia, she reddened under its awful hand, she burned, and maybe that's why she got up, eyes blank as milk, and left the room – but I prefer to believe that the wind was no more than a coincidence, an excuse; that what happened happened because twelve years of unloved humiliation take their toll, even on an idiot, and there is always a point at which something breaks, even though the last straw cannot be identified with any certainty: was it Good News's marriage worries? Or Raza's calmness in the face of shrieking Bilquìs? Impossible to say.

She must have been sleepwalking, because when they found her she looked rested, as if she'd had a good deep sleep. When the wind died and the household awoke from its turbulent afternoon slumber Shahbanou noticed the empty cot at once and raised the alarm. Afterwards nobody could work out how the girl had escaped, how she managed to sleepwalk through an entire houseful of government furniture and sentries. Shahbanou would always say that it must have been quite a wind, it sent soldiers to sleep at the gate and wrought a somnambulist miracle of such potency that Sufiya Zinobia's passage through the house, into the garden and over the wall acquired the power of infecting anyone she passed, who must have fallen instantly into a wind-sick trance. But it is my opinion that the source of the power, the worker of the miracle, was Sufiya Zinobia herself; there would be other such occasions, when one could not blame the wind . . .

They found her in the aftermath of the Loo, sitting fast asleep under the sun's ferocity in the turkey-yard of the widow Aurangzeb, a little huddled figure snoring gently amidst the corpses of the birds. Yes, they were all dead, every one of the two hundred and eighteen turkeys of Pinkie's loneliness, and people were so shocked that they forgot to clear away the corpses for a whole day, leaving the dead birds to rot in the heat and in the crepuscular gloom of the evening and beneath the ice-hot stars, two hundred and eighteen that would never find their way into ovens or on to dining tables. Sufiya Zinobia had torn off their heads and then reached down into their bodies to draw their guts up through their necks with her tiny and weaponless hands. Shahbanou, who found her first, did not dare to approach her; then Raza and Bilquìs arrived, and soon everybody, sister, servants, neighbours, was standing and gaping at the spectacle of the bloodied girl and the decapitated creatures with intestines instead of heads. Pinki Aurangzeb looked hollowly upon the carnage, and was struck by the meaningless hatred in Bilquìs's eyes; the two women remained silent, each in the grip of a different horror, so that it was Raza Hyder, his watery black-rimmed eyes riveted upon the face of his daughter with her bloodied lips, who spoke first in a voice echoing with admiration as well as revulsion: 'With her bare hands,' the new government minister trembled, 'what gave the child such strength?'

Now that the iron hoops of the silence had been snapped Shahbanou the ayah began wailing at the top of her voice: 'Ullu-ullu-ullu!', a gibberish lament of such high pitch that it dragged Sufiya Zinobia out of her lethal sleep; she opened those eyes of watered milk and on seeing the devastation around her she fainted, echoing her own mother on that far-off day when Bilquìs found herself naked in a crowd and passed out cold for shame.

What forces moved that sleeping three-year-old mind in its twelve-year-old body to order an all-out assault upon feathered turkey-cocks and hens? One can only speculate: was Sufiya Zinobia trying, like a good daughter, to rid her mother of the gobbler plague? Or did the anger, the proud outrage which Raza Hyder ought to have felt, but refused to do so, preferring to make allowances for Pinkie, find its way into his daughter instead? – What seems certain is that Sufiya Zinobia, for so long burdened with being a miracle-gone-wrong, a family's shame made flesh, had discovered in the labyrinths of her unconscious self the hidden path that links *sharam* to violence; and that, awakening, she was as surprised as anyone by the force of what had been unleashed.

The beast inside the beauty. Opposing elements of a fairy-tale combined in a single character . . . Bilquìs did not, on this occasion, faint. The embarrassment of her daughter's deed, the ice of this latest shame lent a frozen rigidity to her bearing. 'Be quiet,' she ordered the ululating ayah, 'go in and bring out scissors.' Until the ayah had completed her enigmatic errand Bilquìs would let nobody touch the girl; she circled her in a manner so forbidding that not even Raza Hyder dared go near. While Shahbanou ran for scissors Bilquìs spoke softly, under her breath, so that only a few words wafted as far as the watching husband, widow, younger daughter, servants, anonymous passers-by. '. . . Tear your hair . . . birthright . . . woman's pride . . . all fuzzy-wuzzy like a *hubshee* female . . . cheapness . . . loose . . . crazy,' and then the scissors came, and still nobody dared intervene, as Bilquìs grabbed hold of great clumps of her daughter's savaged tresses, and cut, and cut, and cut. At last she stood up, out of breath, and working the scissors absently with her fingers she turned away. Sufiya Zinobia's head looked like a cornfield after a fire; sad, black stubble, a catastrophic desolation wrought by maternal rage. Raza Hyder picked his daughter up with a gentleness born of his infinite puzzlement and carried her indoors, away from the scissors that were still snipping at air in Bilquìs's uncontrollable hand.

Scissors cutting air mean trouble in the family.

'O, Mummy!' Good News giggled with fear. 'What did you do? She looks like . . .'

'We always wanted a boy,' Bilquìs replied, 'but God knows best.'

In spite of being shaken, timidly by Shahbanou and more roughly by Good News, Sufiya Zinobia did not awaken from her faint. By the next evening a fever had mounted in her, a hot flush spread from her scalp to the soles of her feet. The fragile-looking Parsee ayah, whose sunken eyes made her seem forty-three years old but who turned out to be only nineteen, never moved from the side of the great barred cot except to fetch fresh cold compresses for Sufiya's brow. 'You Parsees,' Good News told Shahbanou, 'you've got a soft spot for mental cases, seems to me. Must be all your experience.' Bilquìs showed no interest in the application of compresses. She sat in her room with the scissors that seemed to be stuck to her fingers, snipping at empty air. 'Wind fever,' Shahbanou called her charge's nameless affliction, which had made that shorn head blaze; but on the second night it cooled, she opened her eyes, it was thought that she had recovered. The next morning, however, Shahbanou noticed that something frightful had begun to happen to the girl's tiny body. It had started to come out in huge blotchy rashes, red and purple with small hard pimples in the middle; boils were forming between her toes and her back was bubbling up into extraordinary vermilion lumps. Sufiya Zinobia was over-salivating; great jets of spittle flew out through her lips. Appalling black buboes were forming in her armpits. It was as though the dark violence which had been engendered within that small physique had turned inwards, had forsaken turkeys and gone for the girl herself; as if, like her grandfather Mahmoud the Woman who sat in an empty cinema and waited to pay for his double bill, or like a soldier falling on his sword, Sufiya Zinobia had chosen the form of her own end. The plague of shame – in which I insist on including the unfelt shame of those around her, for instance what had not been felt by Raza Hyder when he gunned down Babar Shakil – as well as the unceasing shame of her own existence, and of her hacked-off hair – the plague, I say, spread rapidly through that tragic being whose chief defining characteristic was her excessive sensitivity to the bacilli of humiliation. She was taken to hospital with pus bursting from her sores, dribbling, incontinent, with the rough, cropped proof of her mother's loathing on her head.

What is a saint? A saint is a person who suffers in our stead.

On the night when all this happened, Omar Khayyam Shakil had been beset, during his brief sleep, by vivid dreams of the past, in all of which the white-clothed figure of the disgraced teacher Eduardo Rodrigues played a leading role. In the dreams Omar Khayyam was a boy again. He kept trying to follow Eduardo everywhere, to the toilet, into bed, convinced that if he could just catch up with the teacher he would be able to jump inside him and be happy at long last; but Eduardo kept shooing him away with his white fedora, slapping at him and motioning to him to go, get lost, buzz off. This mystified the doctor until many days later, when he realized that the dreams had been prescient warnings against the dangers of falling in love with under-age females and then following them to the ends of the earth, where they inevitably cast you aside, the blast of their rejection picks you up and hurls you out into the great starry nothingness beyond gravity and sense. He recalled the end of the dream, in which Eduardo, his white garments now blackened and tattered and singed, seemed to be flying away from him, floating above a bursting cloud of fire, with one hand raised above his head, as if in farewell . . . a father is a warning; but he is also a lure, a precedent impossible to resist, and so by the time that Omar Khayyam deciphered his dreams it was already far too late to take their advice, because he had fallen for his destiny, Sufiya Zinobia Hyder, a twelve-year-old girl with a three-year-old mind, the daughter of the man who killed his brother.

You can imagine how depressed I am by the behaviour of Omar Khayyam Shakil. I ask for the second time: what kind of hero is this? Last seen slipping into unconsciousness, stinking of vomit and swearing revenge; and now, going crazy for Hyder's daughter. How is one to account for such a character? Is consistency too much to ask? I accuse this so-called hero of giving me the most Godawful headache.

Certainly (let's take this slowly; no sudden moves, please) he was in a disturbed state of mind. A dead brother, rejection by his best friend. These are extenuating circumstances. We shall take them into account. It is also fair to assume that the vertigo which assailed him in the taxi returned, over the next few days, to knock him even further off balance. So there is some sort of flimsy case for the defence.

Step by step, now. He wakes up, engulfed in the emptiness of his life, alone in the insomnia of the dawn. He washes, dresses, goes to work; and finds that by burying himself in his duties he can manage to keep going; even the vertigo attacks are kept at bay.

What is his area of expertise? We know this: he is an immunologist. So he cannot be blamed for the arrival at his hospital of Hyder's daughter; suffering an immunological crisis, Sufiya Zinobia is brought to the country's leading expert in the field.

Carefully, now. Avoid loud noises. To an immunologist in search of the calm that comes of challenging, absorbing work, Sufiya Zinobia seems like a godsend. Delegating as many of his responsibilities as possible, Omar Khayyam devotes himself more or less full-time to the case of the simpleton girl whose body's defence mechanisms have declared war against the very life they are supposed to be protecting. His devotion is perfectly genuine (the defence refuses to rest): in the succeeding weeks, he makes himself fully acquainted with her medical background, and afterwards he will set down in his treatise *The Case of Miss H.* the important new evidence he has unearthed of the power of the mind to affect, 'via direct nervous pathways', the workings of the body. The case becomes famous in medical circles; doctor and patient are forever linked in the history of science. Does this make other, more personal links more palatable? I reserve judgement. Go on one step:

He becomes convinced that Sufiya Zinobia is willing the damage upon herself. This is the significance of her case: it shows that even a broken mind is capable of marshalling macrophages and polymorphs; even a stunted intelligence can lead a palace revolution, a suicidal rebellion of the janissaries of the human body against the castle itself.

'Total breakdown of the immune system,' he notes after his first examination of the patient, 'most terrible uprising I ever saw.'

Now let us put this as kindly as possible for the moment. (I have more accusations, but they will wait.) Afterwards, no matter how furiously he concentrates, trying to summon up every last detail of those days from the poisoned wells of memory, he is unable to pinpoint the moment at which professional excitement turned into tragic love. He does not claim that Sufiya Zinobia has given him the least encouragement; that would, in the circumstances, be patently absurd. But at some point, perhaps during his night-long bedside vigils, spend monitoring the effects of his prescribed course of immunosuppressive drugs, vigils in which he is joined by the ayah Shahbanou, who consents to wear sterile cap, coat, gloves and mask, but who absolutely refuses to leave the girl alone with the male doctor – yes, perhaps during those preposterously chaperoned nights, or possibly later, when it is clear that he has triumphed, that the praetorian revolt has been quelled, the mutiny suppressed by pharmaceutical mercenaries, so that the hideous outcrops of Sufiya Zinobia's affliction fade from her body and the colour returns to her cheeks – somewhere along the line, it happens. Omar Khayyam falls stupidly, and irretrievably, in love.

'It's not rational,' he reproaches himself, but his emotions, unscientifically, ignore him. He finds himself behaving awkwardly in her presence, and in his dreams he pursues her to the ends of the earth, while the mournful remnant of Eduardo Rodrigues looks down pityingly at his obsession from the sky. He, too, thinks of the extenuating circumstances, tells himself that in his distressed psychological condition he has become the victim of a mental disorder, but he is too ashamed even to think of taking advice . . . no, damn it! Headache or no headache, I will not let him get off as lightly as this. I accuse him of being ugly inside as well as out, a Beast, just as Farah Zoroaster had divined all those years ago. I accuse him of playing God or at least Pygmalion, of feeling he had rights of ownership over the innocent whose life he had saved. I accuse that fat pigmeat tub of working out that the only chance he had of getting a beautiful wife was to marry a nitwit, sacrificing wifely brains for the beauty of the flesh.

Omar Khayyam claims his obsession with Sufiya Zinobia has cured his vertigo. Poppycock! Flim-flam! I accuse the villain of attempting a shameless piece of social climbing (he never felt giddy when he did that!) – ditched by one great figure of the period, Omar Khayyam seeks to hitch himself to another star. So unscrupulous is he, so shameless, that he will court an idiot in order to woo her father. Even a father who gave the order which sent eighteen bullets into the body of Babar Shakil.

But we have heard him mumble: 'Babar, life is long.' – O, I'm not fooled by that. You conceive of a revenge plot? – Omar Khayyam, by marrying the unmarriageable child, is enabled to stay close to Hyder for years, before, during and after his Presidency, biding his time, because revenge is patient, it awaits its perfect moment? – Piffle! Wind! Those sick (and no doubt whisky-soaked) words of a fainting whale were no more than a fading, hollow echo of the favourite threat of Mr Iskander Harappa, our hero's erstwhile patron, fellow-debauchee and chum. Of course he never meant them; he is not the avenging type. Did he feel anything at all for that dead brother whom he never knew? I doubt it; his three mothers, as we shall see, doubted it. This is not a possibility one can take seriously. Revenge? Pah! Huh! Phooey! If Omar Khayyam thought about his brother's demise, it is more likely that he thought this: 'Fool, terrorist, gangster. What did he expect?'

I have one last, and most damning, accusation. Men who deny their pasts become incapable of thinking them real. Absorbed into the great whore-city, having left the frontier universe of Q. far behind him once again, Omar Khayyam Shakil's home-town now seems to him like a sort of bad dream, a fantasy, a ghost. The city and the frontier are incompatible worlds; choosing Karachi, Shakil rejects the other. It becomes, for him, a feathery insubstantial thing, a discarded skin. He is no longer affected by what happens there, by its logic and demands. He is homeless: that is to say, a metropolitan through and through. A city is a camp for refugees.

God damn him! I'm stuck with him; and with his poxy love.

Very well; let's go on. I've lost another seven years of my story while the headache banged and thumped. Seven years, and now there are marriages to attend. How time flies!

I dislike arranged marriages. There are some mistakes for which one should not be able to blame one's poor parents.

8

BEAUTY AND THE BEAST

'Just imagine having a fish up your fundament, an eel that spits at your insides,' Bilquìs said, 'and you won't need me to tell you what happens on a woman's wedding night.' Her daughter Good News submitted to this teasing and to the tracing of henna patterns upon the ticklish soles of her feet with the demure obstinacy of one who is guarding a terrible secret. She was seventeen years old and it was the eve of her wedding. The womenfolk of Bariamma's family had assembled to prepare her; while Bilquìs applied henna, mother and daughter were surrounded by eager relatives bearing oils for the skin, hairbrushes, kohl, silver polish, flatirons. The mummified figure of Bariamma herself supervised everything blindly from her vantage point of a takht over which a Shirazi rug had been spread in her honour; gaotakia bolsters prevented her from toppling over on to the floor when she guffawed at the horrifically off-putting descriptions of married life with which the matrons were persecuting Good News. 'Think of a sikh kabab that leaks hot cooking fat,' Duniyazad Begum suggested, old quarrels bright in her eyes. But the virgins offered more optimistic images. 'It's like sitting on a rocket that sends you to the moon,' one maiden conjectured, earning a rocket from Bariamma for her blasphemy, because the faith clearly stated that lunar expeditions were impossible. The women sang songs insulting Good News's fiancé, young Haroun, the eldest son of Little Mir Harappa: 'Face like a potato! Skin like a tomato! Walks like an elephant! Tiny plantain in his pant.' But when Good News spoke up for the first and last time that evening, nobody could think of a single word to say.

'Mummy dear,' Naveed said firmly into the scandalized silence, 'I won't marry that stupid potato, you just see if I do.'

Haroun Harappa at twenty-six was already accustomed to notoriety, because during the one year he had spent at an Angrez university he had published an article in the student paper in which he had described the private dungeons at the vast Daro estate into which his father would fling people for years on end. He had also written about the punitive expedition which Mir Harappa once led against the household of his cousin Iskander, and of the foreign bank account (he gave the number) into which his father was transferring large quantities of public money. The article was reprinted in *Newsweek*, so that the authorities back home had to intercept the entire shipment of that subversive issue and rip out the offending pages from every copy; but still the contents became common knowledge. When Haroun Harappa was expelled from his college at the end of that year, on the grounds that after three terms studying economics he had failed to master the concepts of supply and demand, it was generally supposed that he had written his article out of a genuine and innocent stupidity, hoping, no doubt, to impress the foreigners with his family's acumen and power. It was known that he had spent his university career almost exclusively in the gaming clubs and whorehouses of London, and the story went that when he entered the examination hall that summer he had glanced at the question paper without sitting down, shrugged, announced cheerfully, 'No, there's nothing here for me,' and strolled out to his Mercedes-Benz coupé without more ado. 'The boy's a dope, I'm afraid,'

Little Mir told President A., 'no need to take steps against him, I hope. He'll come home and settle down.'

Little Mir made one attempt to persuade Haroun's college to keep him on. A large filigree-silver cigar box was presented to the Senior Common Room. The fellows of the college refused, however, to believe that a man as distinguished as Mir Harappa would try to bribe them, so they accepted the gift and chucked his son out on his ear. Haroun Harappa came home with numerous squash rackets, addresses of Arab princes, whisky decanters, bespoke suits, silk shirts and erotic photographs, but without a foreign degree.

But the seditious *Newsweek* article had not been the product of Haroun's stupidity. It had been born of the profound and undying hatred the son felt for his father, a hatred which would even survive Mir Harappa's terrible death. Little Mir had been a sternly authoritarian parent, but that in itself was not unusual and might even have engendered love and respect if it had not been for the matter of the dog. On Haroun's tenth birthday, at Daro, his father had presented him with a large parcel, done up in green ribbon, from which a muffled barking could clearly be heard. Haroun was an inward and only child who had grown fond of solitude; he did not really want the long-haired collie puppy who emerged from the package, and thanked his father with a perfunctory surliness that irritated Little Mir intensely. In the next few days it became obvious that Haroun intended to leave the dog to be cared for by the servants; whereupon Mir with the foolhardy stubbornness of his irritation issued orders that nobody was to lay a finger on the animal. 'The damn hound is yours,' Mir told the boy, 'so you look after it.' But Haroun was as obstinate as his father, and did not so much as give the puppy a name, so that in the bitter heat of the Daro sunshine the puppy had to forage for its own food and drink, contracted mange, distemper and curious green spots on the tongue, was driven mad by its long hair and finally died in front of the main door to the house, emitting piteous yelps and leaking a thick yellow porridge from its behind. 'Bury it,' Mir told

Haroun, but the boy set his jaw and walked away, and the slowly decomposing corpse of the unnamed pooch mirrored the growth of the boy's loathing for his father, who was thereafter forever associated in his mind with the stench of the rotting dog.

After that Mir Harappa understood his mistake and went to great lengths to regain his son's affection. He was a widower (Haroun's mother had died in childbirth) and the boy was genuinely important to him. Haroun was outrageously spoiled, because although he refused to ask his father for so much as a new vest Mir was always trying to guess what was in the boy's heart, so that Haroun was showered with gifts, including a complete set of cricket equipment comprising six stumps, four bails, twelve sets of pads, twenty-two white flannel shirts and trousers, eleven bats of varying weight and enough red balls to last a lifetime. There were even umpires' white coats and score-books, but Haroun was uninterested in cricket and the lavish present languished, unused, in a forgotten corner of Daro, along with the polo gear, the tent pegs, the imported gramophones and the home-movie camera, projector and screen. When he was twelve the boy learned to ride and after that was to be found gazing longingly at the horizon beyond which lay the Mohenjo estate of his uncle Iskander. Whenever he heard that Isky was visiting his ancestral home Haroun would ride without stopping to sit at the feet of the man who ought by rights, he believed, to have been his father. Mir Harappa did not protest when Haroun expressed a wish to move to Karachi; and as he grew up in that mushrooming city Haroun's infatuation with his uncle mushroomed too, so that he began to affect the same dandyism and bad language and admiration for European culture that were Isky's trademarks before his great conversion. This was why the young man insisted on being sent to study abroad, and why he passed his time in London engaged in whoring and gambling. After his return he went on in the same way; it had become a habit by then and he was unable to give it up even when his idolized uncle renounced such unstatesmanlike activities, so that the gossip in the town was that a little Isky had taken over where the big one left off. Mir Harappa continued to foot the bill for his son's outrageous behaviour, still hoping to win back the love of his only progeny; to no avail. Haroun in his habitually intoxicated state began to talk too much, and in loose-mouthed company. He spouted, drunkenly, the revolutionary political notions that had been current among European students during his year abroad. He castigated Army rule and the power of oligarchies with all the enthusiastic garrulity of one who despises every word he is saying, but hopes that it will wound his even more detested parent. When he went so far as to mention the possibility of mass-producing Molotov cocktails, none of his cronies took him seriously, because he said it at a beach party while astride the shell of a weeping Galapagos turtle which was dragging itself up to the sand to lay its infertile eggs; but the state informant in the gathering made his or her report, and President A., whose administration had become somewhat rocky, flew into a rage so terrible that Little Mir had to prostrate himself on the floor and beg for mercy for his wayward son. This incident would have forced Mir into a confrontation with Haroun, which he greatly feared, but he was spared the trouble by his cousin Iskander, who had also heard about Haroun's latest outrage. Haroun, summoned to Isky's split-level radiogram of a house, shifted from foot to foot under the brilliantly scornful eyes of Arjumand Harappa while her father spoke in gentle, implacable tones. Iskander Harappa had taken to dressing in green outfits styled by Pierre Cardin to resemble the uniforms of the Chinese Red Guards, because as the Foreign Minister in the government of President A. he had become famous as the architect of a friendship treaty with Chairman Mao. A photograph of Isky embracing the great Zedong hung on the wall of the room in which the uncle informed his nephew: 'Your activities are becoming an embarrassment to me. Time you settled down. Take a wife.' Arjumand Harappa stared furiously at Haroun and obliged him to do as Iskander asked. 'But who?' he inquired lamely, and Isky waved a dismissive hand. 'Some decent girl,' he said, 'plenty to choose from.'

Haroun, realizing that the interview was at an end, turned to go. Iskander Harappa called after him: 'And if you're interested in politics you better stop riding sea-turtles and start working for me.'

The transformation of Iskander Harappa into the most powerful new force on the political scene was by this time complete. He had set about engineering his rise with all the calculated brilliance of which Arjumand had always known him to be capable. Concentrating on the high-profile world of international affairs, he had written a series of articles analysing his country's requirements from the great powers, the Islamic world and the rest of Asia, following these up with an arduous programme of speeches whose arguments proved impossible to resist. When his notion of 'Islamic socialism' and of a close alliance with China had gained such wide public support that he was effectively running the nation's foreign policy without even being a member of the cabinet, President A. had had no option but to invite him into the government. His enormous personal charm, his way of making the plain, bolster-chested wives of visiting world leaders feel like Greta Garbo and his oratorical genius made him an instant hit. 'The thing that satisfies me most,' he told his daughter, 'is that now we've given the go-ahead to the Karakoram road to China, I can have fun kicking around the minister for public works.' The works minister was Little Mir Harappa, his old friendship with the President having failed to outweigh Iskander's public appeal. 'That bastard,' Iskander said to Arjumand with glee, 'is finally under my thumb.'

When the A. regime started losing popularity, Iskander Harappa resigned and formed the Popular Front, the political party which he funded out of his bottomless wealth and whose first Chairman he became. 'For an ex-foreign minister,' Little Mir told the President sourly, 'your protégé seems to be concentrating pretty heavily on the home front.' The President shrugged. 'He knows what he's doing,' said Field-Marshal A., 'unfortunately.'

Rumours of the government's corruption provided the fuel; but Isky's campaign for a return to democracy was perhaps unstoppable anyway. He toured the villages and promised every peasant one acre of land and a new water-well. He was put in jail; huge demonstrations secured his release. He screamed in regional dialects about the rape of the country by fat cats and tilyars, and such was the power of his tongue, or perhaps of the sartorial talents of Monsieur Cardin, that nobody seemed to recall Isky's own status as a landlord of a distinctly obese chunk of Sind . . . Iskander Harappa offered Haroun political work in his home district. 'You have anti-corruption credentials,' he told the youth. 'Tell them about the *Newsweek* article.' Haroun Harappa, offered the golden opportunity of running down his father on their home turf, took the job at once.

'Well, Abba,' he thought happily, 'life is long.'

Two days after Haroun lectured an egg-laying turtle about revolution, Rani Harappa at Mohenjo was telephoned by a male voice so muted, so crippled by apologies and embarrassment that it was a few moments before she recognized it as belonging to Little Mir, with whom she had had no contact since his looting of her home, although his son Haroun had been a regular visitor. 'God damn it, Rani,' Little Mir finally admitted through the spittle-heavy clouds of his humiliation, 'I need a favour.'

Rani Harappa at forty had defeated Iskander's formidable ayah by the simple method of outliving her. The days of irreverently giggling village girls rummaging through her underwear were long past; she had become the true mistress of Mohenjo by dint of the unassailable calm with which she embroidered shawl after shawl on the verandah of the house, persuading the villagers that she was composing the tapestry of their fate, and that if she wished to she could foul up their lives by choosing to sew a bad future into the magical shawls. Having earned respect, Rani was strangely content with her life, and maintained cordial relations with her husband in spite of his long absences from her side and his permanent absence from her bed. She knew all about the end of the Pinkie affair and knew in the secret chambers of her heart that a man embarking on a political career must sooner or later ask his wife to stand beside him on the podium; secure in a future which would bring her Isky without her having to do a thing, she discovered without surprise that her love for him had refused to die, but had become, instead, a thing of quietness and strength. This was a great difference between her and Bilquìs Hyder: both women had husbands who retreated from them into the enigmatic palaces of their destinies, but while Bilquìs sank into eccentricity, not to say craziness, Rani had subsided into a sanity which made her a powerful, and later on a dangerous, human being.

When Little Mir rang, Rani had been looking towards the village where the white concubines were playing badminton in the twilight. In those days many of the villagers had gone West to work for a while, and those who returned had brought with them white women for whom the prospect of life in a village as a number-two wife seemed to hold an inexhaustibly erotic appeal. The number-one wives treated these white girls as dolls or pets and those husbands who failed to bring home a guddi, a white doll, were soundly berated by their women. The village of the white dolls had become famous in the region. Villagers came from miles around to watch the girls in their neat, clean whites giggling and squealing as they leapt for shuttlecocks and displayed their frilly panties. The number-one wives cheered for their number-twos, taking pride in their victories as in the successes of children, and offering them consolation in defeat. Rani Harappa was deriving such gentle pleasure from observing the dolls at play that she forgot to listen to what Mir was saying. 'Fuck me in the mouth, Rani,' he shouted at last with the fury of his suppressed pride, 'forget our differences. This business is too important. I need a wife, most urgently.'

'I see.'

'Ya Allah. Rani, don't be difficult, for God's sake. Not for me, what do you think, would I ask? For Haroun. It's the only way.'

The desperation with which Little Mir stammered out the need for a good woman to stabilize his wayward son overcame any initial reluctance Rani might have felt, and she said at once, 'Good News.' 'Already?' Little Mir asked, misunderstanding her. 'You women don't waste any time!'

How a marriage is made: Rani suggested Naveed Hyder, thinking that a wedding in the family would do Bilquìs good. By that time the telephone link between the two women was no longer a means by which Rani found out what was going on in the city, no longer an excuse for Bilquìs to gossip and condescend while Rani humbly snatched from her friend's conversation whatever crumbs of life it offered. Now it was Rani who was strong, and Bilquìs, her old regal dreams in ruins since Raza's sacking from the government, who needed support, and who found in the unchanging solidity of Rani Harappa the strength to sustain her through her increasingly bewildered days. 'Just what she needs,' Rani thought with satisfaction, 'trousseau, marquees, sweetmeats, too much to think about. And that daughter of hers can't wait to get hitched.'

Little Mir consulted the President before agreeing to the match. The Hyder family had become accident-prone of late: the old rumours from Q. still circulated, and it had not been easy to keep the incident of the dead turkeys out of the papers. But now, in the mountainous coolness of the new northern capital, the President had begun to feel the chilly winds of his unpopularity, and agreed to the marriage, because, he decided, it was time to draw the hero of Aansu close to him again, like a warm blanket or shawl. 'No problem,' A. told Little Mir, 'my congrats to the happy pair.'

Mir Harappa visited Rani at Mohenjo to discuss the details. He rode up stiff with embarrassment and behaved with bad-tempered humility throughout. 'What a father will do for a son!' he burst out at Rani as she sat on the verandah working on the interminable shawl of her solitude. 'When my boy is a daddy himself he will know how a daddy feels. I hope this Good News of yours is a fertile girl.'

'Proper sowing ensures a good harvest,' Rani replied serenely. 'Please take some tea.'

Raza Hyder did not object to the betrothal. In those years when his only responsibility was to oversee the intake and training of raw recruits, when the fact of his decline stared him in the face every day, multiplied, replicated in the gawky figures of youths who didn't know which end of a bayonet meant business, he had been observing the rise of Iskander Harappa with barely suppressed envy. 'The time will come,' he prophesied to himself, 'when I'll have to go begging that guy for an extra pip.' In the turbulent climate of the government's instability Raza Hyder had been wondering which way to jump, whether to come out in support of the Popular Front's demand for elections, or to put what remained of his reputation behind the government in the hope of preferment. The offer of Haroun Harappa for a son-in-law gave him the chance of having it both ways. The match would please the President: that much had been made clear. But Raza also knew of Haroun's hatred for his father, which had placed the boy firmly in Isky Harappa's pocket. 'A foot in both camps,' Raza thought, 'that's the ticket.'

And it is possible that Raza was delighted to be able to get rid of Good News, because she had developed, as she grew, something of the full-mouthed insouciance of the late Sindbad Mengal. Haroun's mouth was also thick and wide, a part of his family inheritance. 'Two fat-lip types,' Raza Hyder told his wife in tones more jovial than he normally used when addressing her, 'made for each other, na? The babies will look like fishes.' Bilquìs said, 'Never mind.'

How a marriage is made: I see that I have somehow omitted to mention the views of the young persons concerned. Photographs were exchanged. Haroun Harappa took his brown envelope to his uncle's house and opened it in the presence of Iskander and Arjumand: there are times when young men turn to their families for support. The monochrome photograph had been artistically retouched to give Good News skin as pink as blotting-paper and eyes as green as ink.

'You can see how he's made her pigtail longer,' Arjumand pointed out.

'Let the boy make up his own mind,' Iskander reproved her, but Arjumand at twenty had conceived a strange dislike of the picture. 'Plain as a plate,' she announced, 'and not so fair-skinned as all that.'

'It's got to be somebody,' Haroun stated, 'and there's nothing wrong with her.' Arjumand cried, 'How can you just say that? Got eyes in your head or ping-pong balls?' At this point Iskander ordered his daughter to be quiet and told the bearer to bring sweetmeats and celebratory glasses of lime juice. Haroun went on staring at that photograph of Naveed Hyder, and because nothing, not even the paintbrush of a zealous photographer, could mask Good News's unquenchable determination to be beautiful, her fiancé was quickly overpowered by the iron will of her celluloid eyes, and began to think her the loveliest bride on earth. This illusion, which was entirely the product of Good News's imagination, entirely the result of the action of mind over matter, would survive everything, even the wedding scandal; but it would not survive Iskander Harappa's death.

'What a girl,' said Haroun Harappa, driving Arjumand from the room in disgust.

As for Good News: 'I don't need to look at any stupid photograph,' she told Bilquìs, 'he's famous, he's rich, he's a husband, let's catch him quick.' 'His reputation is bad,' Bilquìs said, as a mother should, offering her daughter the chance to withdraw, 'and he is bad to his daddy.'

'I'll fix him,' Good News replied.

Later, alone with Shahbanou as the ayah brushed her hair, Good News added some further thoughts. 'Hey, you with the eyes at the bottom of a well,' she said, 'you know what marriage is for a woman?'

'I am a virgin,' Shahbanou replied.

'Marriage is power,' Naveed Hyder said. 'It is freedom. You stop being someone's daughter and become someone's mother instead, ek dum, fut-a-fut, pronto. Then who can tell you what to do? – What do you mean,' a terrible notion occurred to her, 'do you think I'm not a virgin also? You shut your dirtyfilthy mouth, with one word I could put you on the street.'

'What are you talking, bibi, I only said.'

'I tell you, how great to be away from this house. Haroun Harappa, I swear. Too good, yaar. Too good.'

'We are modern people,' Bilquìs told her daughter. 'Now that you have accepted you must get to know the boy. It will be a love match.'

Miss Arjumand Harappa, the 'virgin Ironpants', had rejected so many suitors that although she was barely twenty years old the city's matchmakers had already begun to think of her as being on the shelf. The flood of proposals was not entirely, or even primarily, the result of her extreme eligibility as the only child of Chairman Iskander Harappa; it had its true source in that extraordinary, defiant beauty with which, or so it seemed to her, her body taunted her mind. I must say that of all the beautiful women in that country packed full of improbable lovelies, there is no doubt who took the prize. In spite of bound and still-apple-sized breasts, Arjumand carried off the palm.

Loathing her sex, Arjumand went to great lengths to disguise her looks. She cut her hair short, wore no cosmetics or perfume, dressed in her father's old shirts and the baggiest trousers she could find, developed a stooped and slouching walk. But the harder she tried, the more insistently her blossoming body outshone her disguises. The short hair was luminous, the unadorned face learned expressions of infinite sensuality which she could do nothing to control, and the more she stooped, the taller and more desirable she grew. By the age of sixteen she had been obliged to become expert in the arts of self-defence. Iskander Harappa had never tried to keep her away from men. She accompanied him on his diplomatic rounds, and at many embassy receptions elderly ambassadors were found clutching their groins and throwing up in the toilet after their groping hands had been answered by a well-aimed knee. By her eighteenth birthday the throng of the city's most coveted bachelors outside the gate of the Harappa house had become so swollen as to constitute an impediment to traffic, and at her own request she was sent away to Lahore to a Christian boarding college for ladies, whose anti-male rules were so severe that even her father could see her only by appointment in a tattered garden of dying roses and balding lawns. But she found no respite in that prison populated exclusively by females, all of whom she scorned for their gender; the girls fell for her just as hard as the men, and final-year students would clutch at her behind when she passed. One lovelorn nineteen-year-old, despairing of catching Ironpants's eye, pretended to sleepwalk into the empty swimming pool and was removed to hospital with multiple fractures of the skull. Another, crazed by love, climbed out of the college compound and went to sit at a café in the famous red-light district of Heeramandi, having decided to become a whore if she could not have Arjumand's heart. This distressed girl was abducted from the café by the local pimps, who forced her father, a textile magnate, to pay a ransom of one lakh of rupees for her safe return. She never married, because although the pimps insisted that they had their honour, too, nobody believed she had not been touched, and after a medical inspection the college's devoutly Catholic headmistress absolutely refused to concede that the wretch might have been deflowered upon her antiseptic premises. Arjumand Harappa wrote to her father and asked him to take her away from the college. 'It's no relief,' the letter said. 'I should have known girls would be worse than boys.'

The return from London of Haroun Harappa unleashed a civil war inside the virgin Ironpants. His remarkable physical resemblance to photographs of her father at twenty-six unnerved Arjumand, and his fondness for whoring, gambling and other forms of debauchery convinced her that reincarnation was not simply a crazy notion imported by the Hyders from the country of the idolaters. She attempted to suppress the idea that beneath Haroun's dissolute exterior a second great man, almost the equal of her father, lay concealed, and that, with her help, he could discover his true nature, just as the Chairman had . . . refusing even to whisper such things to herself in the privacy of her room, she cultivated in Haroun's presence that attitude of scornful condescension which quickly persuaded him that there was no point in his trying where so many others had failed. He was not insensible to her fatal beauty, but the reputation of the virgin Ironpants, when combined with that terrible and uninterruptedly disgusted gaze, was enough to send him elsewhere; and then the photograph of Naveed Hyder bewitched him, and it was too late for Arjumand to change her approach. Haroun Harappa was the only man, other than her father, whom Arjumand ever loved, and her rage in the days after his betrothal was awful to behold. But Iskander was preoccupied in those days, and failed to pay any attention to the war inside his child.

'God damn,' Arjumand said to her mirror, unconsciously reflecting the former habit of her mother alone in Mohenjo, 'life is shit.'

It was once explained to me by one of the world's Greatest Living Poets – we mere prose scribblers must turn to poets for wisdom, which is why this book is littered with them; there was my friend who hung upside-down and had the poetry shaken out of him, and Babar Shakil, who wanted to be a poet, and I suppose Omar Khayyam, who was named for one but never was – that the classic fable *Beauty and the Beast* is simply the story of an arranged marriage.

'A merchant is down on his luck, so he promises his daughter to a wealthy but reclusive landowner, Beast Sahib, and receives a lavish dowry in exchange – a great chest, I believe, of broad pieces of gold. Beauty Bibi dutifully marries the zamindar, thus restoring her father's fortunes, and naturally at first her husband, a total stranger, seems horrible to her, monstrous even. But eventually, under the benign influence of her obedient love, he turns into a Prince.'

'Do you mean,' I ventured, 'that he inherits a title?' The Great Living Poet looked tolerant and tossed back his silvery shoulder-length hair.

'That is a bourgeois remark,' he chided me. 'No, of course the transformation would have taken place neither in his social status nor in his actual, corporeal self, but in her perception of him. Picture them as they grow closer to each other, as they move inwards over the years from the opposed poles of Beautyness and Beastdom, and become at last, and happily, just plain Mr Husband and Mrs Wife.'

The Great Living Poet was well-known for his radical ideas and for the chaotic complexity of his extramarital love life, so I thought I would please him by commenting slyly: 'Why is it that fairy-tales always treat marriage as an ending? And always such a perfectly happy one?'

But instead of the man-to-man wink or guffaw for which I'd been hoping (I was very young), the Great Living Poet adopted a grave expression. 'That is a masculine question,' he replied, 'no woman would be so puzzled. The proposition of the fable is clear. Woman must make the best of her fate; for if she does not love Man, why then he dies, the Beast perishes, and Woman is left a widow, that is to say less than a daughter, less than a wife, worthless.' Mildly, he sipped his Scotch.

'Whatif, whatif,' I stammered, 'I mean, uncle, whatif the girl really couldn't bear the husband chosen for her?' The Poet, who had begun to hum Persian verses under his breath, frowned in distant disappointment.

'You have become too Westernized,' he said. 'You should spend some time, maybe seven years or so, not too long, with our village people. Then you will understand that this is a completely Eastern story, and stop this whatif foolishness.'

The Great Poet is unfortunately no longer living, so I cannot ask him whatif the story of Good News Hyder were true; nor can I hope for the benefit of his advice on an even more ticklish subject: whatif, whatif a Beastji somehow lurked *inside* Beauty Bibi? Whatif the beauty were herself the beast? But I think he might have said I was confusing matters: 'As Mr Stevenson has shown in his *Dr Jekyll and Mr Hyde*, such saint-and-monster conjunctions are conceivable in the case of men; alas! such is our nature. But the whole essence of Woman denies such a possibility.'

The reader may have divined from my last whatifs that I have two marriages to describe; and the second, waiting in the peripheries of the first, is of course the long-hinted-at Nikah of Sufiya Zinobia Hyder and Omar Khayyam Shakil.

Omar Khayyam finally screwed up the courage to ask for Sufiya Zinobia's hand when he heard about the betrothal of her younger sister. When he arrived, grey respectable fifty, at her marble home and made his extraordinary request, the impossibly old and decrepit divine Maulana Dawood let out a scream that made Raza Hyder look around for demons. 'Spawn of obscene hags,' Dawood addressed Shakil, 'from the day you descended to earth in the machine of your mothers' iniquity I knew you. Such filthy suggestions you come to make in this house of lovers of God! May your time in hell be longer than a thousand lifetimes.' The rage of Maulana Dawood created, in Bilquìs, a mood of perverse obstinacy. In those days she was still prone to lock doors furiously, to defend herself against the incursions of the afternoon wind; the light in her eyes was a little too bright. But the engagement of Good News had given her a new purpose, just as Rani had hoped; so it was with a fair approximation of her old arrogance that she spoke to Omar Khayyam: 'We understand that you have been obliged to bring your own proposal because of the absence of your family members from Town. The irregularity is forgiven, but we must now consider in private. Our decision will be communicated to you in due course.' Raza Hyder, struck dumb by this reappearance of the old Bilquìs, was unable to disagree until Shakil had left; Omar Khayyam, arising, placing grey hat on grey hair, was betrayed by a sudden reddening beneath the pallor of his skin. 'Blushing,' Maulana Dawood screeched, extending a sharp-nailed finger, 'that is only a trick. Such persons have no shame.'

After Sufiya Zinobia recovered from the immunological catastrophe that followed the turkey massacre, Raza Hyder had discovered that he could no longer see her through the veil of his disappointment in her sex. The memory of the tenderness with which he had lifted her out of the scene of her somnambulist violence refused to leave him, as did the realization that while she was ill he had been beset by emotions that could only be described as arising out of fatherly love. In short, Hyder had changed his opinion of his retarded child, and had begun to play with her, to take pride in her tiny advances. Together with the ayah Shahbanou the great war hero would play at being a train or steamroller or crane, and would lift the girl and throw her in the air as if she really were still the small child whose brain she had been forced to retain. This new pattern of behaviour had perplexed Bilquìs, whose affections remained concentrated on the younger girl ... at any rate, Sufiya Zinobia's condition had improved. She had grown two and a half inches, put on a little weight, and her mental age had risen to about six and a half. She was nineteen years old, and had conceived for her newly loving father a child's version of that same devotion which Arjumand Harappa felt for her father the Chairman.

'Men,' Bilquìs told Rani on the telephone, 'you can't depend on them.'

As for Omar Khayyam: the complexity of his motives has already been discussed. He had spent seven years failing to cure himself of that obsession which relieved him of vertigo attacks, but during those years of struggle he had also arranged to examine Sufiya Zinobia at regular intervals, and had ingratiated himself with her father, building on the gratitude Raza felt towards him for having saved his daughter's life. But a proposal of marriage was something else again, and once he was safely out of the house Raza Hyder began to voice his doubts.

'The man is fat,' Raza reasoned. 'Ugly also. And we must not forget his debauched past.'

'A debauched life led by the child of debauched persons,' Dawood added, 'and a brother shot for politics.'

But Bilquìs did not mention her memory of Shakil drunk at Mohenjo. Instead she said, 'Where are we going to find the girl a better match?'

Now Raza understood that his wife was as anxious to be rid of this troublesome child as he was to see the back of her beloved Good News. The realization that there was a kind of symmetry here, a sort of fair exchange, weakened his resolve, so that Bilquìs detected the uncertainty in his voice when he asked, 'But a damaged child: should we look for husbands at all? Should we not accept the responsibility, wife? What is this marriage business where such a girl is concerned?'

'She is not so stupid now,' Bilquìs argued, 'she can dress herself, go to the pot, and she does not wet her bed.'

'For God's sake,' Raza shouted, 'does that qualify her to be a wife?'

'That frogspawn slime,' Dawood exclaimed, 'that messenger of Shaitan. He has come here with his proposal to divide this holy house.'

'Her vocabulary is improving,' Bilquìs added, 'she sits with Shahbanou and tells the dhobi what to wash. She can count the garments and handle money.'

'But she is a child,' Raza said hopelessly.

Bilquìs grew stronger as he weakened. 'In a woman's body,' she replied, 'the child is nowhere to be seen. A woman does not have to be a brainbox. In many opinions brains are a positive disadvantage to a woman in marriage. She likes to go to the kitchen and help the khansama with his work. At the bazaar she can tell good vegetables from bad. You yourself have praised her chutneys. She can tell when the servants have not polished the furniture properly. She wears a brassière and in other ways also her body has become that of an adult woman. And she even does not blush.'

This was true. The alarming reddenings of Sufiya Zinobia were, it seemed, things of the past; nor had the turkey-assassinating violence recurred. It was as if the girl had been cleansed by her single, all-consuming explosion of shame.

'Maybe,' Raza Hyder slowly said, 'I am worrying too much.'

'Besides,' Bilquìs said with finality, 'he is her doctor, this man. He saved her life. Into whose hands could we more safely place her? Into nobody's, I say. This proposal has come to us from God.'

'Catch your ears,' Dawood shrieked, 'tobah, tobah! But your

God is great, great in his greatness, and so he may forgive such blasphemy.'

Raza Hyder looked old and sad. 'We must send Shahbanou with her,' he insisted. 'And a quiet wedding. Too much hullabaloo would frighten her.'

'Just let me finish with Good News,' Bilquìs said in delight, 'and we will have a wedding so quiet that only the birds will sing.'

Maulana Dawood withdrew from the scene of his defeat. 'Girls married in the wrong order,' he said as he departed. 'What began with a necklace of shoes cannot end well.'

On the day of the polo match between the Army and Police teams Bilquìs shook Good News awake early. The match was not scheduled to begin until five o'clock in the afternoon, but Bilquìs said, 'Eleven hours dolling yourself up to meet your future husband is like money in the bank.' By the time mother and daughter arrived at the polo ground Good News was in such tip-top condition that people thought a bride had abandoned her wedding feast to come and watch the game. Haroun Harappa met them by the little table at which the match commentator sat surrounded by microphones and led them to the chairs he had saved for them; the spectacle of Good News's get-up was so overpowering that he came away with a clearer impression of the design of her nose-jewellery than of the fortunes of the game. Every so often during that afternoon he ran off and returned bearing paper plates heaped with samosas or jalebis, with cups of fizzing cola balanced along his forearms. During his absences Bilquìs watched her daughter like a hawk, to make sure she tried no funny business like catching the eyes of other boys; but when Haroun returned Bilquìs became unaccountably absorbed in the game. The great star of the Police team was a certain Captain Talvar Ulhaq, and in that time of the Army's unpopularity his annihilation of their polo squad that afternoon turned him into something of a national hero, especially as he conformed to all the usual heroic requirements, being tall, dashing, mustachioed, with a tiny scar on his neck that looked exactly like a love-bite. This Captain Talvar was to be the cause of the wedding scandal out of which, it could be argued with some plausibility, the whole of the future grew.

From the stammering and awkward conversation she had with Haroun that day Good News discovered to her consternation that her future husband had no ambitions and a tiny appetite. Nor was he in any hurry to have children. The confidence with which Naveed Hyder had stated, 'I'll fix him,' ebbed out of her in the physical presence of this pudding of a young man, so it was perhaps inevitable that her eyes should become glued to the upright, capering, mythological figure of Talvar Ulhaq on his whirling horse. And maybe it was also inevitable that her excessive dressiness should attract the interest of the young police captain who was famous for being the most successful stud in the city – so maybe the whole thing was Bilquìs's fault for dressing up her daughter – at any rate, Bilquìs for all her vigilance missed the moment when their eyes met. Good News and Talvar stared at each other through the dust and hooves and polo-sticks, and at that moment the girl felt a pain shoot up her insides. She managed to turn the shuddering moan which escaped her lips into a violent sneeze and cough before anyone noticed, and was assisted in her subterfuge by the commotion on the polo field, where Captain Talvar's horse had inexplicably reared and thrown him down into the perils of the flying hooves and sticks. 'I just went stiff all over,' Talvar told Naveed later, 'and the horse lost its temper with me.'

The game ended shortly afterwards, and Good News went home with Bilquìs, knowing that she would never marry Haroun Harappa, no, not in a million years. That night she heard pebbles rattling on her bedroom window, tied her bedsheets together and climbed down into the arms of the polo star, who drove her in a police car to his beach hut at Fisherman's Cove. When they had finished making love she asked the most modest question of her life: 'I'm not so great looking,' she said, 'why me?' Talvar Ulhaq sat up in bed and looked as serious as a schoolboy. 'On account of the hunger of your womb,' he told her. 'You are appetite and I am food.' Now she perceived that Talvar had a pretty high opinion of himself and began to wonder whether she might have bitten off more than she could chew.

It turned out that Talvar Ulhaq had had the gift of clairvoyancy from childhood, a talent which assisted him greatly in his police work, because he could divine where crimes were going to be committed before the thieves had worked it out themselves, so that his record of arrests was unbeatable. He had foreseen in Naveed Hyder the children who had always been his greatest dream, the profusion of children who would make him puff up with pride while she disintegrated under the awesome chaos of their numbers. This vision had made him willing to undertake the extremely dangerous course of action to which he was now committed, because he knew that Raza Hyder's daughter was engaged to be married to the favourite nephew of Chairman Iskander Harappa, that the invitations to the wedding had already gone out, and that by any normal standards his situation was hopeless. 'Nothing is impossible,' he told Naveed, got dressed, and went outside into the salty night to find a sea-turtle to ride. Naveed emerged a little later to find him whooping with joy as he stood on a turtle's back, and while she was enjoying his simple pleasure the fishermen came and grinned at them. Afterwards Naveed Hyder was never sure whether this had been a part of Talvar's plan, whether he had signalled to the fishermen from the back of the weeping turtle, or if he had visited the Cove in advance to plan the whole thing, because after all it was well-known that the fishermen and the police force were great allies, being regularly in cahoots for smuggling purposes ... Talvar, however, never admitted any responsibility for what happened.

What happened was that the fisherman's leader, a patriarch with an honest and open face in which an unblemished set of white teeth gleamed improbably in the moonlight, informed the couple pleasantly that he and his fellows intended to blackmail them. 'Such ungodly goings-on,' the old fisherman said sadly, 'it is bad for our peace of mind. Some compensation, some comfort must be given.'

Talvar Ulhaq paid up without arguing and drove Good News

home. With his help, she managed to climb up the rope of bed-sheets without being discovered. 'I won't see you again,' he said at their parting, 'until you break your engagement and allow what must be to be.'

His second sight informed him that she would do as he had asked, so he went home to prepare for marriage and for the storm which would surely break.

Good News (let us remind ourselves) was her mother's favourite daughter. Her fear of forfeiting this position fought inside her with the equal and opposite fear that the fishermen would continue their blackmail; the insane love she had conceived for Talvar Ulhaq wrestled with the duty she owed to the boy her parents had selected; the loss of her virginity drove her wild with worry. But until the last evening before her wedding she remained silent. Talvar Ulhaq told her afterwards that her inaction had brought him close to the point of insanity, and that he had resolved to turn up at the wedding and shoot Haroun Harappa, whatever the consequences, if she had decided to go through with the match. But at the eleventh hour Good News told her mother, 'I won't marry that stupid potato,' and all hell broke loose, because love was the last thing anyone had been expecting to foul up the arrangements.

O glee of female relatives in the face of unconcealable scandal! O crocodile tears and insincere pummelling of breasts! O delighted crowing of Duniyazad Begum as she dances upon the corpse of Bilquìs's honour! And the forktongued offers of hope: Who knows, talk to her, many girls panic on their wedding eve, yes, she'll see sense, just try only, time to be firm, time to be gentle, beat her up a little, give her a loving hug, O God, but how terrible, how can you cancel the guests?

And when it is clear that the girl cannot be moved, when the delicious horror of it all is out in the open, when Good News admits that there is Someone Else – then Bariamma stirs on her bolsters and the room falls silent to hear her judgment.

'This is your failure as a mother,' Bariamma wheezes, 'so now the father must be called. Go now and bring him, my Raza, run and fetch.'

Two tableaux. In the bridal chamber Naveed Hyder sits immovable and mulish while all around her are women frozen by their delight into living statues, women holding combs, brushes, silver-polish, antimony, staring at Naveed, disaster's source, with petrified joy. Bariamma's lips are the only moving features in the scene. Time-honoured words are dripping out of them: floozy, hussy, whore. And in Raza's bedroom Bilquìs is clinging to her husband's legs as he struggles into his pants.

Raza Hyder awoke to catastrophe from a dream in which he saw himself standing on the parade-ground of his failure before a phalanx of recruits all of whom were exact replicas of himself, except that they were incompetent, they could not march in step or dress to the left or polish their belt buckles properly. He had been screaming his despair at these shades of his own ineptitude, and the rage of the dream infected his waking mood. His first reaction to the news which Bilquìs forced past lips that did not want to let it through was that he had no option but to kill the girl. 'Such shame,' he said, 'such havoc wrought to the plans of parents.' He decided to shoot her in the head in front of his family members. Bilquìs clung to his thighs, slipped down as he began to move, and was dragged from the bedroom, her nails digging into his ankles. The cold sweat of her fear made her pencilled eyebrows run down her face. The ghost of Sindbad Mengal was not mentioned, but O, he was there all right. Army pistol in hand, Raza Hyder entered Good News's room; the screams of women greeted him as he came.

But this is not the story of my discarded Anna M.; Raza, raising his gun, found himself unable to use it. 'Throw her into the street,' he said, and left the room.

Now the night is full of negotiations. Raza in his quarters stares at an unused pistol. Deputations are sent; he remains unbending. Then the ayah Shahbanou, rubbing sleep from black-rimmed

eyes, so like Hyder's own, is dispatched by Bilquìs to plead Good
News's cause. 'He likes you because you are good with Sufiya
Zinobia. He'll listen maybe to you when he won't to me.' Bilquìs
is crumbling visibly, has been reduced to pleading with servants.
Shahbanou holds Good News's future in her hands – Good News,
who has kicked, abused, hit – 'I'll go, Begum Sahib,' Shahbanou
says. Ayah and father confer behind closed doors; 'Forgive my
saying, sir, but don't pile shame on shame.'

At three a.m. Raza Hyder relents. There must be a wedding,
the girl must be handed over to a husband, any husband. That will
get rid of her and cause less of a stir than kicking her out. 'A
whore with a home,' Raza summons Bilquìs to announce, 'is
better than a whore in the gutter.' Naveed tells her mother the
name: not without pride, she says clearly to one and all: 'It must
be Captain Talvar Ulhaq. Nobody else will do.'

Telephone calls. Mir Harappa awoken to be informed of the
change of plan. 'Your bastard family. Fuck me in the mouth if I
don't get even.' Iskander Harappa receives the news calmly, relays
it to Arjumand who is in her nightgown beside the telephone.
Something flickers in her eyes.

It is Iskander who tells Haroun.

And one more call, to a police captain who has not slept a
wink, who like Raza has spent part of the night fingering a pistol.
'I will not tell you what I think of you,' Raza Hyder roars into the
mouthpiece, 'but get your hide here tomorrow and take this no-
good female off my hands. Not one paisa of dowry and keep out
of my sight for ever after.'

'Ji, I shall be honoured to marry your daughter,' Talvar politely
replies. And in the Hyder household, women who can scarcely
believe their luck begin once again to make preparations for the
great day. Naveed Hyder goes to bed and falls sound asleep with
an innocent expression on her face. Dark henna on her soles turns
orange while she rests.

'Shame and scandal in the family,' Shahbanou tells Sufiya
Zinobia in the morning. 'Bibi, you don't know what you missed.'

Something else was happening that night. On university, cam-
puses, in the bazaars of the cities, under cover of darkness, the
people were assembling. By the time the sun rose it was clear that
the government was going to fall. That morning the people took
to the streets and set fire to motor cars, school buses, Army trucks
and the libraries of the British Council and United States Information Service to express their displeasure. Field-Marshal A. ordered
troops into the streets to restore peace. At eleven-fifteen he was
visited by a General known to everyone by the nickname 'Shaggy
Dog', an alleged associate of Chairman Iskander Harappa. General
Shaggy Dog informed the distraught President that the armed
forces were absolutely refusing to fire on civilians, and soldiers
would shoot their officers rather than their fellow-countrymen.
This statement convinced President A. that his time was up, and
by lunchtime he had been replaced by General Shaggy, who
placed A. under house arrest and appeared on the brand-new television service to announce that his sole purpose in assuming
power was to lead the nation back towards democracy; elections
would take place within eighteen months. The afternoon was
spent by the people in joyful celebration; Datsuns, taxi-cabs, the
Alliance Française building and the Goethe Institute provided the
fuel for their incandescent happiness.

Mir Harappa heard about the bloodless coup of President Dog
within eight minutes of Marshal A.'s resignation. This second
major blow to his prestige drained all the fight out of Little Mir.
Leaving a letter of resignation on his desk he fled to his Daro
estate without bothering to await developments, and immured
himself there in a mood of such desolation that the servants could
hear him muttering under his breath that his days were numbered.
'Two things have happened,' he would say, 'but the third is
yet to come.'

Iskander and Arjumand spent the day with Haroun in Karachi.
Iskander on the telephone all day, Arjumand so aroused by the
news that she forgot to sympathize with Haroun about his can-

celled wedding. 'Stop looking so fish-faced,' she told him, 'the future has begun.' Rani Harappa arrived by train from Mohenjo, thinking she was about to spend a carefree day at Good News's Nikah celebrations, but Isky's chauffeur Jokio told her at the station that the world had changed. He drove her to the town house, where Iskander embraced her warmly and said, 'Good you came. Now we must stand together before the people; our moment has come.' At once Rani forgot all about weddings and began to look, at forty, as young as her only daughter. 'I knew it,' she exulted inwardly. 'Good old Shaggy Dog.'

So great was the excitement of that day that the news of the events in the Hyder household was blotted out completely, whereas on any other day the scandal would have been impossible to cover up. Captain Talvar Ulhaq came alone to the wedding, having chosen to involve neither friends nor family members in the shameful circumstances of his nuptials. He had to struggle through streets that were hot with burning cars in a police jeep that mercifully escaped the ministrations of the crowds, and was received by Raza Hyder with glacial formality and scorn. 'It is my earnest intention,' Talvar told Raza, 'to be the finest son-in-law that you could wish for, so that in time you may reconsider your decision to cut your daughter out of your life.' Raza gave the briefest of replies to this courageous speech. 'I don't care for polo players,' he said.

Those guests who had managed to reach the Hyder residence through the unstable euphoria of the streets had taken the precaution of dressing in their oldest, most tattered clothes; nor did they wear any jewellery. They had put on these unfestive rags to avoid attracting the attention of the people, who usually put up with rich folk but might just have elected in their elation to add the city's elite to their collection of burning symbols. The dilapidated condition of the guests was one of the strangest features of that day of strangenesses; Good News Hyder, oiled hennaed bejewelled, looked in that gathering of frightened celebrants even more out of place than she had appeared at the polo match of her inescapable destiny. 'It's like being married in a palace full of beggars,' she whispered to Talvar, who sat flower-garlanded beside her on a little podium beneath the glittering, mirrorworked marquee. The sweetmeats and delicacies of Bilquìs's motherly pride languished uneaten on long whiteclothed tables in the bizarre atmosphere of that horrified and dislocated time.

Why the guests refused to eat: already unbalanced by the dangers of the streets, they had been almost completely deranged by the information, which was conveyed to them on little handwritten erratum slips which Bilquìs had been writing out for hours, that while the bride was indeed the expected Good News Hyder there had been a last-minute change of groom. 'Owing to circumstances beyond our control,' read the little white chitties of humiliation, 'the part of husband will be taken by Police Capt. Talvar Ulhaq.' Bilquìs had had to write this line five hundred and fifty-five times over, and each successive inscription drove the nails of her shame deeper into her heart, so that by the time the guests arrived and the servants handed out the erratum slips she was as stiff with dishonour as if she had been impaled on a tree. As the shock of the coup was replaced on the guests' faces by the awareness of the size of the catastrophe that had befallen the Hyders, Raza, too, became numb all over, anaesthetized by his public disgrace. The presence of the Himalayas of uneaten food struck the chill of shame into the soul of Shahbanou the ayah, who was standing by Sufiya Zinobia in a condition of such extreme despondency that she forgot to greet Omar Khayyam Shakil. The doctor had lumbered into that gathering of millionaires disguised as gardeners; his thoughts were so full of the ambiguities of his own engagement to the halfwit of his obsessions that he utterly failed to notice that he had walked into a mirage from the past, a ghost-image of the legendary party given by the three Shakil sisters in their old house in Q. The erratum slip rested unread in his plump tight fist until, belatedly, the meaning of the uneaten food dawned on him.

It was not an exact replica of that longago party. No food was eaten, but still a wedding took place. Can there ever have been a Nikah at which nobody flirted with anybody else, at which the hired musicians were so overwhelmed by the occasion that they neglected to play a single note? Certainly there could not have been many nuptial feasts at which the last-minute groom was all but murdered on his podium by his newly-acquired sister-in-law.

O dear, yes. I regret to have to inform you that (setting the seal, as it were, on that perfect disaster of a day) the somnolent demon of shame that had possessed Sufiya Zinobia on the day she slew the turkeys emerged once more beneath the mirror-shiny shamiana of disgrace.

A glazing-over of her eyes, which acquired the milky opacity of somnambulism. A pouring-in to her too-sensitive spirit of the great abundance of shame in that tormented tent. A fire beneath the skin, so that she began to flame all over, a golden blaze that dimmed the rouge on her cheeks and the paint on her fingers and toes . . . Omar Khayyam Shakil spotted what was going on, but too late, so that by the time he shouted 'Look out!' across that catatonic gathering the demon had already hurled Sufiya Zinobia across the party, and before anyone moved she had grabbed Captain Talvar Ulhaq by the head and begun to twist, to twist so hard that he screamed at the top of his voice, because his neck was on the point of snapping like a straw.

Good News Hyder grabbed her sister by the hair and pulled with all her might, feeling the burning heat of that supernatural passion scorch her fingers; then Omar Khayyam and Shahbanou and Raza Hyder and even Bilquìs joined in, as the guests sank further into their speechless stupor, aghast at this last expression of the impossible fantasy of the day. The combined efforts of the five desperate people succeeded in detaching Sufiya Zinobia's hands before Talvar Ulhaq's head was ripped off like a turkey's; but then she buried her teeth in his neck, giving him a second scar to balance that famous love-bite, and sending his blood spurting long distances across the gathering, so that all her family and many of the camouflaged guests began to resemble workers in a halal slaughterhouse. Talvar was squealing like a pig, and when they finally dragged Sufiya Zinobia off him she had a morsel of his skin and flesh in her teeth. Afterwards, when he recovered, he was never able to move his head to the left. Sufiya Zinobia Hyder, the incarnation of her family's shame and also, once again, its chief cause, fell limply into her fiancé's arms, and Omar Khayyam had assailant and victim taken immediately to hospital, where Talvar Ulhaq remained on the critical list for one hundred and one hours, while Sufiya Zinobia had to be brought out of her self-induced trance by the exercise of more hypnotic skill than Omar had ever been required to display. Good News Hyder spent her wedding night weeping inconsolably on her mother's shoulder in a hospital waiting-room. 'That monster,' she sobbed bitterly, 'you should have had her drowned at birth.'

A short inventory of the effects of the wedding scandal: the stiff neck of Talvar Ulhaq, which terminated his career as a polo star; the birth of a spirit of forgiveness and reconciliation within Raza Hyder, who found it hard to ostracize a man whom his daughter had almost killed, so that Talvar and Good News were not, after all, cast out of the bosom of that accursed family; also the acceler-ated disintegration of Bilquìs Hyder, whose breakdown could no longer be concealed, even though she became, in the following years, little more than a whisper or rumour, because Raza Hyder kept her away from society, under a kind of unofficial house arrest.

What else? – When it became clear that Iskander Harappa's Popular Front would do extremely well in the elections, Raza paid a call on Isky. Bilquìs stayed at home with her hair hanging loose, railing at the heavens because her husband, her Raza, had gone to abase himself before that blubber-lips who always got everything he wanted. Hyder tried to force himself to apologize for the wedding fiasco, but Iskander said merrily, 'For God's sake, Raza, Haroun can take care of himself, and as for your Talvar Ulhaq, I'm pretty impressed by the coup that fellow engineered. I tell you, he's the man for me!' Not long after this meeting, once the insanity of the elections had passed and President Shaggy Dog had retired into private life, Prime Minister Iskander Harappa made Talvar Ulhaq the youngest police chief in the country's history, and also promoted Raza Hyder to the rank of General and placed him in command of the Army. Hyders and Harappas moved north to the new capital in the hills; Isky told Rani, 'From now on Raza has no option but to be my man. With the amount of scandal sitting on his head, he knows he'd have been lucky to keep his commission if I hadn't come along.'

Haroun Harappa, his heart broken by Good News, flung himself into the party work given him by Iskander, becoming an important figure in the Popular Front; and when, one day, Arjumand declared her love, he told her bluntly, 'Nothing I can do. I have decided never to marry.' The rejection of the virgin Ironpants by Good News's jilted fiancé engendered in that formidable young woman a hatred of all Hyders which she would never lose; she took the love she had intended to give Haroun and poured it like a votive offering over her father instead. Chairman and daughter, Iskander and Arjumand: 'There are times,' Rani thought, 'when she seems more like his wife than I do.' And another unspoken tension in the Harappa camp was that between Haroun Harappa and Talvar Ulhaq, who were obliged to work together, which they did for many years without ever finding it necessary to exchange a single spoken word.

The quiet marriage of Omar Khayyam Shakil and Sufiya Zinobia went off, by the way, without further incident. But what of Sufiya Zinobia? – Let me just say for the moment that what had reawoken in her did not go back to sleep for good. Her transformation from Miss Hyder into Mrs Shakil will not be (as we shall see) the last permanent change . . .

And along with Iskander, Rani, Arjumand, Haroun, Raza, Bilquìs, Dawood, Naveed, Talvar, Shahbanou, Sufiya Zinobia and Omar Khayyam, our story now moves north, to the new capital and the ancient mountains of its climactic phase.

Once upon a time there were two families, their destinies inseparable even by death. I had thought, before I began, that what I had on my hands was an almost excessively masculine tale, a saga of sexual rivalry, ambition, power, patronage, betrayal, death, revenge. But the women seem to have taken over; they marched in from the peripheries of the story to demand the inclusion of their own tragedies, histories and comedies, obliging me to couch my narrative in all manner of sinuous complexities, to see my 'male' plot refracted, so to speak, through the prisms of its reverse and 'female' side. It occurs to me that the women knew precisely what they were up to – that their stories explain, and even subsume, the men's. Repression is a seamless garment; a society which is authoritarian in its social and sexual codes, which crushes its women beneath the intolerable burdens of honour and propriety, breeds repressions of other kinds as well. Contrariwise: dictators are always – or at least in public, on other people's behalf – puritanical. So it turns out that my 'male' and 'female' plots are the same story, after all.

I hope that it goes without saying that not all women are crushed by any system, no matter how oppressive. It is commonly and, I believe, accurately said of Pakistan that her women are much more impressive than her men . . . their chains, nevertheless, are no fictions. They exist. And they are getting heavier.

If you hold down one thing you hold down the adjoining.

In the end, though, it all blows up in your face.

IV

In the Fifteenth Century

9

❦

ALEXANDER THE GREAT

Iskander Harappa stands in the foreground, finger pointing towards the future, silhouetted against the dawn. Above his patrician profile the message curls; from right to left the flowing golden shapes. A NEW MAN FOR A NEW CENTURY. The fifteenth century (Hegiran calendar) peeps over the horizon, extending long fingers of radiance into the early sky. The sun rises rapidly in the tropics. And glinting on Isky's finger is a ring of power, echoing the sun . . . the poster is omnipresent, stamping itself on the walls of mosques, graveyards, whorehouses, staining the mind: Isky the sorcerer, conjuring the sun from the black depths of the sea.

What is being born?–A legend. Isky Harappa rising, falling; Isky condemned to death, the world horrified, his executioner drowned in telegrams, but rising above them, shrugging them off, a compassionless hangman, desperate, afraid. Then Isky dead and buried; blind men regain their sight beside his martyr's grave. And in the desert a thousand flowers bloom. Six years in power, two in jail, an eternity underground . . . the sun sets quickly, too. You can stand on the coastal sandspits and watch it dive into the sea.

Chairman Iskander Harappa, dead, stripped of Pierre Cardin

and of history, continues to cast his shadow. His voice murmurs in his enemies' secret ears, a melodious, relentless monologue gnawing their brains like a worm. A ring finger points across the grave, glinting its accusations. Iskander haunts the living; the beautiful voice, golden, a voice holding rays of dawn, whispers on, unsilenced, unstoppable. Arjumand is sure of this. Afterwards, when the posters have been torn down, in the aftermath of the noose which, winding round him like a baby's umbilical cord, maintained such respect for his person that it left no mark upon his neck; when she, Arjumand, has been shut away in once-more-looted Mohenjo, along with a mother who looks like a grand-mother and who will not accept her dead husband's divinity; then the daughter remembers, concentrating on details, telling herself the time will come for Iskander to be restored to history. His legend is in her care. Arjumand stalks the brutalized passages of the house, reads cheap love-fiction, eats like a bird and takes laxatives, empties herself of everything to make room for the memories. They fill her up, her bowels, her lungs, her nostrils; she is her father's epitaph, and she knows.

From the beginning, then. The elections which brought Iskander Harappa to power were not (it must be said) as straight-forward as I have made them sound. As how could they be, in that country divided into two Wings a thousand miles apart, that fan-tastic bird of a place, two Wings without a body, sundered by the land-mass of its greatest foe, joined by nothing but God . . . she remembers that first day, the thunderous crowds around the polling stations. O confusion of people who have lived too long under military rule, who have forgotten the simplest things about democracy! Large numbers of men and women were swept away by the oceans of bewilderment, unable to locate ballot-boxes or even ballots, and failed to cast their votes. Others, stronger swimmers in those seas, succeeded in expressing their preferences twelve or thirteen times. Popular Front workers, dis-tressed by the general lack of electoral decorum, made heroic attempts to save the day. Those few urban constituencies making returns incompatible with the West-Wing-wide polling pattern were visited at night by groups of enthusiastic party members, who helped the returning officers to make a recount. Matters were much clarified in this way. Outside the errant polling stations large numbers of democrats assembled, many holding burning brands above their heads in the hope of shedding new light on the count. Dawn light flamed in the streets, while the crowds chanted loudly, rhythmically, spurring on the returning officers in their labours. And by morning the people's will had been expressed, and Chairman Isky had won a huge and absolute majority of the West Wing's seats in the new National Assembly. *Rough justice*, Arjumand remembers, *but justice all the same.*

The real trouble, however, started over in the East Wing, that festering swamp. Populated by whom?—O, savages, breeding endlessly, jungle-bunnies good for nothing but growing jute and rice, knifing each other, cultivating traitors in their paddies. Perfidy of the East: proved by the Popular Front's failure to win a single seat there, while the riff-raff of the People's League, a regional party of bourgeois malcontents led by the well-known incompetent Sheikh Bismillah, gained so overwhelming a victory that they ended up with more Assembly seats than Harappa had won in the West. *Give people democracy and look what they do with it.* The West in a state of shock, the sound of one Wing flapping, beset by the appalling notion of surrendering the government to a party of swamp aborigines, little dark men with their unpronounceable language of distorted vowels and slurred consonants; perhaps not foreigners exactly, but aliens without a doubt. President Shaggy Dog, sorrowing, dispatched an enormous Army to restore a sense of proportion in the East.

Her thoughts, Arjumand's, do not dwell on the war that followed, except to note that of course the idolatrous nation positioned between the Wings backed the Eastern bastards to the hilt, for obvious, divide-and-rule reasons. A fearful war. In the West, oil-refineries, airports, the homes of God-fearing civilians bombarded by heathen explosives. The final defeat of the Western forces, which led to the reconstitution of the East Wing as an autonomous (*that's a laugh*) nation and international basket case, was obviously engineered by outsiders: stonewashers and damn-yankees, yes. The Chairman visited the United Nations and bawled those eunuchs out: 'You won't destroy us while I'm alive.' He stormed out of the General Assembly, handsome, intemperate, great: 'My country hearkens for me! Why should I stay in this harem of transvestite whores?'—and returned home to take up the reins of government in what was left of the land of God. Sheikh Bismillah, the architect of division, became chief of the junglees. Later, inevitably, they swarmed into his palace and shot him and his family full of holes. Sort of behaviour one expects from types like that.

The catastrophe: throughout the war, hourly radio bulletins described the glorious triumphs of the Western regiments in the East. On that last day, at eleven a.m., the radio announced the last and most spectacular of these feats of arms; at noon, it curtly informed its audience of the impossible: unconditional surrender, humiliation, defeat. The traffic stood still in city streets. The nation's lunch remained uncooked. In the villages, the cattle went unfed and the crops unwatered despite the heat. Chairman Iskander Harappa, on becoming Prime Minister, correctly identified the national reaction to the astounding capitulation as one of just rage, fuelled by shame. What calamity could have befallen an Army so rapidly? What reversal could have been so sudden and so total as to turn victory into disaster in a mere sixty minutes? 'Responsibility for that fatal hour,' Iskander pronounced, 'lies, as it must, at the top.' Policemen, also dogs, surrounded the home of ex-President Shaggy within fifteen minutes of this decree. He was taken to jail, to be tried for war crimes; but then the Chairman, reflecting, once again, the mood of a people sickened by defeat and yearning for reconciliation, for an end to analyses of shame, offered Shaggy a pardon in return for his acceptance of house arrest. 'You are our dirty laundry,' Iskander told the incompetent old man, 'but, lucky for you, the people don't want to see you beaten clean upon a stone.'

There were cynical people who sneered at this pardon; that is needless-to-say, since all nations have their nihilists. These elements pointed out that Iskander Harappa had been the principal beneficiary of the civil war that ripped his country in half; they spread rumours of his complicity in the whole sad affair. 'Shaggy Dog,' they muttered in their shabby dens, 'was always Harappa's pet; ate out of Isky's hand.' Such negativistic elements are an ugly fact of life. The Chairman treated them with contempt. At a rally attended by two million people, Iskander Harappa unbuttoned his shirt. 'What have I to hide?' he shouted. 'They say I have benefited; but I have lost fully half my beloved country. Then tell me, is this gain? Is this advantage? Is this luck? My people, your hearts are scarred by grief; behold, my heart bears the same wounds as yours.' Iskander Harappa tore off his shirt and ripped it in half; he bared his hairless breast to the cheering, weeping crowd. (The young Richard Burton once did the same thing, in the film *Alexander the Great*. The soldiers loved Alexander because he showed them his battle scars.)

Some men are so great that they can be unmade only by themselves. The defeated Army needed new leadership; Isky packed off the discredited old guard into early retirement, and put Raza Hyder in control. 'He will be my man. And with such a compromised leader the Army can't get too strong.' This single error proved to be the undoing of the ablest statesman who ever ruled that country which had been so tragically misfortunate, so accursed, in its heads of state.

They could never forgive him for his power of inspiring love. Arjumand at Mohenjo, replete with memories, allows her remembering mind to transmute the preserved fragments of the past into the gold of myth. During the election campaign it had been common for women to come up to him, in full view of his wife and daughter, and declare their love. Grandmothers in villages perched on trees and called down as he passed: 'O, you, if I were thirty years younger!' Men felt no shame when they kissed his feet. Why did they love him? 'I am hope,' Iskander told his daughter . . . and love is an emotion that recognizes itself in others. People could see it in Isky, he was plainly full of the stuff, up to the brim, it spilled out of him and washed them clean. – Where did it come from? – Arjumand knows; so does her mother. It was a diverted torrent. He had built a dam between the river and its destination. Between himself and Pinkie Aurangzeb.

In the beginning Arjumand had hired photographers to snap Pinkie secretly, Pinkie in the bazaar with a plucked chicken, Pinkie in the garden leaning on a stick, Pinkie naked in the shower like a long dried date. She left these pictures for the Chairman to see. 'Look, Allah, she's fifty years old, looks a hundred, or seventy anyway, what is kept in her?' In the photographs the face was puffy, the legs vein-scarred, the hair careless, thin, white. 'Stop showing me these pictures,' Iskander shouted at his daughter (she remembers because he almost never lost his temper with her), 'don't you think I know what I did to her?'

If a great man touches you, you age too quickly, you live too much and are used up. Iskander Harappa possessed the power of accelerating the ageing processes of the women in his life. Pinkie at fifty was beyond turkeys, beyond even the memory of her beauty. And Rani had suffered, too, not so badly because she had seen less of him. She had been hoping, of course; but when it became clear that he only wanted her to stand on election platforms, that her time was past and would not return, then she went back to Mohenjo without any argument, becoming once more the mistress of peacocks and game-birds and badminton-playing concubines and empty beds, not so much a person as an aspect of the estate, the benign familiar spirit of the place, cracked and cobwebby just like the ageing house. And Arjumand herself has always been accelerated, mature too young, precocious, quick as needles. 'Your love is too much for us,' she told the Chairman, 'we'll all be dead before you. You feed on us.'

But they all outlived him, as it turned out. His diverted love (because he never saw Pinkie again, never lifted a telephone or wrote a letter, her name never passed his lips; he saw the photographs and after that nothing) splashed over the people, until one day Hyder choked off the spring.

It splashed, too, over Arjumand; for whom it was more than enough. She moved in with him to the Prime Minister's residence in the new northern capital, and for a while Rani kept writing to her, suggesting boys, even sending photographs; but Arjumand would return the letters and the photographs to her mother after ripping them to shreds. After several years of tearing potential husbands in half the virgin Ironpants finally defeated Rani's hopes, and was allowed to continue down her chosen road. She was twenty-three when Isky became Prime Minister, she looked older, and although she was still far too beautiful for her own good the passage of time eroded her prospects, and at last she ran out of suitors. Between Arjumand and Haroun nothing more was said. *He tore me in half long ago.*

Arjumand Harappa qualified in the law, became active in the green revolution, threw zamindars out of their palaces, opened dungeons, led raids on the homes of film stars and slit open their mattresses with a long two-edged knife, laughed as the black money poured out from between the pocketed springs. In court she prosecuted the enemies of the state with a scrupulous ferocity that gave her nickname a new and less ribald meaning; once she arrived at her chambers to find that some joker had broken in during the night and had left, standing in the centre of the room, a mocking gift: the lower half of an antique and rusty suit of armour, a pair of satirical metal legs placed at attention, heels together, on the rug. And laid neatly across the hollow waist, a padlocked metal belt. Arjumand Harappa, the virgin Ironpants.

That night she cried, sitting on the floor of her father's study, her head resting on his knee. 'They hate me.' Iskander grabbed her and shook her until the astonishment dried the tears. 'Who hates you?' he demanded, 'just ask that. It is my enemies who are yours, and our enemies are the enemies of the people. Where's the shame in being hated by those bastards?' She understood then how love engenders hate. 'I am making this country,' Iskander told her quietly, 'making it as a man would build a marriage. With strength as well as caring. No time for tears if you're going to help.' She wiped her eyes and grinned. 'Polygamist,' she punched his leg, 'what an old-fashioned backward type at heart! It's just marriages and concubines you want. Modern man, my foot.'

'Mr. Harappa,' the Angrez television interviewer is asking, 'many commentators would say, there is a widely-held view, some sectors of opinion maintain, your opponents allege, what would you say to the suggestion, that by some standards, from certain points of view, in a way, your style of government might be described as being perhaps, to some extent . . .'

'I see they are sending children to interview me now,' Isky interposes. The interviewer has begun to sweat. Off-camera, but Arjumand remembers.

'. . . patrician,' he finishes, 'autocratic, intolerant, repressive?'

Iskander Harappa smiles, sits back in his Louis Quinze chair, sips roohafza from a cut-glass tumbler. 'You could say,' he replies, 'that I do not suffer fools gladly. But, as you see, I suffer them.'

Arjumand at Mohenjo replays her father's videotapes. Played in the room where it was made, this conversation overwhelms her, this electronic resurrection by remote control. Yes, he suffered them. His name was etched on history in letters of burning gold; why should he go for brassy types? Here they are on the tape, trust a Western journalist to go digging in the cess-tank and come up holding handfuls of scum. He tortured me, they whine, he fired me, he put me in jail, I ran for my life. Good television: make our leaders look like primitives, wild men, even when they have foreign educations and fancy suits. Yes, always the malcontents, that's all they care about.

He never liked arguments. Do as he ordered and do it now, fut-a-fut, or out on your ear you go. This was as it should be. Look what he had to work with – even his ministers. Turncoats, nest-featherers, quislings, timeservers, the lot of them. He trusted none of these characters, so he set up the Federal Security Force with Talvar Ulhaq at its head. 'Information is light,' Chairman Iskander Harappa said.

The clairvoyance of Talvar Ulhaq enabled him to compile

exhaustive dossiers on who-was-bribing-whom, on conspiracies, tax evasion, dangerous talk at dinner parties, student sects, homo-sexuality, the roots of treason. Clairvoyancy made it possible for him to arrest a future traitor before he committed his act of treason, and thus save the fellow's life. The negativist elements attacked the FSF, they would have put out that great cleansing light, so off to jail they went, best place for malcontents. No time for such types during a period of national regeneration. 'As a nation we have a positive genius for self-destruction,' Iskander told Arjumand once, 'we nibble away at ourselves, we eat our children, we pull down anyone who climbs up. But I insist that we shall survive.'

'Nobody can topple me,' Isky's ghost tells the electronic shade of the Angrez journalist, 'not the fat cats, not the Americans, not even you. Who am I? I am the incarnation of the people's love.'

❧

Masses versus classes, the age-old opposition. Who loved him? 'The people', who are no mere romantic abstractions: who are sensible, and smart enough to know what serves them best. Who loved him? Pinkie Aurangzeb, Rani Harappa, Arjumand, Talvar, Haroun. What dissensions among this quintet! — Between wife and mistress, mother and daughter, jilted Arjumand and jilting Haroun, jilted Haroun and usurping Talvar . . . perhaps, Arju-mand muses, his fall was our fault. Through our divided ranks they drove the regiments of his defeat.

They. Fat cats, smugglers, priests. City socialites who remem-bered his carefree youth and could not tolerate the thought that a great man had sprung out of that debauched cocoon. Factory bosses who had never paid as much attention to the maintenance of their workers as they lavished on the servicing of their imported looms, and whom he, the Chairman, forced to accept the unthinkable, that is, unionization. Usurers, swindlers, banks. The American Ambassador.

Ambassadors: he got through nine of them in his six years. Also five English and three Russian heads of mission. Arjumand and

Iskander would place bets on how long each new arrival would survive; then, happy as a boy with a new stick and hoop, he would set about giving them hell. He made them wait weeks for audiences, interrupted their sentences, denied them hunting licences. He invited them to banquets at which the Russian Ambassador was served birds'-nest soup and Peking Duck, while the American got borshch and blinis. He refused to flirt with their wives. With the British Ambassador he would pretend to be a hick just down from the villages, and speak only in an obscure regional dialect; in the case of the United States, however, he took the opposite tack and addressed their legate in incomprehensibly florid French. Embassies would constantly be subjected to power cuts. Isky would open their diplomatic bags and personally add outrageous remarks to the Ambassadors' reports, so that one Russian was summoned home to explain certain unusual theories of his about the parentage of various leading Politburo chiefs; he never returned. The Jack Anderson column in America carried a leaked document in which the U.S. delegate to Iskander's court had apparently confessed that he had long felt a strong sexual attraction towards Secretary Kissinger. That was the end of that Ambassador. 'It took time to get into my stride,' Iskander admitted to Arjumand, 'but once I got the hang of it, those guys never got any sleep.'

He had two-way bugs placed in their telephones and after that the Soviet Ambassador was plagued by interminable recordings of *Hail to the Chief* whenever he picked up his receiver, while the American got the complete thoughts of Chairman Mao. He smuggled a series of beautiful young boys into the British Ambassador's bed, much to the consternation, not to say delight, of his wife, who developed thereafter the habit of retiring to her room very early, just in case. He expelled cultural attachés and agricultural attachés. He summoned the Ambassadors to his office at three in the morning and screamed at them until dawn, accusing them of conspiring with religious fanatics and disaffected textile tycoons. He blocked their drains and censored their incoming mail, depriving the English of their subscription copies of horse-racing journals, the Russians of *Playboy* and the Americans of everything else. The last of the nine Americans lasted only eight weeks, dying of a heart attack two days before the coup which dethroned Isky and ended the game. 'If I last long enough,' the Chairman mused, 'maybe I can destroy the whole international diplomatic network. They'll run out of Ambassadors before I run out of steam.'

In the fifteenth century a great man came to power. Yes, he seemed omnipotent, he could trifle with the emissaries of the might, *look at me*, he was saying, *you can't catch me*. Immortal, invulnerable Harappa. He gave people pride . . . the tenth American Ambassador arrived after Iskander's arrest, and expression of blessed relief on his face. When he presented his credentials to Raza Hyder he murmured quietly, 'Forgive me, sir, but I hope you lack your predecessor's sense of humour.'

'The question of national stability,' Hyder replied, 'is no joke.'

Once, when Arjumand visited her father in his hell-hole of a jail, Iskander, bruised, wasted, sick with dysentery, forced a grin to his lips. 'This tenth bastard sounds like a real shit,' he said painfully. 'I wish I could have made it into double figures.'

In the fifteenth century . . . but the century did not, despite posters, turn in the year of his accession. That happened later. But such was the impact of his coming that the actual change, thirteen hundred into fourteen hundred, felt like an anticlimax when it finally occurred. *His greatness overpowered Time itself.* A NEW MAN FOR A NEW CENTURY . . . yes, he ushered it in, ahead of Time. But it did the dirty on him. Time's revenge: it hung him out to dry.

They hanged him in the middle of the night, cut him down, wrapped him up and gave him to Talvar Ulhaq, who put him into a plane and flew him to Mohenjo, where two women waited, under guard. When the body had been unloaded the pilot and crew of the Fokker Friendship refused to leave the aircraft. The plane waited for Talvar at the top of Mohenjo's runway, giving off a nervous haze, as if it could not bear to stay in that place an instant longer than necessary. Rani and Arjumand were driven by staff car to Sikandra, that outlying zone of Mohenjo where Harappas had always been buried. And saw amid the marble umbrellas of the tombs a fresh, deep hole. Talvar Ulhaq at attention beside the white-swathed body. Rani Harappa, white-haired now, like the phantom of Pinkie Aurangzeb, refused to cry. 'So it's him,' she said. Talvar bowed, stiff-necked, from the waist. 'Prove it,' said Rani Harappa. 'Show me my husband's face.'

'You should spare yourself,' Talvar replied. 'He was hanged.'

'Be quiet,' Rani said. 'Pull back the sheet.'

'I greatly regret,' Talvar Ulhaq bowed again, 'but I have orders.'

'What orders?' Rani did not raise her voice. 'Who can deny me such a thing?' But Talvar said again, 'Sincerely. I regret,' and lowered his traitor's eyes. Talvar and Raza, policeman and soldier: Isky's men.

'Then something is the matter with the body,' Rani said, at which Talvar stiffened. 'Your husband is dead,' he snapped, 'what can be the matter with him now?'

'Then let me kiss him through the sheet,' Rani whispered, and bent down to the swaddled shape. Talvar did not attempt to stop her, until he realized what she was up to, and by then her nails had clawed a great hole in the cloth, and there, staring up at her with open eyes, was Iskander's ash-grey face.

'You didn't even close them,' Arjumand spoke for the first time. But her mother fell silent, staring intently at fleshy lips, at silver hair, until they pulled her away . . . 'Go on,' Rani said, 'bury the evidence of your shame. I have seen it now.' The sun leapt over the horizon as they laid Iskander down.

'When you hang a man,' Rani Harappa said distantly in the returning car, 'the eyes bulge. The face turns blue. The tongue sticks out.'

'Amma, for God's sake.'

'The bowels open, but they could have cleaned that up. I smelled some disinfectant.'

'I won't listen to this.'

'Maybe even the face, they have people to fix such things, to cut off the tongue so that the lips will shut. Maybe make-up artists were employed.'

Arjumand Harappa covered her ears.

'But one thing remains. On a hanged man's neck the rope leaves its mark. Iskander's neck was clean.'

'This is disgusting,' Arjumand said, 'I'll be sick.'

'Don't you understand?' Rani Harappa shouted at her. 'If the rope did not mark him, it must be because he was already dead. Are you to stupid to see? *They hanged a corpse.*'

Arjumand's hands fell to her lap. 'O God.' The mark-free neck: absence of death's visiting card. Seized by a sudden unreason, Arjumand cried, 'Why are you talking so big, Amma? What do you know about hangings and all?'

'You have forgotten,' Rani said mildly, 'I saw Little Mir.'

That day Rani Harappa tried, for the last time, to call her old friend Bilquìs Hyder on the telephone.

'I'm sorry,' a voice said, 'Begum Hyder cannot come to talk.'

'Then it's true,' Rani thought, 'poor Bilquìs. He has her shut away as well.'

Rani and Arjumand were kept under house arrest for six years exactly, two before the execution of Iskander Harappa, four after it. During that time they completely failed to draw closer to each other, owing to the incompatibility of their memories. But the one thing they did have in common was that neither of them ever wept over Iskander's death. The presence at Mohenjo of a small canvas mountain-range of Army tents, which had been thrown up as if by an earthquake in that same courtyard in which Raza Hyder had once staked himself to the ground, kept their eyes dry. That is to say, they were living on usurped soil, in occupied territory, and they were determined not to let the invaders see their tears. Their chief warder, a certain Captain Ijazz, a young barrel of a fellow with toothbrush hair and a persistent fuzz on his upper lip which obstinately refused to thicken into a moustache, at first attempted to goad them into it. 'God knows what you women are,' he shrugged. 'You rich bitches. Your man is dead but you will not wet his grave.' Rani Harappa refused to be provoked. 'You are right,' she replied, 'God knows. And He also knows about young men in uniforms. Brass buttons cannot hide a thing from Him.'

During those years spent beneath the suspicious eyes of soldiers and in the cold breezes of her daughter's solitude Rani Harappa continued to embroider woollen shawls. 'House arrest changes very little,' she admitted to Captain Ijazz at the very beginning, 'speaking for myself. It just means there are new faces around to say a few words to now and then.'

'Don't start imagining I'm your friend,' Ijazz shouted, the sweat glistening on his fuzzy mouth. 'Once we've killed that bastard we'll confiscate this house. All this gold, silver, all those dirty foreign paintings of naked women and of men who are half horse. It must go.'

'Start with the pictures in my bedroom,' Rani advised him. 'They are worth the most money. And let me know if you need help to sort out the real silver from the plate.'

Captain Ijazz was less than nineteen years old when he came to Mohenjo, and in the confusion of his youth he swung violently between the braggadocio born of his embarrassment at being sent to guard such illustrious ladies, and the incompetent awkward shyness of his years. When Rani Harappa offered to assist him with the looting of Mohenjo the flint of his shame ignited the tinder of his pride and he ordered his men to make a pile of valuables in front of the verandah where she sat, her face neutral and composed, and worked upon a shawl. Babar Shakil in his brief youth had burned one heap of relics; Captain Ijazz, who had never heard of the boy who became an angel, reignited that bonfire at Mohenjo, the bonfire in which men burn what oppresses them about the past. And throughout that day of flame Rani Harappa guided the vandalizing soldiers, making sure the choicest pieces of furniture and the finest works of art found their way into the blaze.

Two days later Ijazz came up to Rani, who was in her rocking-chair as usual, and apologized gracelessly for his intemperate deed. 'No, it was a good idea,' she replied, 'I didn't like that old stuff anyway, but Isky would have gone wild if I'd tried to throw it out.' After the fire-looting of Mohenjo, Ijazz started treating Rani Harappa with respect, and by the end of the six years he had begun to think of her as a parent, because he had grown up in front of her eyes. Deprived of a normal life and of the cama-raderie of the barracks, Ijazz took to pouring his heart out to Rani, all his half-formed dreams of women and of a small farm in the north.

'It's my fate,' Rani thought, 'to get mistaken for people's mothers.' She remembered that even Iskander had started making that mistake by the end. The last time he visited Mohenjo he bent down and kissed her feet.

The two women each took their revenge on their captor. Rani made him love her, with the result that he hated himself; but Arjumand began to do what she had never done in her life, that is, she dressed to kill. The virgin Ironpants swung her hips and wiggled her behind and flashed her eyes at all the soldiers, but most of all at the peach-faced Captain Ijazz. The effect of her behaviour was dramatic. Fights broke out in the little canvas Himalayas, teeth were broken, soldiers inflicted knife-wounds on their comrades. Ijazz himself was screaming inwardly, in the grip of a lust so fierce that he thought he would explode, like a balloon full of coloured water. He cornered Arjumand one afternoon while her mother was asleep. 'Don't think I don't know what you're up to,' he warned her, 'you millionaire whores. Think you can do anything. In my village a girl would have been stoned for acting like you do, such cheapness, you know what I mean.'

'Then have me stoned,' Arjumand retorted, 'I dare you.'

One month later Ijazz spoke to her again. 'The men want to rape you,' he yelled helplessly, 'I can see it in their faces. Why should I stop them? I should permit it; you are bringing this shame on your own head.'

'Let them come, by all means,' Arjumand replied, 'but you must be the first.'

'Harlot,' he cursed her in his impotence, 'don't you know you're in our power? Nobody cares one paisa what happens to you.'

'I know,' she said.

By the end of the period of house arrest, when Arjumand had Captain Ijazz imprisoned and tortured slowly to death, he was twenty-four years old; but his hair, like that of the late Iskander Harappa, had gone permanently white as snow. When they took him to the torture chambers he said just three words before he started screaming: 'So, what's new?'

Rani Harappa, rocking on her verandah, completed in six years of embroidery a total of eighteen shawls, the most exquisite pieces she ever created; but instead of showing off her work to daughter or soldiers, she placed each shawl, on completion, in a black metal trunk full of naphthalene balls and fastened the lock. The key to this trunk was the only one she had been permitted to keep. Captain Ijazz kept all the rest on a large ring hanging from his belt, which reminded Rani of Bilquìs Hyder, the Bilquìs who locked doors compulsively under the influence of the afternoon wind. *Poor Bilquìs*. She, Rani, missed their telephone conversations. The deeds of men had severed that link between the women, that nourishing cord which had, at different times, carried messages of support first one way, then the other, along its unseen pulses.

Can't be helped. Rani, phlegmatically, worked on her perfect shawls. At first Captain Ijazz had tried to deny her needles and thread, but she shamed him out of that quickly enough. 'Don't think I'm going to stab myself on account of you, boy,' she told him. 'Or what do you suppose? Will I hang myself, perhaps, by a noose of embroidery wool?' The serenity of Iskander's wife (this was before he died) won the day. Ijazz even agreed to requisition balls of wool in the colours and weights she specified from the military quartermaster-stores; and then once again she began to work, to weave the shawls, those soft fields, and then to raise upon them the vivid and magical crops of her sorceress's art.

Eighteen shawls locked in a truck: Rani, too, was perpetuating memories. Harappa the martyr, the demigod, lived on in his daughter's thoughts; but no two sets of memories ever match, even when their subject is the same . . . Rani never showed her work to anyone until, years later, she sent the trunk to Arjumand as a gift. Nobody ever looked over her shoulder as she worked. Neither soldiers nor daughter were interested in what Mrs Harappa did to while away her life.

An epitaph of wool. The eighteen shawls of memory. Every artist has the right to name her creation, and Rani would put a piece of paper inside the trunk before she sent it off to her newly powerful daughter. On this piece of paper she would write her chosen title: 'The Shamelessness of Iskander the Great.' And she would add a surprising signature: *Rani Humayun*. Her own name, retrieved from the mothballs of the past.

What did eighteen shawls depict?

Locked in their trunk, they said unspeakable things which nobody wanted to hear: the badminton shawl, on which, against a lime-green background and within a delicate border of overlapping racquets and shuttlecocks and frilly underpants, the great man lay unclothed, while all about him the pink-skinned concubines cavorted, their sporting outfits falling lightly from their bodies; how brilliantly the folds of breeze-caught garments were portrayed, how subtle the felicities of light and shade! – the female figures seemed unable to bear the confinements of white shirts, brassières, gymshoes, they flung them off, while Isky lounging on his left flank, propped up on an elbow, received their ministrations, *yes, I know, you have made a saint of him, my daughter, you swallowed everything he dished out, his abstinence, his celibacy of an Oriental Pope, but he could not do without for long, that man of pleasure masquerading as a servant of Duty, that aristocrat who insisted on his seigneurial rights, no man better at hiding his sins, but I knew him, he hid nothing from me, I saw the white girls in the village swell and pop, I knew about the small but regular donations he sent them, Harappa children must not starve, and after he fell they came to me;* and the slapping shawl, Iskander a thousand times over raising his hand, lifting it against ministers, ambassadors, argumentative holy men, mill-owners, servants, friends, it seemed as if every slap he ever delivered was here, *and how many times he did it, Arjumand, not to you, to you he would not have, so you will not believe, but see upon the cheeks of his contemporaries the indelible blushes engendered by his palm;* and the kicking shawl, Iskander booting bottoms and provoking in their owners other feelings than love; and the hissing shawl, Iskander seated in the office of his glory, its details accurate in the most minute degree, so that one could almost smell that awesome chamber, that place of pointed concrete arches with his own Thoughts framed upon the wall, and the Mont Blanc pens like black alps in their holders on his desk, even their white stars picked out by her scrupulous needle; that room of shadows and of power, in which no shadow was empty, eyes glinted in every area of shade, red tongues flicked, silver-threaded whispers susurrated across the cloth: Iskander and his spies, the head spider at the heart of that web of listeners and whisperers, she has sewn the silvery threads of the web, they radiated out from his face, in silver thread she revealed the arachnid terrors of the days, when men lied to their sons and angry women had only to murmur to the breeze to bring a fearsome revenge down upon their lovers, *you never felt the fear, Arjumand, of wondering what he knew;* and the torture shawl, on which she embroidered the foetid violence of his jails, blindfolded prisoners tied to chairs while jailers hurled buckets of water, now boiling hot (the thread-steam rose), now freezing cold, until the bodies of the victims grew confused and cold water raised hot burns upon their skins: weals of red embroidery rose scarlike on the shawl; and the white shawl, embroidered white on white, so that it revealed its secrets only to the most meticulous and squinting eyes: it showed policemen, because he had given them new uniforms, white from head to toe, white helmets with silver spikes, white leather holsters, white jackboots up to the knee, policemen running discothèques in which the booze flowed freely, white bottles with white labels, white powders sniffed from the white backs of gloves, *he turned a blind eye, understand, he wanted the police strong and the Army weak, he was dazzled, daughter, by whiteness*; and the swearing shawl, Iskander's mouth as wide as the Abyss, the oaths represented by foul creatures crawling from his lips, vermilion cockroaches, magenta lizards, turquoise leeches, ochre scorpions, indigo spiders, albino rats, *because he never stopped that either, how selective, Arjumand, your ears*; and the shawls of international shame, Isky grovelling at primrose Chinese feet, Isky conspiring with Pahlevi, embracing Dada Amin; eschatological Iskander, riding an atomic bomb; Harappa and Shaggy Dog like cruel boys slitting the throat of an emerald chicken and plucking the feathers from its east wing, one by one; and the election shawls, one for the day of suffrage that began his reign, one for the day that led to his downfall, shawls swarming with figures, each one a breathtakingly lifelike portrait of a member of the Front, figures breaking seals, stuffing ballot-boxes, smashing heads, figures swaggering into polling booths to watch the peasants vote, stick-waving rifle-toting figures, fire-raisers, mobs, and on the shawl of the second election there were three times as many figures as on the first, but despite the crowded field of her art not a single face was anonymous, every tiny being had a name, it was an act of accusation on the grandest conceivable scale, *and of course he'd have won anyway, daughter, no question, a respectable victory, but he wanted more, only annihilation was good enough for his opponents, he wanted them squashed like cockroaches under his boot, yes, obliteration, and in the end it came to him instead, don't think he wasn't surprised, he had forgotten he was only a man*; and the allegorical shawl, Iskander and the Death of Democracy, his hands around her throat, squeezing Democracy's gullet, while her eyes bulged, her face turned blue, her tongue protruded, she shat in her pajamas, her hands became hooks trying to grab the wind, and Iskander with his eyes shut squeezed and squeezed, while in the background the Generals watched, the murder reflected by a miracle of the needlewoman's skill in the mirrored glasses they all wore, all except one, with deep black circles around his eyes and easy tears on his cheeks, and behind the Generals other figures, peeping over uniformed shoulders, through epaulettes, under armpits, crew-cut Americans and Russians in baggy suits and even the great Zedong himself, they all watched, they didn't have to lift a finger, *no need to look beyond your father, Arjumand, no need to hunt conspirators, he did their work for them, they didn't even have to break wind, I am hope, he used to say, and so he was, but he took off that cloak and turned into something else,* Iskander the assassin of possibility, immortalized on a cloth, on which she, the artist, had depicted his victim as a young girl, small, physically frail, internally damaged: she had taken for her model her memory of an idiot, and consequently innocent, child, Sufiya Zinobia Hyder (now Shakil), gasping and empurpled in Iskander's unyielding fist; and the autobiographical shawl, the portrait of the artist as an old crone, that self-portrait in which Rani had depicted herself as being composed of the same materials as the house, wood, brick, tin, her body merging into the fabric of Mohenjo, she was earth and cracks and spiders, and a fine mist of oblivion clouded the scene; that was the fourteenth shawl, and the fifteenth was the shawl of the fifteenth century, the famous poster recreated in thread, Iskander pointing at the future, only there was nothing on the horizon, no dawn-fingers, just the endless waves of night; and then Pinkie's shawl, on which she committed suicide; and the last two were the worst: the shawl of hell, which, as Omar Khayyam Shakil had discovered as a child, lay in the west of the country in the vicinity of Q., where the separatist movement had grown out of all recognition in the wake of the secession of the East, proliferation of sheep-fuckers, but Iskander had done for them, there it all was in scarlet, scarlet and nothing but scarlet, what he did for the sake of no-more-secessions, in the name of never-another-East-Wing, the bodies sprawled across the shawl, the men without genitals, the sundered legs, the intestines in place of faces, the alien legion of the dead blotting out the memory of Raza Hyder's governorship, or even giving that period, in retrospect, a kindly, tolerant glow, *because there was no comparison, daughter, your man of the people, your master of the common touch, I have lost count of the corpses on my shawl, twenty, fifty, a hundred thousand dead, who knows, and not enough scarlet thread on earth to show the blood*, the people hanging upside down with dogs at their open guts, the people grinning lifelessly with bullet-holes for second mouths, the people united in the worm-feast of that shawl of flesh and death; and Little Mir Harappa on the last of all the shawls, Little Mir buried at the bottom of a trunk, but of course he rose to clasp his cousin in his own phantasmal grip, to drag Iskander Harappa down to hell . . . her eighteenth shawl and her supreme masterpiece, a panoramic landscape, the hard earth of her exile stretched across the cloth, from Mohenjo as far as Daro, villagers balancing buckets on shoulder-poles, horses running free, women tilling the soil, the dawn light kindled in miracles of rose and blue embroidery: Daro was coming awake, and from its great verandah, by the steps, something long and heavy was swinging in the breeze, a single death after the carnage of the seventeenth shawl, Little Mir Harappa dangling by the neck under the eaves of his family home, dead in the first months of the Chairman's reign, his sightless eyes staring down at the very spot where, once upon a time, the cadaver of an unloved dog had been permitted to decay, yes, she had delineated his body with an accuracy that stopped the heart, leaving out nothing, not the disembowelling, not the tear in the armpit through which Mir's own heart had been removed, not the torn-out tongue, nothing, and there was a villager standing beside the corpse, with his bewildered remark sewn in black above his head, 'It looks as if,' the fellow said, 'his body has been looted, like a house.'

It was, of course, for his alleged complicity in the murder of Little Mir Harappa that Iskander was put on trial for his life. Also indicted, for the actual performance of the crime, was the dead man's son Haroun. He, however, was tried *in absentia*, having fled the country, it was thought, although it was possible that he had simply vanished, gone to ground.

No murderers were depicted on Rani's eighteenth shawl . . .

but now that all eighteen have been spread out and admired, it is time to turn away from Harappas, from Rani and Arjumand sequestered in that house whose decay had reached the point at which the water trickled blood-red from rust-corroded taps. Time to turn back the clock, so that Iskander rises from the grave, but recedes, as well, into the background of the tale. Other people have been living lives while Harappas rose and fell.

10

THE WOMAN IN THE VEIL

There was once a young woman, Sufiya Zinobia, also known as 'Shame'. She was of slight build, had a weakness for pine-kernels, and her arms and legs were imperfectly co-ordinated when she walked. Despite this ambulatory awkwardness, however, she would not have struck a stranger as being particularly abnormal, having acquired in the first twenty-one years of life the usual complement of physical attributes, including a small severe face that made her seem unusually mature, disguising the fact that she had only managed to get hold of around seven years' worth of brains. She even had a husband, Omar Khayyam Shakil, and never complained that her parents had chosen for her a man fully thirty-one years her senior, that is to say, older than her own father. Appearances notwithstanding, however, this Sufiya Zinobia turned out to be, in reality, one of those supernatural beings, those exterminating or avenging angels, or werewolves, or vampires, about whom we are happy to read in stories, sighing thankfully or even a little smugly while they scare the pants off us that it's just as well they are no more than abstractions or figments; because we know (but do not say) that the mere likelihood of their existence would utterly subvert the laws by which we live, the processes by which we understand the world.

Lurking inside Sufiya Zinobia Shakil there was a Beast. We have already seen something of the growth of this unspeakable monster; we have seen how, feeding on certain emotions, it took possession of the girl from time to time. On two occasions she fell grievously ill and almost died; and perhaps both illnesses, brain-fever and immunological collapse, were attempts by her ordinary self, by the Sufiya-Zinobia-ness of her, to defeat the Beast, even at the cost of her own life. But the Beast was not destroyed. And maybe somebody should have guessed, after the attack on her brother-in-law, that whatever other-than-Beastly part of her remained was gradually losing its ability to resist the blood-creature within. But when Omar Khayyam's whispering voice finally found the way to unlock her trance, she woke up fresh and relaxed and seemingly unaware of having terminated Talvar's polo-playing career. The Beast had nodded off again, but the bars of its cage had been broken. Still, there was general relief. 'Poor girl got so upset she went wild, that's all,' Shahbanou the ayah told Omar Khayyam, 'but she's O.K. now, thank God.'

Raza Hyder summoned Shakil to a conference and honourably offered him the opportunity of withdrawing from the proposed marriage. On hearing this the antique divine Maulana Dawood, who was also present, refused to remain silent. His original opposition to the nuptials lost in the foggy labyrinths of his great age, the old man whined like a malicious bullet. 'That she-devil and this child of she-devils,' he cried, 'let them make their hell together, in some other place.' Omar Khayyam replied with dignity, 'Sir, I am a man of science; to the devil with this talk of devils. I will not cast off a loved one because she fell ill; it is, rather, my duty to make her well. And this is being done.'

I am no less disappointed in my hero than I was; not being the obsessive type, I find it difficult to comprehend his obsession. – But I must admit that his love for the damaged girl is beginning to seem as if it might be genuine . . . which does not invalidate my criticisms of the fellow. Human beings have a remarkable talent for persuading themselves of the authenticity and nobility of aspects of themselves which are in fact expedient, spurious, base. – At any rate: Omar Khayyam insisted on going ahead with the match.

Bilquìs Hyder, her senses distracted by the events of Good News's wedding day, proved incapable of entering into the spirit of a second marriage. When Sufiya Zinobia left hospital her mother refused to speak to her; but on the eve of the wedding she came to where Shahbanou was oiling the girl and twining her hair, and spoke so ponderously that it was plain that each word was a heavy weight which she was hauling up from the fathomless well of her duty. 'You must think of yourself as the ocean,' she told Sufiya Zinobia. 'Yes, and he, the man, imagine him a sea creature, because that is what men are like, to live they must drown in you, in the tides of your secret flesh.' Her eyes roamed loosely around her face. Sufiya Zinobia pulled a face at these incomprehensible maternal abstractions and replied obstinately in her voice of a seven-year-old girl, which was also the eerily disguised voice of the latent monster: 'I hate fish.'

What is the most powerful impulse of human beings in the face of night, of danger, of the unknown? – It is to run away; to avert the eyes and flee; to pretend the menace is not loping towards them in seven-league boots. It is the will to ignorance, the iron folly with which we exercise from consciousness whatever consciousness cannot bear. No need to invoke the ostrich to give this impulse symbolic form; humanity is more wilfully blind than any flightless bird.

At Sufiya Zinobia's wedding (a private affair; no guests, no marquees; the three mothers of Q. stayed away, Dawood absented himself also, leaving only Hyders and lawyers and Shakil) Raza Hyder forced Omar Khayyam to agree to the insertion in the Nikah contract of a clause forbidding him, Omar, to remove his bride from her parents' home without their prior permission. 'A father,' Raza explained, 'cannot do without the precious pieces of his heart,' from which it can be seen that his new love for Sufiya was burning more brightly than ever, and blinded by the glare of that flame he refused to see the truth of her. In the following years he persuaded himself that by locking up his wife, by veiling her in walls and shuttered windows, he could save his family from the malign legacy of her blood, from its passions and its torments (for if Sufiya Zinobia's soul was in agony, she was also the child of a frenzied woman, and that, too, may be an explanation of a kind).

Omar Khayyam also refused to see. Blinded by science, he married Hyder's daughter. Sufiya Zinobia smiled and ate a plate of laddoos decorated with silver paper. Shahbanou the ayah fussed round her like a mother.

I repeat: there is no place for monsters in civilized society. If such creatures roam the earth, they do so out on its uttermost rim, consigned to peripheries by conventions of disbelief . . . but once in a blue moon something goes wrong. A Beast is born, a 'wrong miracle', within the citadels of propriety and decorum. This was the danger of Sufiya Zinobia: that she came to pass, not in any wilderness of basilisks and fiends, but in the heart of the respectable world. And as a result that world made a huge effort of the will to ignore the reality of her, to avoid bringing matters to the point at which she, disorder's avatar, would have to be dealt with, expelled – because her expulsion would have laid bare what-must-on-no-account-be-known, namely the impossible verity that barbarism could grow in cultured soil, that savagery could lie concealed beneath decency's well-pressed shirt. That she was, as her mother had said, the incarnation of their shame. To comprehend Sufiya Zinobia would be to shatter, as if it were a crystal, these people's sense of themselves; and so of course they would not do it, they did not, not for years. The more powerful the Beast became, the greater grew the efforts to deny its very being . . . Sufiya Zinobia outlived most members of her family. There were those who died for her.

No more dreams of failure, no more square-bashing with green recruits; Raza Hyder got his promotion from Iskander Harappa, and Omar Khayyam Shakil agreed to move north with everyone else. His high medical reputation and Hyder's renewed influence secured for Omar the post of senior consultant at the Mount Hira hospital in the new capital, and then they were off, bedrolls and ayahs and all, and soon they were airborne over the wide northern plateau that lay between two great rivers, the Potwar plateau, the stage on which great scenes were to be played out, seventeen hundred feet above sea-level.

Thin soil over porous pudding-stone . . . but in spite of the soil's thinness the plateau produced improbable quantities of rain-nourished crops; it was a terrain of such unlikely fertility that it had managed to raise a whole new city like a blister on the hip of an old town. *Islamabad* (you might say) out of *Rawalpindi*'s rib.

Maulana Dawood, looking down from the skies and seeing the Potwar plateau with its cities gleaming in the distance, banged on the cabin window in dribbling, half-senile delight. 'Arafat,' he shouted at the top of his voice, alarming a stewardess, 'we are come to Arafat,' and nobody, not Raza his friend, not Bilquìs his enemy, had the heart to set him right, because if the old man had chosen to believe that they were about to land on the holy ground of the Arafat plain outside Mecca Sharif, well, that, too, was a kind of blindness, a fantasy forgivable in the old.

General Raza Hyder inherited from his predecessor a lugubrious seven-foot ADC named Major Shuja, and also an Army so unnerved by its defeat in the former East Wing that it could no longer win so much as a football game. Understanding the intimate relationship between sport and war, the new Commander-in-Chief took it upon himself to attend every possible athletic contest involving his boys, hoping to inspire the teams by his presence. So it was that during the first months of his chieftancy Raza Hyder was present at the most remarkable series of humiliations in the annals of Army sport, beginning with the legendary inter-services cricket game in which the Army XI lost all ten first-innings wickets without scoring a single run off the bat. Their Air Force opponents piled up a formidable reply, because the war had largely been an Army disaster, and so the airmen remained, for the most part, unaffected by the disgrace. The Army cricketers finally lost the game by an innings and 420 runs; it would have been 419 except that one of the Army's second-innings runs was never completed, because the player in question appeared to lose heart in mid-sprint, stopped, scratched his head, stared about distractedly, and failed even to notice when he was run out . . . Hyder witnessed, too, the hockey match in which the Navy boys scored forty times in eighty minutes while the soldiers stared glumly at their curved sticks as if they were rifles, such as the ones surrendered on the day of reckoning in the East; and at the new National Swimming Baths he saw with his own eyes a double tragedy, one Army diver never surfacing after botching a dive so completely that he preferred to drown rather than emerge from the waters of his shame, while another got himself in an even worse tangle, taking off from the high board and landing on his belly with a noise like a gunshot, bursting open like a paint-balloon and forcing the authorities to drain the pool so that they could tidy away his guts. After this the mournful figure of Major Shuja presented itself to the General in his office and suggested that perhaps it would be better, begging for pardon, sir, if the C-in-C Sahib would stay away from such events, as his presence was intensifying the jawans' shame and making matters worse than ever.

'Son of a gun,' Raza cried, 'how come the entire Army turned into a bunch of blushing women overnight?'

'The war, sir,' replied Shuja, speaking from the well of a desolation so profound that he no longer cared about his career prospects, 'and, beg for pardon, General, but you weren't involved in that scrap.'

Now Raza understood that his troops were joined in the terrible solidarity of their shared humiliation, and guessed at last why it was that not one of his fellow officers had ever offered him a fizzy drink in the officers' mess. 'I thought it was jealousy,' he rebuked himself, and said to Shuja, who was waiting glumly at attention for the demotion his insolence deserved: 'O.K., Major; what's your solution?'

The unexpectedness of the question startled Shuja into honesty. 'Permission to speak frankly, sir?' Hyder nodded: 'Man to man. You, me and the gatepost.'

'Then, beg for pardon, sir, but a return to Army rule. Takeover, sir.'

Hyder was amazed. 'Do people always talk treason in this town?'

The gloom surrounding the ADC thickened further. 'The General Sahib asked, sir, and I only said. Young officers are restless, sir, this is an Army town, the Army is used to power, and sir, everyone knows what these politicos are like, no good, sir, not suitable, the officers remember when they had respect, but now they feel so depressed, sir, seems like anyone can kick the Army around these days. Beg for pardon, sir.'

'The devil with your coup,' Hyder told him fiercely, 'the way things are right now half a dozen of Isky Harappa's ex-mistresses could take the whole Army apart.'

'Yes, sir,' Shuja said, and burst, astoundingly, into tears. General Hyder reminded himself that the young giant wasn't much over eighteen; and then his own notoriously over-active tear-ducts began to smart in sympathy, so he said quickly, 'For God's sake, man. Nobody's going to court-martial you. Just get your priorities right. Let's win a few polo matches before thinking of taking over the country.'

'Very good, sir,' Shuja controlled himself, 'I shall convey the General's view to the polo squad, sir.'

'What a life,' Raza Hyder said aloud when he was alone. 'The higher you climb, the thicker the blasted mud.' It was lucky for the country, he mused, that Old Razor Guts was accustomed to standing on his own two feet.

The restoration of the Army's morale, it would be fair to say, was the crowning glory of Raza Hyder's career – it was a tougher job, in my opinion, than anything he undertook when President. How did he do it? – He lost wrestling matches.

The morning after his conversation with Major Shuja he instructed the ADC to select opponents for him, mostly from the common soldiers, but also from a cross-section of the officers. 'I am keen on wrestling,' he lied, 'and it's time I saw what stuff our Army *phaelwans* are made of.'

General Raza Hyder fought with one hundred and eleven soldiers and was thrashed by them all. He made no attempt to win, concentrating, instead, on the far more difficult business of losing against opponents who had forgotten that it was possible to win; of losing, moreover, while giving the impression of struggling for victory with all his might. 'You can see what good it's doing,' he told Omar Khayyam Shakil, who acted as the General's personal physician before and after each bout, and who was alarmed by the phenomenal battering being given to that forty-nine-year-old body. 'Yes,' Omar Khayyam replied, ministering to aching bones and rainbow bruises, 'any fool can see that.' Raza Hyder wept freely as he lay beneath Shakil's probing fingers, but he called them tears of joy.

The wrestling strategy of Raza Hyder gained him a double victory. It helped the Army to accept his leadership, because now he was united with his men in that macabre fellowship of shame. As Old Razor Guts was drop-kicked in the jaw, dumped on canvas with his ankles knotted round his neck, throttled by an infantryman's arm; as his ribs snapped and his arms left their sockets, the old popularity of the hero of Aansu was reborn; cleansed of the dust and anonymity of his Staff College years, it shone once again, like new. Yes, Razor Guts was back, bigger than ever . . . but Raza had been after more than that, and his second purpose was also achieved, because as the soldiers in camp after camp participated in, or witnessed from roaring ringsides, the pulverization of the one genuine war hero left in the Army, they began to regain faith in themselves, they began to believe that if they were good enough to dump the General in the dirt they couldn't be such pathetic fighting men as they had come to imagine. After one year of wrestling Raza Hyder called a halt. He had lost both upper central incisors and sustained countless other injuries. 'I don't have to take this any more,' he told Shuja, whose air of permanent dejection (although somewhat reduced) now stood revealed as a personality flaw and not simply the product of the lost, and now almost forgotten, war.

'Tell those bastards,' Raza instructed him, 'that I expect all personnel to win every competition they enter from now on, or else.' There followed an electrifying improvement in Army sporting results.

I have lingered on this business of Army morale to indicate why it was that during his years as Commander-in-Chief Raza Hyder did not have the time or the mental energy to pay proper attention to what his daughter Sufiya Zinobia was getting up to in the nights.

The politicos and diplomats were in charge of the new city but the Army dominated the old town. The new capital was composed of numerous concrete edifices which exuded an air of philistine transience. The geodesic dome of the Friday Mosque had already begun to crack, and all around it the new official buildings preened themselves as they, too, fell apart. The air-conditioning broke down, the electric circuits shorted, flush water kept bubbling up into washbasins to the consternation of the plumbers . . . O vilest of cities! Those buildings represented the final triumph of a modernism that was really a kind of pre-stressed nostalgia, form without function, the effigy of Islamic architecture without its heart, buildings containing more Mughal arches than the Mughals could ever have imagined, arches reduced by pre-stressed concrete to mere pointy holes in walls. The new capital was in reality the biggest collection of airport terminals on earth, a garbage dump for unwanted transit lounges and customs halls, and maybe that was appropriate, because democracy had never been more than a bird of passage in those parts, after all . . . the old town possessed, by contrast, the confident provinciality of its years. Old, wide, tree-lined streets, chaotic bazaars, slums, the solidly outsized mansions of the departed Angrez rulers. The C-in-C's official residence was a neo-classical palace of stone porticoes with massive fluted pillars supporting mock-Grecian, friezed pediments, and there were little piles of cannonballs lining the grand steps up to the front door; a wheeled gun apocryphally named 'Little Zamzama' guarded the bright-green lawn. The place was spacious that the whole family moved in without any arguments, so that Good News and Talvar Ulhaq, Omar Khayyam and Sufiya Zinobia, Dawood and Shahbanou the ayah, as well as Raza and Bilquìs, pursued their several destinies beneath that ample roof, while the alien gods of Greece and Rome, posing stonily against the high blue sky, looked down on them with supercilious expressions on their faces.

Things did not go well.

'As if this crazy Army isn't bad enough,' Raza told himself in those first northern days, 'here's my own house filling up with mad persons,' and it seemed as though the occupants of that anachronistic palace set about turning his angry exaggeration into the literal truth.

When Maulana Dawood appeared one morning wearing the traditional garb of a pilgrim on the Hajj, in two white cloths, one wound around his loins and the other hooped negligently across his chest, General Raza Hyder was forced to entertain the possibility that the fossilized divine had finally succumbed to the tide of senility which had begun washing over him during their flight into the north. At first he tried to deal kindly with his old ally. 'Maulanaji,' he said, 'if you want to perform the pilgrimage you just have to say the word, I'll fix everything, plane tickets to Arabia and all,' but Dawood only replied, 'Why do I need aircraft when I am already walking upon this sacred ground?' After that the Maulana took to tottering around town with his hands opened before him like a book, intoning verses from the Quran in an Arabic which the loss of his reason led him to adulterate with other, coarser dialects; and in the grip of that senility which made him imagine that he saw the peaks of faraway Abu Qubais, Thabir and Hira behind the town, and which led him to mistake a bicycle factory for the cemetery in which the Prophet's wife lay buried, he began to abuse the townspeople for their irreligious blasphemies, because of course the men were improperly attired and the women were a disgrace, they laughed in his face when he called them whores. He was a mad old man asking the way to the Kaaba, a beardy fool in his second childhood who prostrated himself outside fish-shops as if they were the holy places of Mecca and yelled 'Ya Allah!' In the end his body was brought back to the Hyder residence on a donkey-cart, whose puzzled owner said that the old fellow had expired with the words, 'There it is! – And they are covering it with shit.' He had wandered to the edge of the old town to the place where the new water purification tanks had recently been filled with activated sludge, and Raza Hyder tried hard to pretend that this was the obvious, banal reason for the Maulana's last words; but in reality he was profoundly disturbed, because being a religious man he had never found himself capable of dismissing Maulana Dawood's antics as mere senilities; the *gatta* bruise on Raza's forehead ached and suggested to him that perhaps the old Maulana really had seen a vision of Mecca, a revelation of holiness in the midst of this unholy town, so that his dying words might contain an awful, cryptic warning. 'The Kaaba,' Raza's own voice whispered tremulously in his ear, 'it must have been, he must have seen it at last, and they were pouring excrement on it.' Later, when he was President, he would be unable to get this vision out of his mind.

At the end of the first year of civilian rule, General Raza Hyder became a grandfather. Good News gave birth to fine, healthy twin sons, and the General was so delighted that he forgot all about Sindbad Mengal. Exactly one year later Good News became a mother again; this time she produced triplets. Raza Hyder was a little alarmed and joked nervously to Talvar Ulhaq: 'You said you would be the perfect son-in-law, but, baba, five grandsons is enough, maybe you are overdoing your duty.' Precisely twelve months later Good News brought forth a beautiful quartet of baby girls, whom Hyder loved so much that he decided not to express his concern about the growing numbers of cradles and comforters and washing-lines and rattles clogging up the house. Five more granddaughters turned up one year later to the day, and now

Hyder had to say something. 'Fourteen kids with the same birthday,' he told the couple as sternly as he could manage, 'what do you think you're up to? Haven't you heard of the population problem? You should take, perhaps, certain steps, but at that Talvar Ulhaq drew himself up until his whole body was as stiff as his neck and replied, 'Sir, I never thought to hear you say such a thing. You are a devout man, I thought. Maulana Dawood's ghost would blush if it heard General Hyder recommend such Godless procedures.' So Hyder felt ashamed and shut his mouth, and in the fifth year Good News's womb released six more new lives, three male, three female, because Talvar Ulhaq in the pride of his manhood had chosen to ignore Hyder's remark about too-many-grandsons; and in the year of Iskander Harappa's fall the number rose to twenty-seven children in all, and by that time everyone had lost count of how-many-boys-how-many-girls.

Begum Naveed Talvar, the former Good News Hyder, proved utterly incapable of coping with the endless stream of humanity flowing out between her thighs. But her husband was relentless, insatiable, his dream of children had expanded to fill up the place in his life previously occupied by polo, and owing to his clair-voyant talents he always knew which nights were best for concep-tion. He came to her once a year and ordered her to get ready, because it was time to plant the seed, until she felt like a vegetable patch whose naturally fertile soil was being worn out by an over-zealous gardener, and understood that there was no hope for women in the world, because whether you were respectable or not the men got you anyway, no matter how hard you tried to be the most proper of ladies the men would come and stuff you full of alien unwanted life. Her old personality was getting squashed by the presence of the children who were so numerous that she forgot their names, she hired an army of ayahs and abandoned her offspring to their fate, and then she gave up trying. No more attempts to sit on her hair: the absolute determination to be beau-tiful which had entranced first Haroun Harappa and then Cap-tain Talvar faded from her features, and she stood revealed as the plain, unremarkable matron she had always really been. Arjumand

Harappa, whose hatred of Good News had not been diminished by the years, kept herself informed of her enemy's decline. A photographer who had once taken pictures of Pinkie Aurangzeb was employed to snatch images of Good News; Arjumand showed these slides to Haroun Harappa, carelessly, as if they didn't matter. 'Poor old bachelor boy,' she taunted him, 'to think you could have spent your whole life with this gorgeous floozy if she hadn't found somebody better.'

The Loo does not blow in the north, but still, on some afternoons, Bilquìs would hold the furniture down to stop it blowing away. She roamed the corridors of her new, palatial home mumbling inaudibly under her breath, until one day she raised her voice loud enough for Raza Hyder to hear. 'How does a rocket rise to the stars?' she asked vaguely, because she was really still talking to herself. 'It is never easy to leave the earth. As the machine rises up, it loses parts of itself, they drop off and fall back, until finally the nose, only the nose gets free of the pull of the land.' Raza Hyder frowned and said, 'God knows what you're rambling on about, woman,' but in spite of this remark, and his subsequent suggestion to Omar Khayyam that Bilquìs's mind had begun to wander like her feet, he knew what she had meant, which was that although he had risen, just as she had prophesied, to the very peak of his profession, people had been falling away from him as he rose; other human beings were the burned-out stages of his flight towards shoulder-stars. Dawood, Good News, Bilquìs herself: 'Why should I feel ashamed?' he asked himself. 'I did nothing to them.'

Things had been chipping away at Bilquìs for years, firewinds and pennant-waving knights and murdered cinema managers and not having sons and losing her husband's love and brain-fever and turkeys and erratum slips, but the worst thing of all was to be there, in that palace, that queenly residence of which she had always dreamed, and to discover that that wasn't any good either, that nothing worked out, everything turned to ashes. Ruined by the hollowness of her glory, she was finally broken by the decline of her favourite Good News, who lay suffocating beneath the soft avalanche of her children and would not be comforted . . . one morning they all saw Bilquìs putting on a black burqa, taking the veil or purdah, even though she was indoors and only family members and servants were present. Raza Hyder asked her what she thought she was doing, but she just shrugged and replied, 'It was getting too hot, so I wanted to draw the curtains,' because by now she was scarcely capable of speaking except in metaphors. Her mumbles were full of curtains and oceans and rockets, and soon everybody got used to it, and to that veil of her solipsism, because everyone had their own problems. Bilquìs Hyder became, in those years, almost invisible, a shadow hunting the corridors for something it had lost, the body, perhaps, from which it had come unstuck. Raza Hyder made sure she stayed indoors . . . and the house ran itself, there were servants for everything, and the mistress of the C–in–C's residence became less than a character, a mirage, almost, a mumble in the corners of the palace, a rumour in a veil.

Rani Harappa telephoned occasionally. Bilquìs would sometimes come to the phone, sometimes not; when she did she spoke so quietly and in such slurred accents that Rani found it hard to understand what was being said, discerning only a deep bitterness, as if Bilquìs had begun to resent her friend, as if Hyder's almost discarded wife still had enough pride to dislike the way Iskander had picked up her husband and made him great. 'Your husband, Rani,' she once said, loud and clear, 'he'll never be happy until Raza lies down and licks his boots.'

General Hyder would remember to his dying day the time he had visited Iskander Harappa to discuss the defence budget and been slapped across the face for his pains. 'Expenditure is falling below acceptable levels, Isky,' he informed the Prime Minister, and to his astonishment Harappa banged on his desk so fiercely that the Mont Blanc pens jumped in their holders and the shadows in the corners hissed with alarm. 'Acceptable to whom?' Iskander Harappa shouted. 'The Army does not say what goes, mister. No longer. Get that out of your head. If we allot you fifty paisa a year, then that is what you must make do with. Get that straight and get out.'

'Iskander,' Raza said without raising his voice, 'don't forget your friends.'

'A man in my position has no friends,' Harappa replied. 'There are only temporary alliances based on mutual self-interest.'

'Then you have ceased to be a human being,' Raza told him, and added thoughtfully: 'A man who believes in God must also believe in men.' Iskander Harappa flew into an even more terrifying rage. 'Look out, General,' he shrieked, 'because I can put you back in that dustbin where I found you.' He had rushed out from behind his desk and was screaming right into Raza's face, depositing spittle on the General's cheeks. 'God forgive you, Isky,' Raza murmured, 'you have forgotten that we are not your servants.' It was at this point that Iskander Harappa struck him on a spittle-moistened cheek. He did not strike back, but remarked softly, 'The blushes caused by such blows do not easily fade.' Years later, Rani Harappa would prove his point, by immortalizing such blushes on a shawl.

And in those later years, when Iskander Harappa was safely under the ground and his tough-as-nails daughter was locked away with her mother, Raza Hyder would find himself dreaming about that slap, and about all those years in which Isky Harappa had treated him like dirt. And Arjumand had been even worse, she had stared at him with such open hatred that he believed her capable of anything. Once Isky sent her, in his place, to the annual Army parade, just to humiliate the soldiers by making them salute a woman, and a woman, what was more, who had no official status in the government; and Raza had made the mistake of mentioning his worries to the virgin Ironpants. 'Maybe history has come between our houses,' he said, 'and things have gone wrong, but remember we aren't strangers, Arjumand, we go back along way.'

'I know,' she said witheringly, 'my mother is your cousin, I believe.'

❧

And Sufiya Zinobia?

She was his wife but she was not his wife. In Karachi on his wedding night Omar Khayyam had been prevented by a contractual clause from taking his bride away; instead, he was shown to a room containing a single bed and no Sufiya Zinobia anywhere. Shahbanou the ayah ushered him in and then stood obstinately in the doorway, her muscles tense. 'Doctor Sahib,' she said finally, 'you must tell me what are your intentions.' The fierce solicitude for Sufiya Zinobia which had driven Shahbanou to commit so outrageous a breach of social law, of the master-servant relationship, also prevented Omar Khayyam from becoming angry. 'Don't worry,' he soothed the ayah, 'I know the girl is simple. I have no desire to impose my, to force myself upon, to demand my marital,' whereupon Shahbanou nodded and said, 'That's O.K. for now, Sahib, but how long will you wait? Men are only men.'

'I will wait until my wife is agreeable,' Omar Khayyam replied angrily, 'I am no junglee man.' (But once – we remember – he had called himself a wolf-child.)

Shahbanou turned to go. 'Remember, if you get impatient,' she told him in a matter-of-fact voice, 'that I am waiting to kill you if you try.'

By the time of the move north, it was clear that Omar Khayyam had changed his ways. Like Iskander Harappa, but for different reasons, he gave up his old debauches: Raza Hyder would have settled for nothing less. The new, northern version of Omar Khayyam Shakil lived simply and worked hard: fourteen hours a day at the Mount Hira Hospital, except on those occasions when he stood in the General's corner during wrestling bouts. He returned to the C-in-C's residence only to eat and to sleep, but in spite of all the evidence of reformation, abstinence and dedication, Shahbanou continued to watch him like a hawk, not least because his already ample figure grew ever more corpulent in these days, so that when he joked with the ayah, 'Well, Banou, am I being a good boy or not?', she replied seriously, 'Omar Sahib, I can see you filling up with God knows what, and you are eating so little that it can't be food, so as far as I can tell it's only a matter of time before you lose control or burst. How difficult to be a man,' she said with a grave sympathy in her eyes.

That night he recognized Shahbanou's knock on his bedroom door. He hauled himself out of bed and arrived at the door puffing and patting his heart; to discover the ayah outside, holding a candle, her hair loose, her bony body of a tilyar bird half-visible through her cotton shift. 'What are you thinking of?' Omar Khayyam demanded in surprise, but she pushed her way past him and sat down solemnly on the bed.

'I don't want to kill anybody,' she explained in neutral tones, 'so I thought, better I do this instead.'

'How much you must love her,' Omar Khayyam marvelled. 'More than you,' she answered without criticism and quickly removed her shift.

'I'm an old man,' he told her later, 'so three times is at least two too many. Maybe you want to kill me anyway, and this is a simpler method.'

'It is not simple, Omar Sahib,' she replied, 'and you're not such a wreck as you say.'

After that she came to him every night, except during her times of the month and the days of fertility, and on those seven or eight nights he lay in the grip of his voluntary insomnia imagining her body like a wire beside him in the bed, and wondering about the strange destiny which had led him to marry one wife and to acquire quite a different one. After a while he realized that he had started to lose weight. The pounds were beginning to drop off him, and by the time of Harappa's fall he had become not exactly slim, because he would never be that, but he had shrunk out of all his suits (so it will be seen that his life and Isky's were still linked, because Isky, too, lost weight . . . but again, for different reasons. For different reasons); under the spell of the Parsee ayah he had diminished to remarkably normal dimensions. 'I may be no movie star,' he told his mirror, 'but I have also ceased to be a cartoon.' Omar Khayyam and Shahbanou: our peripheral hero has acquired a shadow bride, and his own shadow has been enabled, as a result, to grow less.

And Sufiya Zinobia?

. . . lies in bed squeezing her eyelids shut with her fingers hoping for the sleep she knows may never come. Feels on the skin of her eyelids the prickle of Shahbanou's stare. The ayah on the mat, watching waiting. Then she, Sufiya Zinobia, decides sleep is impossible, relaxes completely, drops her hands, pretends. She has found that this mimicry, this simulacrum of sleep, makes other people happy. She does it automatically now, has had plenty of practice, her breathing settles into a certain rhythm, there is a certain way of shifting the body at certain intuited intervals, a certain pattern to the behaviour of the eyeballs beneath the lids. After some time she hears Shahbanou rise from her mat, slip out of the room, go a few steps down the passage, knock. Insomnia sharpens the ears. She hears bedsprings, his exhalations, her bony cries. There is a thing that people do at night. Her mother told her oceans and fish. Behind her eyes she sees the Parsee ayah metamorphosing, becoming liquid, flowing outwards until she fills the room. Melted Shahbanou, salty, immense, and a transmogrifying Omar growing scales, fins, gills and swimming in that sea. She wonders what it's like afterwards, when they change back, how they tidy up the mess, how everything gets dry. (One morning she slipped into her husband's bedroom after he left for the hospital and Shahbanou went to count dirty garments with the dhobi. She felt the sheets with her hands, found damp patches. But an ocean should leave its mark: she scanned the floor for starfish, seaweed, shells. And found none: a mystery.)

She likes it now that she is sometimes left alone and the things can happen in her head, the favourite things she keeps in there, locked up; when people are present she never dares to take the things out and play with them in case they get taken away or broken by mistake. Big clumsy people all around, they don't mean to break things but they do. Inside her head the precious fragile toys. One of the best inside-things is when her father picks her up. Hugs, smiles at, cries over her. Says things she doesn't really understand but the sounds are nice. She takes him out of her head and makes him do it over and over, all of it, like having a bedtime story told six times running. You can't do that with the things outside your head. Sometimes they only happen once and you have to be quick and grab them and stuff them away in your secret place. Sometimes they never happen at all. There is a thing she has inside that has never happened anywhere else: her mother skips with her. Bilquìs holds the skipping rope and the two of them jump together, fasterfaster, until they are going so fast you can't see who is who any more, they could be one person held within the circle of the rope. It tires her out to play with this toy, not because of the skipping but because of the difficulty of doing things inside that you haven't brought there from the outside. Why are these inside-only things so much harder to do? And almost impossible to repeat overandover.

A special teacher comes most days and she likes that. She, the teacher, brings new things and Sufiya Zinobia puts some of these inside her head as well. There is a thing called the world that makes a hollow noise when you knock your knuckles on it or sometimes it's flat and divided up in books. She knows it is really a picture of a much bigger place called everywhere but it isn't a good picture because she can't see herself in it, even with a magnifying glass. She puts a much better world into her head, she can see everyone she wants to there. Omar Shahbanou Bilquìs Raza tiny on the tin. She waves down, the little ant family waves back up. Also writing, she can do that, too. In her secret place her favourite letters, the bumpy *sìn*, hockeystick *làm*, *mìm* with its chest puffed out like a turkey, write themselves over and over.

She packs her head full of good things so that there won't be room for the other things, the things she hates.

A picture of herself with dead birds. Who put that in there? And another one: she is biting somebody, hard. Sometimes these badnesses start repeating themselves like stuck records and it isn't easy to push them away and pick up her father's smile or the skipping rope instead. She knows she used to be ill and maybe these bad toys got left over from them.

And there are other things that don't seem to be from any-where. They come most often during the sleepless nights, shapes that make her feel like crying, or places with people hanging upside-down from the roof. She feels the things that get inside her must be her own fault. If she were good the bad things would go elsewhere, so that means she is not good. Why is she so bad? What makes her rotten, evil? She tosses in her bed. And pouring out from inside the fearsome alien shapes.

Often she thinks about *husband*. She knows what a *husband* is. Her father is a *husband*, also Talvar Ulhaq, and now she has one, too. What does that mean, to *have* a *husband*? What are they for? She can do most things for herself and Shahbanou helps with the rest. But she *has* a *husband*. It is another mystery.

Before the marriage she asked Shahbanou about this and put Shahbanou-answering into her head. She takes the ayah out and hears her say, overandover: 'They are for money and babies. But don't worry, bibi, money is no problem and babies aren't for you.' She can't understand this, no matter how often the picture plays. If money is no problem you shouldn't need husbands for it. *And babies aren't for you*. Why? 'Just, I say so.' But why? 'O shoo. Why why why away you fly.' It always ends like that, without explaining anything. But this husband business is important. She *has* one. Everyone else must know but she doesn't. Again her own stupid fault.

The best thing that has happened recently is the babies, her sister's babies. She, Sufiya, plays with them as often as she can. She likes watching them crawl, fall over, make funny noises, likes knowing more than them. She skips for them: O the wonder in their eyes. She puts them in her head and brings them out when the sleep won't come. Good News never plays with the babies. Why? No point asking. 'Why why pudding and pie.' In her head the babies laugh.

Then the bad shapes again, because if she has a husband, and a husband is for babies, but babies-aren't-for-you, then something must be wrong. This gives her a feeling. Just like a blush, all over, hot hot. But although her skin tingles and her cheeks burn it is only happening on the inside; nobody notices these new internal blushes. That is strange also. It makes the feeling worse. Sometimes she thinks, 'I am changing into something,' but when those words come into her head she doesn't know what they mean. How do you change into a something? The bad, wrong words and the feeling sharper and more painful. Go away go away go away. Go away.

There is a thing that women do at night with husbands. She does not do it, Shahbanou does it for her. *I hate fish.* Her husband does not come to her at night. Here are two things she does not like: that he does not come, that's one, and the thing itself makes two, it sounds horrible, it must be, the shrieks the moans the wet and smelly sheets. Chhi chhi. Disgusting. But she *is a wife.* She *has a husband.* She can't work this out. The horrible thing and the horrible not-doing-the-thing. She squeezes her eyelids shut with her fingers and makes the babies play. There is no ocean but there is a feeling of sinking. It makes her sick.

There is an ocean. She feels its tide. And, somewhere in its depths, a Beast, stirring.

The business of the disappearing children had been going on in the country's shanty-towns and slums for many years. There were various theories about these disappearances. It was suggested that the children were being abducted to the Gulf to provide cheap labour or to be exploited by Arab princelings in worse, unnamable ways. Some people maintained that the parents were the culprits, that they were doing away with the unwanted members of their outsize families. The mystery had never been solved. No arrests made, no slave-trade conspiracies unearthed. It became a fact of life: children simply vanished, in broad daylight, into thin air. Poof!

Then they found the headless bodies.

It was the year of the general election. After six years in power, Iskander Harappa and the Popular Front were campaigning hard.

Opposition was fierce, however: Isky's rivals had united to give him a tough fight. Economic criticisms were made; but also suggestions-of-Godlessness, vilification-of-arrogance, insinuations-of-corruption. It was widely supposed that the Front would lose every frontier constituency, both in the northwest and around Q. Also many seats in the towns. In short, people had plenty on their minds without worrying about a few dead paupers.

The four bodies were all adolescent, male, pungent. The heads had been wrenched off their necks by some colossal force: literally torn from their shoulders. Traces of semen were detected on their tattered pants. They were found in a rubbish dump near a slum. It seemed that the four of them had died more or less simultaneously. The heads were never found.

The election campaign was at fever-pitch. The murders barely made the newspapers; they were not reported on the radio. There were rumours, some gossip, but people were quickly bored. All kinds of God knows what-all could happen in those slums.

This is what happened.

The woman in the veil: a horror story.

Talvar Ulhaq was flying back to the capital from Q. when he had the vision. In those days the chief of the Federal Security Force was a busy man, hardly sleeping, racing around the country. It was election time, and Talvar was a member of Iskander Harappa's trusted inner circle, his act of betrayal was still in the future. So he was fully occupied, because Isky relied on the FSF to keep him one jump ahead of his opponents, to discover their plans, to infiltrate fifth-columnists into their headquarters and subvert their arrangements, to find grounds for arresting their leaders. He was busy with such matters in that aeroplane, so that when the damaged ligaments in his neck began to play up like the very devil, he gritted his teeth and ignored them, because he was running his eyes carefully over certain photographs of separatist Frontier politicos in bed with attractive young men who were, in fact, loyal employees of the FSF, working courageously and selflessly for their country. But then the vision came, and Talvar had to look up from his work, because it seemed to him that the cabin shimmered and dissolved, and then he was standing like a shadow on the wall of the Hyder residence, at night, watching the figure of Bilquìs Hyder, veiled as usual in a head-to-toe black burqa, moving towards him down a darkened corridor. As she passed him without glancing in his direction he was appalled to see that her burqa was sodden and dripping with something too thick to be water. The blood, black in the unlit corridor, left a trail down the passage behind her.

The vision faded. When Talvar got home he checked things out and discovered that nothing seemed amiss at the Hyder house, Bilquìs had not left the premises and everyone was fine, so he put the matter out of his mind and got on with his job. Later he confessed to General Raza Hyder, 'It's my mistake. I should have seen at once what was going on; but my thoughts were on other things.'

The day after his return from Q. Talvar Ulhaq heard about the four headless bodies, by the purest chance: two of his men were joking about the murders in the FSF canteen, wondering if they could pin the killings on well-known homosexual opposition bosses. Talvar went cold and cursed himself. 'You idiot,' he thought, 'no wonder your neck was hurting.'

He drove immediately to the Army GHQ, and asked Raza to accompany him into the gardens, to make sure they were not overheard. Hyder, in some confusion, did as his son-in-law requested.

Once they were outside in the heat of the afternoon Talvar recounted his vision, and admitted shamefacedly that he should have known that the figure he had seen had been too physically small to have been Bilquìs Hyder. It seemed to him, to, that on reflection there had been something a little loose and uncoordinated about its walk . . . 'Forgive me,' he said, 'but I think that Sufiya Zinobia has been sleepwalking again.' Such was the respect for his clairvoyant powers that Raza Hyder listened giddily, but without interruption, as Talvar continued, expressing the opinion that were Sufiya Zinobia to be subjected to a medical examination she would be found not to be virgo intacta, which would be highly indicative, because they all knew that her husband did not share her bed. 'Pardon my bluntness, sir, but I believe she had intercourse with the four young goondas before tearing off their heads.'

The image of his deranged daughter surrendering to that multiple deflowering, and then rising in her vengeance to rip her lovers to shreds, made Raza Hyder feel physically ill . . . 'Please understand, sir,' Talvar was saying respectfully, 'that I do not wish to proceed in this matter, except in accordance with your precise instructions. This is a family business.'

'How was I to know?' Raza Hyder, his voice arriving almost inaudibly from a great distance. 'Some birds, a bad temper at a wedding, then nothing for years. Kept thinking, what problem? Would go away, had gone. Fooled ourselves. Fools,' and then he was silent for several minutes. 'Could be the finish for me,' he added eventually, 'funtoosh, kaput, good night.'

'Can't be allowed, sir,' Talvar objected. 'The Army needs you, sir.'

'Good fellow, Talvar,' Raza mumbled, and then drifted off again until his son-in-law coughed and asked, 'So, how to proceed, sir?'

General Hyder snapped out of it. 'What do you mean?' he inquired. 'What is this proceed? What evidence is here? Only theory and mysticism. I will have none of it. How dare you make allegations on such a basis? To hell with this tomfoolery, mister. Don't waste my time.'

'No, sir.' Talvar Ulhaq came to attention. Tears were in the General's eyes as he put his arm around the younger man's braced shoulders.

'Got the message, hey, Talvar, boy? *Chup*: mum's the word.'

In the depths of the ocean the sea-Beast stirs. Swelling slowly, feeding on inadequacy, guilt, shame, bloating towards the surface. The Beast has eyes like beacons, it can seize insomniacs and turn them into sleepwalkers. Sleeplessness into somnambulism, girl into fiend. Time moves differently for the Beast. The years fly past like birds. And as the girl grows, as her understanding increases, the Beast has more to eat . . . Sufiya Zinobia at twenty-eight had advanced to a mental age of approximately nine and a half, so that when Shahbanou the ayah became pregnant that year and was dismissed from service on the grounds of her immorality, Sufiya knew what had happened, she had heard the night-time noises, his grunts, her birdlike cries. In spite of her precautions the ayah had conceived a child, because it's easy to miscalculate dates, and she left without a word, without attempting to apportion blame. Omar Khayyam kept in touch with her, he paid for the abortion and made sure she did not starve afterwards, but that solved nothing; the damage had been done.

Sufiya Zinobia stiff as a board in bed. Trying to bring the good things out of her head, babies, her father's smile. But instead there is only the thing inside Shahbanou, the thing that husbands make, because he did not give me the baby she took it inside her instead. She, Sufiya, possessed by fault and shame. That woman who loved me. And my husband, who can blame him, he never had a wife. Overandover in her empty room; she is a tide rising towards flood, she feels something coming, roaring, feels it take her, the thing, the flood or perhaps the thing in the flood, the Beast bursting forth to wreak its havoc on the world, and after that she knows nothing, will remember nothing, because it, the thing, is free.

Insomnia into somnambulism. The monster rises from the bed, shame's avatar, it leaves that ayah-empty room. The burqa comes from somewhere, anywhere, it has never been a difficult garment to find in that sad house, and then the walk. In a replay of the turkey disaster she bewitches the nocturnal guards, the eyes of the Beast blaze out of hers and turn the sentries to stone, who knows how, but later, when they awake, they are unaware of having slept.

Shame walks the streets of night. In the slums four youths are transfixed by those appalling eyes, whose deadly yellow fire blows like a wind through the lattice-work of the veil. They follow her to the rubbish-dump of doom, rats to her piper, automata dancing in the all-consuming light from the black-veiled eyes. Down she lies; and what Shahbanou took upon herself is finally done to Sufiya. Four husbands come and go. Four of them in and out, and then her hands reach for the first boy's neck. The others stand still and wait their turn. And heads hurled high, sinking into the scattered clouds; nobody saw them fall. She rises, goes home. And sleeps; the Beast subsides.

General Raza Hyder searched his daughter's room himself. When he found the burqa it was crackly, starched by the dried-on-blood. He wrapped it in newspaper and burned it to ashes. Then he threw the ashes out of the window of a moving car.

It was election day, and there were many fires.

11

MONOLOGUE OF A
HANGED MAN

Chairman Iskander Harappa developed a toothache thirty seconds before the jeeps surrounded his home in the capital of unwanted airport terminals. His daughter Arjumand had just said something that tempted fate, and whenever anybody did that it made all of Iskander's betel-blackened teeth howl with superstitious anguish, especially after midnight, when such things are even more dangerous than they seem in the daylight. 'The steam has gone out of the opposition,' Arjumand had suggested, much to her father's alarm. He had been musing in a contented after-dinner fashion about the rumoured escape of an albino panther in the wooded hills of Bagheeragali some forty miles away; forcing his thoughts out of those haunted woods he scolded his daughter, 'God knows how to wash off this optimism of yours; I'll have to dunk you in the reservoir behind the Barrage Dam.' Then his teeth began giving him hell, worse than ever before, and he said aloud in his surprise what he had suddenly thought: 'I am smoking the last but one cigar of my life.' No sooner had the prophecy left his lips than they were joined by an uninvited guest, an Army officer with the saddest face in the world, Colonel Shuja, for six years ADC to General Raza Hyder. The Colonel saluted and informed the Prime Minister of the coup. 'Beg for pardon, sir, but you must accompany me at once to the Bagheeragali rest house.' Iskander Harappa realized that he had failed to grasp the meaning of his reverie, and smiled at his own stupidity. 'You see, Arjumand,' he said, 'they want to feed me to the panther, isn't it so?' Then he turned to Shuja and asked who had given such orders. 'Chief Martial Law Administrator, sir,' the Colonel replied. 'General Hyder, sir, beg for pardon.'

'Look at my back,' Iskander told his daughter, 'and you will see a coward's knife.'

Thirty minutes later General Salmàn Tughlak, the Joint Chief of Staff, was hauled out of a noisy nightmare, in which the débâcle of the East Wing war was being replayed in slow motion, by the insistence of his telephone bell. General Tughlak was the only member of President Shaggy Dog's high command to have escaped the Harappa overhaul of the upper echelons of the Defence establishment, and for a moment the bad dream refused to leave him, so that he yelled distractedly into the telephone, 'What's up? Have we surrendered?'

'We've done it,' the voice of Raza Hyder said in some confusion.

General Tughlak was equally puzzled: 'Done what, for God's sake?'

'Ya Allah,' Raza Hyder panicked, 'didn't anybody tell you?' Then he began to stammer, because of course the Joint Chief was his superior officer, and if the boss refused to bring the Navy and Air Force out in support of the Army's initiative things could get pretty nasty. Thanks to the indecipherable stammer of his fear and the lingering mist of sleep enveloping General Tughlak, it took Raza Hyder over five minutes to make the Joint Chief understand what had happened that night.

'So?' Tughlak said at last. 'What now?'

Hyder's stammer improved; but he remained cautious: 'Excuse me, General,' he used delaying tactics, 'how do you mean, sir?'

'Damn it, man,' Tughlak exploded, 'what orders are you going to give?'

There was a silence during which Raza Hyder understood that it was going to be all right; then he said meekly, 'Tughlakji, you know, with your previous martial law experience and all . . .'

'Spit it out,' Tughlak commanded.

'. . . frankly, sir, we were hoping you could help us with that.'

'Bastard amateurs,' old Tughlak muttered happily, 'take over a government and you don't know your pricks from your sticks.' The opposition had never accepted the election results. Mobs in the cities cried corruption; there were fires, riots, strikes. The Army was sent to fire on civilians. Jawans and young officers murmured mutinous syllables, which were drowned at first by rifle-shots. And Arjumand Harappa tempted fate.

It is said that General Hyder was at first reluctant to move, doing so only when his colleagues gave him the choice of deposing Harappa or falling with him. But President Hyder denied this: 'I'm the type,' he said, 'who sees a mess and can't help cleaning it up.'

On the morning after the coup Raza Hyder appeared on national television. He was kneeling on a prayer-mat, holding his ears and reciting Quranic verses; then he rose from his devotions to address the nation. This was the speech in which the famous term 'Operation Umpire' was first heard by the people. 'Understand,' Raza said briskly, 'the Army seeks to be no more than an honest ref or ump.'

Where was Raza's right hand while he spoke? On what, while he promised fresh-elections-within-ninety-days, did his fingers rest? What, leatherbound and wrapped in silk, lent credibility to his oath that all political parties, including the Popular Front of 'that pluckiest fighter and great politician' Iskander Harappa, would be allowed to contest the rerun poll? 'I am a simple soldier,' Raza Hyder declared, 'but scandal is scandal, and unscandalling must be accomplished.' The television camera travelled down from his *gatta*-bruised face, down along his right arm, until the nation saw where his right hand rested: on the Holy Book.

Raza Hyder, Harappa's protégé, became his executioner; but he also broke his sacred oath, and he was a religious man. What he did later may well have been the result of his desire to cleanse his sullied name in the eyes of God.

That was how it began. Arjumand Harappa was packed off to Rani at Mohenjo; but Haroun Harappa was not caught. He had fled the country or gone underground . . . whichever it was, it seemed, in those first days, like a considerable over-reaction. Raza Hyder joked to General Tughlak: 'That is one heck of a stupid boy. Does he think I'm going to cut off his thing just because he wasn't good enough to marry my daughter?'

Chairman Iskander Harappa was detained in some comfort at the government rest house in Bagheeragali, where of course he was not eaten by a panther. He even retained the use of a telephone, for incoming calls only; the Western newspapers found out the number and Iskander gave long, eloquent interviews to many overseas journalists. In these interviews he made detailed accusations, casting numerous doubts on Raza Hyder's good faith, moral fibre, sexual potency and legitimacy of birth. Still Raza remained tolerant. 'That Isky,' he confided to Colonel Shuja, 'highly-strung bloke. Always was. And the chap is naturally upset; I'd be the same in his shoes. Also one must not believe everything one reads in the Christian press.'

'Suppose you hold elections and he wins, sir,' Colonel Shuja ventured as his face acquired the most dolorous expression Raza had ever seen on that unhappy countenance, 'beg for pardon, sir, but what'll he do to you?'

Raza Hyder looked surprised. 'What is this *do*?' he cried. 'To me? His old comrade, his family member by marriage? Have I tortured him? Have I thrown him in the public lock-up? Then what is there for him to do?'

'Family of gangsters, sir,' Shuja said, 'those Harappas, everyone knows. Revenge crimes and what-all, it's in their blood, beg for pardon, General.'

From that moment Raza Hyder's bruised forehead acquired deep furrows of thought, and two days later he announced to his ADC, 'We're going to see that fellow pronto and just sort everything out.'

Afterwards Colonel Shuja would swear that until the meeting between Raza and Iskander the General had never thought of assuming the Presidency. 'That stupid man,' he always stated when asked, 'brought his fate on his own head.' Shuja drove with General Hyder to Bagheeragali, and as the staff car climbed the hill roads their nostrils were assailed by the sweet scents of pine-cones and beauty, those aromas which had the power of lifting the heaviest hearts and making one think that nothing was insoluble. And at the Bagheeragali bungalow the ADC waited in an antechamber while the fateful conference took place.

Iskander Harappa's premonition about the cigars had come true, because in spite of all the air-conditioning units and cut-glass goblets and Shirazi rugs and other creature comforts at the rest house he had been unable to locate a single ashtray; and when he asked the guards to have a box of his favourite Havanas sent from his home they had politely told him it was impossible. The smoking ban possessed Isky's thoughts, wiping out his appreciation of his comfortable bed and good meals, because it was plain that somebody had ordered the guards to deny him his smokes, so he was being told something – *watch out* – and he didn't like it, no sir. The absence of cigar-smoke left a rancid taste in his mouth. He began to chew betel-nut non-stop, deliberately spitting the juice out on the priceless rugs, because his rage had begun to overcome the fastidious elegance of his true nature. The paans made his teeth hurt even more, so what with everything that had gone wrong inside his mouth it wasn't surprising his words turned bad as well ... Raza Hyder could not have been expecting the reception he got, because he went into Iskander's room with a conciliatory smile on his face; but the moment he shut the door the cursing began, and Colonel Shuja swore that he saw wisps of blue smoke emerging from the keyhole, as if there were a fire inside, or four hundred and twenty Havana cigars all smoking away at the same time.

Seducer of your grandmother's pet mongrel bitch, seller of your daughters at low prices to the bastard offspring of pimps, diarrhoeic infidel who shits on the Quran – Isky Harappa cursed Raza for an hour and a half without permitting any interruption. Betel-juice and the absence of tobacco added to his already enormous vocabulary of imprecations a deadlier rancour than it had ever possessed in the days of his rakehell youth. By the time he finished the walls of that room were spattered from top to bottom with betel-juice, the curtains were ruined, it looked as if a herd of animals had been slaughtered in there, as if turkeys or goats had been struggling wildly in their death-throes, rushing around the room with the blood spewing from the red smiles on their throats. Raza Hyder came out with paan-juice dripping off his clothes, his moustache was full of it and his hands shook as the red fluid dribbled off his fingertips, as if his hands had been washed in a bowl of Iskander's lifeblood. His face was paper-white.

General Hyder did not speak until the staff car pulled up outside the C-in-C's residence. Then he said casually to Colonel Shuja: 'I have been hearing some terrible things about Mr Harappa's period in office. That man does not deserve to be set loose. He is a menace to the country.'

Two days later Talvar Ulhaq made the statement in which, under oath, he accused Iskander Harappa of arranging for the murder of his cousin, Little Mir. When Colonel Shuja read this document he thought, wonderingly: 'Just look where bad language will get you.'

In those days the Chief Martial Law Administrator's home had begun to resemble an orphanage more than a seat of government, owing to Good New's inability to stem the annual flood of children issuing from her loins. Twenty-seven children aged between one and six puked, dribbled, crawled, drew with crayons on the walls, played with bricks, screamed, spilled juice, fell asleep, tumbled down stairs, broke vases, ululated, giggled, sang, danced, skipped, wet themselves, demanded attention, experimented with bad language, kicked their ayahs, refused to clean their teeth, pulled the beard of the religious teacher engaged to teach them handwriting and the Quran, tore down curtains, stained sofas, got lost, cut themselves, fought against vaccination needles and tetanus jabs, begged for and then lost interest in pets, stole radios, and burst into top-level meetings in that demented house. Meanwhile Good News had expanded yet again, and she was so big she looked as if she'd swallowed a whale. Everyone knew with a terrible certainty that the progression was continuing, that this time no fewer than eight babies would be produced, and that next year there would be nine, and after that ten, and so on, so that by her thirtieth birthday she would have given birth to no fewer than seventy-seven children; the worst was still to come. It is possible that if Raza and Talvar had not been thinking of other things they might have guessed what she would do; but maybe nobody would have stopped her anyway, because the oppression of the children had started to unhinge everyone who lived amid the uproar of their numbers.

O, this Talvar Ulhaq: what uneasinesses, what ambiguities hung around the stiff-necked chief of the Federal Security Force! Hyder's son-in-law, Harappa's right-hand man . . . after the fall of Iskander Harappa, Raza Hyder came under considerable pressure to do something about his daughter's husband. The FSF was not a popular organization; Raza had no option but to disband it. But still there were cries for Talvar's head. So it was just as well that the former polo star chose this moment to prove that he had meant every syllable of his loyal vow to be the perfect son-in-law. He handed Raza Hyder his secret, detailed dossier on the Mir Harappa killing, from which it was obvious that Haroun Harappa had committed the murder, out of his ancient hatred for his father; and that the evil genius behind the unsavoury affair had been none other than the Chairman of the Popular Front, who had once murmured, patiently: 'Life is long.'

'There is evidence that he misused public money developing the tourist trade, for his own benefit, in Aansu,' Raza Hyder briefed General Tughlak, 'but this is much better. This will finish him completely.'

The act of loyal treason committed by Talvar Ulhaq changed everything. The Popular Front was banned from the elections; then the elections were postponed; then postponed again; then shelved; then cancelled. It was in this period that the initials CMLA, standing for Chief Martial Law Administrator, acquired a new meaning. People began to say what they really stood for was *Cancel My Last Announcement*.

And the memory of a right hand on a Book refused to fade.

Chairman Iskander Harappa was taken from Bagheeragali rest house to the Kot Lakhpat jail in Lahore. He was kept there in solitary confinement. He suffered from malaria and from infections of the colon. There were bouts of severe influenza. His teeth began to fall out; and he lost weight in other ways as well. (We have mentioned that Omar Khayyam Shakil, his old companion in devilry, was also slimming down in this period, under the benign influence of a Parsee ayah.)

The trial took place in the High Court at Lahore, before five Punjabi judges. Harappa, it will be recalled, hailed from the Mohenjo estate in Sind. The testimony of ex-FSF Chief Talvar Ulhaq was central to the prosecution's case. Iskander Harappa gave evidence in his own defence, accusing Talvar of fabricating evidence to save his own skin. At one point Iskander used the phrase, 'Damn it,' and was reprimanded for the use of bad language in court. He apologized: 'My state of mind is not good.' The Chief Justice replied: 'We don't care.' This made Iskander lose his temper. 'I've had enough,' he cried, 'of insults and humiliations.' The Chief Justice ordered police officers: 'Take that man away until he regains his senses.' Another judge added the following remark: 'We cannot tolerate this. He thinks he is the former Prime Minister, but we do not care for him.' All this is on the record.

At the end of the six-month trial, Iskander Harappa and also the absent Mr Haroun Harappa were sentenced to hang by the neck until dead. Iskander was immediately moved into the death-cell at Kot Lakhpat jail. He was given just seven days, instead of the usual thirty, to lodge an appeal.

Iskander announced: 'Where there is no justice, there is no point in seeking it. I shall not appeal.'

That night Begum Talvar Ulhaq, the former Good News Hyder, was found in her bedroom at the Hyder residence, hanged by the neck, dead. On the floor beneath her dangling feet lay the broken rope of her first attempt, snapped by the enormous weight of her pregnancy. But she had not been deterred. There was jasmine in her hair and she had filled the room with the fragrance of Joy by Jean Patou, the most expensive perfume in the world, imported from France to cover up the smell of her bowels opening in death. A suicide note had been attached to the obscene globularity of her midriff by a baby's safety-pin. It referred to her terror of the arithmetical progression of babies marching out of her womb. It did not mention what she thought of her husband, Talvar Ulhaq, who would never be brought to trial on any charge.

At the funeral of Naveed Talvar, Raza Hyder kept staring at the cryptic and estranged figure of his wife Bilquìs in her black burqa; he remembered all at once how he had first come upon her in that distant fortress full of refugees, how she had been as naked then as she was clothed now; he saw her history as a slow retreat from that early nudity into the secrecy of the veil.

'Ai, Bilquìs,' he murmured, 'what happened to our lives?'

'You want to feel bad?' she answered, much too loudly. 'Then feel bad for the life that has been lost. I blame you for this. Shame, shame, poppy-shame.'

He understood that she was no longer the luminous girl with whom he had fallen in love in a different universe, her reason had gone, and so he made Colonel Shuja escort her home before the funeral rites were completed. Sometimes he thinks the walls are throbbing, as if the water-stained concrete has developed a tic, and then he allows himself to close his eyelids which are as heavy as iron shields, so that he can tell himself who he is. In the armour of this blindness he recites: I, Iskander Harappa, Prime Minister, Chairman of the Popular Front, husband of Rani, father to Arjumand, formerly devoted lover of. He has forgotten her name and forces his eyelids open, he has to use his fingers to push them up, and the walls are still pulsating. Cockroaches dislodged by the movement fall down upon his head; they are three inches long and when he brushes them to the floor he has to crush them with his bare heels; they crackle like pine-kernel shells on the cement. There is a drumming in his ears.

What is the shape of death? Death's cell is ten feet long, seven wide, eight high, twenty point seven four cubic yards of finality beyond which there awaits a certain courtyard, a last cigar, silence. *I will insist on Romeo y Juliettas. That story also ends in death* . . . They call this solitary confinement but he is not alone, there are flies fornicating on his toenails and mosquitoes drinking from the pools of his wrists, putting the blood to some use before it all goes to waste. Four guards in the corridor, too: in short, plenty of company. And sometimes they let his lawyers pay a call.

Through the door of the iron bars comes the stink of the latrine. In the winter he shivers but the low temperature takes the edge off that brown and foetid smell. In the hot season they switch off the ceiling fan and the odour bubbles and swells, stuffing its putrid fingers up his nose, making his eyes bulge even though his tear ducts are dry. He goes on hunger strike and when he is almost too weak to move they hang a blanket over the latrine door and switch on the fan. But when he asks for drinking water they bring it boiling hot and he has to wait many hours for it to cool.

Pains in the chest. He vomits blood. There are nosebleeds, too.

Two years from fall to hanging, and almost the whole time spent in the enclosed space of death. First in Kot Lakhpat, then in the District Jail from which, if he had a window, he could see the palace of his former glory. When they moved him from the first death-cell to the second he formed the giddy conviction that no move had taken place, that although he had experienced the sack over the head, the shovings, the sensations of travel, of flight, they had simply done it to disorient him, and brought him back to his starting-place. Or finishing-place. The two cells were so alike that he would not believe he had been moved to the capital until they let his lawyers in to tell him so.

They keep him chained around the clock. When he turns too suddenly in his sleep the metal cuffs bite into his ankles. For one hour a day they remove the chains; he shits, walks. And is shackled once again. 'My morale is high,' he tells his lawyers, 'because I am not made of the wood whick burns easily.'

The death-cell, its proportions, its contents. He focuses his mind on what is concrete, tangible, there. These flies and mosquitoes and cockroaches, they are his friends, he counts them, they can be touched or crushed or borne. These iron bars enclosing him, one to six. This flea-bag mattress, provided after he made a fuss daily for five months, it is a victory, perhaps his last. These chains, that lotah pot full of water too hot to touch. Something is meant here, something intended. The death-cell holds the key to the mystery of dying. But nobody scratched a code on any wall.

If it is a dream, and sometimes in the fever of his days he thinks it is, then (he also knows) the dreamer is someone else. He is inside the dream, or he would not be able to touch dream-insects; dream-water would not burn him ... someone is dreaming him. God, then? No, not God. He struggles to remember Raza Hyder's face.

Comprehension comes before the end. He, Harappa, brought the General from the wilderness into the world. The General of whom this cell is one small aspect, who is general, omnipresent, omnivorous: it is a cell inside his head. Death and the General: Iskander sees no difference between the terms. *From darkness into light, from nothingness into somethingness. I made him, I was his father, he is my seed. And now I am less than he. They accuse Haroun of killing his father because that is what Hyder is doing to me.*

Then another step, which takes him beyond such aching simplicities. The father should be superior and the son, inferior. *But now I am low and he, high.* An inversion: the parent become the child. *He is turning me into his son.*

His son. Who emerged dead from the womb with a noose

about his neck. *That noose seals my fate.* Because now he understands the cell, the throbbing walls, the smell of excrement, the drumbeat of a foul invisible heart: death's belly, an inverse womb, dark mirror of a birthplace, its purpose is to suck him in, to draw him back and down through time, until he hangs foetal in his own waters, with an umbilical cord hung fatally round his neck. He will leave this place only when its mechanisms have done their work, death's baby, travelling down the death canal, and the noose will tighten its grip.

A man will wait a lifetime for revenge. The killing of Iskander Harappa avenges the still-born child. *Yes: I am being unmade.*

Iskander Harappa was persuaded by his lawyers to lodge an appeal against the High Court's sentence of death. The appeal was heard by a bench of seven judges sitting in the Supreme Court in the new capital. By the time the Supreme Court hearings ended he had been in captivity for a year and a half; and a further six months were to pass before the body of the former Prime Minister arrived at Mohenjo in the care of Talvar Ulhaq, who had, by then, been returned to active police duty.

Elections were not held. Raza Hyder became President. All this is well know.

And Sufiya Zinobia?

Back goes the clock once again. It was election day and there were many fires. Raza Hyder pouring ashes from the window of a moving car. Isky Harappa unaware of the death-cells of the future. And Omar Khayyam Shakil in a blue funk.

After the dismissal of Shahbanou the Parsee ayah, Omar Khayyam grew afraid, because he saw the shapes of his early life rising up to haunt his adulthood. Once again a Parsee girl had been made pregnant; once again, there was a mother with a fatherless child. The idea that there could be no escape wrapped itself round his head like a hot towel and made it hard for him to breathe; and on top of that he was extremely nervous of what

General Hyder might do now that the ayah had been dismissed for the crime of pregnancy and it was no longer possible to keep the secret of whom Shahbanou had been visiting every night. What was out in the open: the most grievous of faults, the infidelity of a husband beneath his wife's father's roof. A betrayal of salt.

But Raza Hyder was just as agitated as Omar Khayyam, and was not thinking about salt. After the burning of the blood-encrusted veil he had been assailed by the thought that perhaps Talvar Ulhaq was just a little too good to be true with his pose of ideal son-in-lawship. Whose neck got bitten? Whose polo career was vampirically terminated? Who might, very plausibly, have bided his time and waited for revenge? 'Fool that I am,' Raza cursed himself, 'I should have had the blood analysed. Maybe it was only a goat's; but now it's all up in smoke.'

O reluctance of a father to accept his daughter's Beastliness! Up in smoke: certainty, obligation, responsibility. Raza Hyder considered the option of forgetting the whole thing . . . that night, however, he was visited by a dream of Maulana Dawood, and the dead divine yelled at him that it was about time he started believing that a devil had got inside his daughter, because the whole business was a test of his faith devised by God, and he had better choose what he really cared about, his daughter's life or the eternal love of the Deity. Maulana Dawood, who had apparently gone on ageing after death and was more decrepit-looking than ever, added unkindly that if it was any help he could assure Hyder that Sufiya Zinobia's antics would get worse rather than better, and in the end they would certainly terminate Raza's career. Raza Hyder woke up and burst into tears, because the dream had shown him his true nature, which was that of a man who was prepared to sacrifice everything, even his child, to God. 'Remember Abraham,' he told himself as he mopped his eyes.

So Hyder and Shakil were both distressed, that morning, by the sense of being out of control of their lives – by the stifling presence of Fate . . . Raza realized that he had no option but to talk to Sufiya Zinobia's husband. Never mind that foolishness with the ayah; this was serious, and the fellow had a right to know.

When the General's ADC presented himself to Omar Khayyam
Shakil and said sadly and in some puzzlement that the C-in-C
required the doctor's presence on a little fishing expedition, Omar
began to quake in his boots. What could be so important as to
make Hyder spend the day with him while the city was exploding
with post-electoral fireworks? 'This is it,' he thought, 'that ayah
has done for me.' On the drive into the Bagheeragali hills he was
too afraid to open his mouth.

Raza Hyder told him that they were going to a stream that was
famous both for the beauty of the surrounding wooded slopes and
for the legend that its waters were haunted by a fish-hating ghost
of such ferocity that the many plump mahaseer trout who passed
that way preferred to leap on to the hooks of any anglers who
fished there, no matter how incompetent they were. That day,
however, neither Raza nor Omar Khayyam would succeed in
landing a single fish.

Rejection by mahaseer trout: why did the fish not bite? What
made the two distinguished gentlemen less appealing than the
ghostfish? Being unable to enter into the imagination of a trout, I
offer my own (fishy enough) explanation. A fish seeks, in a
fishhook, a kind of confidence, the hook communicating its
inevitability to fishlips. Angling is a battle of wits; the thoughts of
the fishermen pass down rods and lines, and are divined by finny
creatures. Who, on this occasion, found haunted waters easier to
stomach than the ugly descending thoughts . . . well, accept don't
accept, but facts are facts. A day in wading boots and empty bas-
kets at the end of it. The fish delivered their verdict on the men.

Two men in water discussed impossible things. While all
around them koels, pine-trees, butterflies added a fantastic
improbability to their words . . . Raza Hyder, unable to get
revenge-plots out of his mind, found himself thinking that he was
placing his fate in the hands of a man whose brother he had exter-
minated. O suspect sons-in-law! Doubt and gloom hung over
Hyder's head and scared away the fish.

But – even though Iskander Harappa in his death-cell believed that men would wait a lifetime for revenge — even though I am going to have to reopen this blasted possibility, because Hyder has got it into his head — I simply cannot bring myself to see our hero as a brooding, biding-his-time menace out of a revenge tragedy. I have conceded that his obsession with Sufiya Zinobia might have been genuine; beyond that, or even because of that, I stick to my guns. Too much time has passed without any hint from Omar Khayyam that some terrible deed of retribution was in the offing; it seems to me that he has made his choice, choosing Hyders, rejecting family; that Omar-the-husband, Omar-the-son-in-law, has long since disposed of the shade of Omar-the-brother, mourning for the sibling he never knew, darkest of horses, waiting for his chance. — It is tiresome when one's characters see less clearly than oneself; but I have his three mothers on my side. — And Raza can't have taken his own worries too seriously, because he ended up telling Omar Khayyam everything, the headless boys, the semen traces, the veil. — And if he didn't, well, then, nor shall we..

Two men in a fast-flowing stream, and over their heads thunderclouds, invisible to human eyes but alarming to fishy ones. Omar Khayyam's bladder had begun to ache with fear, the fear of Sufiya Zinobia replacing his fear of Raza Hyder, now that he had realized that Raza was turning a blind eye to the Shahbanou affair; and a third fear, too, the fear of what Raza Hyder was proposing.

The sacrifice of Abraham was mentioned. The painless, fatal injection. Tears streamed from Hyder's eyes, plopped into water, their saltiness further discouraging the already scornful fish. 'You are a doctor,' Hyder said, 'and a husband. I leave it up to you.'

The action of mind over matter. In a hypnotic trance the subject can acquire what seems like superhuman strength. Pain is not felt, arms become as strong as iron bars, feet run like the wind. Extraordinary things. Sufiya Zinobia could enter such a state, it seemed, without external help. Perhaps, under hypnosis, a cure could be effected? The wellsprings of the rage located, burned away, drained ... the source of her anger discovered, and made still. Let us recall that Omar Khayyam Shakil was an illustrious medical man, and the professional excitement had led him to Sufiya Zinobia years ago. That old challenge had been renewed. Raza and Omar Khayyam: both men felt themselves being tested, the one by God, the other by his science. And it is common for males of the species to be incapable of resisting the idea of a test . . . 'I shall watch her closely,' Omar Khayyam said. 'There is a possible treatment.'

Nobody does anything for just one reason. It is not possible that Omar Khayyam, for so long shameless, was made brave by a twinge of shame? That his guilt over the Shahbanou business made him say, 'There is a treatment,' and so face the worst danger of his life? – But what is undeniable, what I do not attempt to deny, is that courage was shown. And courage is a rarer thing than evil, after all. Credit where it's due.

But what confusion swept over Raza Hyder! A man who has decided to do away with his daughter for religious reasons does not relish being told he has been too hasty.

'You're a fool,' General Hyder told his son-in-law. 'If the devil comes out again she will tear off your stupid head.'

To come to the point: for some days Omar Khayyam watched Sufiya at home, playing with the numberless children, skipping for them and shelling pine-kernels, and he could see that she was getting worse, because this was the first time that the violence bursting from her had left no after-effects, no immune-disorder, no comatose trance; she was becoming habituated to it, he thought in fright, it could happen again at any time, the children. Yes, he saw the danger, now that he was looking for it he caught the flickers in her eyes, the coming and going of little pricks of yellow light. He was watching her carefully so he saw what casual eyes would have missed, which was that the edges of Sufiya Zinobia were beginning to become uncertain, as if there were two beings occupying that air-space, competing for it, two entities of identical shape but of tragically opposed natures. From the flickering points of light he began to learn that science was not enough, that even though he rejected possession-by-devils as a way of denying human responsibility for human actions, even though God had never meant much to him, still his reason could not erase the evidence of those eyes, could not blind him to that unearthly glow, the smouldering fire of the Beast. And around Sufiya Zinobia her nephews and nieces played.

'It's now or never,' he thought, and spoke to her in the fashion of an old-fashioned husband: 'Wife, kindly accompany me to my quarters.' She rose and followed him without a word, because the Beast was not in charge; but once they were there he made the mistake of commanding her to lie down on the bed, without explaining that he had no intention of forcing her to, of demanding his marital, so of course she misunderstood his purpose and at once the thing began, the yellow fire burning from her eyes, and she leapt from the bed and came at him with her hands stuck out like hooks.

He opened his mouth to scream but the sight of her sucked the breath from his lungs; he stared into those eyes of Hell with his mouth open like asphyxiating fishlips. Then she fell to the floor and began to writhe and to gag, and purple bubbles formed on her protruding tongue. It was impossible not to believe that a struggle was taking place, Sufiya Zinobia against the Beast, that what was left of that poor girl had hurled itself against the creature, that the wife was protecting her husband against herself. This was how it came about that Omar Khayyam Shakil looked into the eyes of the Beast of shame and survived, because although he had been paralysed by that basilisk flame she had snuffed it out long enough to break the spell, and he managed to shake himself free of its power. She was flinging herself around the floor so violently that she splintered the frame of his bed when she collided with it, and while she thrashed about he managed to reach his medicine bag, his fingers managed to reach the hypodermic and the sedative, and in the very last instant of Sufiya Zinobia's struggle, when for a fraction of a second she acquired the serene air of a slumbrous infant, just before the final assault of the Beast, which would have

destroyed Sufiya Zinobia Shakil for ever, Omar Khayyam stuck
the needle, without benefit of local anaesthetic, deep into her
rump and pushed the plunger, and she subsided into unconsciousness with a sigh.

There was an attic room. (It was a house designed by Angrez
architects.) At night, when the servants were asleep, Raza Hyder
and Omar Khayyam carried the drugged form of Sufiya Zinobia
up attic stairs. It is even possible (difficult to see in the dark) that
they wrapped her in a carpet.

Omar Khayyam had refused to administer the final, painless
injection. *I will not kill her. Because she saved my life. And because,
once, I saved hers.* But he no longer believed treatment was possible; he had seen the golden eyes of the most powerful mesmerist
on earth. Neither kill nor cure . . . Hyder and Shakil agreed that
Sufiya Zinobia was to be kept unconscious until further notice.
She was to enter a state of suspended animation; Hyder brought
long chains and they padlocked her to the attic beams; in the
nights that followed they bricked up the attic window and fastened huge bolts to the door; and twice in every twenty-four
hours, Omar Khayyam would go unobserved into that darkened
room, that echo of other death-cells, to inject into the tiny body
lying on its thin carpet the fluids of nourishment and of unconsciousness, to administer the drugs that turned her from one
fairy-tale into another, into sleeping-beauty instead of beauty-
and-beast. 'What else to do?' Hyder said helplessly. 'Because I
cannot kill her either, don't you see.'

The family had to be told; nobody's hands were clean. They
were all accomplices in the matter of Sufiya Zinobia; and the
secret was kept. The 'wrong miracle' . . . she disappeared from
sight. Poof! Like so.

When it was announced that the Supreme Court had upheld the
death sentence by a split decision, four to three, Iskander
Harappa's lawyers told him that a pardon was assured. 'Impossible
to hang a man on such a split,' they said. 'Relax.' One of the

judges who had voted for acquittal had said, 'All's well that ends well.' Legal precedent, Iskander was told, obliged the Head of State to exercise clemency after a vote of this type. Iskander Harappa told his lawyers: 'We shall see.' Six months later he was still in the death-cell when he was visited by the unchangingly glum-faced Colonel Shuja. 'I have brought you a cigar,' the ADC said, 'Romeo y Juliettas, your favourite, I think.' Iskander Harappa guessed as he lit up that he was going to die, and began to say his prayers in beautiful Arabic; but Shuja interrupted, 'Some mistake, beg for pardon, sir.' He insisted that he had come for quite a different reason, that Harappa was required to sign a full confession, and after that the question of clemency would receive favourable consideration. On hearing this Isky Harappa summoned the last of his strength and began to swear at the mournful Pathan officer. It was a kind of suicide. His words had never been sharper. The obscenity of his language inflicted stinging blows, Shuja felt them piercing his skin, and understood what Raza Hyder had suffered in Bagheeragali two years earlier; he felt the rage rising within him, he was unable to undergo such humiliation without giving way to the anger, and when Iskander yelled, 'Fuck me in the mouth, pimp, go suck your grandson's cock,' that was it, it didn't matter that Shuja was not old enough to have a grandchild, he stood up very slowly and then shot the former Prime Minister through the heart.

The Beast has many faces. Some are always sad.

A hanging in the courtyard of the District Jail at dead of night. Prisoners howling, banging cups, sang Isky's requiem. And the hangman was never seen again. Don't ask me what became of him; I can't be expected to know everything. He vanished: poof! – And after the body was cut down, the flight to Mohenjo, Rani tearing the death-sheet from the face. But she never saw the chest. And then blind men seeing, the lame walking, lepers cured when they touched the martyr's tomb. It was also said that this tomb-touching was a particularly efficacious remedy for disorders of the teeth.

And Pinkie's suicide; no need to go into all that again. She stayed dead; she never haunted anybody.

President Raza Hyder in a prison courtyard with a dangling corpse remembered what Bilquìs had said. 'They are falling away,' he thought, 'like rocket stages.' Dawood gone to Mecca, Bilquìs and Sufiya lost behind different veils, Good News and now Isky twirling on their ropes. Distrusting his sons-in-law, but bound to them by necessity, Raza felt around him the enclosing emptiness of the void. It was at this moment, when Harappa hung from a noose with a bag over his head, that Raza Hyder heard Iskander's voice. 'Never fear, old boy, it's pretty difficult to get rid of me. I can be an obstinate bastard when I choose.'

The golden voice, clear as a bell. And Raza Hyder in shock shouted, 'The motherfucker isn't dead!' The obscenity from his lips astonished the still-unvanished hangman, and at once in his ear the laughing Isky-voice: 'Don't be silly, yaar. You know what's going on here.'

O unceasing monologue of a hanged man! Because it never left him, from the day of Iskander's death to the morning of his own, that voice, sardonic lilting dry, now advising him not to fire his ADC because that would let the truth out for sure, now teasing him, President sahib, you've got a lot to learn about running the show; words dripping on his ear-drum like Chinese tortures, even in his sleep; sometimes anecdotal, reminding him of tilyars and tied-to-a-stake, at other times taunting, how long do you think you'll last, Raz, one year, two?

Nor was Iskander's the only voice. We have already seen the first appearance of the spectre of Maulana Dawood; it returned to perch, invisibly, on the President's right shoulder, to whisper in his ear. God on his right shoulder, the devil on his left; this was the unseen truth about the Presidency of Old Razor Guts, these two conflicting soliloquies inside his skull, marching leftright left-right leftright down the years.

From *The Suicide*, a play by the Russian writer Nikolai Erdman: 'Only the dead can say what the living are thinking.'

Reappearances of the dead must be offset by disappearances of the living. A hangman: poof! And Pinkie Aurangzeb. And I've saved the worst for last: on the night of the Harappa hanging, Omar Khayyam Shakil discovered that Sufiya Zinobia, his wife, Hyder's daughter, had escaped.

An empty attic. Broken chains, cracked beams. There was a hole in the bricked-up window. It had a head, arms, legs.

'God help us,' said Omar Khayyam, in spite of his uncircumcised, unshaven, unwhispered-to beginnings. It was as though he had divined that it was time for the Almighty to step forward and take charge of events.

12

❦

STABILITY

The great French revolutionary hero Danton, who will lose his head during the 'Terror', is making a rueful remark. '. . . But Robespierre and the people', he observes, 'are virtuous.' Danton is on a London stage, not really Danton at all but an actor speaking the lines of Georg Büchner in English translation; and the time is not then, but now. I don't know if the thought originated in French, German or English, but I do know that it seems astonishingly bleak – because what it means, obviously, is that *the people are like Robespierre*. Danton may be a hero of the revolution, but he also likes wine, fine clothes, whores; weaknesses which (the audience instantly sees) will enable Robespierre, a good actor in a green coat, to cut him down. When Danton is sent to visit the widow, old Madame Guillotine with her basket of heads, we know it isn't really on account of any real or trumped-up political crimes. He gets the chop (miraculously staged) because he is too fond of pleasure. Epicureanism is subversive. The people are like Robespierre. They distrust fun.

This opposition – the epicure against the puritan – is, the play tells us, the true dialectic of history. Forget left-right, capitalism-socialism, black-white. Virtue versus vice, ascetic versus bawd,

God against the Devil: that's the game. *Messieurs, mesdames: faîtes vos jeux.*

I watched the play in a large theatre that was two-thirds empty. Politics empties theatres in old London town. Afterwards, the departing audience made disapproving remarks. The trouble with the play, apparently, was that there was too much of ranting Danton and not enough of sinister Robespierre. The customers bemoaned the imbalance. 'I liked the nasty one,' someone said. Her companions agreed.

I was with three visitors from Pakistan. They all loved the play. 'How lucky you are,' they envied me, 'to live where such things can be put on.' They told me the story of a recent attempt to stage *Julius Caesar* at the University of P. It seems that the authorities became very agitated when they heard that the script called for the assassination of a Head of State. What was more, the production was to be in modern dress: General Caesar would be in full dress uniform when the knives got to work. Extreme pressure was brought to bear on the University to scrap the production. The academics, honourably, resisted, defending an ancient writer with a rather martial name against this assault-of-the-Generals. At one point the military censors suggested a compromise: would the University not agree to mount the whole production, just as scripted, with the single exception of that unpalatable killing? Surely that scene was not absolutely necessary?

Finally, the producer came up with a brilliant, a positively Solomonic solution. He invited a prominent British diplomat to play Caesar, dressed in (British) Imperial regalia. The Army relaxed; the play opened; and when the first-night curtain fell, the house lights went up to reveal a front row full of Generals, all applauding wildly to signify their enjoyment of this patriotic work depicting the overthrow of imperialism by the freedom movement of Rome.

I insist: I have not made this up . . . and I am reminded of a British diplomat's wife whom I mentioned earlier. 'Why don't people in Rome,' she might well have inquired, 'get rid of General Caesar in, you know, the usual way?'

But I was talking about Büchner. My friends and I had liked *Danton's Death*; in the age of Khomeini, etc., it seemed most apposite. But Danton's (Büchner's?) view of 'the people' bothered us. If the people were like Robespierre, how did Danton ever get to be a hero? Why was he cheered in court?

'The point is,' one of my friends argued, 'that this opposition exists all right; but it is an internal dialectic.' That made sense. The people are not only like Robespierre. They, we, are Danton, too. We are Robeston and Danpierre. The inconsistency doesn't matter; I myself manage to hold large numbers of wholly irreconcilable views simultaneously, without the least difficulty. I do not think others are less versatile.

Iskander Harappa was not just Danton; Raza Hyder wasn't Robespierre pure-and-simple. Isky certainly lived it up, perhaps he was something of an epicure, but he also believed that he was always, unarguably, right. And eighteen shawls have shown us that he wasn't averse to Terror, either. What befell him in his death-cell befell others because of him. That is important. (But if we mind about the others, we must also, unfortunately, mind about Iskander.) And Raza Hyder? It is possible to believe that he took no pleasure in what he did, that the pleasure principle was not in operation, even though he claimed to act in the name of God? I don't think so.

Isky and Raza. They, too, were Danpierre and Robeston. Which may be an explanation; but it cannot, of course, be an excuse.

When Omar Khayyam Shakil saw the Sufiya-Zinobia-shaped hole in a bricked-up window, the idea came to him that his wife was dead. Which is not to say that he expected to find her lifeless body on the lawn below the window, but that he guessed that the creature inside her, the hot thing, the yellow fire, had by now consumed her utterly, like a house-gutting blaze, so that the girl whose fate had prevented her from becoming complete had finally diminished to the vanishing point. What had escaped, what now roamed free in the unsuspecting air, was not Sufiya Zinobia Shakil at all, but something more like a principle, the embodiment of violence, the pure malevolent strength of the Beast.

'Damn it,' he told himself, 'the world is going mad.'

There was once a wife, whose husband injected her with knock-out drugs twice daily. For two years she lay on a carpet, like a girl in a fantasy who can only be awoken by the blue-blooded kiss of a prince; but kisses were not her destiny. She appeared to be spellbound by the sorceries of the drug, but the monster inside her never slept, the violence which had been born of shame, but which by now lived its own life beneath her skin; it fought the narcoleptic fluids, it took its time, spreading slowly through her body until it had occupied every cell, until she had become the violence, which no longer needed anything to set it off, because once a carnivore has tasted blood you can't fool it with vegetables any more. And in the end it defeated the drug, it lifted its body up and broke the restraining chains.

Pandora, possessed by the unleashed contents of her box.

Yellow fire behind her closed eyelids, fire under her fingernails and beneath the roots of her hair. Yes, she was dead all right, I'm sure of it, no more Sufiya-Zinobia-ness, everything burned up in that Hell. Throw a body on a funeral pyre and it will jerk, genuflect, sit up, dance, smile; the fire pulls the nerve-strings of the corpse, which becomes the fire's puppet, conveying a ghastly illusion of life amidst the flames . . .

There was once a Beast. When it was sure of its strength, it chose its moment, and sprang through a wall of brick.

During the next four years, that is to say the period of the Presidency of Raza Hyder, Omar Khayyam Shakil grew old. Nobody noticed at first, because he had been grey for years; but once he had turned sixty his feet, which had been obliged for most of their lives to bear the impossible burden of his obesity, staged a revolt, because in the aftermath of the departure of Shahbanou the ayah, when he had been deprived of the mint teas and nocturnal nourishments of her loyalty, he began to put on weight again. Buttons popped off trouser waistbands, and his feet went on strike. Omar

Khayyam's steps became agonies, even when he leaned on the sword-concealing cane which he had carried down all the years, ever since the time of his lecherous alliance with Iskander Harappa. He took to spending hours on end seated in a cane chair in what had once been Sufiya Zinobia's prison cell, staring out through the window which held, in fantastic outline, the red brick after-image of his departed wife.

He retired from Mount Hira Hospital and sent most of his pension money to an old house in Q. inhabited by three old women who refused to die, unlike Bariamma, who had long since done the decent thing and expired, propped up by bolsters, so that it was almost a full day before anyone saw what had happened . . . more money was sent to a Parsee ayah, and Omar Khayyam lived quietly under Raza Hyder's roof, shelling pine-kernels while his eyes, roving outwards through the attic window, seemed to be following someone, although there was nobody there.

Because he was familiar with the theory that susceptibility to hypnosis was the sign of a highly developed imaginative faculty – that the hypnotic trance is a form of inward creativity, during which the subject remakes herself and her world as she chooses – he sometimes thought that Sufiya Zinobia's metamorphosis must have been willed, because even an autohypnotist cannot ask herself to do what she would be unwilling to do. So then she had chosen, she had created the Beast . . . in which event, he ruminated in a cane chair with a mouth full of pine-kernels, her case is an object lesson. It demonstrates the danger of permitting the imagination too free a rein. The rampages of Sufiya Zinobia were the results of a fancy that ran wild.

'Shame should come to me,' he informed the koel perching on the window, 'here I sit doing what I'm criticizing, thinking God knows what, living too much in my head.'

Raza Hyder also thought: 'Shame should come to me.' Now that she was gone his thoughts were plagued by her. That something-too-loose in her muscles, that something-half-coordinated in her gait had stopped him loving her for a time. *She had to almost die before I. And of course it wasn't enough.* His head was bursting with voices: Isky Dawood Isky Dawood. Hard to think straight . . . and now she would take her revenge. Somehow, some time, she would drag him down. Unless he found her first. But who to send, who to brief? 'My daughter, the idiot with brain-fever, has become a human guillotine and started ripping off men's heads. This is her photo, wanted dead or alive, handsome reward.' Impossible. No can do.

O impotence of power. The President persuading himself not to be stupid, she won't survive, she hasn't, nothing heard for some time now, no news is good news. Or she'll turn up somewhere and then we'll hush it up. But still there cropped up in his thoughts the picture of a tiny girl with a face of classical severity; it was an accusation . . . throbbing at his temples, Isky and Dawood whispered and argued, rightleftright. But one can be haunted by the living as well as the dead. A wild look appeared in his eyes.

Like Omar Khayyam Shakil, President Raza Hyder began to shell and eat large quantities of pine-kernels, Sufiya Zinobia's favourite treat, which she had spent long and happy hours releasing from their shells, with crazy dedication, because the shelling of pine-kernels is a form of lunacy, you spend more energy getting the damn things out than they give you when you eat.

'General Hyder,' the Angrez television interviewer asks Raza, 'informed sources opine, close observers claim, many of our viewers in the West would say, how would you refute the argument, have you a point of view about the allegation that your institution of such Islamic punishments as flogging and cutting-off of hands might be seen in certain quarters as being, arguably, according to certain definitions, so to speak, barbaric?'

Raza Hyder smiles at the camera, a courteous smile, the smile of a man of true good manners and no little decorum. 'It is not barbaric,' he replies. 'Why? For three reasons.' He raises a finger for each reason and counts them off. 'Number one,' he explains, 'is that, kindly understand, a law in itself is neither barbaric nor not barbaric. What matters is the man who is applying the law. And in this case it is I, Raza Hyder, who am doing it, so of course it will not be barbaric.

'Number two, let me say, sir, that we are not some savages down from the trees, you see? We will not simply order people to stick out their hands, like this, and go fataakh! with a butcher's knife. No, sir. All will be done under the most hygienic conditions, with proper medical supervision, use of anaesthetic etcetera.

'But the third reason is that these are not laws, my dear fellow, which we have plucked out of the wind. These are the holy words of God, as revealed in sacred texts. Now if they are holy words of God, they cannot also be barbaric. It is not possible. They must be some other thing.'

He had chosen not to move into the President's House in the new capital, feeling more comfortable in the Commander-in-Chief's residence, in spite of the noisy hordes of motherless children bullying ayahs in the corridors. At first he had been willing to spend some of his nights under the Presidential roof, for instance at the time of the Pan-Islamic conference when Heads of State arrived from all over the globe, and they all brought their mothers along, so that all hell broke loose, because the mothers in the zenana wing embarked at once on a tooth-and-nail struggle for seniority, and they kept sending urgent messages to their sons, interrupting the conference's plenipotentiary sessions to complain about mortal insults received and honour besmirched, which brought the world leaders close to starting fist-fights or even wars. Raza Hyder did not have a mother to land him in hot water, but he had worries of his own, because he had discovered on the first night of the conference that while he was in this airport of a palace the voice of Iskander Harappa became so loud in his ears that he could hardly hear anything else. The monologue of the hanged man buzzed in his skull, and it seemed that Isky had decided to give his successor some useful tips, because the disembodied voice had started quoting liberally and in an irritatingly sing-song accent from what it took Raza a long time to work out were the writings of the notorious infidel and foreigner Niccolò Machiavelli. Raza lay awake all that night with the spectral buzzing in his head. 'In taking a state,' Iskander was saying, 'the conqueror must arrange to commit all his cruelties at once, for injuries should be done all together, so that being less tasted, they will give less offence.' Raza Hyder had been unable to prevent an exclamation – 'Ya Allah, shut up, shut up!' – from getting past the Presidential lips, and at once guards came running into his bedroom, fearing the worst, namely an invasion by the endlessly complaining mothers of the world leaders; Raza was obliged to say with shame, 'Nothing, nothing. A nightmare, a bad dream, nothing to worry about.'

'Sorry, Raza,' Iskander whispered, 'only trying to help.'

The moment the conference was over and the mothers had been pulled apart Raza rushed back to his other home, where he could relax, because there Maulana Dawood's voice in his right ear was louder than Isky's in his left. He learned to concentrate all his attention on his right side, and as a result it became possible to live with the ghost of Iskander Harappa, even though Isky kept trying to make his points.

In the fifteenth century General Raza Hyder became President of his country, and everything began to change. The effect of the ceaseless monologue of Iskander Harappa was to drive Raza into the ectoplasmic arms of his old crony Maulana Dawood. Around whose neck had once been placed, by mistake, a certain necklace of shoes. Raza Hyder with his *gatta* bruise was, you recall, the type of *mohajir* who had arrived with God in every pocket, and the more Iskander whispered the more Raza felt that God was his only hope. So when Dawood whined, 'Here in holy Mecca much evil can be seen; the sacred places must be cleansed, that is your first and only duty,' Hyder paid attention, even though it was clear that death had not managed to disabuse the divine of the notion that they had come to the holy heart of the faith, Mecca Sharif, the city of the great Black Stone.

What Raza did: he banned booze. He closed down the famous old beer brewery at Bagheera so that Panther Lager became a fond memory instead of a refreshing drink. He altered the television schedules so drastically that people began summoning repair men to fix their sets, because they could not understand why the TVs were suddenly refusing to show them anything except theological lectures, and they wondered how these mullahs had got stuck inside the screen. On the Prophet's birthday Raza arranged for every mosque in the country to sound a siren at nine a.m. and anybody who forgot to stop and pray when he heard the howling was instantly carted off to jail. The beggars of the capital and also of all the other cities remembered that the Quran obliged the faithful to give alms, so they took advantage of the arrival of God in the Presidential office to stage a series of enormous marches demanding the establishment by law of a minimum donation of five rupees. They had underestimated God, however; in the first year of his rule Raza Hyder incarcerated one hundred thousand beggars and, while he was at it, a further twenty-five hundred members of the now-illegal Popular Front, who were not much better than mendicants, after all. He announced that God and socialism were incompatible, so that the doctrine of Islamic Socialism on which the Popular Front had based its appeal was the worst kind of blasphemy imaginable. 'Iskander Harappa never believed in God,' he declared publicly, 'so he was destroying the country while pretending to hold it together.' The incompatibility doctrine made Raza very popular with the Americans, who were of the same opinion, even though the God concerned was different.

' "Of those who have attained the position of prince by villainy," ' Iskander's voice whispered in his ear, '*Il Principe*, chapter eight. You ought to read it; it's very short,' but by this time Raza had worked out how to ignore his sinister or left-sided dead angel. He blotted out Isky's mischief-making, and instead of noting the historical precedents offered by the histories of Agathocles the Sicilian and Oliverotto da Fermo he listened to Maulana Dawood. Iskander refused to give up, claiming that his motives were selfless, trying to remind Raza of the difference between well and badly committed cruelties, and of the need for cruelties to diminish with time, and for benefits to be granted little by little, so that they might be better enjoyed. But by now Dawood's ghost was in its stride; it had gained in confidence, on account of its preferential treatment by the President, and ordered Raza to ban movies, or at least imported ones for a start; it objected to unveiled women walking the streets; it demanded firm measures and an iron hand. It is a matter of record that in those days religious students started carrying guns and occasionally taking pot-shots at insufficiently devout professors; that men would spit at women in the street if they went about their business with their midriffs showing; and that a person could be strangled for smoking a cigarette during the month of fasting. The legal system was dismantled, because the lawyers had demonstrated the fundamentally profane nature of their profession by objecting to divers activities of the state; it was replaced by religious courts presided over by divines whom Raza appointed on the sentimental grounds that their beards reminded him of his deceased adviser. God was in charge, and just in case anybody doubted it He gave little demonstrations of His power: he made various anti-faith elements vanish like slum children. Yes, the bastards were just rubbed out by the Almighty, they vanished, poof, like so.

Raza Hyder was a busy man in those years, with little time for what remained of his family life. He ignored his twenty-seven grandchildren, leaving them to their father and ayahs; but his devotion to the concept of family was well-known, he made much of it, and that was why he saw Bilquìs regularly, once a week. He had her brought to the television studios in time for his broadcast to the nation. This always began with a prayer session, during which Raza knelt in the foreground renewing his bruise, while behind him Bilquìs prayed too, like a good wife, in soft focus and veiled from head to foot. He would sit with her for a few moments before they went on air, and he noticed that she always brought some sewing along. Bilquìs was not Rani; she embroidered no shawls. Her activities were both simpler and more mysterious, consisting of sewing large expanses of black cloth into shapes that were impossible to decipher. For a long time the awkwardness between them prevented Raza from asking her what the hell she was up to, but in the end his curiosity got the better of him, and when he was sure nobody else was within earshot the President asked his wife: 'So what is all this stitching? What are you making in such a hurry that you can't wait till you get back home?'

'Shrouds,' she answered seriously, and he felt a chill on his spine.

Two years after the death of Iskander Harappa the women of the country began marching against God. These processions were tricky things, Raza decided, they needed careful handling. So he trod cautiously, even though Maulana Dawood screamed in his ear that he was a weakling, he should strip the whores naked and hang them from all available trees. But Raza was circumspect; he told the police to avoid hitting the ladies on the breasts when they broke up the demonstrations. And finally God rewarded his virtuous restraint. His investigators learned that the marches were being organized by a certain Noor Begum, who was going into the tenements and villages and whipping up anti-religious feelings. Still Raza was reluctant to ask God to make the bitch disappear, because you can't ask the Almighty to do everything, after all; so he felt profoundly justified when he was given evidence that his Noor Begum was a notorious character with a history of exporting women and children to the harems of Arab princes. Only now did he send his men off to seize her, because nobody could object to such an arrest, and even Iskander Harappa complimented him: 'You're a quick learner, Raza, maybe we all underestimated your skills.'

This was Raza Hyder's motto: 'Stability, in the name of God.' And after the Noor Begum business he added a second maxim to the first: 'God helps those who help themselves.' To achieve stability-in-God's-name he placed Army officers on the board of every major industrial enterprise in the country; he put Generals everywhere, so that the Army got its fingers deeper into things than it had ever done before. Raza knew his policy had succeeded when Generals Raddi, Bekar and Phisaddi, the youngest and ablest members of his general staff, came to him with hard and fast evidence that General Salmàn Tughlak, in cahoots with Police Chief Talvar Ulhaq, Raza Hyder's son-in-law, and Colonel Shuja, his long-time ADC, was planning a coup. 'Stupid fools,' Raza Hyder murmured, regretfully. 'Whisky addicts, you see? They want their chota pegs and so they are ready to unmake everything we have achieved.' He put on a lachrymose expression as tragic as any of Shuja's; but he was secretly delighted, because he had always been embarrassed by the memory of his inept nocturnal telephone call to General Tughlak; and he had been trying to find a reason for disposing of his ADC ever since the business in the death-cell at the District Jail; and Talvar Ulhaq had ceased to be trustworthy years ago. 'A man who will turn against one boss,' Raza said to young Raddi, Bekar and Phisaddi, 'will turn against two,' but what he really meant was that the clairvoyancy of Talvar scared him stiff, and anyway the fellow knew all about Sufiya Zinobia, and that meant he knew too much . . . Raza clapped the young Generals on their backs and said, 'Well, well, now it is all in the lap of God,' and by the next morning the three conspirators had vanished without even leaving behind the tiniest little puffs of smoke. The twenty-seven orphans of Talvar Ulhaq filled the C-in-C's residence with a curious harmonized scream, all of them shrieking at exactly the same pitch and pausing for breath at the same time, so that everyone had to wear ear-plugs for forty days; then they realized that their father wasn't going to return, and shut up completely, so that their grandfather never noticed them again until the last night of his reign.

The loyalty of his junior Generals showed Raza Hyder that the Army was having too good a time to wish to rock the boat. 'A stable situation,' he congratulated himself, 'everything tickety-boo.'

It was at this point that his daughter Sufiya Zinobia re-entered his life.

May I interpose a few words here on the subject of the Islamic revival? It won't take long.

Pakistan is not Iran. This may sound like a strange thing to say about the country which was, until Khomeini, one of the only two theocracies on earth (Israel being the other one), but it's my opinion that Pakistan has never been a mullah-dominated society. The religious extremists of the Jamaat party have their supporters among college students and so forth, but relatively few people have ever voted Jamaat in an election. Jinnah himself, the Founder or Quaid-i-Azam, doesn't strike me as a particularly God-bothered type. Islam and the Muslim State were, for him, political and cultural ideas; the theology was not the point.

What I am saying will probably be anathematized by the present regime in that hapless country. Too bad. My point is that Islam might well have proved an effective unifying force in post-Bangladesh Pakistan, if people hadn't tried to make it into such an almighty big deal. Maybe Sindhis, Baluchis, Punjabis and Pathans, not to mention the immigrants, would have sunk their differences for the sake of their common faith.

Few mythologies survive close examination, however. And they can become very unpopular indeed if they're rammed down people's throats.

What happens if one is force-fed such outsize, indigestible meals? – One gets sick. One rejects their nourishment. Reader: one pukes.

So-called Islamic 'fundamentalism' does not spring, in Pakistan, from the people. It is imposed on them from above. Autocratic regimes find it useful to espouse the rhetoric of faith, because people respect that language, are reluctant to oppose it. This is how religions shore up dictators; by encircling them with words of power, words which the people are reluctant to see discredited, disenfranchised, mocked.

But the ramming-down-the-throat point stands. In the end you get sick of it, you lose faith in the faith, if not *qua* faith then certainly as the basis for a state. And then the dictator falls, and it is discovered that he has brought God down with him, that the justifying myth of the nation has been unmade. This leaves only two options: disintegration, or a new dictatorship . . . no, there is a third, and I shall not be so pessimistic as to deny its possibility.

The third option is the substitution of a new myth for the old one. Here are three such myths, all available from stock at short notice: liberty; equality; fraternity.

I recommend them highly.

Afterwards, during his terror-stricken flight from the capital, Raza Hyder would remember the story of the white panther that had been in circulation at the time of Iskander Harappa's arrest, and would shudder with recognition and fear. The rumour had died down quickly enough, because nobody ever reported an actual sighting of the fabulous animal, except for one rather unreliable village boy named Ghaffar, and his description had been so cock-eyed that people had decided that the panther had sprung from inside Ghaffar's notoriously untruthful head. The improbable beast of the boy's imagination had been, he said, 'not white all over, it had a black head and no hair anywhere else, like it had gone bald; also, it walked funnily.' The newspapers had reported this statement jokily, knowing that their readers had a tolerant fondness for monster stories; but General Hyder, recalling the affair, was seized by the fearful notion that the white panther of Bagheeragali had been a proleptic miracle, a minatory prophecy, Time's ghost, the future stalking the forests of the past. 'He saw her all right,' Raza bitterly thought, 'and nobody believed.'

She reappeared in this way:

One morning Omar Khayyam Shakil was sitting looking out of the attic window as usual when Asgari the sweeperwoman, who had been driven wild by this habit of his, which obliged her to come up and sweep the floors of that forgotten room, and also by his absent-minded way of dropping pine-kernel shells on the floor while she worked, muttered under her toothless old woman's breath which smelled strongly of the disinfectant *fineel*: 'That beast should come here and finish off all inconsiderate persons who won't let an honest woman finish her job.' The word 'beast' penetrated the mists of Omar Khayyam's reverie, and he alarmed the old lady by demanding loudly, 'What is the meaning of that remark?' Once she had been convinced that he wasn't going to have her fired like Shahbanou, that he did not think of her harm-less sourness as a curse, she relaxed and scolded him, in the manner of old retainers, for taking things too seriously. 'Those stories have started up again, that's all,' she said, 'idle tongues need exercise. No need for the big sahib to get so hot.'

For the rest of that day Omar Khayyam was buffeted by an inner storm whose cause he did not dare to name, even to himself, but at night during his forty-odd winks a dream of Sufiya Zinobia came to him. She was on all fours and stripped as naked as her mother had been by the legendary firewind of her youth – no, more so, because there was nothing clinging to her shoulders, no dupatta of modesty-and-shame. He woke up, but the dream refused to leave him. It hung before his eyes, that spectre of his wife in the wilderness, hunting human and animal prey.

In the following weeks he threw off the lethargy of his more-than-sixty years. In spite of bad feet he became a familiar, eccen-tric figure at the bus depot, where he would limp up to fearsome Frontier types and offer them money in return for certain infor-mation. He hung around the halal slaughterhouses, leaning on his cane, on the days when the peasants brought animals in from the outlying districts. He frequented bazaars and ramshackle cafés, an incongruous figure in a grey suit, supported by a swordstick, asking questions, listening, listening.

Slowly it became clear to him that the stories of the white pan-ther were indeed being told again; but what was remarkable was that they had begun to come from all over the country, in the bus-top bundles of gas-field workers returning from Needle and in the cartridge belts of rifle-toting tribesmen from the north. It was a large country, even without its East Wing, a land of wilder-nesses and marshy deltas studded with mangrove trees and moun-tain fastnesses and voids; and from every out-of-the-way corner of the nation, it seemed, the tale of the panther was travel-ling to the capital. Black head, pale hairless body, awkward gait. Ghaffar's derided description was repeated to Omar Khayyam, over and over again, by illiterate voyagers, all of whom believed the rumour to be unique to their own part of the world. He did not disabuse them of this belief.

Murders of animals and men, villages raided in the dark, dead children, slaughtered flocks, blood-curdling howls: it was the time-honoured man-eater scare, but with a new and terrifying twist: 'What animal', a six-foot Frontiersman asked Omar Khayyam with the innocent awe of a child, 'can tear a man's head off his shoulders and drag his insides out through the hole to eat?'

He heard of villages that had formed vigilante groups, of mountain tribals who had placed all-night sentries on the lookout. Tales of sightings were accompanied by boastful claims of having winged the monster, or even less credible yarns, you'll never believe it, sahib, I hit it right between the eyes with a shikar rifle, but the thing is a demon, it just turned round and vanished into the air, you can't kill such creatures, God protect us ... so it appeared that the white panther was already being mythologized. There were those who said it could fly, or dematerialize, or grow until it was bigger than a tree.

She grew, too, in the imagination of Omar Khayyam Shakil. For a long time he told nobody about his suspicions, but they swarmed round his sleepless nocturnal form, they surrounded the armchair of his pine-kernel-shelling days. He imagined her, it, the Beast, choosing in the craftiness of its spirit to distance itself from cities, knowing, perhaps, that in spite of its, her, colossal strength she was vulnerable, that in cities there were bullets, gases, tanks. And how fast she had become, how much ground she covered, spreading herself so widely across the peripheries of the land that years had passed before her various legends had been able to encounter one another, to be united in his thoughts, forming the pattern which uncovered her night-obscured shape. 'Sufiya Zinobia,' he said to the open window, 'I can see you now.'

On all fours, the calluses thick on her palms and soles. The black hair, once shorn by Bilquìs Hyder, long now and matted around her face, enclosing it like fur; the pale skin of her *mohajir* ancestry burned and toughened by the sun, bearing like battle

scars the lacerations of bushes, animals, her own itch-scratching
nails. Fiery eyes and the stink of ordure and death. 'For the first
time in her life' – he shocked himself by the sympathy in the
thought – 'that girl is free.' He imagined her proud; proud of her
strength, proud of the violence that was making her a legend, that
prohibited anyone from telling her what to do, or whom to be, or
what she should have been and was not; yes, she had risen above
everything she did not wish to hear. Can it be possible, he wondered, that human beings are capable of discovering their nobility
in their savagery? Then he was angry with himself, remembering
that she was no longer Sufiya Zinobia, that nothing was left in her
which could be recognized as the daughter of Bilquìs Hyder, that
the Beast within had changed her for all time. 'I should stop
calling her by her name,' he thought; but found that he could not.
Hyder's daughter. My wife. Sufiya Zinobia Shakil.

When he decided he could not keep his secret any longer and
went to inform Raza Hyder of his daughter's activities, he found
the three Generals, Raddi, Bekar and Phisaddi, emerging from the
President's office wearing identical expressions of slightly stunned
beatitude. They had been walking on cloud nine ever since Hyder
promoted them to his inner cabinet in the aftermath of the
Tughlak coup, but on this occasion they were intoxicated by an
excess of prayer. They had just told Raza that the Russians had
sent an army into the country of A. across the north-west frontier,
and to their astonishment the President had leapt from his chair,
unrolled four prayer-mats on the floor and insisted that they all
give thanks, pronto, fut-a-fut, for this blessing that had been
bestowed on them by God. They had been rising and falling for
an hour and a half, developing on their foreheads the first traces of
the bruise which Raza wore with pride, when he stopped and
explained to them that the Russian attack was the final step in
God's strategy, because now the stability of his government would
have to be ensured by the great powers. General Raddi replied a
little too sourly that the Americans' policy was centred on staging
a dramatic counter-coup against the Olympic Games, but before

Raza could lose his temper Raddi's friends Phisaddi and Bekar began to shake each other's hands and congratulate themselves noisily. 'That fat-arsed Yankee,' Phisaddi shouted, referring to the American Ambassador, 'he'll have to foot the bills now,' and Bekar began to fantasize about five billion dollars' worth of new military equipment, the latest stuff at last, missiles that could fly sideways without starving their engines of oxygen and tracking systems that could detect an alien anopheles mosquito at a range of ten thousand miles. They were so carried away that they conveniently forgot to tell the President the rest of the news; but Raddi remembered, and blurted out before anyone could stop him the intelligence that Mr Haroun Harappa had taken up residence in an elite apartment block situated in the centre of Cabul, the capital city of A. His colleagues, alarmed by Raddi's second misjudgment of the President's mood, tried to cover for him again, reassuring Raza that the report was unconfirmed, all kinds of disinformation were emerging from Cabul in the wake of the Russian occupation; they tried to divert his attention to the question of refugees, but the President just beamed and beamed. 'They can send us ten million refugees,' he cried, 'because by taking that one in they have completed by royal flush.'

Now all three Generals were confused; all three felt obliged to explain that their best information was that Haroun Harappa was being given the full and active support of the new Russian-backed regime over the border, that he was assembling a terrorist group which was being given Soviet arms and Palestinian training, and which he had named Al-Iskander in memory of his beloved uncle. 'Excellent,' Hyder grinned, 'now at last we can show the people that the Popular Front is nothing but a bunch of assassins and bad-mashes,' and he made the three Generals get down and give thanks to God all over again.

So it was that Raza Hyder saw his colleagues to the door of his office with true happiness in his heart, and as the dazed triumvirate staggered off the President greeted Omar Khayyam Shakil with genuine warmth: 'Well, you old dog, what brings you here?'

The appalling good humour of Raza Hyder stirred up curious

emotions inside Omar Khayyam, so that it was almost with pleasure that he answered, 'A most delicate and confidential matter';
and behind the locked doors of the President's office a mood of
grim contentment settled on him while he advised Raza of his
speculations and researches and watched the good news drain out
of the President's face, to be replaced by a grey pallor of fear.

'So, so,' Raza Hyder said, 'I had almost deceived myself she
was dead.'

' "I would compare her to an impetuous river," ' Iskander
Harappa whispered in his ear, ' "that, when turbulent, inundates
the plains, casts down trees and buildings; everyone flees before it,
and everything yields to its fury without being able to oppose it.
So it is with Fortune, which shows her power where no measures
have been taken to resist her, and directs her fury where she
knows that no dykes or barriers have been made to hold her." '

'What barriers?' Raza Hyder cried aloud, convincing Omar
Khayyam that the President was cracking up under stress. 'What
walls can I build against my child?' But Maulana Dawood, his
angel of the right, said nothing.

How does a dictator fall? There is an old saw which states, with
absurd optimism, that it is in the nature of tyrannies to end. One
might as well say that it is also in their nature to begin, to continue, to dig themselves in, and, often, to be preserved by greater
powers than their own.

Well, well, I mustn't forget I'm only telling a fairy-story. My
dictator will be toppled by goblinish, faery means. 'Makes it pretty
easy for you,' is the obvious criticism; and I agree, I agree. But
add, even if it does sound a little peevish: '*You* try and get rid of a
dictator some time.'

When Raza Hyder had been President for nearly four years, the
white panther started coming closer to the capital. That is to say,
the murders and animal-slayings grew closer together, the sightings grew more frequent, the stories linked up with each other
and formed a ring around the city. General Raddi told Raza

Hyder that it was clear to him that these acts of terrorism were the work of the Al-Iskander group commanded by Haroun Harappa; whereupon, to his great surprise, the President thumped him heartily on the back. 'Good show, Raddi,' Hyder roared, 'you aren't such an idiot as I thought.' Raza convened a Presidential press briefing, at which he pinned the blame for the so-called 'headless murders' on those infamous dacoits and gangsters who were being backed by the Russians and acting under the orders of the arch-bandit Haroun, and whose purpose was to sap the moral fibre of the nation, 'to weaken our Godly resolve,' Raza said; 'destabilization is their intention, but I tell you they will never succeed.'

Secretly, however, he was aghast at this latest proof of his help-lessness to resist his daughter. It seemed to him once again that the years of his greatness and of the construction of the great edifice of national stability had been no more than self-delusory lies, that this nemesis had been stalking him all along, permitting him to rise higher and higher so that his fall might be greater; his own flesh had turned against him, and no man has a defence against such treason. Yielding to a fatalistic melancholy born of his certainty of approaching doom, he left the day-to-day running of the govern-ment in the hands of his three elevated Generals, knowing that if Sufiya Zinobia were killed by the large search parties which were now scouring the countryside for terrorists, she would also be identified, and the shame of that naming would bring him down; but if she eluded her pursuers, that would be no help either, because he saw that what she was doing was moving slowly inwards, spiralling inexorably in to the centre, to the very room in which he paced, sleeplessly, crunching with every step the carpet of pine-kernel shells covering the floor, while Omar Khayyam Shakil, similarly insomniac, stared out through the attic window at the menacing night.

Silence in his right ear. Maulana Dawood had vanished, never to speak to him again. Plagued by this silence, which was now as oppressive as the increasingly gloating sibilances of Iskander Harappa on his left side, Raza Hyder sank ever deeper into the quicksands of his despair, understanding that he had been left to his fate by God.

I have not changed my opinion of Mr Haroun Harappa: the man was a buffoon. Time inflicts strange ironies on its victims, however, and Haroun, who had once mouthed insincere revolutionary slogans and cracked jokes about Molotov cocktails while he perched on a sea-turtle's back, was now the incarnation of the thing he had once despised, a notorious gang-leader with a band of desperadoes to command.

Both Rani and Arjumand Harappa were permitted by the authorities to issue public statements from Mohenjo deploring terrorist activity. But Haroun had developed the unstoppable mulishness of the genuinely stupid man; and the death of Isky Harappa had finally cured him of his obsession with the memory of Good News Hyder. It is not uncommon for a dead love to be reborn as its opposite, and nowadays the name 'Hyder' made Haroun see nothing but red. It was a further irony, therefore, that his hijacking of a civilian aircraft on the tarmac of the airport at Q. only served to distract attention, for a few moments, from the scandal of the white panther murders and the crisis of the Hyder regime.

When General Raddi was alerted to the seizure of the aeroplane at Q., he initiated a remarkable plan, instructing the local police authorities to flatter Harappa's men as effusively as possible. 'Tell them that a coup is in progress,' Raddi suggested, amazing himself by the inspiration of his idea, 'that Hyder has been seized and the women of Mohenjo will soon be free.' Haroun Harappa fell for it, the fool, and he kept the aircraft on the ground, with its full complement of passengers, and awaited the call to power.

The day grew hotter. Condensation formed on the roof of the passenger cabin and fell on the occupants like rain. The aircraft's supplies of food and drink ran low, and Haroun in the impatience of his naïvety radioed the control tower and demanded to be sent a meal. His request was greeted with great politeness; he was told that nothing was too good for the future leader of the people, and very soon a banquet of lavish proportions was sent to the aircraft, while the control tower begged Haroun to eat and drink his fill, assuring him that he would be informed the minute it was safe for him to emerge. The terrorists gorged themselves on that food of dreams, on the meatballs of hope-beyond-hope and the fizzy drinks of delusion, and within an hour of finishing they had all fallen fast asleep in the heat, with the top buttons of their trousers open. The police boarded the aircraft and manacled them all without firing a single shot.

General Raddi searched the C-in-C's residence for Hyder, and found him in the attic of his despair. He entered to discover Raza and Omar Khayyam lost in silences. 'Wonderful news, sir,' he announced, but when he had completed his report he realized at once that he had somehow managed to put his foot in it once again, because the President rounded on him and roared: 'So you've got Harappa in the lock-up, eh? So who do you propose to blame for the panther killings now?' General Raddi blushed like a bride and began to apologize, but his puzzlement got the better of him, and he blurted out: 'But sir, surely, the elimination of the Al-Iskander threat means that the headless murders will cease?'

'Go, go, get away from me,' Raza muttered, and Raddi saw that the President's anger was muted, distant, as if he had accepted some secret fate. Nutshells crackled beneath Raddi's departing boots.

The killings continued: farmers, pie-dogs, goats. The murders formed a death-ring round the house; they had reached the outskirts of the two cities, new capital and old town. Murders without rhyme or reason, done, it seemed, for the love of killing, or to satisfy some hideous need. The crushing of Haroun Harappa removed the rational explanation; panic began to mount. The search parties were doubled, then doubled again; still the slow, circling pattern of blood continued. The idea of the monster began to be treated with incredulous seriousness by the newspapers. 'It is as if this beast can bewitch its victims,' one article said. 'Never any sign of a struggle.' A cartoonist drew a picture of a giant cobra mesmerizing heavily-armed, but powerless, mongoose hordes.

'Not long now,' Raza Hyder said aloud in the attic. 'This is the last act.' Omar Khayyam agreed. It seemed to him that Sufiya Zinobia was trying her strength, testing the powers of those hypnotic eyes on larger and larger groups, petrifying her adversaries, who stood incapable of self-defence as her hands closed round their necks. 'God knows how many she can take on,' he thought, 'maybe by now a regiment, the full Army, the whole world.'

Let us state plainly that Omar Khayyam was afraid. Raza had become fatalistically convinced that his daughter was coming for him, but she might just as easily be searching out the husband who drugged and chained her. Or the mother who named her Shame. 'We must run,' he told Raza, but Hyder seemed not to hear; the deafness of acceptance, of silence-in-the-right-ear and Isky-in-the-left had stopped his ears. A man abandoned by his God may choose to die.

When the lid blew off their secret, it began to seem like a miracle to Omar Khayyam that the truth had been kept hidden so long. Asgari the sweeperwoman had vanished without giving notice, unable, perhaps, to put up with the proliferation of pine-kernel shells; or maybe she was just the first of the servants to flee the terror, the first of them to guess what was likely to happen to anyone who stayed in that house . . . it seems probable, at any rate, that it was Asgari who spilled the beans. It was a sign of Raza's declining power that two newspapers felt able to run stories hinting that the President's daughter was a dangerous madwoman whom her father had permitted to escape from his residence some considerable time back, 'without even bothering to advise the proper authorities,' one journal cheekily said. Neither the press nor the radio went so far as to link the disappearance of Sufiya Zinobia with the 'headless murders', but it was in the wind, and in the bazaars and at the bus depots and over the tables of cheap cafés the monster began to be given its true name.

Raza summoned his triumvirate of Generals. Raddi, Bekar and Phisaddi arrived, to hear Hyder dredge up, for the last time, a few shards of his old authority. 'Arrest these subversives!' he demanded, waving newspapers at the Generals. 'I want them in the darkest jail, I want them finished, defunct, kaput!' The three officers waited until he had finished and then General Raddi said with the utter delight of a man who has long looked forward to such a moment: 'Mr President, we do not believe such action would be wise.'

'House arrest will follow in a day or two,' Hyder told Omar Khayyam, 'when they have prepared the ground. I told you: the final curtain. That Raddi, I should have known, I'm losing my grip. When a General dreams up a coup in this blasted country, you can bet he'll try and carry it out, even if he only meant it in the beginning as a sort of joke, or trick.'

How does a dictator fall? Raddi Bekar Phisaddi lift journalistic embargoes. Certain fatal connections are hinted at in print: the dead turkeys of Pinkie Aurangzeb, Good News Hyder's wedding-day fiasco and the stiff neck of Talvar Ulhaq, theories about the dead boys in the slums make the news at last. 'The people are like dry wood,' Raza Hyder says. 'These sparks will start a fire.'

Then the last night comes.

All day a crowd has been gathering around the compound walls, growing angrier as it grows larger. Now it is night and they hear it milling around: chants, shouts, jeers. And sounds from further away like whistles, the glow of fires, shrieks. Where is she, Shakil wonders, will she come now, or when? How will it end, he muses: with the mob surging into the palace, lynchings, lootings, flames — or in the other, the stranger way, the people parting like mythological waters, averting their eyes, allowing her through, their champion, to do their dirty work: their Beast with her fiery eyes? Of course, he thinks insanely, of course they have not sent soldiers to guard us, what soldier would set foot in this house of imminent death . . . and then he hears in the corridors below the soft rat-like sounds, the susurrations of servants fleeing the house, their bedrolls on their heads: bearers and hamals and sweeper-boys, gardeners and odd-job men, ayahs and maids. Some of them are accompanied by children, who might in the daylight look too well-fed for their ragged clothes, but who will pass, in the night, for the offspring of the poor. Twenty-seven children; as he hears them go he counts, in his imagination, their padding steps. And feels, from the invisible night-mob, an expectancy, filling the air.

'For pity's sake,' he pleads with Raza, 'let's try and get out.' But Hyder is a crushed figure, incapable for the first time in his life of producing moisture from his eyes. 'Impossible,' he shrugs, 'the crowds. And beyond them there will be troops.'

The door creaks; a woman's feet crush scattered empty shells. Approaching across the pine-kernel droppings is – is the forgotten figure of Bilquìs Hyder. Who is carrying a heap of shapeless garments, a selection from the work of her isolated years. Burqas, Omar Khayyam realizes, as hope bursts inside him; head-to-toe cloaks of invisibility, veils. *The living wear shrouds as well as the dead.* Bilquìs Hyder says simply, 'Put these on.' Shakil seizes, rushes into his womanly disguise; Bilquìs pulls the black fabric over her husband's unresisting head. 'Your son became a daughter,' she tells him, 'so now you must change shape also. I knew I was sewing these for a reason.' The President is passive, allows himself to be led. Black-veiled fugitives mingle with escaping servants in the darkened corridors of the house.

How Raza Hyder fell: in improbability; in chaos; in women's clothing; in black.

Nobody questions women wearing veils. They pass through the mob and the ring of soldiers, jeeps, trucks. Finally Raza speaks: 'So what now? Where to go from here?'

And because Omar Khayyam is filled with the sense of having walked out into the middle of a dream, he hears himself replying: 'I think I know a place.'

And Sufiya Zinobia?

She did not attack the empty palace. She was not caught, nor killed, nor seen again in that part of the country. It was as if her hunger had been satisfied; or as though she had never been more than a rumour, a chimaera, the collective fantasy of a stifled people, a dream born of their rage; or even as if, sensing a change in the order of the world, she had retreated, and was prepared to wait a little longer, in that fifteenth century, for her time.

V

JUDGMENT DAY

I t is almost over.

Veiled, bumping on buses, cowering in the shadows of bus stations, they head south and west. Always on the short-haul routes, the stopping buses, avoiding the Trunk Road mail expresses. Off the Potwar plateau, down into the riverine plains, their faces set towards the land-border beyond Q. They have only the money they find in their pockets, so they eat little, drink as much as possible: livid green cordials, pink tea scooped out of large aluminium pots, water drawn from yellow lakes in which enervated water-buffalo sprawl. For days they scarcely speak, and force themselves to remain impassive when policemen walk squinting along queues of waiting travellers at small-town depots, tapping their lathis against short-trousered thighs. For Shakil and Hyder, the humiliation of the ladies' latrines. There is no country poorer than Escape.

They are not caught; nobody expects a fleeing President to be found in women's clothing on a rutputty third-class bus. But there are sleepless days and nights; there is fear, and despair. A flight through an exploding land. In the lassitudinous heat of the rural areas bus radios interrupt the swooning agonies of singers to speak

of riots and gunshots. On two occasions they sit in buses surrounded by demonstrators, and wonder if they are to die in an
anonymous sandy town, engulfed by petrol fire. But the buses are
allowed to pass, and slowly the border approaches. And beyond
the border, the possibility of hope: yes, there might be sanctuary
across the frontier, in that neighbouring country of priest-kings,
godly men who would surely give refuge to a fallen leader with a
bruise upon his brow. And then they might even be far enough
from *her*, from feral nemesis, from the revenge of flesh against
flesh. Raza Hyder, unmanned by wife-sewn veils, clings to such
optimistic straws.

The border is impossible to police. Concrete posts marching
across the wastes. Omar Khayyam remembers the stories of people
crossing it at will, of old man Zoroaster impoverished by that
open frontier, deprived by wasteland of all supplements to his
income. The memory of Farah Rodrigues which this recollection
triggers almost chokes him, mingling in his gullet with the history
of the ayah Shahbanou; then the dizziness begins. As he recalls the
cloud which descended along the frontier and frightened him so
badly that he fainted in Farah's arms, he realizes that his old vertigo is returning to torment him, it rushes upon him as he sits in a
jolting bus with chickens pecking at his neck and travel-sick
sharecroppers in the aisles, vomiting on his toes. The vertigo
carries him back to his childhood and shows him once again
the worst of all his nightmares, the gaping mouth of the void. The
deepest parts of Omar Khayyam are stirring once more, the
dizziness is churning them up, they are warning him that
whatever anyone says he ought to know that the border is the
edge of his world, the rim of things, and that the real dreams are
these far-fetched notions of getting across that supernatural
frontier into some wild hallucination of a promised land. Get
back into 'Nishapur', the inner voices whisper, because that's
where you've been heading, all your life, ever since the day
you left.

Fear fights off the vertigo; it gives him the power not to faint.

The worst moment comes almost at the end. They are climbing aboard the last of the buses of their flight, the bus which is to bear them to the depot at Q., when they hear the terrifying joke. 'Look where we've got to in this country,' the bus-driver sneers, he is enormous, with tree-trunk arms and a face like a horsehair cushion, 'even the transvestites are going into purdah now.' At once the busload of gas-miners and bauxite quarrymen starts up a racket of wolf-whistles, dirty laughs, obscenities, ulula-tions, songs; hands reach out to pinch the *hijra* bottoms. 'This is it,' Omar Khayyam thinks, 'done for, trapped, funtoosh,' because he is sure that someone will tear off their veils, and Hyder's is a famous face, after all – but just then Bilquìs Hyder speaks up and silences the passengers completely. 'Shame should come to you, she cries in her unquestionably female voice, 'have the men in this region sunk so low that ladies must be treated like whores?' A hush of embarrassment in the bus. The driver, blushing, orders three farm labourers to vacate their seats at the very front of the vehicle, 'to make sure, begums, that you are not molested further; yes, it is a question of honour for me, the dignity of my autobus has been dirtied.'

So: in a silent and apologetic bus, and after surviving a bad scare, Omar Khayyam Shakil and his two companions arrive, soon after midnight, at the bus station in the outskirts of Q. Hobbling on bad feet, unsupported by the stick he has been obliged to leave behind, exhausted, he leads them through unlit streets to a large building between the Cantonment and the bazaar, where he unveils himself and emits a certain whistle, repeating it until he sees the movement at an upstairs window; and then the contrap-tion of Mistri Yakoob Balloch begins its descent, and they are raised into 'Nishapur', the mother-country, home, like buckets drawn from a well.

When Omar Khayyam's three mothers understood who had been brought into their presence they emitted little sighs, as if after many years they had been released from some particularly constricting garments, and settling down comfortably side-by-side on their creaky old swing-seat they began to smile. The smile was beatific, innocent, but somehow its replication on the three identically ancient mouths gave it a quality of distinct, though indefinable, menace. It was the middle of the night, but one of the three old ladies, whom Omar Khayyam in the exhaustion of his travels had barely recognized as Chhunni-ma, ordered him to go at once into the kitchen and boil some tea, as if he had just come in after popping out for a couple of minutes. 'No servants any more,' Chhunni Shakil apologized gracefully to Raza Hyder, who had torn off his burqa and collapsed into a chair in a dazed condition for which fatigue was only a partial explanation, 'but our first visitors for over fifty years must take a welcoming cup.' Omar Khayyam lumbered off and returned with the tray, only to be scolded affectionately by a second mother, the withered remnant of Munnee-in-the-middle: 'Hopeless, I swear. What pot are you bringing, boy? Go to the almirah and fetch out the best.' He followed her pointing finger to a large teak cupboard in which he discovered, to his great amazement, the long-lost thousand-piece china service from the Gardner works in Tsarist Russia, those miracles of the crockery-maker's art which had faded into mere legends as long ago as his childhood. The revenant dishes and plates brought a hot flush to his face, filling his spinning thoughts with a nostalgic terror, inspiring in him the fleeting but awesome idea that he had come back to a household populated only by ghosts. But the blue-and-pink cups and saucers and quarterplates were solid enough; he arranged them on his tray with a shiver of disbelief.

'Now go quickly to the Peek Frean tin and bring out cake,' commanded his youngest mother, Bunny, her octogenarian voice trembling with a delight she made no effort to explain; Omar Khayyam muttered something puzzled and inaudible and limped away in search of the stale chocolate gâteau which added the final touch of quaint improbability to that *takallouf*-ridden nightmare of a tea-party. 'This is more like it,' Chhunni approved as she cut and handed out slices of dried-out cake. 'For such honoured guests, this is the usual way.'

Omar Khayyam observed that while he had been out of the room fetching the cake his mothers had obliged Bilquìs Hyder, by the inexorable force of their courtly charm, to remove her burqa. Her face, eyebrowless, dust-pale, sleep-starved, was a death-mask, with only the high points of red colour on her cheekbones to indicate that she was alive; it made the bad feelings Omar Khayyam had been having even worse than before. His teacup rattled on its saucer while his heart was squeezed by a renewed fear of the cryptic atmosphere of his childhood home, which could turn living persons into the mirrors of their ghosts; then Bilquìs spoke, and he was jerked out of these exhausted fantasies by her expression of a most peculiar idea.

'Once there were giants,' Bilquìs Hyder carefully, and wistfully, pronounced.

The laws of *takallouf* had forced her to make conversation, but it had been too long since Bilquìs had indulged in chit-chat; she had lost the knack of it, and there was the tension and debilitation of the long escape to consider besides, to say nothing of the eccentricity of her latter years. Sipping tea as she spoke, smiling brightly in response to the triple smile of her hostesses, she seemed to imagine herself to be recounting some tiny, amusing anecdote, or expatiating wittily upon a sophisticated point of fashion. 'Once giants walked the earth,' she repeated, emphatically. 'Yes, titans absolutely, it's a fact.'

Three mothers creaked and swung with expressions of fascinated absorption upon their smiling faces; but Raza Hyder took no notice, closed his eyes, grunted from time to time. 'Now the pygmies have taken over, however,' Bilquìs confided. 'Tiny personages. Ants. Once he was a giant,' she jerked a thumb in the direction of her somnolent husband, 'you would not believe to look, but he was. Streets where he walked shook with fear and respect, even here, in this very town. But, you see, even a giant can be pygmified, and he has shrunk now, he is smaller than a bug. Pygmies pygmies everywhere, also insects and ants – shame on the giants, isn't it? Shame on them for shrinking. That's my opinion.' Three old ladies nodded gravely while Bilquìs made her lament; then they hastened to agree with her. 'Quite right,' Chhunni pronounced courteously, and Munnee chimed in, 'Giants, how true, there must have been,' and then Bunny Shakil concluded: 'Because after all there are angels also, they are still around, oh yes, we are sure of that.'

An unnaturally high colour suffused Bilquìs's face as she sipped her tea, annihilating the image of the death-mask; she was apparently determined to find solace in that appalling scene, to convince herself of her safety by forging a desperate and over-rapid intimacy between herself and the three creaking ancients . . . but Omar Khayyam had stopped noticing things, because at the moment when his youngest mother mentioned angels he had understood the strange high spirits of the Shakil sisters. His three mothers were improvising this instant of demented theatre so as to avoid having to mention a certain dead youth; there was a hole at the heart of their smiling hospitality, and they were skirting around its periphery, around that void such as escaping creatures make in bricked-up windows, that absence the shape of the unnamable Babar Shakil. Yes, that was it, they were in a state of elation, because they had Raza Hyder in their clutches at last, and could see no reason except one for Omar Khayyam to have brought the fellow here; so they were trying not to spoil things, seeking to lull their victims into a sense of false security, they didn't want the Hyders to get worried and try to run away. And at the same time they were sighing happily, convinced it was finally going to happen, revenge, right under their noses. Omar Khayyam Shakil's head swam with the knowledge that the three of them would force him to do it – remorselessly and in cold blood to do Raza Hyder to death under his mothers' roof.

The next morning he awoke to the sound of Bilquìs Hyder slamming windows. Omar Khayyam struggled out of a bed which was unaccountably soaked in perspiration, his legs weaker, his feet more painful than usual, and hobbled off to see what was happening. He found his three mothers watching Bilquìs as she stormed around the house, pulling windows shut, fiercely, as if she were angry about something; she fastened shutters and lowered chick-blinds. It struck Omar Khayyam as if for the first time how tall his mothers were, like arms stretched up into the sky. They stood in attitudes of mutual solicitude, supporting each other at the elbows, making no attempt to interfere with Bilquìs's window-shutting frenzy. Omar Khayyam wanted to stop her, because as the windows closed the air inside the house became thicker and lumpier, until he felt as if he were inhaling mulligatawny soup, but his three mothers motioned him to be still. 'She is our guest,' whispered Chhunni-ma, 'so she can stay for ever if she likes,' because the old woman had divined that Bilquìs's behaviour was that of a woman who has gone far enough already, too far, a woman who has ceased to believe in frontiers and whatever-might-lie-beyond. Bilquìs was barricading herself against the outside world in the hope that it might go away, and that was an activity which the Shakil sisters could understand without a word being said. 'She has suffered,' Munnee Shakil stated with a mysterious smile, 'but she is welcome to be here.'

Omar Khayyam felt the air congeal into soup, and the germs of claustrophobia began to breed. But other germs, too, were in the air, and when Bilquìs collapsed in a boiling stupor Omar Khayyam guessed the meaning of his own morning weakness, the hot flushes, the rubbery legs. 'Malaria,' he made himself say, and then the vertigo swirled around him and he fell down beside Bilquìs Hyder, out cold and blazing hot.

At that very instant Raza Hyder awoke from a sick dream in which the several pieces of the late Sindbad Mengal had appeared to him, all joined up in the wrong way, so that the dead man's head was in the middle of his stomach and his feet stuck out, soles upward, like asses' ears from his neck. Mengal had not recriminated at all, but had warned Raza that the way things were going the General sahib would be sliced up himself in a few days. Old Razor Guts, still half-asleep, rose from his bed crying danger, but the disease had begun to burn inside him, too, and he fell back gasping for air and shivering as if it were winter. The Shakil sisters came and stood beside his bed to watch him shake.

'How nice,' Bunny Shakil said comfortably, 'the General seems to be in no hurry to depart.'

The fever was a fire that made you cold. It burned away the barriers between consciousness and sleep, so that Omar Khayyam never knew whether things were really happening or not. At one point as he lay in a darkened room he thought he heard Bilquìs shouting something about brain-fever, about visitations and judgments, the sickness that crippled her daughter being visited upon her parent in the city of her shame. He thought, too, that he heard Raza yelling for pine-kernels. And at another time he was sure that the forgotten figure of the schoolteacher Eduardo Rodrigues had been standing accusingly by his bedside holding a dead baby in its arms – but that couldn't be true, that must have been the delirium. There were moments of what felt like lucidity, during which he called for his mothers and dictated the names of drugs. He had memories of receiving medication, he recalled arms lifting his head and popping white pills into his mouth, but when he bit one by mistake it tasted of calcium, so that the suspicion was born in his fevered brain that his mothers had not sent for the drugs at all. His thoughts heated up to the point at which he could entertain the sick possibility that the Shakil sisters were happy to let the malaria do their dirty work for them, that they were willing to sacrifice their surviving son if he took the Hyders along with him. Either they are mad or I am, he thought, and then the fever took him again and made all thinking impossible.

Sometimes, he believed, he had gained consciousness and heard through the closed and shuttered windows snatches of angry

voices below, also shots, explosions, breaking glass, and unless that
had been part of the delirium too it meant that troubles were
erupting in the town, yes, he could remember certain cries clearly,
for instance *The hotel is on fire*. Was it or wasn't it? Memories
lurched back towards him through the marshes of the disease, he
was almost positive now that he had heard the hotel burn, the
crash of the collapsing golden dome, the last suffocating squawks
of an orchestra crushed beneath the falling masonry. There had
been a morning on which the ash cloud of the dead hotel
had managed to get inside 'Nishapur', in spite of shutters and
windowpanes it had insinuated itself into his bedroom, covering
everything with the grey powder of the hotel's death and
strengthening his feeling of being stricken down in a house of
phantoms. But when he asked one – which? – of his three
mothers about the burning hotel she – who? – had replied, 'Close
your eyes now and don't worry. Ash everywhere, what an idea.'

He persisted in his belief that the world was changing outside,
old orders were passing, great structures were being cast down
while others rose up in their place. The world was an earthquake,
abysses yawned, dream-temples rose and fell, the logic of the
Impossible Mountains had come down to infect the plains. In his
delirium, however, in the burning clutches of the sickness and the
foetid atmosphere of the house, only endings seemed possible. He
could feel things caving in within him, landslips, heaves, the patter
of crumbling masonry in his chest, cog-wheels breaking, a false
note in the engine's hum. 'This motor,' he said aloud somewhere
in that halted time, 'will not run any more.'

Three mothers creaked on their swing-seat at his bedside. No,
how had they moved it, what was it doing here, it was a ghost, a
mirage, he refused to believe in it, closed his eyes, squeezed them
tight, reopened them a minute or a week later, and they were still
there in the seat, so it was clear that the sickness was worse, the
hallucinations were gaining in confidence. The sisters were
explaining sadly that the house was no longer as big as it had once
been. 'We keep on losing rooms,' the spectre of Bunny mourned,

'today we mislaid your grandfather's study. You know where it used to be, but now if you go through that door you turn up in the dining room, which is impossible, because the dining room is supposed to be on the other side of the passage.' And Chhunni-ma nodded, 'It's so sad, son, look how life treats old people, you get used to a certain bedroom and then one day, poof, it goes away, the staircase vanishes, what to do.' 'The place is shrinking,' middle-Munnee fumed. 'Honestly, too bad, like a cheap shirt. We should have had it Sanforized. Soon the whole house will be smaller than a matchbox and we will be out on the street.' And Chhunni-ma had the last word. 'In that sunlight, without walls,' the phantasm of his eldest mother prophesied, 'we will not be able to survive. We will turn to dust and be blown away by the wind.'

Then he was unconscious again. When he surfaced there was no swing-seat, there were no mothers, he was alone in that four-poster bed with serpents coiled round the columns and Paradise embroidered on the canopy. His grandfather's deathbed. He realized that he felt as strong as a horse. Time to get up. He jumped out of bed and had wandered barefoot and pajama-clad out of the room before it occurred to him that this was only another illusion, but by then he couldn't stop himself, his feet, which had stopped hurting, walked him along the cluttered passages full of hatracks and stuffed fishes in glass cases and broken ormolu clocks, and he saw that far from having shrunk, the house had actually expanded, it had grown so vast that it held within its walls every place in which he had ever been. The sum of all his possibilities: he opened one cobwebbed door and shrank back from the little, brightly-lit group of white-masked figures stooping over a body. It was an operating room at the Mount Hira Hospital. The figures were beckoning to him in a friendly way, they wanted him to help with the operation but he was afraid to see the patient's face. He turned abruptly and felt pine-kernel shells crunching beneath his heels as the rooms of the Commander-in-Chief's official residence began to form around him. At some point he began to run, trying to find his way back to bed, but the corridors kept turning corners without warning, and he arrived panting at a mirror-worked marquee in which a wedding banquet was being held, he saw the bride's face in a fragment of mirror, she wore a noose around her neck, and he shouted out, 'You should have stayed dead,' making all the guests stare at him. They were all dressed in rags because of the dangers of going well-dressed into the turbulence of the streets and they were chanting in unison, shame, shame, poppy-shame, all the girls, know your name. Then he was running again, but slowing down, he was getting heavier, his chins flopped sweatily down from his jaw until they touched his nipples, the rolls of his obesity hung over his knees, until he could not move, no matter how hard he tried, he was sweating like a pig, the heat the cold, no escape, he thought, and tumbled backwards as a shroud fell softly over him, white, soaking wet, and he realized that he was in bed.

He heard a voice, which he identified, after a struggle, as Hashmat Bibi's. She spoke from within a cloud: 'Only child. Always they live too much in their poor head.' But he had not remained an only child.

Burning, burning in that cold fire. Brain-fever. Bilquìs Hyder at his bedside pointed angrily to the Peek Frean tin. 'Poison,' she accused, 'germ poison in the cake. But we were hungry, we could not resist and so we ate.' Upset by this slur on his family name, he began to defend his mothers' hospitality, no, not the cake, it was stale but don't be ridiculous, think of the bus-journey, look what we drank, green pink yellow, our defences were low. Bilquìs shrugged and went over to a cupboard and pulled out every piece of the Gardner china collection, one by one, and smashed them all into pink-and-blue dust on the floor. He shut his eyes, but eyelids were no defence any more, they were just doors into other places, and there was Raza Hyder in uniform with a monkey on each shoulder. The monkey on the right had the face of Maulana Dawood and its hands were clasped over its mouth; on the left shoulder sat Iskander Harappa scratching his langoor's armpit. Hyder's hands went to his ears, Isky's, after scratching, covered his eyes, but he was peeping through the fingers. 'Stories end, worlds end', Isky the monkey said, 'and then it's judgment day.' Fire, and the dead, rising up, dancing in the flames.

During recessions in the fever he remembered dreaming things that he could not have known were true, visions of the future, of what would happen after the end. Quarrels between three Generals. Continued public disturbances. Great powers shifting their ground, deciding the Army had become unstable. And at last Arjumand and Haroun set free, reborn into power, the virgin Ironpants and her only love taking charge. The fall of God, and in his place the myth of the Martyr Iskander. And after that arrests, retribution, trials, hangings, blood, a new cycle of shamelessness and shame. While at Mohenjo cracks appear in the earth.

A dream of Rani Harappa: who chooses to remain at Mohenjo, and sends Arjumand, one day, a gift of eighteen exquisite shawls. These shawls ensure that she will never leave the estate again: Arjumand has her own mother placed under guard. People engaged in building new myths have no time for embroidered criticisms. Rani remains in that heavy-eaved house where the water flows blood-red; she inclines her head in the direction of Omar Khayyam Shakil. 'Seems the world can't be a safe place,' she pronounces her epitaph, 'if Rani Harappa's on the loose.'

Stories end, worlds end; and then it's judgment day.

His mother Chhunni says: 'There is something you should know.'

He lies helpless between wooden serpents, burning, freezing, red eyes wandering in his head. He gulps air; it feels somehow fuzzy, as if he has been buried by divine justice beneath a gigantic woollen mountain. He is beached, gasping, a whale pecked at by birds. But this time the three of them are really there, no hallucination, he is sure of it, they sit on his bed with a secret to reveal. His head swims; he closes his eyes.

And hears, for the first time in his life, the last family secret, the worst tale in history. The story of his great-grandfather and his brother, Hafeezullah and Rumi Shakil. Each married a woman the other found unsuitable, and when Hafeez spread it around town that his sister-in-law was a female as loose as a baggy pajama whom Rumi had plucked out of the notorious Heeramandi red-light district, the break between the brothers was complete. Then Rumi's wife took her revenge. She convinced her husband that the cause of Hafeez's sanctimonious disapproval was that he had wanted to sleep with her, after her marriage, and she had turned him down flat. Rumi Shakil became as cold as ice and went at once to his writing-desk, where he composed an anonymous, poison-pen letter to his brother, in which he accused Hafeez's wife of having extramarital relations with a famous sitarist of the time, an accusation which was lethal because it was true. Hafeez Shakil had always trusted his wife blindly, so he turned pale when he read the letter, which he recognized instantly as having been written in his brother's hand. When he questioned his wife she confessed at once. She said she had always loved the sitarist and would have run away with him if her parents hadn't married her off to Hafeez. Omar Khayyam's great-grandfather took to his bed and when his wife came to see him, holding their son in her arms, he put his right hand on his chest and addressed his last words to the baby boy.

'This motor,' he said sadly, 'will not run any more.'

He died that night.

'You said the same thing,' Munnee Shakil tells Omar Khayyam, 'in your fever, when you didn't know what you were talking about. The same thing in the same words. Now you know why we told you the story.'

'You know everything now,' Chhunni-ma continues. 'You know this is a family in which brothers have done the worst of things to brothers, and maybe you even know that you are just the same.'

'You also had a brother,' Bunny says, 'and you have treated his memory like mud.'

Once, before he went out into the world, they had forbidden him to feel shame; now they were turning that emotion upon him, slashing him with that sword. 'Your brother's father was an anarchangel,'

Chhunni Shakil whispered at his bedside, 'so the boy was too good for this world. But you, your maker was a devil out of hell.' He was sinking back into the swamps of the fever, but this remark hit home, because none of his mothers had ever spontaneously raised the subject of fathers before. It became obvious to him that his mothers hated him, and to his surprise he found the idea of that hatred too terrible to be borne.

The illness was lapping at his eyelashes now, offering oblivion. He fought against it, a man of sixty-five overwhelmed by motherly disgust. He saw it as a living thing, huge and greasy. They had been feeding it for years, handing it morsels of themselves, holding out pieces of their memories of dead Babar to their hateful pet. Who gobbled them up, snatching them greedily from the sisters' long bony fingers.

Their dead Babar, who, during his short life, had never been permitted to forget his inferiority to his elder brother, the great man, the success, the man who enabled them to shoo away the pawnbroker, to save their past from ending up on the shelves of Chalaak Sahib. The brother whom he, Omar Khayyam, had never known. Mothers use their children as sticks — each brother a rod with which to chastise the other. Asphyxiated by the hot wind of his mothers' worship of Omar Khayyam, Babar fled into the mountains; now the mothers had changed sides, and the dead boy was their weapon against the living. *You married into the murderer's family. You licked the shoes of the great.* Behind his eyelids Omar Khayyam saw his mothers placing, around his neck, the garland of their hatred. This time there was no mistake; his sweat-drenched beard rubbed against the frayed laces, the tattered leathery tongues, the laughing mouths of the necklace of discarded shoes.

The Beast has many faces. It takes any shape it chooses. He felt it crawl into his belly and begin to feed.

General Raza Hyder awoke one morning at dawn with his ears full of a tinkling, splintering sound like the breaking of a thousand windows, and realized that it was the noise of the sickness breaking. He took a deep breath and sat upright in bed. 'Fever,' he said happily, 'I beat you. Old Razor Guts isn't finished yet.' The noise ended and he had the feeling of floating across a lake of silence, because the voice of Iskander Harappa had fallen silent for the first time in four long years. He heard birds outside; they were only crows, but they sounded as sweet as bulbuls. 'Things are on the mend,' Raza Hyder thought. Then he noticed the state he was in. They had left him to rot in the bog of his own juices. It was obvious that nobody had been to see him for days. He was lying in the pestilential squashiness of his own excrement, in sheets turned yellow by perspiration and urine. Mould had begun to form on the bedclothes, and there was green fungus on his body as well. 'So this is what they think of me,' he exclaimed to the empty room, 'those witches, I'll give them what for.' But in spite of the hideous condition of the sick-bed his new mood of optimism refused to be punctured. He stood up on legs which were only slightly wobbly and threw off the stinking garments of his illness; then, with great delicacy and distaste, he gathered together a bundle of suppurating linen and dropped it out of a window. 'Hags,' he chuckled to himself, 'let them get their own dirty laundry from the street, it serves them right.' Naked now, he went into the bathroom and showered. As he soaped away the fever-stink a daydream of a return to power flitted across his mind. 'Sure,' he told himself, 'we'll do it, why not? Before anyone knows what's what.' He felt a great surge of fondness for the wife who had rescued him from the jaws of his enemies, and was filled with the desire to make things right between the two of them. 'I treated her badly,' he accused himself guiltily, 'but she came up trumps all right.' The memory of Sufiya Zinobia had become little more than a bad dream; he was not even sure of its basis in fact, half-believing it was just one of the many hallucinations which the disease had sent to torment him. He stepped out of the shower, wrapped a towel around himself and went in search of clothes. 'If Bilquìs hasn't recovered yet,' he vowed, 'I'll nurse her night and day. I'm not leaving her to the mercy of those three crazy vultures.'

There were no clothes anywhere. 'God damn it,' Raza blasphemed, 'couldn't they have left me a shalwar and a shirt?'

He opened the door of his room and called out, 'Anyone there?' But there was no reply. The lake of silence filled the house. 'O.K.,' thought Raza Hyder, 'then they'll just have to take me as they find me.' Wrapping his towel firmly around his waist, he set off in search of his wife.

Three empty, darkened rooms and then a fourth which he knew was the right place by the smell. 'Bitches!' he yelled savagely to the echoing house. 'Have you no shame?' Then he went inside.

The stench was even worse than it had been in his own room, and Bilquìs Hyder lay still in the obscenity of her shit. 'Don't worry, Billoo,' he whispered to her, 'Raz is here. I'll clean you up good and proper and then you'll see. Those animal women, I'll make them pick up turds with their eyelashes and stuff them up their nostrils.'

Bilquìs did not reply, and it took Raza a few moments to sniff out the reason for her silence. Then he smelt the other smell beneath the putrid odours of waste matter, and he felt as if a hangman's knot had smashed him in the back of the neck. He sat down on the floor and began drumming his fingers on the stone. When he spoke it came out all wrong, he hadn't meant to sound bad-tempered, but what came out was this: 'For God's sake, Billoo, what are you up to? I hope you are not acting or something. What's the meaning of this, you're not supposed to die?' But Bilquìs had crossed her frontier.

After his querulous words had come out to embarrass him he looked up to find the three Shakil sisters standing in front of him with scented handkerchiefs over their noses. Chhunni-ma also held, in her other hand, an antique blunderbuss which had once belonged to her grandfather Hafeezullah Shakil. She was pointing it at Raza's chest, but it was waggling about so much that her chances of hitting him were remote, and anyway the piece was so impossibly old that it would probably blow up in her face if she pulled the trigger. Unfortunately for Raza's chances, however, her sisters were also armed. Handkerchiefs were in their left hands, but in Munnee's right was a fierce-looking scimitar with a jewelled haft, while Bunny's fist was closed around the shaft of a spear with a badly rusted, but undeniably pointy, head. Optimism left Raza Hyder without bothering to say good-bye.

'You should be dead instead of her,' Chhunni Shakil declared. The anger had gone out with the optimism. 'Go ahead,' he encouraged the sisters. 'God will judge us all.'

'He did well to bring you here,' Bunny reflected, 'our son. He did well to wait for your fall. There is no shame in killing you now, because you are a dead man anyway. It is only the execution of a corpse.'

'Also,' Munnee Shakil said, 'there is no God.'

Chhunni waved the blunderbuss in the direction of Bilquìs. 'Pick her up,' she ordered. 'Just as she is. Pick her and bring her quick.' He rose to his feet; the towel slipped; he made a grab for it, missed, and stood naked before the old women, who had the grace to gasp . . . freshly showered, and wholly undressed, General Raza Hyder carried the stinking, mould-encrusted body of his wife through the corridors of 'Nishapur', while three sisters hovered around him like carrion crows. 'You must go in here,' Chhunni stated, pushing the barrel of the blunderbuss into his back, and he entered the last room of all the rooms in his life, and recognized the dark bulk of the dumb-waiter hanging outside the window and blocking most of the light. He had resolved to remain silent whatever happened, but his surprise made him speak: 'What's this?' he asked. 'Are you sending us outside?'

'How well known the General must be in our town,' Munnee mused. 'So many friends eager to meet you again, don't you think? What a reception they will make when they find out who is here.'

Raza Hyder naked in the dumb-waiter beside Bilquìs's corpse. The three sisters moved to a panel on the wall: buttons switches levers. 'This machine was built by a master craftsman,' Chhunni explained, 'in the old days, when nothing was beyond doing. A certain Mistri Balloch; and at our request, which we conveyed to him through our dear departed Hashmat Bibi, he included in the contrivance some extra fitments, which we now propose to use for the first and last time.'

'Let me go,' Raza Hyder cried, understanding nothing. 'What are you wasting time for?'

They were his last words. 'We asked for these arrangements,' Munnee Shakil said as the three sisters each placed a hand upon one of the levers, 'thinking self-defence is no offence. But also, you must agree, revenge is sweet.' The image of Sindbad Mengal flashed into Raza's mind as the three sisters pulled down the lever, acting in perfect unison, so that it was impossible to say who pulled first or hardest, and the ancient spring-releases of Yakoob Balloch worked like a treat, the secret panels sprang back and the eighteen-inch stiletto blades of death drove into Raza's body, cutting him to pieces, their reddened points emerging, among other places, through his eyeballs, adam's-apple, navel, groin and mouth. His tongue, severed cleanly by a laterally spearing knife, fell out on to his lap. He made strange clicking noises; shivered; froze.

'Leave them in there,' Chhunni instructed her sisters. 'We will not be needing this contraption any more.'

The contractions were coming regularly, squeezing his temples, as if something were trying to be born. The cell was swarming with malaria-bearing anopheles mosquitoes, but for some reason they did not seem to be biting the stiff-necked figure of the inter-rogator, who wore a white helmet and carried a riding whip. 'Pen and paper is before you,' the interrogator said. 'No pardon can be considered until a full confession has been made.'

'Where are my mothers?' Omar Khayyam asked piteously, in a voice that was in the process of breaking. It soared-high-plunged-low; he was embarrassed by its antics.

'Sixty-five years old,' the other sneered, 'and acting like a baby. Get a move on, I haven't got all day. I am expected at the polo ground very shortly.'

'A pardon is really possible?' Omar Khayyam inquired. The

interrogator shrugged in a bored way. 'Anything is possible,' he replied, 'God is great, as you will doubtless be aware.'

'What shall I put,' Omar Khayyam wondered, picking up the pen, 'I can confess to many things. Fleeing-from-roots, obesity, drunkenness, hypnosis. Getting girls in the family way, not sleeping with my wife, too-many-pine-kernels, peeing-tommery as a boy. Sexual obsession with under-age brain-damaged female, resultant failure to avenge my brother's death. I didn't know him. It is difficult to commit such acts on behalf of strangers. I confess to making strangers of my kin.'

'This is not helpful,' the interrogator interrupted. 'What kind of man are you? What type of bounder will wriggle out of his guilt and let his mothers take the rap?'

'I am a peripheral man,' Omar Khayyam answered. 'Other persons have been the principal actors in my life-story. Hyder and Harappa, my leading men. Immigrant and native, Godly and profane, military and civilian. And several leading ladies. I watched from the wings, not knowing how to act. I confess to social climbing, to only-doing-my-job, to being cornerman in other people's wrestling matches. I confess to fearing sleep.'

'We are getting nowhere.' The interrogator sounded angry. 'Evidence is beyond dispute. Your swordstick, gifted to you by Iskander Harappa, the victim's arch-enemy. Motive and opportunity, plenty of both. Why keep up this pretence? You bided your time, for years you lived a false life, you won their trust, finally you drew them to the killing ground. Promising flight across the frontier to lure them on. Most effective bait. Then you pounced, stab stab stab, over and over. This is all obvious to see. Cut the cackle now, and write.'

'I am not guilty,' Omar Khayyam began, 'I left the swordstick at the C-in-C's,' but just then his pockets started feeling very heavy, and the interrogator stretched out his hands to pluck out what-weighed-pockets-down. When Omar Khayyam saw what Talvar Ulhaq was holding out to him on an accusing palm, his voice turned falsetto. 'My mothers must have put them in there,' he shrieked, but there was no point in going on, because staring up at him from his inquisitor's hand were the terrible exhibits, pieces of Raza Hyder, neatly sliced, his moustache, his eyeballs, teeth.

'You are damned,' Talvar Ulhaq said, and, raising his pistol, shot Omar Khayyam Shakil through the heart. The cell had begun to burn. Omar Khayyam saw the abyss open up beneath his feet, felt the vertigo come as the world dissolved. 'I confess,' he cried, but it was too late. He tumbled into the black fire and was burned.

Because they had grown accustomed to ignoring the house, it was not until that evening that someone noticed a change, and shouted out that the great front doors of the Shakil mansion were standing open for the first time that anybody could remember; but then they all knew at once that something important had happened, so that it hardly seemed like a surprise when they found the congealing pool of blood below the dumb-waiter of Mistri Balloch. For a long while they stood transfixed by the open doors, unable to go inside, even for a peep, in spite of their curiosity; then all in a moment they rushed in, as if some unseen voice had given them permission: cobblers, beggars, gas-miners, policemen, milkmen, bank clerks, women on donkeys, children with metal hoops and sticks, gram vendors, acrobats, blacksmiths, wives, mothers, everyone.

They found the dejected palace of the sisters' haughty pride standing defenceless, at their mercy, and they were amazed by themselves, by their hatred of the place, a hatred which oozed out of sixty-five-year-old, forgotten wells; they ripped the house to pieces as they hunted for the old women. They were like locusts. They dragged the ancient tapestries off the walls and the fabric turned to dust in their hands, they forced open money-boxes which were full of discontinued notes and coins, they flung open doors which cracked and fell off their hinges, they turned beds upside-down and ransacked the contents of silver canteens, they tore baths from their moorings for the sake of their gilded feet and pulled out the stuffing from the sofas in search of hidden treasure, they threw the useless old swing-seat out of the nearest window. It was as if a spell had been broken, as if an old and infuriating conjuring trick had finally been explained. Afterwards, they would look at each other with a disbelief in their eyes that was half proud and half ashamed and ask, did we really do that? But we are ordinary people . . .

It grew dark. They did not find the sisters.

They found the bodies in the dumb-waiter, but the Shakil sisters had vanished, and nobody would ever see them again, not in 'Nishapur' nor anywhere on earth. They had deserted their home but they kept their vows of retreat, crumbling, perhaps, into powder under the rays of the sun, or growing wings and flying off into the Impossible Mountains in the west. Women as formidable as the three sisters Shakil never do less than they intend.

Night. In a room near the top of the house they found an old man frowning in a four-poster bed with wooden snakes winding around the columns. The noise had woken him up; he was sitting bolt upright and muttering, 'So, I'm still alive.' He was grey all over, ashen from head to foot, and so eaten up by sickness that it was impossible to say who he was; and because he had the air of a spirit who had returned from the dead they backed away from him. 'I'm hungry,' he said, looking surprised, and then peered at the cheap electric torches and smouldering firebrands of the invaders and demanded to know what they were doing in his quarters; whereupon they turned and fled, shouting to the police officers that someone was up there, maybe alive, maybe dead, but at any rate someone in that house of death, sitting up in bed and acting smart. The police officers were on their way up when they heard a sort of panic starting in the street outside, and they ran off to investigate, blowing their whistles, leaving the old man to get up and put on the grey silk dressing-gown which his mothers had left neatly folded at the foot of his bed, and to take a long drink from the jug of fresh lime-juice which had been there just long enough for the ice-cubes to melt. Then he, too, heard the screams.

They were strange screams. He heard them rise to their peaks and then die with uncanny abruptness, and then he knew what was coming into the house, something that could freeze a shriek in the middle, something that petrified. Something that would not, this time, be sated before it reached him, or cheated, or escaped from; that had entered the night-streets of the city and would not be denied. Something coming up the stairs: he heard it roar.

He stood beside the bed and waited for her like a bridegroom on his wedding night, as she climbed towards him, roaring, like a fire driven by the wind. The door blew open. And he in the darkness, erect, watching the approaching glow, and then she was there, on all fours, naked, coated in mud and blood and shit, with twigs sticking to her back and beetles in her hair. She saw him and shuddered; then she rose up on her hind legs with her forepaws outstretched and he had just enough time to say, 'Well, wife, so here you are at last,' before her eyes forced him to look.

He struggled against their hypnotic power, their gravitational pull, but it was no use, his eyes lifted, until he was staring into the fiery yellow heart of her, and saw there, just for an instant, some flickering, some dimming of the flame in doubt, as though she had entertained for that tiny fragment of time the wild fantasy that she was indeed a bride entering the chamber of her beloved; but the furnace burned the doubts away, and as he stood before her, unable to move, her hands, his wife's hands, reached out to him and closed.

His body was falling away from her, a headless drunk, and after that the Beast faded in her once again, she stood there blinking stupidly, unsteady on her feet, as if she didn't know that all the stories had to end together, that the fire was just gathering its strength, that on the day of reckoning the judges are not exempt from judgment, and that the power of the Beast of shame cannot be held for long within any one frame of flesh and blood, because it grows, it feeds and swells, until the vessel bursts.

And then the explosion comes, a shock-wave that demolishes the house, and after it the fireball of her burning, rolling outwards to the horizon like the sea, and last of all the cloud, which rises and spreads and hangs over the nothingness of the scene, until I can no longer see what is no longer there; the silent cloud, in the shape of a giant, grey and headless man, a figure of dreams, a phantom with one arm lifted in a gesture of farewell.

ACKNOWLEDGMENTS

This book was written with the financial assistance of the Arts Council of Great Britain. It also owes a good deal to the entirely non-financial assistance of many others, my gratitude to whom will perhaps best be expressed by leaving them unnamed.

The unattributed quotation on page 126 has been taken from *The Life Science* by P.B. and J.S. Medawar (Wildwood House, 1977). The italicized line on page 181 is from Saul Bellow's *The Adventures of Augie March* (Weidenfeld and Nicolson, 1954). I have also quoted from *The Book of Laughter and Forgetting* by Milan Kundera, translated by Michael Henry Heim (Faber and Faber, 1982); from the Muirs' translation of *The Trial* by Franz Kafka (Victor Gollancz, 1935); from *The Prince* by Niccolò Machiavelli, in the translation by Luigi Ricci, edited by E.R.P. Vincent, for World's Classics, Oxford University Press (1935); from N.J. Dawood's translation of *The Koran* (Penguin Classics, 1956); and from the plays *The Suicide* by Nikolai Erdman, translated by P. Tegel (Pluto Press, 1979), and *Danton's Death* by Georg Büchner, in the version by Howard Brenton from a translation by Jane Fry (Methuen, 1982). My thanks to all concerned; and to the many journalists and writers, both Western and Eastern, to whom I am indebted.

My gratitude, too, to Walter, for letting go; and finally, and as always, to Clarissa, for everything.

PHOTO: Beowulf Sheehan/PEN American Center

SALMAN RUSHDIE is the author of a number of ac-
claimed novels: *Grimus; Midnight's Children* (which was
awarded the Booker Prize in 1981, and, in 2008, was
voted the "Best of the Booker," the best novel to have
won that prize in the award's forty-year history); *The
Enchantress of Florence; The Satanic Verses* (winner of the
Whitbread Prize for Best Novel); *Haroun and the Sea of
Stories* (winner of the Writers Guild Award); *The Moor's
Last Sigh* (winner of the Whitbread Prize for Best
Novel); *The Ground Beneath Her Feet* (winner of the
Eurasian section of the Commonwealth Prize); *Fury* (a
New York Times Notable Book); and *Shalimar the Clown*
(a *Time* Book of the Year). He is also the author of a
book of stories, *East, West,* and works of nonfiction—
*Imaginary Homelands, The Jaguar Smile, The Wizard of Oz,
Step Across This Line* and his memoir, *Joseph Anton.* He is
co-editor of *Mirrorwork,* an anthology of contemporary
Indian writing.